DRAGON MOUNT

JENNIFER M. EATON

DRAGON MOUNT © 2018 Jennifer M. Eaton

Published by Galactic Razor
Cover by Victoria Cooper

For Glenn.

Years ago you told me
I had what it takes to be a bestseller.
Dragon Mount is the first release showing off
My new USA Today Best Selling Author title.
I know you're smiling, saying, "See, I told you so."
I wish you were here so I could see that wonderful smirk.
I hope the French fries are great in Heaven, my friend.

Miss you.

Anna didn't need a man. What she needed was a dragon—a big, hulking, nasty dragon fully capable of biting the head off of any jerk who even thought of hurting her. As she breathed in the essence of moonflowers drifting on the breeze, she knew this would be the place to find what she was looking for.

Well, she might not exactly find a dragon in New Zealand, but maybe enough magic to help her forget and start over.

A woman on the street corner spun a rack of postcards displaying pictures of the country's pristine landscape. Anna's stomach soured as she tucked back the dark hair that blew into her eyes. She and Andrew had dreamed of sitting in a little café, filling out postcards just like those, writing *Wish you were here, suckers!* over and over again. A hint of a smile touched her lips, before it fell away.

When they first started planning this vacation it was a pipe dream—the mutual *coup de gras* of their bucket lists. It was supposed to be their honeymoon.

Until a honeymoon was no longer needed.

"Stop thinking about him." Her sister didn't even look up from her fistful of pamphlets. "I can smell you brooding from here."

The sun slipped toward the peaks in the distance, ending a day filled with terminals, planes, and busses. Anna shielded her eyes as the sky exploded with an orange and pink glow.

"It says here that those mountains you're staring at are called *Aoraki*." Sybil pointed to the text. "The original settlers believed that the sons of the sky god got their canoe stuck on a reef. They froze to death and became the mountains." She smiled. "That's kind of creepy. Right up your alley."

Anna took a step toward the postcard vendor and stopped herself. Postcards were meaningless, but fun. They'd always been a favorite part of every vacation. But maybe not anymore.

She closed her eyes. How many things would she have to give up because they reminded her of *him*?

"Right now these Maori people are celebrating some sort of ancient fertility festival called the Seventeen Year." Sybil snorted. "Fertility, huh? Sounds like my kind of party."

Of course it was. Anything her sister could relate to sex was a good time. How could she be so flippant about things like that when guys...

Sybil lowered the pamphlets. "Stop. Thinking. About. Him."

Anna sighed. How could she stop? She was standing on a street in New Zealand, where they'd dreamed of going since forever.

A fistful of brochures slapped Anna's cheek. She stood stunned, gaping.

"You are going to enjoy this vacation if it kills me." Sybil pointed the pamphlets at her like a sword.

Leave it to her sister to drag them both back to elementary school tactics.

A laugh popped out of Anna's mouth as she splayed her hands. "I'm sorry. This is just harder than I thought it would be." That was the hugest of understatements. "But I'm okay." She nodded to herself. "I need this."

More like she needed *to do* this. New Zealand wasn't only her and Andrew's dream. It was her dream. That didn't change because he was out of the picture.

"What you need is a nice, stiff drink."

Anna smiled. It probably couldn't hurt. "I think I need some time for all this to soak in."

"Then let's call this a good start." Sybil raised her hand into the air. "Taxi!"

"Wait. Where are we going?"

Her sister glanced back at her. "Like I said, to get a drink."

"Is there something wrong with the hotel bar?"

Sybil waved at one of the approaching yellow cars. "Yes, it's packed with tourists. I want to meet some New Zealanders."

Her sister, the quintessential party girl. "We haven't even unpacked and you already want to go bar hopping?"

"Oh, come on." Sybil was inside the cab before Anna could argue. "Believe me, once this vacation is over, you'll be a new person."

Was there something wrong with her old person? Anna didn't think so.

Well, not her *old*-old person. Growing up, she'd been ready for anything. She and Andrew were going to take on the world together.

Until she caught him in bed with someone else.

Mom had always called Anna a miniature explosion, ready to take on the world. The firecracker inside Anna had extinguished that night, and she hadn't found a way to rekindle the spark.

She closed her eyes and swallowed the painful ball building in her throat. She was here to forget—to erase the bad and come home as a clean slate, ready to start over. This started by proving to herself that life no longer revolved around one guy.

In the distance, a large black bird soared toward the mountains. It circled as if it flew for the pure pleasure of feeling the wind in its feathers. That's what she needed, the confidence to spread her wings and glide toward the horizon.

Sybil glared at her. "Don't make me drag you into this car."

Anna sucked in a deep breath before she slipped onto the worn, black seat beside her sister. "One drink. Promise."

Her sister made a spectacle of rolling her eyes.

"Where to?" The driver's accent made it sound like *Wayer-tou.*

Sybil leaned up and handed a brochure to him. She pointed to a handwritten note on the top of the page. "Do you know where this is?"

He snorted. "Kinda off the beaten path for a couple of Sheilas."

Sybil flopped back in her seat. "Sounds perfect."

Off the beaten path? Was she out of her mind?

Anna leaned closer as the cab pulled from the sidewalk. "This is crazy. We are in a foreign country with—"

"Not a care in the world." She tapped Anna's knee. "Relax. Trust me. We're going to see where real New Zealanders hang out."

Great. Just great.

Anna stared out the window as they left civilization behind. The approaching dusk cast a deepening haze over the hillside as clean, undisturbed green stretched out as far as the eye could see. The tension eased from Anna's shoulders as she lost herself in undefiled nature.

She hated to admit it, but those rolling fields reached inside and mended part of the hole torn in her heart. She couldn't imagine living somewhere with so much incredibly beautiful *nothing.*

"I have a surprise for you." Sybil nudged her shoulder. "We're not taking the movie site tour tomorrow."

Anna spun toward her. "We're not?"

"Nope. I changed our date to Monday."

"Why?"

"Because tomorrow morning, you and your favorite sister are taking the plunge off Kawarau Bridge."

Anna nearly choked. "What?"

"Yup. It's all set up. They're picking us up at our hotel at 8:30."

"Are you out of your mind? I am not bungee jumping!"

"Yes, you are. It's already bought and paid for. No refunds, no excuses."

No excuses? Anna had a great big gaping excuse. Even back home in the US she erred on the cautious side. She really didn't have a choice.

Eight years ago, she woke up after a car accident and found out she had a rare blood type. The hospital had to have plasma flown in from another state, and the delay almost killed her. Ever since, she'd been warned to take it easy and cautioned against foreign travel, but here she was, vacationing in New Zealand with a nutty sister who wanted them to plummet to their deaths tied to the ends of rubber bands.

"There is no way I'm jumping off a bridge."

Sybil snickered as the cab pulled to a stop. "We'll see."

Her sister paid the cabbie as Anna stepped onto worn, colorful cobblestones. The black sconces encircling the weathered rock buildings and the matching streetlamps flared to life simultaneously. Anna jumped as one of them blew out.

"Surprise!" Sybil said.

Anna looked up and down the deserted street. "Surprise what?"

"Don't you recognize it? This is the street they modeled Bree after."

Anna looked again. "It is?"

"Yup. I found it on Wikipedia under little-known *Lord of the Rings* sites." She narrowed her eyes. "One of these places is supposed to look just like the Prancing Pony inside."

Anna took in the gnarled, wooden signs. She could barely read the names on some of them. At the far end of the road, four men in long coats entered a bar with a carved rooster hanging above the door. It seemed warm for coats that long. Must be a Kiwi thing.

Sybil grabbed Anna's wrist and tugged her along the bumpy, colorful walkway toward a worn, timber door with wide, black hinges. "This place looks as good as any to start."

Anna pulled out of her grip. "To start? I agreed to one drink."

Sybil held her chest, feigning hurt. "Of course we'll only have one drink." She pulled Anna through the door. "Per bar."

Anna sighed. With Sybil, there was always a loophole.

Inside, the tavern looked nothing like the Prancing Pony. It looked more like the bar in that old show *Cheers* that her father watched on Netflix. A circular bar dominated the center of the room. Its white-tiled surface clashed with the dark paneling. Flickering candles on cherrywood tables nestled against the wall cast a yellowish glow throughout the room. Inside the serving-circle, a dark-skinned man placed a glass into a huge wooden fixture hanging precariously over the bar.

"Welcome, ladies. Please, have a seat." He gestured across the nearly empty bar and the mostly open tables. So much for meeting the locals.

Anna had to admit the tavern had its charm, though. The hotel bar had all the appeal of a meat market, while this place oozed culture.

An old man wearing a multi-colored, patchwork shirt sat alone at the table closest to the door. His tunic matched the vibrant weavings hanging from the walls like he was a part of the decor.

Combine him with the dead animal heads mounted above the entrance, and Anna felt as if she'd stepped back in time. If she could convince them to trash the plasma television screen, this place would be the perfect retreat.

She and Sybil settled on stools at the bar and ordered drinks. From the opposite side of the serving circle, a very light-skinned platinum-blond guy flashed a smile. His eyes mirrored the over-head lighting, making everything about him seem paler, as if he were dusted in white powder. Anna quickly looked away. She settled her eyes on the Malibu Bay Breeze the barkeep handed her, forcing her gaze to remain there so she didn't stare.

"Is it always so quiet here?" Sybil asked the bartender.

"You missed the happy hour crowd. People have been staying in after dusk the past few days."

Sybil frowned. "I guess we'll have to come back earlier tomorrow."

Or not.

Sybil had to notice that this *wasn't* the Prancing Pony. Absorbing culture was fine and all, but Anna had her first taste of New Zealand on the car ride over here. She wanted to see more, not spend her time drinking.

The bartender walked to the other side of the counter and spoke to the blond guy. After a moment, they both turned toward Anna. She nearly choked on her drink before she looked away.

Her cheeks heated. The blond must have mentioned that she'd been staring at him. With skin that pale, he must have people stare at him all the time, and here she was, the gawking American, jumping on the bandwagon.

Anna concentrated on the ice cubes in her glass, trying to not look like she was aware the two men were still chatting.

About her? No, of course not.

But what if they were?

If she and Sybil had stayed at the hotel bar, like she'd wanted, she could've just caught the next elevator to her room and hid from all this awkwardness.

She leaned toward her sister. "This obviously isn't the right place. Maybe we should go."

"Come on, Sis. There's more to sightseeing than movie loca-tions. There's a lot about the local culture I'd like to sample, too." She spun her stool toward a table of three guys near the wall and sipped her drink through the thin, red stirring straw. Her lips turned up in a wry grin.

Anna's eyes widened. "You came all the way to New Zealand to get laid?"

"Well, not only to get laid. But it's on my to-do list."

"What's wrong with the guys in New Jersey?"

Sybil shrugged. "I might run into them again. I hate that. This will be more fun. No strings attached." She smacked Anna playfully. "Not to mention New Zealand accents. Yum."

Anna shook her head. "You're crazy."

"Me? And it's not crazy to sit home every Saturday night?"

Hanging out at home was a perfectly respectable thing to do on the weekend. She and Andrew…

Anna cringed, closed her eyes, and refocused. There was no more *she and Andrew*. Not since she left for college. Not since she came home to surprise him on his birthday.

College had become her life after that night. Classes and studying. Nothing more.

Nothing more than lying awake at night, crying.

She gritted her teeth. She was not *that girl* anymore. She didn't need a guy, and she didn't need to go out on the weekend to look for another shitfaced, lying bastard. Anna worked her tail off studying all week. She needed to decompress and relax on her days off. Alone.

Anna cringed, then straightened. She didn't want to be alone. Not really. But she wasn't ready to get out there and date again. Andrew had been her world since middle school. She didn't know how to be with anyone else.

Sybil would never understand that. Her sister's plan was to play the field and be married to her cushy corner executive office for the rest of her life. There was nothing wrong with that, for *her*. Anna wanted the best of both worlds—a family and a job. She wasn't going to find that hooking up with a guy she'd never see again.

"I don't understand how you can even think of sleeping with a guy you've just met." Anna sipped her drink and set it back on the bar.

"Believe me. It's a heck of a lot easier than getting tied down in a relationship. Guys get crazy when they hang around too long. They get all protective and..." The word cheat hung on the edge of her lips before she copped out by sipping her drink.

Anna crumpled her napkin and threw in on the bar. "I don't know, I think I still want what Mom and Dad had—the love of my life, job, and two point five kids?"

"Point five?"

"Yeah, my dog." Anna watched the condensation drip down her glass. "Is it so wrong to want a guy that will do almost anything for me?"

"You're dreaming, little sister. He doesn't exist. I gave up looking for him years ago."

But Dad existed. Could it be true that their generation hadn't spawned any great guys?

The bartender adjusted the volume on the television.

A news reporter brushed back a lock of her dark hair and brought a microphone to her lips. "So there you have it. This small village, the third in as many nights, now lays in shock after this morning's gruesome discovery. The identities of the women have not been made public yet, but NZN News has learned that two of the victims lived here in Wellington, and the third was a Norwegian tourist. Neighboring towns have called for a seven o'clock curfew tonight, as all of New Zealand prays for an end to this senseless killing spree."

"They were disemboweled, just like the last two," one of the guys at the table said. "I saw it on the internet. This bloke is a sadist or something."

Last two? Holy crap! Were they anywhere near Wellington?

The bartender changed the channel. "I hope they catch him soon."

"There be no one to catch," the old guy in the colorful garb mumbled. "They look for a man. They need to turn their eyes to the sky. They seek what they are not prepared to find."

A shiver ran down Anna's spine. The tavern was oddly reminiscent of an old horror flick, and this weathered, creepy guy was the trope old codger that knew the truth, but no one believed him until they were running for their lives. If he was about to say that all of New Zealand was haunted by ancient bloodthirsty spirits, she was *so* out of here.

The guy at the other table turned in his seat. "What are you talking about, pop, some Maori legend?"

The old man's eyes darkened. "Is no legend. We in a Seventeen Year. They should not be looking for a man."

The table of guys laughed. "So what are they looking for, a dragon? I think you've had a few too many."

"Every seventeen years the dragons fly. They search New Zealand for mates." He pointed to the television. "This be the work of a gray dragon, the worst of them all."

"Yeah, and Aoraki and his brothers got stranded on a reef and became the mountains." One of the guys laughed into his beer.

Anna took in the old man's colorful attire, remembering the brochure Sybil read to her. It seemed crazy that people still believed that kind of folklore.

The elder remained stoic. "How do you know they did not become the mountains, if you were not there?"

Anna bit back her smile. The ominous cloud in the room lifted as the table of guys snickered. It was sad they made fun of the old man, though. He couldn't help what he'd been brought up to believe, no matter how ridiculous.

The bartender leaned across the counter toward her. "The bloke on the flipside would like to buy you a drink."

Anna cringed. The guy she'd been staring at? She glanced around the barkeep. Blondie smiled at her.

"Umm, no thanks. Tell him no offense, I'm just passing through. I'm not going to be here that long."

Sybil elbowed her. "What's wrong with you?"

"He's not my type."

"What, he doesn't have a pulse?"

"Shut up."

Someone settled beside her, and Anna tensed. She turned her head slowly until her gaze met eerie, light blue eyes and even lighter skin.

Blondie smiled. "Hello, I'm sorry. I heard you turn down my drink. You're not from around here, I suppose?" The New Zealand accent dripped from his pale lips. The package didn't seem to fit together.

"Um, no. We're from New Jersey."

He tilted his head. "In England?"

"No. New Jersey as in the United States."

His eyes widened. "Oh, that makes sense. You didn't look or sound English. Anyway, in these parts, it's customary for a man to buy a woman a drink to say hello. I was only being courteous. I didn't mean to offend you."

Sybil left her chair and sat on the other side of Blondie. She scribbled something on a napkin.

Anna shifted her weight. "In America, a guy buys a girl a drink if he's trying to pick her up."

"Pick her up?"

"As in a date."

His eyes widened, showing more of the creepy glass-like pupils, which maybe, now that she looked closer, were eerily beautiful.

"That would be a bit presumptuous of me, wouldn't it?" he asked. "I don't even know your name."

Sybil held up the napkin she'd been toiling over. It read:

Platinum blond babies are beautiful

Anna laughed. Well, no, it came out more like an embarrassing snort, but Blondie didn't seem to notice, thank goodness.

She offered him her hand. "My name is Anna."

Instead of shaking, he flipped her palm down and kissed her knuckles. Who in God's name was this guy?

"It is a pleasure to meet you, Miss Anna of the great continent of America. My name is Joesephutus."

She shuffled her feet, trying to ward off the odd tingle in her toes. "Wow, that's quite a name. Do you mind if I just call you Joe?"

His smiled seeped into her. "Only if you allow me to buy you that drink."

Sybil gave a thumbs up over his head, and then returned to her place beside Anna.

Yeah, little sister Anna getting picked up in a bar would make Sybil's day. Anna would never hear the end of it.

As she gazed into Joe's haunting, crystal eyes, though, she couldn't help but want to know more about this interesting man. She'd gone from being completely freaked out about his appearance, to enthralled.

Too bad 11,000 miles was too far for a long distance relationship. She needed to nip this in the bud before it went any further. "I'm sorry, but I'm really not interested." An ache welled in her belly. She bit her lower lip to keep from retracting her words as Joe lowered his eyes.

His lips thinned. "No problem. Enjoy your time in New Zealand." He bowed his head and returned to his seat.

Anna nearly stepped off her chair to stop him. After all, it was only a drink, and he seemed nice. Shoot, why couldn't she be more like Sybil and okay with things like this?

An elbow in the back returned her attention to her sister. "What's wrong with you?" Sybil said. "He was cute."

"I don't know." And she didn't. Anna's stomach continued to whirl. Her skin ached, as if tugging her toward the other side of the bar, nudging her back to where Joe slipped into his seat and cradled his drink between his palms.

He'd been sweet and didn't come on too strong like the asses in bars back home. The poor guy was probably just shy, and she'd totally turned him down.

Sybil was right, what *was* wrong with her?

A cool breeze whipped in when someone opened the door. Anna was glad for the touch of chill as she turned toward her sister.

"Holy hell," Sybil whispered, her gaze fused to the entrance.

A man walked, no—slid through the entrance, but not in a slimy, snake-like way. It was more like gliding across the surface of a pond. He towered over everyone, well over six feet. Stopping in the center of the room, he placed his hand on his chest and bowed to the old man, who straightened, beaming.

The newcomer turned back to the bar, and Anna's heart triple beat as his gaze brushed over her. His long, dark hair shifted slightly as he walked, coming close to falling over one eye, but not quite covering it. Anna had seen this man before, on the cover of hundreds of romance novels. He seemed painted; perfect, as if molded by an artist. She quivered, warming in all the most embarrassing places.

He smiled at Anna, before turning his attention to Sybil. As soon as his gaze left hers, a sweep of relief flooded Anna, as if she'd been held by something, but then let go.

Sybil blanched, her eyes wide as the stranger slipped his fingers over hers.

"Please forgive my forwardness." He kissed the back of her hand, just like Joe had. "But you are the most beautiful thing I've ever seen." He leaned up, still holding her fingers. "You must allow me the honor of your company."

His gaze darted over the bar, where Joe leaned back on his stool with a dumbfounded look on his face. The hot guy smiled before returning his attention to Anna's sister.

Sybil blinked as if waking from a stupor. "Of course, please, sit."

The man eased onto the seat beside them, his gaze never leaving Sybil's. How was it that no matter where they were in the world, her sister managed to be a beacon for beefcake? It wasn't fair. Well, not like Anna wanted to be eaten alive by a guy's eyes, but damn, did her sister wear *come and take me* perfume or something?

"I'm Sybil. This is my sister, Anna."

He lowered his head. "Miss Anna, a flower equally as lovely."

Sure, but you went for the one that looked and dressed like a runway model. Hot guys never went for the plain ones. Not that she wanted him to leech onto her, but, you know.

"My name is Quenor." He kissed Sybil's knuckles again, this time hesitating as his lips touched her skin.

Sybil cleared her throat. "Quay-noor? You mean, like, Connor?"

His eyes bored into her like he hadn't eaten in a month and she was a hot fudge sundae. "Connor sounds lovely with your accent."

Wow, his own accent sang from his lips. Anna could listen to his voice forever. She had to tear her eyes away from him. Taking a deep breath, she placed her chilled glass to her temple to try to cool herself down. She definitely needed to get a grip.

"Can I get you something to drink?" the bartender asked Connor.

"Whatever the lovely Sybil is having is fine for me."

Their gazes remained locked. Sybil seemed tongue-tied.

Icy fingers itched up Anna's back. Something wasn't quite right about this guy. There was hot, and then there was *too hot*. And then there was Connor. The attraction Anna felt when he looked at her, the attraction she still felt, even when he'd obviously chosen Sybil, bordered on hypnotic.

The bartender reached up and grasped a wineglass from the fixture hanging over the bar. As he pulled the cup down, the contraption tilted. Several of the glasses slipped from their housing and fell, shattering on the bar top.

Sybil cried out, and Anna gasped as a strong shove sent her stumbling off her seat. The bartender stood, gaping at the mess, while Blondie's right knee angled up on the bar, and his other foot balanced on the stool that Anna had occupied. His left hand still held her from harm's way, while his right held the fixture from falling at the same time. How had he gotten across the bar so quickly?

"I have this end." Connor reached up, his long arms easily grabbing the other side of the fixture.

"Thanks," the bartender said, helping them ease the wooden frame safely to the floor. His face contorted and reddened with the effort, while Joe and Connor lowered the fixture to the floor without difficulty.

Sybil held her hand to her chest, but her eyes remained glued to her new date.

Don't worry, sis, no glasses hit me. No reason to check and make sure I'm all right or anything.

The barkeep grabbed a dustpan and saluted Joe and Connor with the sweeper brush. "Your drinks are on the house, mates."

"Thank you, but that's not necessary." Joe turned to Anna, and his eyes widened. "You're bleeding."

She blinked in surprise. "What?"

He grabbed her hand, raising her red, glistening fingertip. "You've been cut."

"It's not that bad."

His gaze centered on her fingertip. His brow furrowed as a red bead dripped down to her palm.

She trembled. "Umm, you can let go of me, now."

His gaze flicked to hers and held. He leaned closer. Her pulse throbbed in her ears like she was underwater. The room spun, but dizziness didn't overcome her. The beat of her heart seemed to slow while every inch of her yearned to lean closer and breathe this beautiful stranger in.

Breathe him in? What in God's name had gotten into her, and why was this guy still holding her wrist?

She tried to push him away, but slipped, smearing blood across his cheek. He hardened his grip, as another red droplet beaded on her fingertip.

Her gaze drew back to his light blue, crystalline eyes. She needed to scream, to slap him in the face, to run. She couldn't move, though. Her breaths came shallow and raspy. Part of her longed to kiss away the crimson stain that tainted the edge of his pale lip.

Wait. What?

The brightness of the blood against his milky skin caused flashes of Edward Cullen to run through her mind. The idea was ridiculous, of course. No one believed in vampires. That was almost as stupid as believing in fairies.

But he was fairy-like, now that she thought about it, with those icy blue eyes and white hair. He actually pulled off his albinism with an air of sex appeal. Well, not the dripping screw-me sexy like Connor, but there was definitely something about this guy who was still... fixating on her bloody cut like a deranged lunatic.

He released her.

She nearly stumbled, but grabbed the edge of her stool instead. "What is wrong with you?"

He blinked as if clearing his eyesight. "I-I don't know." He stared at her finger like it might bite him.

Okay, so, yes—this guy was cute, but he obviously had some serious issues.

She grabbed a napkin and wrapped her wound. "In case you were wondering, that is *not* the way to get an American girl's attention."

"I know, I-I'm sorry." He rubbed his temples. "I-I didn't mean to offend."

Connor left Sybil's side and grabbed Joe's shoulder. "Joese-phutus, are you all right?"

He wiped the blood from Joe's face with his bare hand and then stared at his fingers.

"Wait, you two know each other?" Anna asked.

The taller man whipped his face in her direction. His gaze focused on her with an intensity that made her want to cower in the corner. Connor leaned closer and drew in a deep breath. Was he… smelling her?

Joe became pale. Well, pale-er if that was even possible. He took a stilted breath before elbowing Connor's considerably larger bulk out of the way and taking Anna's uninjured hand. "Anna, I would really, really like to buy you that drink."

His grip tightened. Not painful, but strange. Possessive. Every part of her screamed to tug her hand from his, but all she could do was stare into those glassy, light eyes.

Connor laughed, tapping Joe on the back. "I can't believe it. You are one lucky little…"

The door to the bar flung open and slammed against the wall as if it had been kicked.

The cool breeze thickened the air.

Connor nudged Joe.

"I feel it," Joe said.

Holding Sybil's shoulder, Connor glanced at Anna, then Joe. "We need to get your little lass out of here."

"I'm aware of that." Joe turned to the barkeep. "Do you have a back exit?"

"Too late," Connor whispered.

Joe grumbled under his breath, tightening his grip on Anna's arm. He leaned close to her ear. "If you get the opportunity, run like your life depends on it." He glanced at the door. "Because it does."

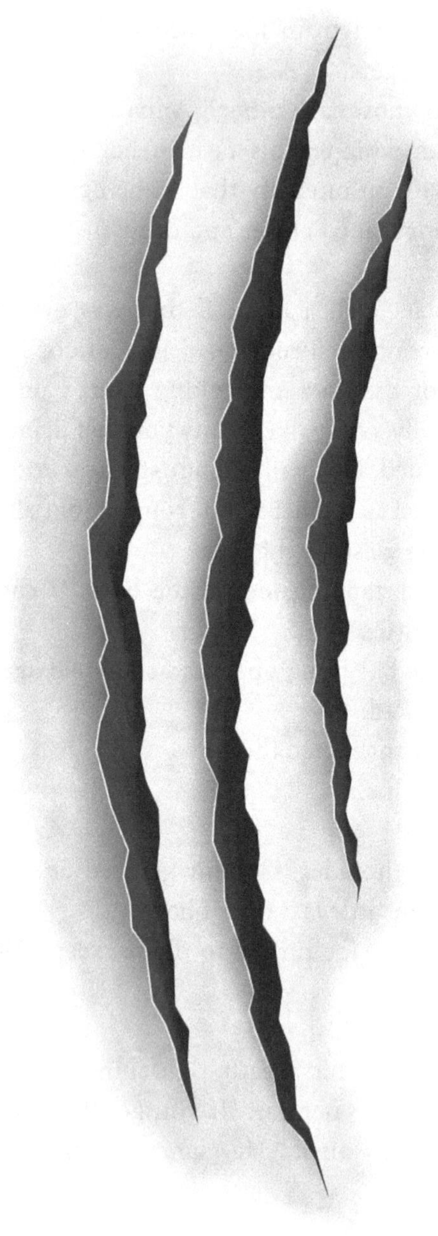

CHAPTER 2

Four men entered. Their long, gray jackets shifted with a life of their own.

Two of the men remained on either side of the door, as if standing guard. One walked to the table of guys that had made fun of the old man. Anna expected him to strike up a conversation. Instead, he stared at them.

An itchy sensation crawled up her spine as the guys at the table fidgeted and cast panicked glances at each other. After a moment, one stood, threw a few bills on the table, and scurried between the two men standing by the door. Seconds later, the other guys at the table followed.

The fourth newcomer stopped mid room and drew his fingers through his short, brunette hair as he scanned the tables.

The old man's lips thinned before he stood. "You are not welcome here." His accent tripped over a marked shake in his voice. His hands formed fists.

The guy in the center of the room lifted his nose into the air and sniffed as the third shoved the old man back into his seat.

Asshole. Anna moved to intervene, but Joe drew her back.

"This is a Seventeen Year, elder," the third guy said. "We'll search where it pleases us."

"Enough." The one in the center of the room set his gaze on Sybil. "The elder deserves honor, whether or not his tongue is forked."

The old man shifted in his seat. His gaze jumped between the two newcomers. "You'll not find the South's hopeful in these villages. They are at the base of *Aoraki*. You waste your time here."

"We'll see." The one who seemed to be the ring-leader sauntered toward Sybil with a gait not unlike Connor's. He reached out and fingered one of her curls.

Sybil gasped, but didn't move until Connor edged between her and the lead asshole, who probably had six inches on her date's already impressive height. "This one is mine, Galeptopnor. You can look elsewhere."

The guy—was his name Gale Topner?—laughed. His dark gray coat shifted around his waist. "Brave words, for a twilight born." He leaned past Connor, taking a deep breath, as if smelling Sybil behind him. "Luckily for you she is nothing." He straightened. "Unlike the careless, languid greens, the children of the mountain take the Seventeen Year seriously. We'll entertain ourselves once the hunt is over."

Connor reached back, shoving Sybil further behind him. "Then get on with it, and let the rest of us enjoy our night of freedom." He pointed his chin toward the old man. "As the elder said, the offerings are on *Aoraki*."

Gale stepped back. "As they always are, but it has been ten cycles since they've presented anything of value."

Offerings? Value? What in goodness name were these people talking about?

The newcomer stepped toward Anna, and Joe jumped between them in an awkward recreation of Connor's protection of Sybil. Gale towered over him by over a foot. Anna smashed against the bar as Joe backed into her.

"We-we're not in the hunt," Joe said. "Just leave us to our entertainment."

Anna cringed. Entertainment? She was no one's entertainment, thank you very much.

Anna pressed her palms against Joe's back, ready to shove him away, but he didn't budge. She could feel the sculpted ridges of muscle beneath his T-shirt, and her attention drew from the man advancing, to the one standing between them. His skin warmed under her hands as if his body reached toward her, beckoning. Her sight blurred before refocusing on Joe's back, and his thick, distinct platinum hair.

Gale smirked. "What are you hiding back there, runt?"

Joe straightened, trying to make himself bigger.

Where did he get off trying to be her protector? She'd dealt with assholes before. She didn't need some guy to jump in like a knight in shiny platinum armor.

"Cain." Gale's word came out as a command, and the jerk who'd scared off the guys grasped Joe by the shoulders, picked him up, walked him across the room, and set him down beside the empty table.

A chill swept through the door, sending a shiver across Anna's skin as Gale gazed down on her.

She was vaguely aware of Cain pointing at Joe as he shouted: "Stay."

Joe's eyes saddened before he lowered his gaze to the floor. Part of her felt naked without him sheltering her; which was ridiculous since they'd only met a few minutes ago.

Her breath hitched as the tall stranger reached for her. She willed her hands into fists. She tried to punch, but her body didn't react. She stood frozen as Gale twirled her hair around his fingers.

"That one's just a child, a plaything," Connor said. "Leave her to the runt. Maybe she'll keep him busy and out of your way."

"I have no need to keep a runt out of my way." Gale continued his perusal. "His participation in the Seventeen Year is a waste of his people's meaningless hope." He leaned closer to Anna, his nose grazing her neck as he breathed her in. "You, though, precious one." He cupped Anna's cheeks. "You are *very* interesting."

The pupils in his eyes seemed to swirl, dragging her to infinity. Something deep in her mind prodded that she wanted to push him away, to stand up, pull back her shoulders and tell this asshole that she wouldn't just stand there and let him… let him…

Let him what?

Damn, he was handsome, and his hands, so warm against her skin. She could melt under his touch. Anna eased toward him, but someone batted Gale's hands from her. The room instantly chilled.

"Back off," Joe said. "She's mine."

The two men guarding the door snickered, while Gale's face twisted into a snarl.

"He's right," Connor said. "The boy found her. He has first rights."

"Really?" Gale shoved Joe, slamming him against the bar as if he weighed no more than a loaf of bread. "Are you willing to fight me for her, runt?"

Joe lunged for the taller man, but Connor shoved an arm between them, grabbing Joe.

"This is not the place," Connor said.

Gale crossed his arms. "Would you rather we challenge on the mountain? I can humiliate him now, or eviscerate him later. It makes no difference to me."

Joe twisted in Connor's grip. "Let go of me."

"Calm down, little one," Connor said. "There's no reason to die today."

All three of them glanced at Anna, and she could tell from the looks on their faces that there was probably a perfectly good reason to die today, as far as they were concerned. Whatever it was, she didn't travel all the way to New Zealand to get in the middle of some stupid pissing match with the locals.

She shuddered, eyeing the door.

If you get the opportunity, run like your life depends on it.

The other two men still blocked the exit. Had the bartender answered when they asked about a back door? Why were they all still staring at her?

"Enough." Gale turned to Connor. "Keep your little pet grounded or I will ground him for you." He grabbed Anna's wrist and wrenched her toward the exit.

The soles of Anna's shoes slid along the slick hardwood. "Wait. I'm not leaving with you."

Gale didn't turn. He just pulled harder.

"Stop!" Sybil cried out. "That's my sister."

The night air chilled Anna's face as the tavern door closed behind them. "Please let me go. I don't have any money."

Well, not much anyway, but she'd give it to him, if he'd just leave her be.

Gale pulled her behind the building and shoved her against the wall beside the dumpster. He pressed her shoulders into the cool brick. A huge, flattened courtyard sprawled out behind him, big enough to house a bazaar or a circus, but now lay eerily empty. Damn that freaking curfew.

He stared into her eyes, and the tension slipped from her muscles.

He ran his nose up the side of her neck, again. "Your scent is intoxicating."

Her scent?

Gale held her face. A trace of smoke carried on his breath. "You are special, did you know that? Your blood is very hard to find."

"My-my blood?" Her blood was a hindrance, a curse. What was he talking about?

"But now that I've found it, you will be mine."

Anna's head lolled to the side. She groaned as he dragged his tongue along her collarbone.

Something deep within her screamed. This man was insane. Yet she eased closer to him, languishing in his touch. She slipped her hand behind his neck and ran her fingers through his soft hair. Voices shouted somewhere in the distance, but she tuned it out, soaking in only the sound of Gale's breath, heated to a pant.

"For the next ten months, you will be queen." His eyes consumed her. She couldn't move. "Would you like that," he asked. "Do you want me?"

"No, she doesn't want you."

A bored expression crossed Gale's face before he turned and faced Joe standing in the courtyard behind him. "Haven't you learned, runt? Bugger off before I put you down."

"Let her go. This isn't right."

The cold air swept through her now that she was devoid of Gale's warmth. She pawed at the back of his coat.

He slipped his arm around her shoulder, and she cuddled into his embrace.

"See," he said. "Does she look unhappy?"

Unhappy? How could she be unhappy with such strength around her, such warmth?

"She has no idea what she feels. You're compelling her." Joe stepped closer.

Anna smiled at him. He was sweet, but she didn't need him anymore. Gale was what she needed, no one else.

Sybil appeared, screaming Anna's name while Connor held her back. She must be jealous. She must want Gale, too, but it was too late. Anna had already given herself to him.

"Let her go," Joe repeated.

Gale snickered, walking behind Anna. "Here she is," he said. "Come and take her."

Anna swayed, lost like a dandelion puff drifting on the breeze as an odd sweeping crackle sounded in the darkness behind her.

Any other day she'd be terrified of the courtyard's darkness, but Gale was here. She belonged to him. He'd protect her.

A scream shrieked from Sybil's lips. Still in Connor's grip, she reached for Anna, pointing.

Anna blinked, startled when the cool air touched her cheek.

What were they doing outside?

A deep, guttural growl echoed through the courtyard. Anna spun toward the sound and froze. A huge figure loomed inches from her, dwarfing her slight form. Monstrous gray wings fluttered on the edge of the darkness before two bright, yellow eyes fixed on her.

Time froze for a moment while her mind took stock and tried to separate fantasy from reality.

What she saw wasn't possible. It wasn't real.

That certainly didn't change the fact that something huge and sinister stared back at her.

Heart racing, she ran, passing Connor and her sister, heading back toward the front of the tavern.

As she cleared the corner, Cain snatched her in a vise-like grip. "Don't leave now," he said. "The excitement has barely started."

He shoved her back toward the rear of the building, where the huge gray beast reared up, bellowing in fury over a smaller, silvery-white... God, could she even say it?

They were DRAGONS.

Cain's grip on her tightened. "Do you know how few human beings have seen dragons spar?" He whispered in her ear, "You should be honored."

Honored? Was this asshole out of his mind? Two more gray dragons dropped from the sky, one on either side of the small, pale dragon.

"When they disembowel the sniveling runt, Galeptopnor will offer you his seed to seal your union."

This was insane. She must have gotten a spiked drink at the bar.

Connor leaned out from behind a stack of empty vegetable crates and beckoned to her. She struggled, but Cain's grip dug deeper into her biceps.

Further inside the courtyard, the smaller dragon snarled and snapped, whipping one of the larger creatures with the edge of his tail. The gray howled, backing away, while the first dragon lashed out with one muscular, clawed arm.

A dull thud sounded through the air as the largest gray slammed its reptilian arm into the little dragon's chest. Cain yanked Anna back as the small dragon stumbled, but its wing hit them with the force of a baseball bat. Cain lost his grip and Anna thudded to the ground.

She ignored the pain, scrambled to her feet, and sprinted toward the stack of crates.

Connor held out a hand to her while dragging Sybil behind him. He grabbed onto Anna like a vise.

"Dra-dragons," Anna whimpered.

"So I see." Connor yanked, propelling her into a sprint beside him.

Sybil grunted with each clop of her chunky heels on the pavement. Anna thanked God for the foresight to wear sneakers.

As they slipped from the alley, Connor skidded to a stop a few feet from a line of three more men in gray fanned out in front of the tavern. The door opened, and the bartender stuck his head out. "I've called the police."

Connor didn't even glance in his direction. "Fine. Get inside and pull down the shades."

When they were alone, one of the gray-clad men smiled. "Hello Quenor."

Connor's nose flared. "Zeph." He backed Anna and Sybil up a step.

"So, that's your game, is it?" Zeph walked toward them. "Wait until Gale is busy with the runt, and you slip out with the prize? That's not playing fair."

Connor tugged the women closer. "That's not what's happening here." He glanced at Anna. "She's too young for my tastes."

Zeph held his hands out to his sides. "Yet here we are."

The silence seemed to echo along the sidewalk as Connor's gaze roamed the streets. If he was looking for a way out, Anna prayed he'd find it.

Zeph's face morphed into a feral sneer. "Hand the girl over. You know this won't end well for you, my friend."

Sirens sounded in the distance, drawing Zeph's attention away from them. Connor shoved Anna and Sybil down the alley opposite the tavern. "Run. Don't look back."

The wood and brick walls provided little protection from the biting wind, and even less from the roaring snarls that filled the night behind them.

Anna and Sybil stopped beside a dumpster.

"Oh, God. What were those things?" Sybil clutched her chest. "Who were those guys?"

Anna shook her head. She didn't give a damn about the guys, but she'd gotten a damn clear look at the creatures fighting behind the tavern. And no, she hadn't been hallucinating. There were actually dragons in New Zealand!

Sybil started to hyperventilate, and Anna grabbed her shoulders. "Stop. I need you to focus. Can you do that?"

Tears streamed from her sister's eyes. "Those things, they were monsters."

"I know, but we have to get out of here. Panicking isn't going to save us." She looked over her shoulder. No one else came down the alley, but the roars of the creatures heightened, as if there were even more of them now. She turned back to her sister. "We need to get to those sirens. I need you to run with me."

Sybil gulped, then nodded.

"Okay then, let's go."

They sprinted down the alley. Pungent smells from the dumpsters rose through the air, turning Anna's stomach. She ran faster, dragging her sister behind her. Their only chance was to find protection, and the sirens seemed as good a chance as any. She darted to the right, and down a deserted street.

Whooting beats filled the air, sounding like someone repeatedly snapping a towel. Anna blotted out the sound and concentrated on the sirens. If she dwelled on what might be flying toward her, she might succumb to a sobbing hysteria.

Something dug into her shoulders. She cried out as sharp claws punctured her flesh.

This wasn't real. This couldn't be happening. Why wasn't she waking up?

Her stomach flipped as the ground dropped out from below her. Sybil screamed, falling to her knees, looking up and reaching for Anna as she rose into the sky.

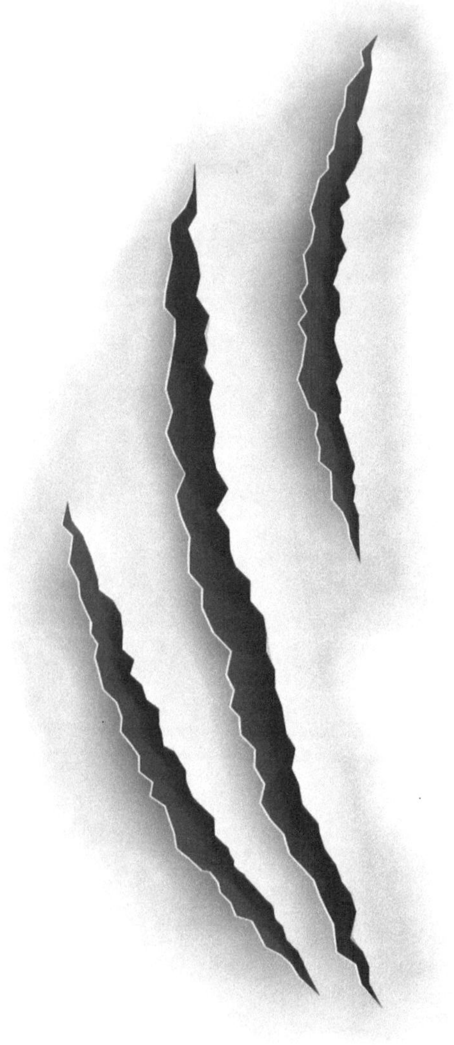

CHAPTER 3

The town drifted from sight as the wind whipped through Anna's hair and lashed her cheeks. The whooting beat of the creature's wings thudded in time with her erratic breathing. She twisted and slammed her fists against the gray-scaled talons digging into her shoulders. The pain and the blood oozing from her wounds seemed distant, lost in the wave of horror and her need to get free.

As they rose higher, her lungs burned, and her arms grew heavy. Dizzy, she hung limp and helpless in the huge creature's claws, watching the pinpoint lights of the towns below drift past. The air around her hummed like a frigid vacuum, mottled by the sound of the creature's relentless wings. Time could have stilled for all she knew, and the lights passing below could be just a mirage. Her eyes fluttered closed. Maybe if she slept for just a little while...

The beast holding her pitched to the side, and pain ripped through her shoulders. Anna hung on and prayed for this new torture to stop.

Her abductor howled into the night. Blinking away the tears,

Anna caught an immense, dark form in the moonlight seconds before it slammed into her captor's hide.

Anna gasped as the creature above released its grip.

She seemed to hang for a moment before gravity took hold, pulling her back to the ground where she belonged.

The lights of the town below raced toward her. The frigid wind cut into her skin. All pain whisked to the recesses of her mind as she flailed, her scream frozen in her throat.

Coherent sound vanished. The howling of the wind was her only companion, before a cascade of warm green fluttered around her, bumping her back up in the air. She struggled to catch her breath and a scream finally wrenched from her throat as she began to fall again. Her stomach balled as she grappled for unseen purchase.

The green shroud encompassed her again, before a gentler grip took her by the arms and pulled her back into the sky. The lights below grew distant once more. Anna pawed at the warm talons wrapped around her arms. Her shoulders screamed, but the pain paled in comparison to the merciless grip of her former captor. She struggled for breath and leaned her head against the claw gripping her left arm, thankful for the few second's rest despite being flown off by a different beast.

Somehow, though, she didn't feel threatened as she had by the gray dragon, as if this huge, gentle creature above meant no harm. Deep emerald-green scales sparkled in the moonlight as her new captor spun, heading away from the mountain.

Her wounds started to throb despite the gentle touch. A whoosh of breath escaped her lips, and she drew in another. Even though they were turned away from the mountain, heading back toward the populated areas, she was still the prisoner of a giant, flying reptile.

The beast slowed, hovering.

Anna blinked the sting from her eyes until the mist cleared and a gray dragon came into focus, beating its huge, bat-like wings. What took her breath away, though, was the pale, limp form of her sister dangling from the creature's talons.

"Sybil!"

The green dragon holding Anna bellowed in fury. Anna cringed, her ears ringing from the deafening sound. The gray howled once in return, and Anna could swear the beast smiled before opening its talons, dropping her best friend and only sister.

The sky became a nightmare as the green craned its wings and fell, careening toward Sybil's falling body. One of the dragon's claws released Anna as it grabbed for her sister, snatching her wrist. They jerked as Sybil's limp form jolted to a stop. The dragon's wings beat furiously, but they continued to fall.

Ignoring the pain in her shoulder, Anna screamed down to her sister. "Sybil! Sybil, wake up. Sybil!"

When would this insane nightmare end?

They spiraled toward the ground, the dragon beating its wings in a mad fury. Anna thought the creature looked at her, sorrow in its huge, dark eyes as it grunted with the extra weight of two women in its claws. It made a pitiful, whining sound before Anna's arm slipped from its grip.

Her stomach lurched as she fell, undeterred. Screaming, she looked up to see the beast wrapping its other claw around Sybil before night enveloped them. Anna flailed her arms and legs as the lights below screamed toward her.

They were beautiful, those lights, almost serene from above. Too bad she'd never know which town they were.

Another roar echoed through the darkness, and she slammed into something hard and warm. The breath knocked from her lungs. She coughed as she started to ascend like she'd landed on the floor of an elevator.

Her breathing slowed as a sense of safety rolled over her, but that was ridiculous, because the warm, gray-scaled hide beneath her hands *was not* an elevator. Anna trembled as the creature beat its wings, gaining altitude. A deep sense of calm fell over her like a veil. She closed her eyes and languished in it, until another hulking form slammed against her savior's hide.

Wait. Savior? This was another dragon!

She blinked away her stupor seconds before another huge, dark hide slammed against them. Anna wrapped her arms around her dragon's neck as it reared back. Her dragon inhaled, and night became day as a stream of blue and yellow flames spewed from the creature's mouth.

Holeee… Anna cringed back from the heat, but held tighter as the beast's neck warmed beneath her hands.

Something else slammed them from the side. The dragon balked and Anna lost her grip. She tumbled across the dragon's rigid spine and pawed at the creature's tail before careening toward the ground again.

Her scream echoed over the growls and roars of the multi-colored creatures whisking about, clawing at each other. She fell through them and back into the solace of darkness. Three seconds of relief was replaced by the shock of the lights below screaming toward her once more. Her head spun, the lights clouding into a haze as they got bigger.

It didn't matter anymore, nothing did. She closed her eyes and embraced the frigid air.

Something growled, joggling Anna out of her stupor as a streak of white flew past her. With the lines of the town below in view, Anna screamed as the blur bumped her from below, slowing her fall before white, glowing talons wrapped around her biceps, raising her into the air and dragging her feet across a sloped rooftop.

Dazzling white wings sparkled above, robbing the sky of moonlight and infusing the stars' brilliance into its own. Over-head, a green and a gray dragon beat their wings, snapping and spewing fire at each other before her white rescuer whisked her away from the mayhem and turned them once again toward the mountains in the distance. Those high peaks that only moments ago sparked terror through her core, now looked more like solace and salvation.

The dragon above her was small, maybe half the size of the others, but even more gentle than the green. He craned his neck to look at her, and what she saw stole her breath—not the soulless eyes of a beast, but concern, tenderness.

She closed her eyes and turned away. It was a trick. Somehow the creature had pushed her terror aside, masking her primal instincts and forcing her to be calm—probably making it easier for the beast to carry her to her death. She wouldn't give in.

The white dragon growled and coughed. They faltered, falling slightly before gaining altitude again. One of its wings flapped erratically, a dark fluid dripped from a jagged rip from the outer edge, clear through to the wing bone. Anna shuddered, remembering the clawing and hissing mass of dragons that were... fighting over her? All of this was too insane to comprehend.

With a final grunt, her sparkling savior stopped struggling. The bright wings wrapped around her and tightened. Her world became a glowing pearlescent tourniquet, tight and constricting. She struggled to breathe as dragons bellowed their fury somewhere in the distance.

The white dragon's heartbeat drummed in her ears, belaying a terror that may have matched her own, before the all-too familiar sensation of falling flayed what was left of her resolve. She pressed against the warm, tense wings nearly suffocating her, carrying them both to their death.

She yearned for the lights of the town, for the comforting presence of anyone human in these last few fleeting seconds; when the brief cry of dozens of muffled voices seeped through the creature's wings.

A moment of hope dissolved into a horrific crash, slamming her against the base of the dragon's still-clenched wings. Anna's head throbbed. Her chest stung. Dizzy, she was unable to suck in a breath, as the dragon's heartbeat faded to nothing.

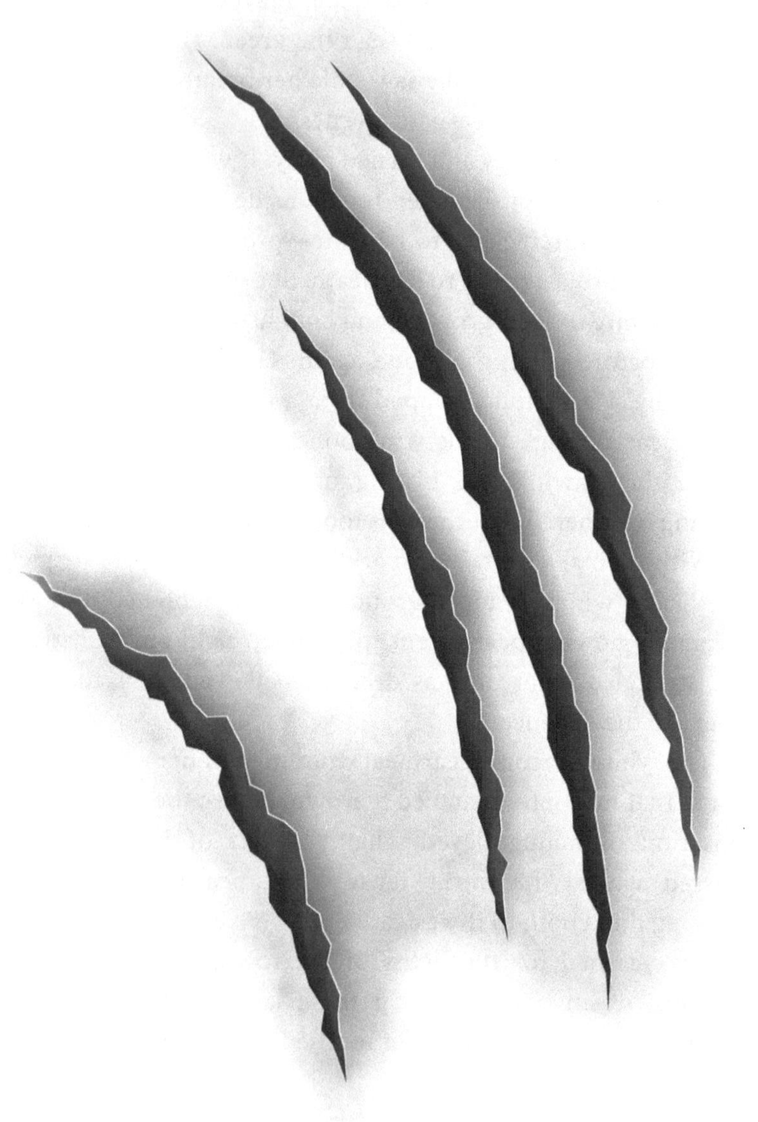

CHAPTER 4

*D*ragons didn't exist. If Nik could get his grandparents to believe that, living in the twenty-first century would be so much easier on them.

He scratched his head as his grandfather ascended the creaking wooden steps of the platform Nik had helped build earlier in the day. The majestic peaks of Mount Cook, or *Aoraki* as the old folks called the sacred mountain, glowed in the moonlight, casting an eerie backdrop to the ancient ceremony.

Shifting his weight, Nik bumped into one of the hundred or so onlookers lined up on the meadow as Pops lit the torches lining the stage, smiling at each of the teenage girls being offered up for the Seventeen Year sacrifice.

Nik shook his head and searched the girls' expressions. Most of the *sacrifices*, barely able to call themselves women, chatted amongst themselves, smiling. One tapped on her cellphone screen, while another was brazen enough to have her phone to her ear and her back to the onlookers.

They didn't believe in this ridiculous ceremony any more than he did. If a single one of them thought there was even a remote possibility that a dragon would swoop out of the sky and snatch them off the platform, they'd be running for the hills, screaming. They, like he, were there to make their parents happy—or in Nik's case, his grandparents.

There were dozens of places he'd rather be on a Friday night. He counted them off in his mind and blinked them away. Pops would notice if he was *woolgathering*, as his grandparents called it. The old man had an uncanny ability to know when Nik was procrastinating, or daydreaming, or lying; name the sin. The creepy skill grated on Nik's nerves, but he loved the old guy, despite his archaic religious beliefs.

His grandfather started chanting toward the sky as if the stars might actually answer him for the first time in his life. You had to give the old man kudos for his trust in the ancient ways. Nanna and Pops believed without question that dragons existed, even though they admitted to never seeing one.

They were both descendants of the ancient Maori clans that roamed New Zealand before it appeared on any modern-day maps. Every thought, every decision they made was deeply rooted in Maori tradition. Honoring the past was a duty, and not one they took lightly. Their history was a part of them, and as ridiculous as this ceremony was, Nik could afford to stand in the middle of nowhere once every seventeen years, if that's what made his grandparents happy.

Well, *normally* he could afford to waste time. This, unfortunately, hadn't been a red banner year for him. Not that the year before had been much better.

He eyed the makeshift shelters lining the outer edge of the ceremony—a crude ancient Maori village recreated every seventeen years for this event. His family's tent rose from the ground only a few paces away. It would provide the perfect solace to get some real work done.

However, he owed his grandparents this night of stupidity after they raised him from a tot. Truth was, he would do anything for them. Except tell them the truth, that he was penniless and about to lose the apartment they'd cosigned for him. If he didn't find a job in the next few days, he'd have to bury what was left of his dignity and move back in with them. Again.

Life had turned to crap after the plant closed two years ago. He hadn't eaten a real meal in days, which was why the more practical side of him knew he couldn't just stand here and watch this senseless ceremony while he should be looking for a way to earn a living.

The elders lifted their torches to the night sky and joined his grandfather's chant in the Maori tongue. The odd words rang out in a choppy, but melodious crescendo. Nik recognized a word here and there. Among the crowd, the blank expressions told him he wasn't the only one who didn't understand most of it. Maori was a dying language from a dying culture. He had no idea why the elders clung to their ancient language and tradition. It was irrational. Modern ways and English had swept across New Zealand eons ago. Why they refused to adapt was a mystery to him.

When his grandfather closed his eyes and reached up to the heavens, Nik inched to the back of the crowd and slipped into their tent.

He pulled out his cell phone and held it high, smiling when he got a connection. He called up his *Career Digger* app and scrolled through the new job listings. At this point, he'd pick up dog crap if there was a steady paycheck in it.

A scream outside turned his blood to ice. He shoved his phone in his pocket and brushed open the slit in the tent. Someone stumbled by the opening as the teenage girls scrambled down the platform stairs, while others jumped into the fleeing crowd.

In the darkness above, a whooting sound, like a helicopter in slow motion, created a choppy breeze that fanned the flames of the torches. Nik blinked, sure his eyes deceived him when the edge of a huge blue wing caught the torchlight before the flames whisked out.

"Hold!" His grandfather was the only one left on the platform. "Hold! We have nothing to fear."

The chaos told Nik otherwise. Above them, shots of fire lit up the darkness, as if two men floated above dueling with flamethrowers. A dark form moved overhead, much closer than the blasting flames. The breeze caused by the huge shape extinguished all but the torch held by his grandfather.

A shriek among the stars stunned the Maori, freezing most and drawing their eyes to the sky. The flamethrower fight above began anew—but something fell toward them. Something large.

"Pops get down!" Nik lunged for the platform, his heart throttling as his grandfather stood motionless, watching the object speed toward him.

He'd be crushed. God, no. He'd be crushed!

The remainder of the crowd scattered as the object, white and round, careened to the surface. The ground quaked as the projectile slammed to the Earth between Nik and the platform.

Nik skidded to a stop, choking on the rising dust. "Pops!"

The world slowed around him. The dull thud of Nik's own heart throbbed in his ears. Pops had been his world, his everything for as long as he could remember. He'd taught Nik how to ride a bicycle, and how to drive a car. He'd been there for him through school and sports and a long line of failed relationships. Nik should have been out here, paying attention to the ceremony. He should have been close enough to get to his grandfather, to save the man who had raised him.

The powdery cloud settled, revealing first the still-blazing torch, then his grandfather's wide eyes as he stood on the crippled, leaning platform. The old man's gaze drew to the sky, and a horrified look overcame his consternation.

"The tarp." Pops gestured to those who had not fled. "Quickly."

A man wearing a traditional bright red, green, and blue mottled vest reached under the platform. A second joined him and pulled out a large, silvery-black roll. A third arrived as they struggled to unravel what looked like a thick blanket.

"Nikau, help them." His grandmother parted the crowd gathered on the fringe of the spectacle and jostled him forward.

Blinking away his surprise, and the dust caking his eyes, Nik grasped an edge of the tarp and pulled with the others, surprised by the heavy weight of the fabric.

"What are we doing?" Nik asked.

"We need to cover it, quickly," the man in the vest said.

Okay, not quite the depth of explanation he was hoping for, but Nik carried their burden toward the smoking fallen—Meteor? Boulder? Where in God's name had it fallen from, and why was everyone acting like it needed to be hidden?

A roar filled the night sky. Maybe many roars. Shit.

Shit shit shit! What the hell was up there?

They unrolled the tarp, and the guy beside him helped Nik attach the corner of the fabric on the edge of a pole while another group had hastily assembled more poles around the smoking, white *thing*.

As he paused, the others worked as a cohesive unit, stretching out the tarp over the poles to cover the smoldering object.

What did these people do, train daily on the off chance that a giant rock would fall out of the sky?

A firm grip shoved him forward. "Come Nikau. Our time has come." Pops led him into the hastily made structure as the others pulled seams taut from the outside.

The exterior lights went dark, leaving only the ghostly glow of his grandfather's torch flickering against the tent walls. Pops checked the support poles, nodding as he pushed on each.

"Our time has come for what?" Nik asked.

Pops extinguished his torch, and the tent sealed shut behind him, leaving them in darkness. "Our Destiny."

CHAPTER 5

"*Help.*" *Nikky wiped the tears from his eyes and struggled against the belts restraining him against his booster car seat.*

His arms fell down toward the front of the car. His mother's hand caught the edge of the moonlight.

"Mommy?" he whispered between tears, but she didn't respond.

Nikky craned his neck to see past the back of the driver's seat, but his father was hidden from view. Above, a bank of clouds shrouded the moon. He wasn't afraid. He was a big boy. It was just the dark. Only babies were afraid of the dark.

A ball twisted in his throat as the sound of an owl carried through the shattered front windshield. "Mommy, please wake up." He wiped tears from his eyes. "Daddy?" The darkness crept in from all sides. He sobbed into the fold of his booster seat until exhaustion overtook him.

NIK CRINGED AS THE STENCH OF WET FIREPLACE ACCOSTED HIS nose. He turned over and tried to grab his pillow, but his hands found nothing but dirt and stone.

What the hell?

He bolted upright, squinting in the haze around him until his grandfather's smiling face came into focus.

"Pops?"

"Morning is finally here. Are you ready?"

"Pops, I told you last night, I have no freaking clue what you're talking about."

Nanna had insisted on Nik drinking some kind of cider as soon as she and the rest of the elders had been sealed inside this makeshift tent with rockus-giganticus. Three sips and he had a vague memory of someone catching him. He rubbed his aching temple. If he didn't know better, he'd say he'd been drugged.

Pops tapped his shoulder. "Come, let us begin."

Nanna approached and handed her grandson another mug. Nik stepped back, eyeing the dark drink.

She smiled. "Coffee this time. Extra shot. This will wake you up in two snaps of a dragon's tail."

His eyes narrowed. "You drugged me last night."

She shrugged. "Nothing new. How do you think I got you to stay in bed as a toddler?"

The dusty air dried his tongue before he shut his mouth. Despite her smile, Nanna wasn't the joking type. She probably wasn't kidding.

His head spun again, and he grabbed the coffee and chugged it down in three gulps. Wiping his mouth with his sleeve, he stood beside Pops as two of the men from last night drew a light sheet from the boulder. The surface of the object sparkled like uniform shards of glass hard woven into the outer facing in a flowing pattern of veined ridges.

The boulder twitched.

What the...?

Nik stepped back, but reset himself, realizing he was the only one who reacted. His grandfather stepped toward the boulder.

"Pops, wait."

The older man raised his chin. "We've waited far too long already."

Nik's breath hitched as Pops ran his hand over the surface of the—God, what? He gaped, measuring the awestruck expressions of those around him.

"You don't realize what this is, do you?" Nanna stepped beside him.

Nik shook his head. "I sure wish someone would fill me in."

Pops placed both hands on the object. "Dawn rises, Great One. The battle is done. Let daylight and your people protect you from those who may do you harm."

The stone rumbled and broke apart on one side. No, it didn't break apart. It shivered and unraveled, like it was *alive*.

The rock groaned. Half of it broke apart and draped along the ground like a thick, veined sheet. A jagged rip sliced through what looked far too much like a wing. A giant, shimmering, white wing!

Nanna squeezed his arm. "Yes, dear one. It's a dragon."

Nik flinched. She'd spoken so matter of fact, like saying, "Yes, Nik, the sky is blue," or "Rain falls from the clouds." Didn't she have any idea what this meant?

She turned to the man beside her, a middle-aged bloke sporting a thick, dusky beard and worn jeans. "What do you think, Tyler?"

He scratched his mustache, dropping to his haunches beside the unfurled wing. "He's hurt pretty bad. If the ancient tomes are true, he's small, even for a crystal dragon." Tyler brushed his fingers beside the torn edge. "What were you doing out there, young buck? Those big dragons nearly made a meal of you."

He drew his fingers closer to the wing bone, and the closed part of the boulder rippled with a flash of white light. A huge snout filled with gleaming teeth appeared, growling and hissing in Tyler's face. Nik stumbled back as the creature's icy blue eyes lanced each of them.

Tyler remained on his haunches, still. Maybe not even breathing. After about five seconds, he eased his head down and bared his neck to the mythical monster. Was he out of his mind?

Nanna had held her place despite the monstrous alligator-shaped jaws pointed at her. She spread her hands. "We are your people, Great One. We have waited long for the opportunity to serve. Please, let us help you."

A rumble manifested deep within the beast's throat.

She took a step forward.

"Nanna, don't," Nik said.

"Hush." Another step, her arms still splayed and palms showing. "Let us prove ourselves to you. You are hurt. We have supplies. Tyler is a veterinarian. Let us heal you."

Tyler slowly elevated his head as the white snout sniffed his hair.

Nanna pointed at the injured wing. "Do we have your permission?"

The beast lowered its nose before tucking its snout back inside the other wing, like a bird snuggling into its nest.

Now he'd seen it all. That thing had actually listened to her.

Tyler returned his attention to the wing. "Elaina, fetch my bag."

"On it." A young blonde girl who couldn't be more than sixteen skirted to the other side of the tent.

"Will you be able to help him?" Nanna asked.

"Sure," Tyler said. "It's just like working on a really big, winged cow."

She smacked his head. "I'm serious."

"So am I. I have no clue." He rubbed the back of his head where she'd slapped him. "I can clean out the injury and stitch up the ripped wing, but the histories of the dragon healers were lost. I'll only be guessing."

"And your guess is?"

He stood. "In my opinion, it will be days before he can shift, and weeks before he can fly again."

Nanna grimaced, sharing a glance with Pops. Neither of them looked happy with that response.

Elaina returned with an old-fashioned black leather doctor's bag. "Here, Dad."

The vet grabbed the satchel. "Thanks, Sweetie."

Pops gently levied the injured wing off the ground, and Elaina held the ripped edges of the thin membrane together as Tyler poured water over the tear and painstakingly stitched the jagged edges together.

The dragon only twitched a few times before Tyler puffed out a relieved breath and eased away from his patient. "There you have it. For now, that's all I can do."

Everyone exchanged glances. A huge *so-now-what* stare bounced between them. The silence bled into the air before a whimper rose up from within the still-folded wing; not a deep, menacing sound, but a frightened, high pitched...

"Hello?" A small voice called from within. "Is someone out there?"

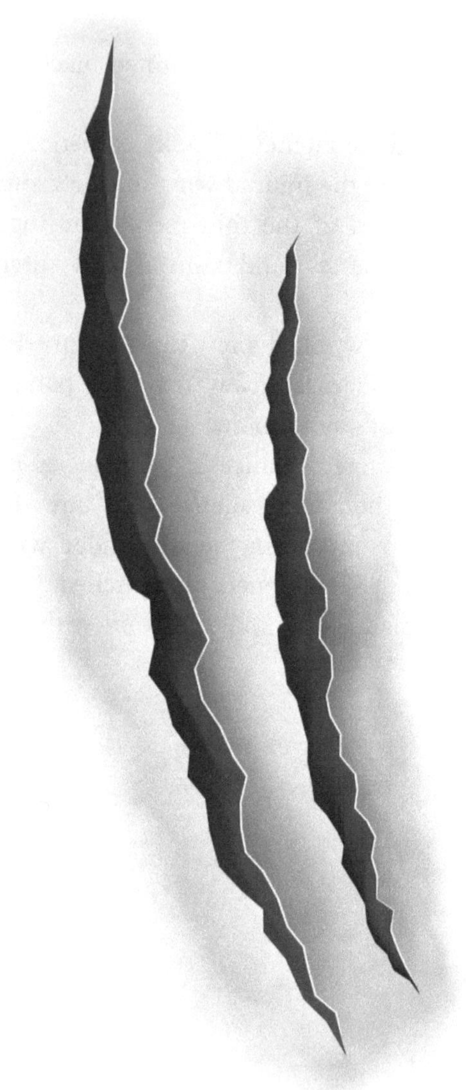

CHAPTER 6

*P*ops returned his hands to the side of the dragon.

"Could it be possible?" Nanna fell to her knees beside her husband.

Pops closed his eyes, pressing his hands on the dragon's outer hide as if listening through the touch. "There is an extra heartbeat. Not Draconic."

Nanna reached up and caressed the point where the dragon's head had disappeared. "Do you have a prize, Great One? Is that why the others attacked you? Had you won the game?"

"Please be careful," Nik said, but he couldn't bring himself to do more than stand and watch. Were they both out of their minds? That was a giant reptile, teeth and all.

Sobs carried up from within the dragon's folded wing.

Nanna continued her stroking. "We have been taught that the crystal dragons were the oldest and wisest of the Draconi. They ruled when our land was free and pure. If you have a prize, we welcome her and rejoice with the great Sky Father, *Rakinui*. Let us make sure she is unharmed for you."

Rakinui? She was spouting ancient gibberish when there was a giant, wounded animal inches from her, ready to lash out at any moment.

"Please, help me," the girl's voice pleaded.

Nik shuddered. The voice seemed so small and alone. His heartbeat quickened. His breath came in slow, staggered gasps.

Nikky rubbed his eyes as the sunlight shone through the car window. His arms ached, sore where his seatbelt gripped him to the car booster seat. The back of Daddy's hand on the dashboard came into focus, then the back of his mother's head, leaning against the broken windshield below him.

"Mommy?"

She didn't move.

"Mommy!"

He struggled, shaking his seat until the car moaned and creaked. The metal frame shifted and the car jolted forward—or down.

Nikky's grip hardened on his seatbelt. His breath stuck in his throat as the side of the mountain spread out before him, and the meadow, miles away, seemed to laugh at him from so far below. Afraid to breathe, let alone move, his head spun.

Voices sounded from above. "Help," he whispered, but the sound barely squeaked from his mouth.

"Is anybody down there?" someone called.

Nikky trembled, clinging to his seatbelt.

The meadow, so far away.

His parents, why didn't they answer?

Why was the big window broken?

Who were those people?

All the while, the meadow called, waiting for Nikky to fall.

Nik straightened, taking in a slow, deep breath. He, better than anyone, knew that no one deserved to be alone and afraid.

"We need to get her out of there." He stomped toward the shimmering mound and grabbed the edge of the fold where the head had disappeared.

"Nikky, no!" Nanna and Pops shouted in unison.

The warm, rough hide shifted, and a puff of hot, smoky air blasted across Nik's face. He froze, staring into two white nostrils the size of fists hovering mere inches from his eyes. A low grumble resounded from somewhere below.

"Don't move," Pops said.

He wasn't planning on moving. At the moment, breathing wasn't top of his list, either.

"He means no harm, Great One." Nanna's voice was soft, placating. "He only wants to make sure the girl is all right. We want her safe, just as you do."

Nanna stroked the lizard's scaly snout, mere inches away from teeth longer than Nik's fingers. Why was everyone acting like this godforsaken thing could understand them?

The creature reared back and roared in Nik's face. He fell, and the vet dragged him back, slamming them both to the dirt floor.

Tyler wiped his brow with his sleeve. "Life lesson, kid. Don't piss off a dragon."

Nik pushed him away. "No shit." He stood, but the dragon stretched his long neck, his fierce gaze meeting Nik's.

"Get on your knees," Tyler said. "Lower you head in submission."

"Are you out of your fucking mind?"

The dragon growled.

Nanna kept her hand on the beast's neck as she turned to him. "He thinks you are challenging him for the girl. This is a fight you cannot win, Nikau. You must show him you acquiesce."

Heat and smoke spewed from the creature's mouth. Dragons breathing fire, that had to be myth, right? But the idea of dragons, in itself, was a myth.

The creature's growl deepened. Its eyes narrowed—such a human response, so knowing.

"Please, Nikky," Nanna said. "For once in your life, listen to reason."

Reason? There was no room for reason in a world where Nikau Smith was staring down the gullet of a dragon.

The beast moved closer. Maybe she was right. Picking a fight with something five times his size was not smart. But they had to save that girl. If he had to bow to a stinking animal to make that happen, so be it.

Nik dropped to his knees and lowered his head. "Is this enough? Maybe I should just distract it so someone can snatch the girl."

The dragon roared at the tent's ceiling. The hidden girl screamed from within its furled wings.

Pops dropped to his knees beside Nik. "Please forgive, Great One. No one is going to take her from you. You have my promise in this."

"Why do you keep talking like this stupid thing can understand you?"

A puff of hot air blasted his face again.

"Because this is not a dumb lizard," Pops said. "This is a living, breathing, sentient dragon lord. *Our* dragon lord. The new king, if we can help him take the throne."

The dragon leaned back.

Pops stood slowly, hands splayed to the dragon. "We are here to serve. My grandson is young, arrogant, and unschooled in our ways. I take the blame for that. The world has changed innumerably. If you are here to restore balance to your island, you will face many challenges. Please, let us help you."

The dragon rustled, shaking its glowing white mane and growling like a dog asking to be fed. Nik hoped it wasn't really asking to be fed, because right now these crazy old people looked pretty darn pissed at the only young, arrogant kid in the tent.

Nanna moved between Nik, Pops, and the dragon. The creature lowered his head to meet her eyes. "We don't understand, Great One, but as you know, there is a way we can communicate." She looked back at her husband.

"Carolyn, no," Pops whispered.

She held up her hand. "There is no other way." She turned back to the dragon. "I am a *Kotahi*, the last of my line. I am, and always will be, your servant."

The dragon tilted its head.

"Do you know what the *Kotahi* are, Great One?"

It lowered its head to the ground and craned its neck away from her.

Tyler placed his hand on her arm. "Carol, this is insane. The *Kotahi* were all taken young, and even then, half of them died."

"Never at the strike of a crystal dragon. Deaths are recorded from the reds and the grays." She slid her hand along the dragon's head. "We need to talk to him. We need to give him a voice."

Nik sighed. "Would someone please explain what the hell you people are talking about? There is a girl hidden in there." He pointed to the dragon's wing. "We need to get her out."

Tyler dragged his fingers through his bangs. "Your grandmother wants to let the dragon bite her."

"What?"

Nanna lifted her chin. "To make a bond that will allow me to speak for him. Our family has held this station for generations. *Kotahi* means *One* in Maori. As in two minds, one voice. *Kotahi Reo*, the voice of the dragon."

"You are *not* letting that thing bite you."

The dragon straightened and bumped her back. When she turned, it shook its head like a giant puppet saying 'no'.

That did it. Nik had to be dreaming.

"Dragons have venom, like a snake," Tyler explained. "It's written that the bite of a dragon, on the right host, creates a connection, and yes, the *Kotahi* have been dragon speakers in all the Draconic histories, but Carol, with your heart, and your age…" He placed his hand on her arm. "You can't."

"I must." She turned to the dragon. "We can't help each other with yes and no answers. We need to talk to you." She rolled up her sleeve and reached her bare arm to the beast.

Nik batted her arm away. "Like hell. You are not letting that thing bite you."

"There is no other way."

Nik turned to the dragon. "Do *you* want to bite her?"

It shook its head again.

Yeah, damn, this had to be some kind of freaky dream.

"Good." He turned to Nanna. "See? The dragon doesn't even want to do it."

Tyler narrowed his eyes, staring at Nik. "*You* can do it."

Nik retreated, before realizing he had nearly backed into the dragon. "What?"

"You share the same bloodline. You have *Kotahi* blood, too."

Nik's eyes widened. "You want me to let the dragon bite me?" He looked at each of them. "You people are all certifiable, you know that?"

Nanna pushed him. "Then get out of my way." She held out her arm to the dragon, again.

The creature looked from her, to Nik, before shoving her to the side with its snout once more.

"It knows you won't survive, Carol," Tyler said. "The Great Ones care about humanity. They always have. That's what made them such accomplished rulers. If he were a gray, you'd probably be dead already."

She shoved her arm closer to the dragon, but it snorted and turned away.

The voice within the beast's folded wing fell to hysterical sobs.

Nik stepped toward the dragon. "Okay, listen, you can obviously understand what we're saying. How about you take your sentient badass comprehension for a ride and let that girl go before she has a heart attack."

It shook its head for the third time.

"Great." Nik turned to Tyler. "How about tranquilizers. Can't you just shoot the damn thing?"

The dragon roared.

Tyler held up his hands. "I would never think of it, Great One."

"P-p-please," the voice sobbed.

"Enough," Nanna said.

Nik stepped between her and the dragon, and took a deep breath. "So, is this true? If you bite one of us, we'll be able to understand you?"

Smoke whisked from the beast's nostrils before it looked down.

For all Nik knew, the dragon-whisperer portion of the Maori legends was the only part of all this insanity that wasn't accurate. But as he took in the solid, determined profile of the woman who raised him as her own, he couldn't help but wonder if maybe all of their stories, all the myths, all the bedtime tales they'd shared with him were true. What if there really was a way to communicate? This could be the start of an incredible journey—or a damnable end.

Either way, this lovely, wonderful woman who'd given up so much for him was not going to risk her life. Not while he was still breathing.

"Take me," he told the dragon. "I'll be your guinea pig."

The beast snorted as Nik rolled up his sleeve.

Nik glanced at the vet. "How bad is this going to hurt?"

Tyler shrugged. "I have no idea. No one has seen a live dragon in a thousand years."

Great. Just great.

Nik held out his arm. The dragon stared at him, then Nanna, then the vet. It took in a deep breath, then released it. If Nik didn't know better, and he probably didn't, he'd think that was a sigh.

The beast head-butted Nik in the chest, sprawling him into the dirt with a thud.

"What the hell, you..." Nik forgot what he was about to say as the dragon took his sneaker in his mouth, and dragged his body closer. It nosed his leg twice.

"The femoral artery," Tyler said. "Your leg is probably a better conduit for the venom."

Venom. Dammitall. This was insane. Letting this thing bite his arm was one thing, but bite his leg? There was a hell of a lot more flesh to gnaw on down there.

Behind the vet, Pops slipped his arm around Nanna's shoulder. She leaned into him, but her eyes were on Nik. A smile beamed from her face.

Nik had struggled through school and sports and life in general. He'd been such a burden on them. But he owed them so much for taking him in after the accident. They'd shown him love when there was no one else in his life left to give him that comfort. They'd been so patient with him through every pitfall. They always encouraged, rarely scolded. But it occurred to him now, taking in her expression, that he'd never seen pride in her eyes.

As terrified as he was, his heart lifted.

Tyler pointed to Nik's belt buckle. "You're going to need to take off your pants."

"I know where the femoral artery is." *I'm not a total idiot.*

He shifted out of his pants, thankful for choosing a nondescript pair of boxers yesterday morning. The dragon loomed above him.

God, he had to be out of his mind. This was stupid. Dumb. Insane.

The dragon lowered its head and took Nik's leg into its mouth. Coarse teeth dragged across his flesh. A damp heat swathed his skin.

This was it. He wiped the sweat from his brow.

What was he thinking by agreeing to this collective insanity? How was he going to…? He winced and dug his fingers into the dry, trampled grass as two simultaneous pricks entered his skin.

CHAPTER 7

$\mathcal{N}$ik clamped his jaw shut, determined not to scream as the bite deepened. He grunted, taking shallow breaths, until the dragon abated, easing away from him.

That was it?

He puffed out a laugh. "That wasn't so bad."

A pencil appeared in front of his face. "Bite on this," Tyler said.

Well, it was a little late for that.

His grandmother came into focus behind the end of the eraser. She gestured to the pencil. "Do it, quickly."

"Okay, but it's over. It hardly even hurt." He shoved the pencil between his teeth, just before the world spun. He dug his fingers further into the earth, but his nails broke off and bled. He screamed as the soil boiled, dragging his hands into its depths before he yanked them free and jumped to his feet. Night had fallen like a thick mist around them. The world became a blur of dark, slow moving shapes.

A shadowy figure wrapped around him, dragging him back to the rolling terrain. Nik kicked and spat, jerking free as he jammed his knee into the shadow's groin.

Somewhere in the distance, a man grunted and cursed, but

Nik sprinted toward a bright beacon shining over the horizon. The light was warm, safe, he needed to get there before… A giant, winged creature reared up before him, shimmering in the darkness. Nik fell, and a thousand hands grasped his arms, yanking him back and holding him to the ground. He screamed and kicked as two huge, glowing eyes materialized in the endless night sky. A hot puff of smoky breath wafted over his face.

Wait. There had been a dragon.

No, but that was ridiculous. Dragons weren't real.

The hands around him tightened. He twisted and kicked as he sunk deeper into the earth. The soil bubbled up and over his head, churning as it dragged him down. He screamed, but dirt filled his mouth, silencing him as the darkness covered everything.

"Nikky." Nanna's voice, a fleeting call from a time long gone, beckoned in the distance.

He was far away. Floating.

Blue sky and clouds shot past his face. Wind whipped through his hair as he soared through the sky. He laughed as the mountains passed far below. But man wasn't meant to fly. He couldn't be up here. It was impossible. Inconceivable.

A burst of wind hit his side. His stomach dropped out as he fell. The peak of Mount Cook came rushing toward him—merciless, unrelenting earth waiting to squash him on impact.

"Nikky!"

He lurched, lost in a world of pitch black. He screamed, fighting a grip far stronger than his own. A deep, pressing weight crushed him, drilled him back into the soil, and he squeaked out a dry scream as his eyes shot open, blinded by a blazing sun filtered through the creases in the thick canvas and silhouetting the outline of a…

Oh God, it hadn't been a dream.

The three-inch claws of a dragon held him down while a gray-haired woman slapped his face.

"Nikky!"

He puffed out a breath. "I'm here." He blinked against the light. "I'm here."

The dragon removed its foot, and Nanna drew Nik into her arms. Nik heard Pops whisper, "Thank you, Great One."

Thank you? The goddamn thing bit me!

Pushing out of his grandmother's arms, he grabbed his pants and pulled them up slowly over his injured leg. This had to rate up there with the stupidest things he'd ever done. He zipped his fly and shot his attention back to the dragon's one folded wing.

Shit. The girl.

He eased off the ground and took a stumbling step.

Tyler steadied him. "Take it easy. You've been unconscious for nearly an hour."

The dragon rumbled a challenge deep within its throat.

But Nik was tired of bowing and scrabbling at this creature's scaly feet. It was nothing more than a winged alligator, and if they had to make this stupid animal into a suitcase to save whoever this thing was holding, then so be it.

"All right, you sack of shit. I let you poison me. Now give up the girl."

Mine. Need. Find.

Nik's head spun, and Tyler grabbed him again.

What the hell was that?

Home. Pain. Hurt. Take.

Nik's stomach churned. He leaned over and heaved. His dry throat rasped as a cough overtook him.

Nanna placed her hand on his back. "You need to open yourself, Nikau. Let the dragon in."

Let the dragon in? Had this woman always been certifiable? What in God's name was she talking about now?

Another rumble, and the huge nostrils appeared by the side of his face again. *Respect.*

Nik turned away. "Great. Now I'm hearing things."

"Do you hear him?" Nanna asked.

No. It wasn't possible.

Nik gulped, and looked down the snout of the looming beast. "Did you just say something?"

Insolent. Ungrateful.

Nik grabbed his temples and leaned over. Those weren't his words.

But that was impossible.

Nanna placed her hand on his back. "What does the Great One say? Will he let us see the girl? Tell him we mean no harm."

Nik concentrated on the new sensations whirling through his mind. "It's not like that. He doesn't talk. It's more like emotions. Feelings. Well, no, it *is* words, but emotion words. He's not really talking. It's more like he's thinking what he feels."

Nanna took his face in her hands. "You are still fighting it. Open yourself to your *Kotahi* heritage. Be *one* with the dragon."

One with the dragon. Great. Were we going to start yoga chants now?

The dragon snorted.

Wait, did that thing just laugh? He hadn't said that out loud, right?

Another whimper from within the creature's wing. The beast lowered its head. Its eyes seemed sad.

She afraid. I afraid.

"Holy shit," Nik whispered.

"Yes," Nanna said. "Open yourself. Allow the dragon to flow through you."

Flow? He didn't know jack shit about flow, but his blood tingled, sparkling through his veins.

Nik straightened. A sense of power coursed through him, a power he knew wasn't his own. As insane as it all seemed, Nanna was right. He could *feel* the dragon, and the emotions streaming through him were not the senseless thoughts of a wild beast, but the rational, discerning thoughts of an intelligence that matched —hell, probably *surpassed* his own.

This wasn't an animal that they were dealing with, not in the sense he'd thought. As the essence of this creature surged through him, he had to admit, this was something more. It was time for him to step up and take the reins.

Nik held out his hands to the dragon. "We get that you're afraid. But so is she."

This was crazy. Stupid. He was talking to a lizard. His mind whirled, struggling to come to terms with what his rational brain saw, and the swirl of clear, analytical thought and emotion coursing through him. Animal, yet not. Uncanny. Strange.

Biped talk stranger. The words loomed in his head, as if they rose up from a space deep within him, hovered, and slipped away as quickly as they'd manifested.

Shit. That was enough to drive anyone nuts. But if Nik was hearing the dragon's thoughts, could the dragon hear him?

Some. Erratic. Hard. The dragon shifted, and the girl screamed again.

Nik raised his hands higher. "Then search my mind. Know that we wouldn't hurt her."

That was the truth, at least. He needed to get her free if they had any chance of smuggling her off this mountain.

The dragon growled deep within its chest.

Nik pushed his thoughts away. This was going to be harder than he thought. "Okay, let's agree not to trust me." He pointed to the Maori around him. "But you can trust these people. They want to help. They may all be certifiable, but they are along for this crazy ride. They're going to do everything in their power to do what's right by you. All they want to do right now is make sure the girl is all right, and then give her right back to you. Okay?"

The dragon craned his neck. *She will run. She is afraid.*

Damn, its sentences were getting clearer by the second. Nik sighed. "Do you blame her? God knows where you grabbed her from, and you've had her tucked in your wing all night."

Safe.

"Yeah, maybe, but terror can really mess a person up in the head." He shivered, remembering the small child trapped in the car seat as he took a step toward the beast. "Just let us take a look at her. I promise I won't try to take her away."

Not yet, at least. One step at a time.

The dragon growled again.

Dammit, Nik needed to keep his thoughts in check. He stared into the beast's eyes. If he was going to be his grandparent's *Kotahi*, he was going to be the best damn *Kotahi* that ever lived. He wouldn't let this dragon manipulate him.

The creature hobbled to the left on three legs, one still holding the girl within its wing. If its muscles were anything like a human's, the dragon had to be hurting after clutching someone for so long. And the angry red swelling around the stitches in its wing had to ache.

All that aside, if the lizard didn't drop the girl, they would be at a stalemate, and if what he remembered about the Seventeen Year ritual was true, this thing only had a few days to return to its lair, or wherever the hell dragons came from; and that wing looked pretty screwed up in his uneducated opinion.

Nik furrowed his brow. If the dragon was as smart as he seemed, he knew his limitations, and he knew better than anyone how hurt he was. No matter how proud this creature might be, he needed help.

Nik glanced at the creature's primary caregiver. Tyler was a human being before he became veterinarian to a mythical beast. Nik was fairly certain that he could coerce the man into not treating the dragon unless their demands were met; and right now, they needed to convince this thing to drop the girl. Period.

He opened his mouth to say as much, when the dragon blinked, puffed out a hot breath, and unfurled its left wing.

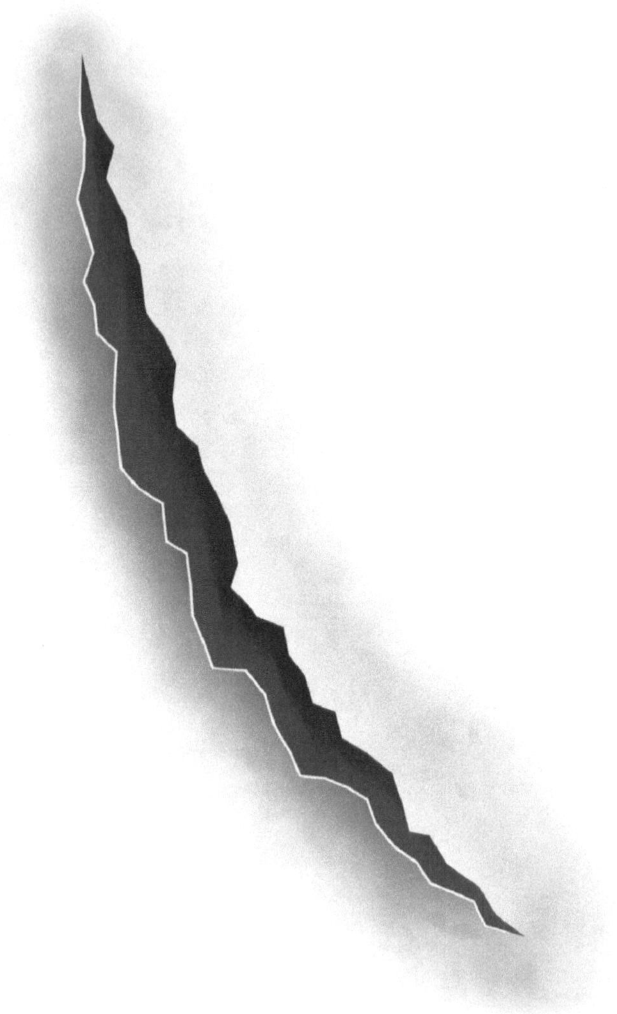

CHAPTER 8

*A*nna gasped as she tumbled into the cool air and slammed into the dirt. Sand kicked up around her face, and she coughed as someone threw a blanket around her shoulders.

An old woman wiped her forehead with a cool, damp cloth. "Shhh," she said. "You're fine. Everything is going to be fine."

Fine? She'd never be fine again.

Anna drew in a deep breath and let it out slowly. Those had been dragons last night. She'd witnessed an entire hoard of fairy-tale beasts fighting in the middle of town. If she hadn't been there, she'd never have believed it.

The old woman pulled her closer, cooing something in her ear and rocking her like a child. She trembled, relishing the warm, gentle touch of a human being.

This was real, right? She wasn't dreaming this time; she was actually here with this lady, wherever here was.

Last night was real too, no matter how hard she tried to discount it.

Anna had run into the alley with Sybil. Something grabbed her and she'd lifted into the sky. The houses and shops had looked so small, like they shrank before her eyes.

She shuddered. Anna could have been something's dinner right now if it hadn't been for... for who?

It seemed like hours of frigid air chilling her skin and a thousand beats of massive wings before they were attacked by another group of dragons. During the scuffle, she'd dropped from the creature's talons. A terror worse than being snatched by a mythical beast lashed through her as the wind, so loud and cold, whipped past her in the night sky. Endless darkness had spread out below. She could sense, more than see the Earth as she careened toward her death, until a roar filled the sky, and a large hand wrapped around her arm.

She blinked away the horror of the memory.

It hadn't been a hand. Claws had wrapped around her arm, but they didn't dig into her flesh like the other dragon's. They'd grasped gently, despite the creature's haste.

Leaning away from the woman, Anna took in the wafting, tan tent walls around her.

When she'd been plucked out of the sky, she'd been shoved inside some kind of sack, and they'd continued to fall. The warm, soft bag whisked away the night chill, until it constricted, clamping around her as they crashed to the ground. She'd blacked out, and woke with the warm fabric still swaddling her.

"Take slow, deep breaths," the older woman cautioned. "We're going to take care of you. Everything will be fine."

But it hadn't been a blanket at all, or a bag. The fabric had twitched in the night, as if alive. A heartbeat lulled her in and out of sleep.

And now she was here, with this woman, and all these strangers staring at her.

Sensing movement behind her, she hazarded a look over her shoulder.

Some moments freeze in time. Some unforgettable moments are joyous, while others stick with you for very different reasons.

Seeing two huge, crystalline eyes peering at you from over a shimmering silver snout was one of those inexplicable moments.

A scream ripped from her throat.

She was awake now; she was sure of it. But here she was, face to face with another creature that wasn't supposed to exist.

The dragon's eyes widened. It pushed back, scrambling away from her and sitting like a dog. The beast towered shoulders, neck, and head above the men surrounding her—men who seemed more interested in her than the fact that a huge, mythical monster sat among them.

The dragon cocked its snout to the right, reminiscent, again, of a puppy.

One of the men stepped toward her. "He didn't mean to scare you."

"How do you know? That's a-that's a…"

"Dragon." The woman behind Anna ambled forward. "A crystal dragon, to be exact: the wisest, purest, and most noble of the Draconi. You are a lucky girl."

Anna glanced back at her before returning her gaze to the massive, looming beast. "Lucky?"

"To be chosen. Dozens of young girls came here last night to present themselves to the dragons, yet you fell to us from the sky. You must be special indeed."

"Are you out of your mind? I was snatched off the street."

The man came closer. "He said he saved you from the…" He squinted. "I'm seeing really big, gray dragons."

The old woman gasped. "Nikau, do you speak the truth?" She stood and faced the beast. "Did you fight the mountain dragons? Is that how you were hurt?" She rubbed her face. "Grace of *Aoraki*, you are lucky to be alive."

"He says he didn't have a choice. They'd taken the girl from him, he couldn't let them have her."

The old woman walked toward the towering beast and placed her hand on its lowered snout.

The creature leaned in to accept what looked like a caress, and nuzzled her shoulder.

Anna blinked twice and stared. She wasn't crazy. That thing was actually nuzzling the old lady. It arched its back and a translucent wing scattered what little light came through the tent. The movement projected a multi-colored kaleidoscope on the fabric wall.

The other wing lay limp, spread out along its right side. A series of stitches raked up a pink, puffy line that ran from the outer edge of the wing to its base.

So, it was hurt. That didn't explain why they were all there, though. Had the woman trained the dragon somehow? Was it her pet?

The man; Nikau, the woman had called him, still stood a few feet from her, rubbing his eyes. A small tear in his jeans marred his left thigh, and dark, grimy streaks blemished his face, as if he'd slept in the dirt. They all looked that way, come to think of it. Maybe this was some kind of dragon loving, camping cult.

She closed her eyes, collecting herself. The cult part wasn't really what worried her. There was still a real, live dragon just a few feet away.

Nikau dropped his fingers from his eyes. "Sorry, I know this is a little strange. This is all new to me, too." He glanced back to the dragon. "He doesn't want you to be afraid."

"Okay, reality check. Is that really a dragon?"

The group nodded as Nikau helped Anna to her feet.

She squeezed his hands. "And you, how do you know it doesn't want me to be afraid?"

He pulled free from her grasp and rubbed his face, again. "As crazy as it sounds, I am his *Kotahi*. It's sort of like a translator. I can hear him." He tapped his temple twice. "Up here."

"I'm supposed to believe you can read the dragon's mind?"

"Like I said, I know it sounds crazy."

The dragon growled, nosing the air.

"Hang on, boss," Nik said. "You're hurt and we still need to check your girlfriend out."

Anna took a tentative step toward the creature. "What did it say?"

"That he needs to get going, but with that wing, and those gray dragons out there ready to turn him into sushi, I think that's a pretty bad idea."

A taller, broad man with dark hair and a gray-peppered beard pointed at her shoulder. "I'd like to take a look at those wounds."

Anna fingered the grayish-red stains on her blouse. Shifting, she winced. "Are you a doctor?"

"I'm a DVM." He smiled when she cocked a brow. "Doctor of Veterinary Medicine."

"You're a vet?" She leaned away.

"Yes, ma'am. But if you prefer…" He pointed over his shoulder. "Tom is an accountant, Jim is a mechanic, and Nanna and Pops are both retired cooks. You can have one of them look you over, if you prefer."

He was kidding, right?

Nikau shrugged when she met his gaze. "Don't look at me, I'm currently unemployed."

The dragon limped toward her, dragging his right wing behind him.

"Careful there." The vet lifted the creature's wing off the ground.

"He says he can help heal her," Nik said.

Anna stepped back. "Oh, please dragon tears?"

The creature cocked its head to the left.

"He's a little confused," Nik said. "I'm getting a feeling that the dragon tear legend is a myth." He squinted. "But I'm getting a vision of him licking you. I guess it's like a dog licking a wound?"

She grabbed her shoulder. "Eww."

"You'll need to take off your shirt." The old woman—what had the vet called her—Nanna? Removed her jacket and held it in front of Anna like a screen. "Everyone not needed, get out. That would be all but me, Doc Tyler, the dragon, and Nikau to translate."

Oh, God. She was actually serious about this. "I'm not letting that thing lick me. What if it likes the way I taste?"

The woman pursed her lips. "If he was going to eat you he would have done so already."

"I don't even like it when my dog licks my face." Anna clutched her shoulders as the rest of the people filed out of the tent without comment. Outside, a flurry of voices questioned them.

"I know you're uncomfortable," the veterinarian said. "At a bare minimum, I need to take a look." He pulled the blanket from her shoulders. "We can't let that get infected."

She couldn't really argue with that. Wincing, she allowed him to help slide her blouse over her head and bit her lip against the collective gasp.

Deep red, weepy, swollen wounds and dark purple bruises covered her skin. She could barely recognize her own body. She needed a hospital. Probably surgery. Stitches at least. God, did they even have her stupid blood type in this country? What if she really needed surgery, could she get back to the States in time?

The dragon moved behind her. Heat emanated from its silvery-white scales. But that couldn't be right. Reptiles were cold-blooded, weren't they?

"Hold still," Nikau whispered.

Anna leaned against the old woman, her head down. Was she really going to let them do this?

A moist heat rolled over her right shoulder. The tongue scratched lightly against her skin and dragged across her back and along the wounds on her front. Anna gulped down the bile building in her throat. This couldn't be sanitary. She was going to die here.

And what would she even tell a doctor if she found one? *Oh, you see, there was this dragon, and I let it lick me. Sorry the injuries are infected even worse now.*

God, they'd think she was crazy.

She winced, her muscles throbbing, until the heat swept over her, through her, and into her, tingling through her skin until suddenly the pain eased away. She clung to the old woman, shaking, until the dragon drew back.

Nanna's eyes lit up as she surveyed the wounds. "Incredible. Absolutely incredible."

Anna straightened, forgetting to hide her bra from the strangers around her as she checked her shoulders.

The deep gashes had covered over, glistening with a sticky goo. The swelling had already gone down. It wasn't as dramatic as the dragon tear-miracle depicted in the movies, but it was darn close.

She looked up at the mythical creature. It wasn't huge like the dragons in movies, but it was definitely the largest animal she'd ever stood this close to without being terrified. The other dragons from last night, they'd been bigger than elephants. One was taller than a giraffe. Maybe that was why she'd been carried away with such ease.

When this smaller dragon finally snatched her from the sky, it had struggled in the air. She remembered the sensation of rising and falling, until the dragon had roared, and then they'd fallen. Was that when he was injured? Did they rip his wing in retaliation for him saving her?

She stood and reached for his nose. The creature startled, then lowered its snout closer to her hand. Its scales were hard, but sleek. They shimmered, even within the tent's mottled light.

Anna realized no pain had raked through her shoulder as she reached up to touch him. He'd saved her in more ways than one. "Thank you."

The creature quivered, pressing its nose into her hair.

"He says, *always*." Nik's eyes reddened. "The sense of warmth, it's overwhelming."

Shimmering tears had formed in the dragon's eyes as well. Was it possible? Could this huge reptilian beast *feel*?

The creature moved its snout beneath her chin and rubbed. She laughed, scratching it behind a short, pointed ridge where its ears should have been.

Tyler mopped his brow. "It's getting too hot to stay in the tent. Are you able to walk in the sun, Great One?"

The dragon lifted its head and faced him.

"It doesn't seem like the sun is a problem," Nik said. "Why do you ask?"

"There are stories about dragons not coming out in the daytime. Some accounts made it sound like sunlight might be painful."

Nik looked at the dragon and nodded. Was he really talking to it inside his head?

He turned to Tyler. "Apparently the gray ones can't see in the sunlight, so they only come out at night. The rest of them have no problem with the daylight."

"That is good news for us," the old woman said. "But this tent won't fool them again. Tonight, they will search in earnest."

"The glow worm caves," Tyler said. "They are more than large enough to hide a dragon."

"Waitomo Caves are on the North Island," Nik said. "We'll never get there before nightfall, especially with an injured dragon."

The old woman smiled. "Waitomo Caves are a tourist trap. There are wonders on South Island the Maori have kept to themselves." She reached up and ran her hand down the dragon's neck. "We have the perfect place to hide you, Great One."

CHAPTER 9

The tent exit loomed just inches away. In a few moments, everyone outside would see with their own eyes what had fallen from the sky last night.

Nik stood on the Dragon's right and held the injured wing just off the ground. "Is this okay? Am I hurting you?"

The dragon's voice bubbled up from within. *It's fine. But you don't need to serve me.*

"No, but it's a little easier to handle this mind-meld thing when your pain isn't lancing through my cranium."

The creature turned toward him. *I'm sorry. It's not my intent to hurt you.*

Anna was cradled between the un-injured wing and the dragon's hide. She wasn't quite a hostage, but she was close enough that the dragon could furl her back inside his wing at the slightest hint of danger.

Or her trying to run away.

I don't think she's going to run. Where would she go? Nik pulled back the opening of the tent and peeked outside.

"Is it talking to you?" Anna asked.

"Yeah. He's a little nervous about what's going to happen outside."

Tyler exited, and Nik stole a glance through the tent flap. Outside, many of the people who'd fled the previous evening mulled about. Nik could tell from the look on most of the younger people's uninterested carriages that they still didn't believe their elders had saved a real-live dragon last night. They were all going to pee their pants when they found out everything they've been discounting for years was actually true. He let the flap fall closed.

"Does he have a name?" Anna traced her fingers down the ridge on the dragon's neck.

Ummm. Nik turned toward the creature. "I feel incredibly stupid for never asking you that."

The dragon preened his scales. *It hadn't mattered, but she should know.* He lowered his snout and nuzzled her cheek. *She knows me. Tell her I am Joesephutus.*

"Ja-who-what-is?"

Anna laughed. "Is it hard to say?"

"Yeah. I guess it's Draconic."

Tell her it's Joe.

"Joe?"

Anna took a step back, her eyes wide.

"What's wrong?"

She continued to stare at the dragon.

Tell her not to be afraid.

Nik reached for her. "Are you okay?"

Anna slapped him away. "This isn't funny. Do you know Joe? Were you in the bar last night? Did you watch them take me?"

Nik held out his hands in surrender. "I have no idea what you're talking about. The dragon said that he knows you, and his name is Joe."

She turned to Puff. Her nose flared as her face reddened. "You *are not* the cute guy from the bar."

Cute? A smug flush rushed from the dragon.

I'm not sure that's what we should be focusing on right now.

She needs to trust me. She needs to understand.

Nik turned to the girl "He says…"

Her face twisted into a sneer. "I *am not* calling it Joe."

Nik's heart raced as the dragon moved from side to side.

It lowered its head. *She's angry.*

Yeah, I'm getting that.

She doesn't believe me.

Nik couldn't really blame her. Dragons were one thing, but magic? *I'm not really sure I believe it, either.*

The dragon jerked his head up.

Nik Shrugged. *Well, if you really are this Joe person she knows, then go ahead and shift. Show her.*

The beast lowered his snout. Its nose wrinkled and it clawed the earth several times before Nik's right arm and shoulder exploded in pain. His sight blurred. Then the pain—No, the *agony* disappeared like someone had thrown a switch.

The dragon held his right claw off the ground. He trembled, his breaths staggered.

I can't shift. The pain is too much.

Nik massaged his own arm and side. "Yeah, I'm getting that."

Boss raised his head as the girl approached and reached for him.

She held the dragon's face. "He's making all of this up, isn't he?"

Seriously? "You think I'm lying?"

Tell her yes. The dragon pulled himself back up to standing. *She can't know I'm weak, and I can't chance her being angry.*

"But—"

Tell her!

"Okay, okay." Nik huffed out a breath. "Yeah, I made it all up. He's just a dragon. His name is Joes-hopping-with-figs or something like that."

A puff of hot, smoky air blew from the dragon's nose, but the creature's irrational anxiety about what this girl thought of him melted when Anna smiled.

She ran her palm down the creature's jawline. "How about we call you Puff?"

"Puff?"

"Puff the Magic Dragon. I like it."

Nik narrowed his eyes. "That's kinda stupid." The dragon growled at him. Nik held up his hands. "Okay, okay. Apparently if you're happy, he's happy. Puff it is."

Anna petted the dragon's mane like a horse. She whispered something into the creature's ear that Nik couldn't make out. Warmth spread through Nik's chest as the boss lifted his nose to allow her to scratch under his chin.

Nik folded his arms. *I thought you wanted her to know you were this Joe person.*

The creature lowered his gaze to Nik. *I do, but it was too much, too soon. I can't chance any negative emotion now. Besides...* He lifted his chin again.

Anna laughed as she scratched under his muzzle with vigor.

This feels so incredibly good.

Nik smiled. If he were being honest, he wouldn't want to piss off a girl who was running her hands up and down his body, either. So, Puff it is, for now.

From outside, Nanna pulled back the tent flap. "It is time, Great One."

Nik held up the injured wing as a collective gasp, followed by a numbing hush, fell over those outside. The dragon stepped into the light, and Nik walked alongside, squinting. The wing barely weighed a pound. He could practically see through the thin membrane once the light enveloped them.

A middle-aged woman in the crowd swayed. The man standing beside her caught her as she fell, but his gaze remained fixed to the creature as they emerged.

Pops stood alongside the opening, brandishing the extinguished torch he'd held the night before like a scepter. "Behold, the dragon lord who fell to his people last night. Once again, the Maori are called to stand with the Draconi."

"Is it dangerous?" someone asked.

"Look at the size of it."

The dragon recoiled. *Even among humans I'm looked down on for my size.*

Nik gazed up at Puff. "I don't think they're remarking on how small you are. You're kind of scary, to be honest."

"I don't think he's scary." Anna patted the creature's shimmering hide.

Puff turned to her. The injured wing twitched beneath Nik's fingers as a raging warmth trickled across their bond. Sweat beaded at the *Kotahi's* temples, and he let go for a moment to wipe his brow.

Beside the dragon, Anna's hair glistened in the sunlight. Her smile reached into him, warming him with an abandon that riddled each cell in Nik's body before it settled, throbbing against his zipper.

This was not the time to be thinking about bending this girl over the arm of a sofa, yet his hand twitched as he considered dragging her back into the tent and showing her what a real man could...

He shook his head to clear it. What was wrong with him? This girl was barely out of high school.

A numbness swirled around him as he watched the dragon's talon twitch in time with the tick in his own hand. By God, these weren't his thoughts, but the dragon's. This Seventeen Year thing was serious.

You really snatched her to be your mate?

Puff startled before turning away from the girl. *That is the basic idea, but I never dreamed I'd actually find one.*

So it's true? All you have to do is find a girl and you become king?

Not just any girl. We need to find a match, one whose genetics can support the Draconi. He looked back to Anna, warming again before he returned his attention to Nik. *The odds against finding a match are astronomical. That is why the grays tried to take her from me. They knew the chances of them finding their own were slim.*

The people started to move in. Each bowed before they came too close.

Why her? What makes her special?

Her blood is different from yours and from anyone's. As your blood-line can be elevated to Kotahi, her blood allows a Draconic breeding match.

A few reached out their hands to be sniffed like a dog. Idiots. They had no idea how incredible this creature truly was.

The dragon tilted his head toward Nik. *You think I'm incredible?*

"Don't get a big head." Nik smiled. "Well, don't get a big-*ger* head."

Puff snorted then lowered his snout so the people could touch him.

It was amazing, the more Nik thought about it. Last night, most of these people were just playing a game or appeasing the elders. Then they were running for their lives. He doubted half of them really believed that what had fallen from the sky was a dragon, yet they'd stayed. Now here they were, paying homage to this thing like a god.

The creature jolted its head back up with a growl. The onlookers backed away. A few cried out.

I am not a god. I'm just a Draconi.

"Well, yeah, but you have to understand the magnitude of this. I mean, most people think dragons are a myth. Being here to see this, it's the opportunity of a lifetime."

Pops raised his voice above the clatter. "The Seventeen Year continues tonight. More dragons will come, hoping to find and overpower the Great One." He paused, surveying the gawkers.

"We cannot allow that to happen. This Seventeen Year will see the crystal dragons rise once again."

The older people in attendance cheered. The younger ones seemed dazed.

Nik leaned towards the dragon. "We're not really talking about you ruling the islands, right?"

I don't really want to rule the dragons, let alone the humans. A deep-seeded disgust rolled over the bond between them. It didn't seem like disgust of humans, though. In fact, a small sparkle of pride swept through the air between them when the dragon's gaze roamed over the smiling faces. So, if not the humans, than who?

"Are these other dragons really that bad?" Nik asked.

Puff shuddered, but remained silent.

Pops turned toward Mount Cook's great peaks. "We need all who are able to make the journey up the mountain to join us. Tonight, we shelter with the dragon lord within Ruma Marama."

Nik balked. "I thought The Light Chamber was a myth?"

Pops smiled. "So are dragons."

CHAPTER 10

Making her way through the rocky terrain, Anna squinted in the midday sun, shielding her eyes as she looked for some sign of a cave. The dragon shifted his wing over her, shading her face.

Damn, if this thing wasn't more of a gentleman than most of the men she'd met. "Thank you." She rubbed the base of his wing. "But you're probably going to get sore if you keep doing that."

Nik lifted Puff's right wing. "There's shade over here if you want to hold his wing for a while."

The dragon growled, and Nik held up his free hand in capitulation. "Okay, boss, okay. The girl doesn't work. I get it."

The older man, Pops, Nik had called him, took the wing from his grandson. "Allow me to serve, Great One."

"We named him Puff," Nik said.

Pops flared his nose. "I will not name a dragon lord after a fairy tale character."

Anna cringed. Apparently the old man didn't get the irony. The dragon didn't seem to mind his name, though, and that was good enough for her.

They moved on in silence, following a line of people led by

Tyler in the front, and, from the volume of the talking, a large number of people behind them concealed by the bulk of the dragon.

"Do I have to go all the way to the top with you?" Anna asked. "Can't someone just drive me back to my hotel?"

Pops laughed. "No one is going back down."

Well that was just great. Why couldn't she be saved by a dragon and then dropped into a crowd of people heading down the mountain, rather than up?

Anna stopped. Her stomach hardened.

She'd been flown toward these mountains by a dragon, but she wasn't the only one.

A hazy vision of Sybil's unconscious body in the grip of that dark green dragon materialized in her mind. Anna took a steadying breath. That dragon had been trying to save them. If he flew her away, Sybil was safe. Anna had to believe that. The other options were unthinkable.

Sybil was fine. She had to be.

Anna repeated the words in her head, shivering. Yes, she was fine, and wherever she was, she was most likely busting a few brain cells looking for her baby sister.

Puff looked at her, concern wrinkling his reptilian brow. She flashed a tentative smile, and kept walking.

She caught Nik's gaze. "Can I borrow a cell phone or something? I need to call my sister and let her know I'm all right." And to make sure Sybil was okay, as well. She needed to hear her sister's voice, to center herself back into reality.

"I've checked for service a few times," Nik said. "I had some Wi-Fi back at camp, but there's nothing up here."

Wonderful. Just terrific. All her muscles ached. This was nothing a good night's sleep wouldn't help—the kind that needed a bed, not the rocky floor of a cave.

The dragon nuzzled her. She giggled.

"He said he will keep you warm tonight, if you're worried about the cold," Nik said.

Puff lowered one eye to her level. His gaze seemed so wise, so human. Were dragons pre-historic? Were they always intelligent, or had they evolved that way, like man evolving from apes?

Part of her wanted to get away, to run down the mountain and find her way back to her hotel and hopefully thwart Sybil's impending sisterly breakdown. But something more than curiosity kept her beside this incredible creature. She felt drawn to him, as if an evening furled within his wings had created an irrevocable bond between them. Somehow, she knew that this majestic creature would always be there for her.

The crowd at the front of the procession cheered.

"At last, we have arrived," Pops said. "We will have you safe in no time, Great One."

They'd arrived? Arrived where?

Pops handed the injured wing back to Nik and scurried ahead as the rest of them remained behind with the dragon. This part of the mountainside looked no different than any other part they'd passed.

Tyler and his team spread blankets and drove unlit torches in the ground as the rest of the procession funneled in. Glancing around her own group, Anna was relieved to see a few modern flashlights attached to several belt-bags, and tucked inside webbed backpacks. Torches took this whole retro-dragon motif a little too far.

Nik's grandmother shouted directions as people mulled about, several pitching tents, some starting small campfires while others broke out propane grills.

Anna's belly rumbled. The dragon's gaze darted to her midriff, and then to her eyes.

"Puff asked if you're hungry," Nik said.

She nodded to the dragon. "We humans usually eat breakfast

first thing in the morning." Was she actually talking to a dragon? Part of her waited for someone to jump out and say "April Fools."

Nik turned to Pops. "The boss wants food for his—" He glanced at Anna. His lips parted, as if he'd stopped mid-thought. "For his new friend."

Why did he look at her like that?

Within moments a blonde girl, maybe three or four years younger than Anna, handed her a plate of bread and apples. "Here you go. We'll get you something more substantial once we get settled." She curtsied to Puff. "How's your wing, Great One?"

The dragon lowered his snout and nuzzled her hair.

Nik smiled. "He says it's better, and thanks for helping stitch him up."

The girl ran her fingers under Puff's chin before turning to Anna. "He's magnificent, isn't he?"

Magnificent, magical, unbelievable… name your over-expressive adjective; nothing could really describe standing next to an actual living, breathing dragon.

"My name is Elaina, by the way, if you need anything."

She bowed to Puff again and took another plate from a young child. Two men placed a large trough of water on the ground by Puff's feet.

The dragon lapped the water slowly, seeming afraid to spill the basin that looked more like a saucer now that it was dwarfed by the dragon's snout.

Elaina handed Nik the plate of food.

"Thanks." He smiled again. "From both of us."

Puff sat up and lowered his head to Elaina and the men who'd brought the water.

One reached up and ran his palm along the dragon's neck. "I can't believe you're real."

"He's glorious," the other said.

A pink flush flooded the area around Puff's eyes. He turned away. Was he embarrassed by the compliment? How cute!

"We need your help at the doorway," Nanna told the men. She turned to Nik. "You, too."

Nik swallowed a bite of apple. "But I need to translate."

"The dragon is smarter than all of us combined. I'm sure he'll manage."

She grabbed Nik's arm and led him away, still clutching his plate.

Elaina pulled her hair into a ponytail. "I guess I'll get going, too." She waved her fingers at Puff as she started toward the mountain.

Anna ate in silence, probably the only one not stealing a look at the pearlescent creature seated beside her. Was she supposed to make conversation? Maybe. They all seemed to think the creature was far more intelligent than an animal should be.

She talked to her dog all the time. Little Dixie was a great listener, wagging her tail when Anna was excited, giving sad eyes when she was upset. Maybe all animals were inherently in-tune to human emotion.

That's what could be happening with the dragon. It made the most sense, anyway. Either that, or these people were right, and there was more to this creature than modern thought could comprehend.

Puff gazed down at her, his eyes casting the same devotion she saw from Dixie every day. Damn, it was insane, but she could see how people would think this thing was capable of coherent thought.

The dragon certainly seemed to understand that they were trying to help him, though, and despite his size, and his teeth, the creature didn't seem horrifying. Not like the gray ones from last night.

Back in the street behind the tavern, this little silver dragon had stood up to the others even though they'd towered over him. He could have been killed; but he'd fended them off, giving Anna, Sybil, and Connor time to run.

She rubbed her healing shoulder. This dragon was different from the ones he'd saved her from. She just wasn't sure why.

Puff pushed her plate with his nose.

"Are you hungry?" she asked.

He balked, then shook his head.

"What, then?"

A light billow of smoke wafted from his nostrils.

Maybe taking his translator away wasn't the best idea. But was Nik really translating, or was the guy full-of-it and making this all up?

Anna always imagined conversations with Dixie. It was pretty easy telling what her little pooch thought at times. Actually hearing words in your head, though, that was just crazy.

Puff's scales glistened, hundreds of hues brightening his silvery-white hide.

Yes, hearing voices was crazy, but no worse than sitting beside a dragon.

She picked up an apple slice and held it out. "Are you sure you're not hungry? They're pretty tasty."

The dragon nudged the fruit back to her.

"I feel bad, not sharing. Please, try some."

Puff blinked twice, sniffed the fruit, and slowly bared a row of small, human-looking front teeth just under his nostrils. Anna held her breath as he eased the apple away from her, tossed it up, and snapped the wedge of fruit out of the air. Anna didn't even see a swallowing motion.

"Didn't your mother ever tell you to chew your food?"

He tilted his head and stared at her.

"I guess not."

Nik returned with his grandmother.

"Great One." Nanna bowed. "We need to ask a favor." She looked back to the mountainside, where people were pulling vines from what looked like the result of an old rockslide. "We have to clear the entrance to the cave, and then reseal the chamber before nightfall." She looked at the ground before returning her gaze to Puff. "Unfortunately, most of the rocks are too large to move. You won't be able to fit through the opening the Maori normally use unless you shift." She took in a deep breath, and released it through pursed lips. "I'm sorry, we never considered the possibility of harboring a full sized dragon."

Puff stood and brushed Nanna's cheek with the side of his nose.

"He says don't worry about it." Nik shoved his hands in his pockets. "He thinks we're all doing a great job."

The dragon cocked his head and looked at his interpreter. Anna wondered how much was getting lost in translation.

Puff poked his nose in the air twice, shuddered, and groaned before lowering his head.

"No, no." Nik patted the dragon's neck. "It's not your fault. Don't worry about it. We'll figure this out."

"What?" Nanna and Anna said in unison.

"He can't shift. Something about concentration, and pain, and something else about his ripped wing. I can't get it all. He's sort-of rambling."

Anna pursed her lips. Maybe Nik was the one rambling. She hoped they weren't going to try to convince her that the dragon was the guy from the bar, again.

Nik glanced back to Puff. "He's scared. Probably a lot more than he wants anyone to know."

Puff jerked upright, nose to nose with Nik before the creature roared in his translator's face.

Anna screamed, falling to her knees and covering her ears. Were they all wrong about this beast? Would it turn on them now?

Nik's knees wobbled, but he didn't back down. "What are you going to do, eat me for telling the truth? You're scared, I get that. I've been in your big-ass reptilian head." He shoved the dragon's snout back. "I saw it all in your memories. I saw them attack you. I saw how big they were. I felt their talons rip through your wing. Shit, I'd be scared, too if I knew they were coming for me. But you know what?" He pointed to the people around the camp, and those at the mountainside, all of who had stopped and stared when the dragon roared. "These people don't care that you're scared. Being scared is normal. Human. They get that as well as I do. Let them help you." He took a step closer and took the beast's muzzle into his hands. "Let *me* help you."

Anna's heart pounded as the dragon and the human stared at each other. Puff had seemed so nice a few moments ago, but then to act out like that, was he really safe to be around?

Nik exhaled and touched his head to Puff's nose. "I know," he whispered. "I'm sorry."

He was sorry? Sorry for what?

Nik turned. "It was wrong of me to tell you he's scared. That was something *personal*." He looked back to the dragon, but the creature looked away.

Anna gulped, not quite ready to believe the dragon wasn't about to pounce on one of them.

Nik turned from the creature and faced the people who'd gathered around them. "You've all heard the legends. We've heard how the gray mountain dragons stole the crown from the crystal dragons eons ago. Well, apparently it's worse than we'd thought." The people in the crowd glanced at each other. "The Draconi are dying." A few people gasped. "The crystal dragons have been lobbying to return to the skies, to ask the humans for peaceful coexistence like they had with our ancestors." He looked at the ground. "I can't put into words what he's shown me from his memories; what those huge gray dragons have done to the rest of the Draconi, it's unfathomable."

Anna bit her lip. The gray dragons were the ones who had snatched her off the street, whose talons had bit into her flesh. She could appreciate anyone, any*thing* being terrified of them.

Nik looked at Puff again.

The hush over the crowd loomed like a weight pressing them against the mountain. Anna rubbed her arms, warding off a phantom chill.

If there really was an entire race of dragons, where had they been hiding all these years?

Nik wiped his eyes and turned back to the crowd. "The gray dragons have been killing any bucks even remotely strong enough to win the Seventeen Year." He ran his hand down the side of Puff's glistening neck. "Our dragon wasn't even on their radar. He's too young to compete, but he was the crystal dragons' only hope to break the cycle of terror." Nik sighed, closing his eyes as if listening. "He's only about seventeen years old." Nik opened his eyes. "And they sent him out against huge males three and four times his age. They have to be desperate."

Anna blinked. *Seventeen years old.* He was only a few years younger than she was, and his people had sent him out against those huge dragons? Were they insane?

Puff got to all fours. He growled in low, subtle tones and purrs. The crowd listened, rapt. Anna waited for the translation.

"He never expected to survive, let alone win." Nik glanced at Puff's injury. "But he needs to heal. He thanks us for our assistance."

Puff walked toward the mountain. The people parted for him, following once he passed.

Nik held his arm out to Anna. "Coming?"

"I guess." Where else would she go? And she was dying to see what would happen.

Nanna took Nik's other arm. Her eyes glistened and her chin tilted a smidge higher when she looked at her grandson. Pops held an equally bright smile as they followed the dragon to the mountainside. What would it be like, knowing your grandson could talk to dragons? Especially since these people seem to have been waiting for this moment their whole lives. Even though no one was ever going to believe any of this, Anna was thrilled to be a part of something so momentous.

Puff fluttered his good wing when he reached the pile of rocks. He growled a few times, not a menacing sound, but more like the sound Dixie made when she wanted to go out.

Nik turned to Pops. "He wants to know if this is the right place."

Pops nodded. "Our people walled the cavern up hundreds of years ago, when foreigners started to invade." He looked back to the rocks. "Ruma Marama is one of our most sacred places. We couldn't bear to see it defiled."

He walked to the right edge, where a grouping of smaller rocks lay stacked like a totem pole. Pops and Tyler removed four large rocks from the top of the pile, revealing an opening about a foot and a half wide. "This is the entrance we use."

The dragon approached, took a boulder in his massive jaws, and drew it from the hole, setting it a few yards from the opening."

Pops beamed. "Thank you, Great One."

So that's what they meant when they asked the dragon to shift. They wanted him to move the rocks for them. But why not just come out and ask him for help?

Pops turned toward the crowd. "If everyone takes what they can carry, we will be inside in no time. We only need a hole large enough to get the dragon through." He glanced at the sun, which had peaked, and now started its slow afternoon descent. "We must be within and have the camouflage back in place before sunset."

Sunset—when the gray dragons would come looking for Puff.

The scars on Anna's shoulders pulsed with a dull ache. It would be a long time before she'd forget the searing bite of the gray dragon's claws piercing her flesh, if she was *ever* able to forget.

A child, probably no older than seven ran to the pile, grabbed a small stone, and set it beside the boulder the dragon had moved.

The girl laughed when Puff nuzzled her, and she ran to grab another rock.

Puff turned, his gaze falling on Anna. She still wanted to fight the idea that this magnificent beast was anything more than an animal, but it was becoming harder and harder. Those eyes held wisdom, and the more she stared at them, the more she realized the devotion within them seeded so much deeper than modern thought would allow her to admit.

Her heart fluttered, and she had to fight the desire to reach out and stroke the dragon's hide, to touch him and wallow in his warmth. No, this was not just an animal, or even just a dragon.

She took a step toward him and he lowered his head. He was in so much danger, up against such ridiculous odds, all with the slim hopes of saving his people from some sort of homicidal oligarchy.

Anna trembled, remembering the gray megalith rearing up, and the echo of the beast's roar through the streets. Did this little dragon have a chance against anything so huge, when he was injured and unable to fly?

Three more children ran past, some working in tandem alongside the adults moving the rocks. The laughter from the children, the determined looks on the people's faces, infused her. It had been ages since she'd seen so many people come together with a common purpose; unless they'd been paid to do so, that is.

If those huge dragons were coming, all these people were in as much danger as the dragon, yet they didn't run. They labored on without question.

Puff limped toward the mountain and pulled out another boulder that no human seemed able to budge. All the smaller rocks above the boulder rolled away from the opening, widening the hole.

The people cheered, and Anna clapped with them. Near the opening, Nik took a large stone from his grandfather, while Nanna brought water to those laboring in the sun. Everyone seemed to have a job. Everyone but Anna, that was. Yet none gave her notice, or showed signs of annoyance at her lack of effort.

She pushed the fog from her mind. She really *was* the only one standing here, doing nothing. What was wrong with her? She was one of the few who'd seen what those gray dragons could do. She should be at the front of the line to help.

The children ran back toward the pile for more rocks. If Anna had been their parents, she would have dragged them down the mountain at the first mention of dragons. But their moms and dads were probably among those who toiled with the others. None of them worried about finishing in time. They just continued to work, many with smiles on their faces. They knew, without a doubt, that they would be safe within that mountain tonight, because they worked together toward that goal. She should be no different.

Anna moved toward the pile.

"Puff says stay back." Nik placed the rock he'd been carrying on the ground. "He doesn't want you hurt."

She looked back to the dragon who stood with a boulder in his mouth.

"Screw that," Anna said. "I'm in as much danger as everyone else." She walked past the dragon. "Besides, I owe you my life, in case you've forgotten. What kind of girl would I be if I didn't return the favor?"

Anna grabbed the biggest stone she could carry, and hauled it from the pile.

CHAPTER 11

*K*nackered, Nik slipped to the floor and accepted a cup of water as the last of the rocks hiding the cavern were replaced by the men who had volunteered to remain outside.

The sun is nearly down. Will they have time to find shelter?

Nik found Pops among those sitting. "Puff is worried about the people outside."

Pops glanced at the door as the final stone slid into place, cutting them off from the fading sunset. "The old ways are dead, but the heart of the Maori lives on. These mountains are our friends. They will find somewhere to hide until morning."

Nik supposed it would be easier to hide three men than it would be to hide a dragon. Especially one with a crowd of followers.

They shouldn't follow me. They should get as far away from me as possible.

Buckley's chance of that.

A little girl handed Nik a flashlight. He flicked it on.

These people love you already, and you haven't even officially won the Seventeen Year yet.

Puff tossed his mane before wrapping his wing around Anna. *Ask her if she is warm enough.*

The girl was already gazing up at him, smiling. "Thanks." She drew his wing closer and leaned against Puff's side. She closed her eyes and breathed deeply.

"I think she just answered your question."

Despite being inside the beast's head and being the first to know what the huge creature was thinking, Nik wasn't so sure he'd be as cozy as Anna was with a dragon. Was her comfort a natural reaction, or was the dragon doing some kind of magic to her?

Puff's gaze drifted from the girl, to Nik. *How could you even think that?*

It's a valid question. I mean, look at her.

She cuddled in closer.

See? This morning she was screaming and clawing to get away from you.

The dragon looked away. *I have not compelled her.*

Interesting. Since you have a word for it, can I assume that you could compel her if you wanted to?

A quiver started at Puff's nose and rattled along his hide until shaking through his tail. *The gray dragons are masters of compulsion. Taking away another's free will is a game to them.*

A vision of a young, glassy-eyed, green buck stumbling toward a gray dragon filled Nik's mind. The smaller dragon jerked as if waking up just seconds before three gray dragons descended on him. The largest tore out the fledgling's throat.

Nik grimaced. So that's how they take out their competition. Cowards. But why don't the other dragons stand up to them?

The grays always provide justification for their actions. All those who question them tend to disappear.

That was no way to live. Dragons were supposed to be huge, domineering beasts. How could they allow themselves to be subjugated like that?

"Just how big are the other dragons?

A memory flashed between them. Nik saw through Puff's eyes as a gray dragon reared up, towering over the smaller dragon like a German shepherd over a kitten. Jesus, no wonder the other dragons were so scared.

"Yet you joined the competition, knowing what they were capable of."

Someone had to. The crystal dragon's next choice would have been my father.

"You didn't want your dad flying?"

Puff shook his head. *He is not a fast flyer, and he and my mother are one of only fifteen fertile Draconic pairs left. They are the only remaining pair among the crystal dragons. I couldn't let him, or my kind, make that sacrifice.*

If the Draconi are really dying out, it's suicide for the grays to be picking off their competition. Unless their size shrinks their brains, they have to understand they need to increase their numbers.

They only target young males. The two females that have been born over the past three mating cycles they have allowed to live.

Nik snorted. Yeah, and I suppose the grays are making a harem for themselves.

Puff tilted his head, but Nik could tell at least part of what he said was true. Crap like that shouldn't happen anymore. Even though they were dragons, they should have modernized like the rest of the free world. Being killed just because you've been deemed competition, or living just so you can breed—he couldn't fathom any society, or any people in that society, standing for that.

Puff shifted his weight. Nanna and Pops seemed very excited about Puff being a crystal dragon. All the storybooks talk about the celebrated days when the crystal dragons were in power. Maybe they were right. Maybe what the Draconi needed was someone to step up and be brave enough to say *no more*.

However, if the grays were really as huge as Puff had shown

him, this little dragon surviving the ones roaring in the sky last night was nothing less than a miracle. Maybe *Aoraki* really *had* smiled on him.

Or maybe he'd been chosen.

Maybe the land had been waiting for the right dragon to be born to bring the world back into balance. It was the basis of a thousand legends.

Puff licked the swollen edge of his stitched wing. He certainly didn't look like a hero, but some of the best heroes were underdogs. It had been a long time since the world had a David bring down a Goliath. Why not now?

Unease rolled across their bond. Deep down, Nik could tell the little dragon wanted to help his people. Short fantasies of him winning the competition and saving his kind flittered on the edge of his Draconic psyche.

In that, maybe they weren't so different.

Twelve-year-old Nik peered through the bush he'd hidden behind when the Iculi brothers showed up at his secret hideout in the forest.

The younger brother, Jason, placed a white bucket on the ground. The stench of gasoline filled the woods when the older brother, Mike, poured a clear liquid into the pail. Something moved within, shifting the bucket.

"This is gonna be good." Mike pulled a lighter from his pocket. "You ready?"

Jason kicked the bucket over, and a black and white cat, paws bound, spilled out.

Nik tensed. They wouldn't.

Jason clipped a lead onto the cat's collar. "Hold on. It's more fun when they run around."

The cat howled as he cut the bindings on its hind legs. Once the front legs were free, the cat bounded away, only to be stopped by the lead. The animal howled, pulling against the tether.

"You can run, but you can't hide." Mike flicked the lighter. A yellow flame mirrored in the kid's psychotic eyes. "Show time."

"Stop!" Nik jumped out from behind the bush. Taking advantage of their surprise, he grabbed the cat. The creature clawed and hissed, scratching his arms as he pulled the cat free of the collar and threw the gasoline-soaked animal into the trees. The cat landed on its paws before bounding out of sight.

"Stupid fuck." Mike raised the lighter. His scowl turned into a smile.

"Wait!" Jason screamed.

Nik gasped, realizing that the struggle with the cat had left his own clothes drenched in gasoline.

Grown-up Nik ran his fingers over the burn scars on his wrists. Mike and Jason were so much bigger than him. Teenagers. He could have been killed.

Younger Nik sniffed. "I was stupid. I should have run away as soon as I saw them."

Pops placed a cool cloth over the burn.

"What would running have accomplished?"

"I wouldn't have gotten hurt." Tears welled in his eyes. "Sorry I was so dumb."

Pops cocked his head. "I think there is a cat out in the woods who is happy you were so dumb."

Nik looked up from his wrist to the dragon's wing. They'd both be scarred for life for doing what was right.

However, little Nik had acted on instinct. If he'd had time to think of the possible outcomes, he probably wouldn't have saved the cat.

Pops's words stuck with him, though. He'd gone from feeling

like a fool, to feeling like a hero. That day had been a turning point for him. He was no longer the orphan kid, hiding in the corner fearing ridicule. He stood up for himself. More importantly, he stood up for others.

He couldn't begrudge Puff his fears, though. Those dragons were a hell of a lot bigger than Mike and Jason.

An asshole was an asshole, though. The bigger they come, the harder they fall. If Puff wanted to win this thing, he needed to believe in himself. Moreover, he needed to believe that he could make a difference.

"You're going to change things." Nik said. "You're going to make everything right again."

I hope to, if I live long enough.

Pessimism wasn't going to help this situation. Did Puff really believe, deep down, that he was sacrificing himself for the greater good? Did he really expect to die last night?

The dragon locked gazes with him. Guilt swept along their bond with a deep, twisting pain in the chest.

Shit. He really did expect to die.

Better me than my father.

"How can you say that?"

Puff held up his good wing. *Look at me.*

Anna blinked, her eyes heavy, before Puff covered her again.

I am small even among the crystal dragons. My father is large, strong, and most importantly, virile. If he fell during the competition, it would have been catastrophic to the crystal dragons. He looked away. *My loss would be inconsequential.*

"That's why they left you alone. They didn't think you were a threat."

They were right.

"Yet here you are, with a beautiful girl under your wing."

Puff fluttered the thin membrane concealing Anna. *I got lucky. I wasn't even... I didn't...* He closed his eyes and lowered his muzzle.

A memory skidded along the edge of their bond. The essence of the dragon within Nik fought, toiled, and rolled as if trying to pull the recollection back before solid figures took shape. The dull fog around the vision faded into the depths, leaving Nik high in the night sky with frigid air chilling his face.

Puff flew far behind a gaggle of multicolored dragons. The blue, gold, red, and green dragons glided in a clump to the right, leaving the grays in the distance to themselves. Puff wasn't the only dragon to know it was safer to leave some contenders at the head of the flock.

A large dragon, so deeply green it was almost black, broke from the front of their group and dropped to the rear beside him, blocking the light of the moon.

"You shouldn't be back here with me, Quenor," Puff said in Draconic. "You are fast and strong. You could be king."

The green twisted his wings, causing the huge beast to roll playfully through the night sky. "Except I don't want to be king."

"Then why are you flying?"

"The same reason I always fly. So I can find a beautiful, young girl to lose myself inside for a few hours."

"You are incorrigible."

"Of course I am. I'm a green." Quenor arched his wings, gliding through the starry night. "And what about you? You can fly much faster than a gray. I've seen you."

Nik concentrated on the memory and realized Puff wasn't even winded, as if he were out for a slow stroll, rather than flying through the air.

"If they see me as a threat, I'm dead." Puff snorted. "I can outfly one, but all seven?"

"You are a good friend, Joesephutus. But you'd be an even better king." Quenor reared up before he banked down, careening toward the glistening lights in the town below.

King?

The notion that any of them could stand against the grays and survive was a foolish dream. They were all safer keeping their heads bowed.

The older dragons held too many dreams of past glory. The life they remember probably never even existed.

They all whispered in the shadows of the proud days of the crystal dragons, but those whispers were dealt with harshly.

Puff fluttered his wings as the wind pushed him higher.

The crystal dragons have always been small, and the grays have always been massive. Domination by the strongest is the only life Puff knew. Being ruled by the smartest, it made no sense.

You are a good friend, Joesephutus.

But you'd be an even better king.

The words hung in the air. Every young buck dreamed of taking the crown. Puff was no different. But reality showed him the strength of the grays. There was a reason they were in power, and an even bigger reason not to oppose them.

Still hovering, Puff squinted into the night sky as the last of the flock faded into the distance. It would take some time to catch up, but he needed to convince Quenor to return to the air, as well.

Puff drew his wings back, pointed down, and followed his friend to a grassy patch in a large deserted courtyard outlined by several human buildings.

"What are you doing?" he asked.

"Hunting."

Puff cocked his head. "This isn't where the sacrifices are."

"No, but there are human females here. Pretty, ripe, plump females fresh for the plucking." Quenor stretched his neck and arched his wings. His colossal form faded into that of a man before he drew human clothing from a pack he had held in his rear talons.

Nik shuddered. So they really *could* shift into human form. They could be anyone, anywhere, and no one would have any idea.

"You always ask where I disappear to every few weeks." He held up his arms. "This is one of my favorite places"

Puff shrank down to a similar height. "You hunt outside of mating season? Why?"

Quenor pulled on dark jeans. "Because mating is fun. Greens have always played mating games between seasons."

Puff dragged his fingers through platinum blond, nearly white hair. "But this actually is mating season. We're supposed to pick from the women offered."

"What fun is that?" He pointed to the rear of one of the buildings. "Have you ever been to a tavern, my friend? They are a great place to find companionship, or maybe, in your case, a place to nest quietly with your nose under your tail for a few hours."

"I'm not sticking my nose under my tail. I followed you down here, my friend."

Quenor pulled his shirt over his head and tugged the hem down over his waist. "Then leave, stay, I don't care. I, personally, am looking for a nice warm human girl to spend the rest of the evening with, and unlike the rest of you, I don't care if she can carry my child." He turned away and headed for the bar on the right. He pointed toward the rear door of a different building. "That place is always quiet. Hide there for a few hours and I'll come back for you when I'm done." He turned the corner and disappeared.

He was actually serious.

Quenor had no intentions of competing in the hunt.

Then again, neither did Joesephutus.

He took in the wispy cloud bank hiding a stretch of twinkling stars. The other dragons would be half way to Aoraki by now. If either of them had a chance in this competition, it was gone, now.

His gaze carried over the weathered wooden door behind the tavern. If he'd already lost, a short rest and a drink or two certainly couldn't hurt.

He yanked the pack from his shoulder and pulled out a shirt, pants, and shoes.

NIK FOLDED HIS ARMS. "YOU WERE HIDING."

Puff balked. Anna stirred, but didn't wake. *I was not hiding.*

Sure he wasn't. "So this extended break, is this where you found Anna?"

The dragon nodded. *I was seated at the bar, and she just walked in.* His gaze fell to the ground. *I felt drawn to her, even before I realized she was compatible.*

"You're an incredibly lucky dragon."

That's what Quenor said. He preened his injured wing. *But I was foolish to think I could protect her long enough to get us back to Dragon Mount.*

"But that's why we're here helping you heal, so you can get back to your mountain." This wasn't just about Puff. The horrors the little dragon had shown him had to stop.

Yes, they do.

But trepidation skidded along their bond; fear not just of dying, but the horror of the consequences of failure.

Puff shivered, and a vision of two silvery-white dragons lying in a pool of blood winked out as quickly as the image appeared. Not a memory, but a fear of what could happen if Puff challenged the ruling dragons and failed. They wouldn't just kill Puff. They'd punish his parents and maybe all the crystal dragons.

Nik ran his fingers beneath Puff's chin. "I'm here for you. We all are. Once you are king, no one will hurt your people."

Puff's neck rolled in a gulping motion. *I'm not sure if that will be enough.*

"Maybe not." Nik looked over his shoulder, where Nanna and Pops seemed to be making plans for exiting at first light. "But they believe it's enough. Maybe you need to believe in yourself as much as they do."

$\mathcal{A}$nna's eyes fluttered open to figures moving within a flickering light, skewed by the thin, silver warmth swaddling her. She took in a deep breath and let it out slowly.

Dragons were real, and a dragon had comforted her all night, blanketing her with his wing. No matter how many times she repeated it, the whole idea seemed too fantastic to be true.

She stretched and the wing around her lifted. A shiny silver nose came down and touched hers.

"He says good morning." Nik handed her a warm mug.

The sweet essence of chocolate infused her. "Hot cocoa?"

"What can I say? The Maori know how to throw a party." He sat beside her. "Puff wants to know if you slept okay."

Anna snorted a laugh. "Darn considerate dragon, isn't he?"

Nik's gaze flashed to Puff, then back to her. "Believe it or not, he's genuinely concerned."

Yeah, she needed to get used to the idea that the giant cuddly reptile was actually a person.

Or like a person.

Crap, the whole idea was enough to make a girl crazy.

Nik held his own mug to the side and leaned closer. Anna

flinched, leaning back into Puff as Nik buried his nose in her hair. What the hell was he doing?

He took a deep breath. His eyes met hers. "Okay, that was pretty awkward. Sorry."

"Did you just smell me?"

Pink flooded his cheeks. "Umm, yeah." He looked up at the dragon. "Strawberries and dirt. Next time, if you want to know what she smells like, sniff her yourself." He locked gazes with Puff before turning to her. "Apparently he was afraid you might be upset if he smelled you. He wants to know if he can sniff you, himself."

Puff lowered his head and hunched his huge shoulders. The area around his eyes flashed red as it had the day before when the girl complimented him.

Anna narrowed her eyes. "I-I guess that would be okay."

Puff fluttered his good wing around her. Her hair shifted, tickling her neck as the creature drew in a deep breath. Puff hummed as he exhaled, and a slight tingle ran over her, as if the dragon's breath had seeped through her skin, stroking her from somewhere deep inside.

Her mind fogged and she leaned toward him, ready to lose herself back within the safety of his soft, warm embrace.

"Just like I told you," Nik said. "Strawberries. The dirt, I guess, is a given."

He held up his filthy hands, and Anna lurched as if waking suddenly from a daze, spilling some of her drink. The cocoa soaked into the dirt floor, making a murky paste.

Idiot. When had she gotten so clumsy? She set the mug on the ground and covered the spill with fresh dirt.

"Sorry," Nik said. "I didn't mean to startle you."

She looked at the dragon. "You didn't startle me, Puff."

"No, I meant me. I startled you," Nik said.

Anna flushed. "Oh, I'm sorry. This is getting a little confusing."

Nik smiled. "I get it. I *totally* get it."

The dragon's gaze scanned the Maori making small clusters around lit flashlights. Each group bowed to him as they noticed they held his interest. So odd. Nanna noticed his attention and approached.

Puff lowered his neck and laid his large head on the ground.

"What's wrong?" Nanna rubbed sand on her hands and let it fall to the floor.

"I think he's worried about living up to everyone's expectations," Nik said.

Nanna smiled. "A humble king."

The dragon glanced at her and snorted.

"I don't think he feels like a king," Nik said.

"Yet a king you will be—as soon as you bring this wonderful woman back to the mountain with you."

"Wait. What?" Anna scampered back, kicking her mug and spilling the rest of the contents across the dirt floor. "Bring who back where?"

Nanna placed her hand on the girl's shoulder. "As I told you, you're a lucky girl."

Anna stood, her eyes scanning the small cave. "What are you talking about? I only stayed the night until it was safe. Today someone is going to take me back down the mountain."

Nik stood beside her. His lips formed a thin line. "We need to tell her. She doesn't know about the Seventeen Year."

Anna straightened. "Seventeen years of what?"

The calm, sweet sincerity of Nanna's gaze would have been comforting, if three men hadn't just moved in front of the door to the cave.

Come on, did they think she could move all those boulders by herself and run for it?

"Every seventeen years, the dragons take flight in search of mates. On rare occasion, they find one." Nanna eased down to the dirt between Anna and Puff. "It is a contest of sorts. The ones who bring back suitable mates spar until a winner is chosen. The victor is made king for the next seventeen years."

Bile rose in Anna's throat. She checked the exit again. Still blocked.

"More often than not, only one dragon is successful and fighting is unnecessary." Nanna looked back to the dragon. "We have not had a change in rule in hundreds of years, and it's been over a thousand since we had the honor of a crystal dragon's wisdom."

Anna opened her mouth several times to speak, but no words left her lips. She closed her eyes and took a deep breath. "This is a joke, right?"

Nanna continued to smile.

The dragon, leaning on one paw, then the other, trembled beside Nik.

Nik raised his hands. "He doesn't want you to be afraid."

"No? But he wants to *mate* with me?" She pointed at the beast. "That is a dragon. I'm not letting that thing touch me." She turned away from them, but Pops grabbed her.

"The Draconi do not mate with humans in dragon form," Pops said. "They are shapeshifters."

Anna stopped struggling and stared at him. *Shapeshifting,* again. These people were certifiable.

"Female dragons became rare. No one knows why. The few that still live usually bear male offspring."

Anna's eyes became dry, but she couldn't blink.

"Dragons are magical creatures, so they began shifting form, seeking an alternate solution. They found that certain human females could mother the genetic code of the Draconi, so every mating season, every seventeen years, the dragons fly hoping to find suitable mates."

Anna grimaced. "I don't know how many times I have to say it. I am not having sex with a Dragon."

"I understand your trepidation, but as we've said, they are

shifters. Our dragon can walk, talk, smell, feel, and even mate like a human being."

Anna's gaze carried over the deep, yearning sincerity in Puff's eyes, and over his shimmering, white mane that was, now that she thought about it, the same color as the guy's hair in the bar.

The dragon said that he knows you, and his name is Joe.

Wait. No.

Not only no, but hell no. She wasn't going to let them suck her into this insanity. Dragons, okay, seeing is believing, but being able to magically transform from one creature to another?

Nik turned to Puff. "I know your wing is hurt, but can you shift at all? Can you show her something to help her believe?"

It wasn't a surprise when the dragon shook his snout. Dragons were one thing. She could deal with the idea of a creature that had remained hidden all these years. After all, they were finding new species in the rainforests all the time. But magic? Shapeshifting?

"The crystal dragons have always been harbingers of peace," Nanna said. "I meant it when I said you were a lucky girl."

Anna covered her ears. "Stop saying that. You're all nuts, you know that?"

Puff lowered his snout to her.

"He says he'd never hurt you." Nik closed his eyes and rubbed the bridge of his nose.

Anna stopped struggling. "Magic, hidden kingdoms, shapeshifters—you have to listen to yourselves. This is ludicrous." She turned to the dragon. "Please let me go. I just want to go home."

Nik paled. He grabbed his neck as his eyes reddened.

"This isn't just about our dragon," Pops said. "His kind are counting on him."

"Our Great One is far younger than I feared." Nanna scratched behind a darker set of scales where his ear might be. "The crystal dragons betray their desperation. They sent their only hopeful into the fray, with such slim chances at success. They must have great faith that *Aoraki* would look favorably on them, and invite the wise ones back to rule these islands." She looked back to Anna. "And so they have, by offering you."

Tears streamed down her cheeks. "But I'm not even from New Zealand. I'm from New Jersey." She wiped her face. "There has to be someone else."

"There is no other." Nik winced, then rose slowly, as if fighting his own movement until he stood with a rigid posture Anna hadn't seen from him before. His gaze latched to hers. Anna stiffened, her attention drawn to Puff.

"I need you." The dragon's sparkling eyes never left Anna. His tail slid across the dirt behind him. "You're already a part of me. You have been since we met." Puff took a step toward her, his presence commanding, as Nik's voice resonated through the chamber. "Can't you feel it? Can't you feel *me*?"

Anna was vaguely aware of Nik in her peripheral vision, grabbing his temples, growling, and shaking his head as if to fight something off. But it was the dragon's gaze that kept her centered. A hum filled her ears, drawing her in. She yearned to be back beneath his wing, safe, wanted and needed. Everything she'd ever wanted was here, yet behind the desire swirling across her skin, itched a terror waiting to be set free. Nonetheless, she found herself taking a step toward the beast.

"Wait a Goddamn minute." Nik pushed between them. "You winged bastard, you just took me over." He kept his back to Anna, still facing the dragon. His shirt rose and fell as if he had trouble catching his breath. From the tilt in Puff's head to the tick in Nik's fist they appeared to be fighting, but without words.

"Yeah, well I'm your translator, so let me translate. That wasn't cool."

Anna gulped. The dragon had taken control of him? Or at least

Nik thought he'd taken control. But that wasn't possible, right? If Puff could do that to Nik, could he control Anna as well?

Nanna took Anna's hand, startling her. "You are the link to the future." She glanced at Nik, then back to the dragon. "Imagine a world where man and dragon can live alongside each other once again." She smiled. The light in her eyes was contagious, if it weren't Anna's future they were discussing. "The world was in balance when the crystal dragons ruled, and it will be in balance again."

That all sounded great, but they were missing the point.

Anna closed her eyes. "They can rule all they want, as long as I'm sitting on my couch back home. I want nothing to do with this."

CHAPTER 13

*P*uff stomped his front talons on the cave floor. His menacing growl reverberated through the room. The crowd retreated, some reaching the back of the cavern.

Nik splayed his hands. "Whoa, boss, get a grip. No one is going anywhere." He turned toward Anna. "He says if you leave, the other dragons will find you."

Puff grunted. A vision of a woman lying in a pool of blood with a newborn dragon beside her flashed through Nik's mind. He froze as the memory focused on her wide, vacant eyes. A large gray dragon lumbered forward, nudged the baby toward the corpse, and coerced the fledgling to eat. Nik dropped to the floor and retched.

The memory darkened as the dragon's muzzle touched Nik's side. *I won't let that happen to her.*

Shit, this was serious. Those gray dragons killed their mates when they were done with them. Anna needed to know Puff was the safer choice, but freaking her out more than she already was wasn't the best idea, either.

Nik took a towel offered by someone and wiped his face before he looked up. "Anna, I get that you're scared."

Her eyes were wild. "Do you? You're all nuts. Every stinking one of you. I want to go home." She twisted in Pop's grip. Tears welled in her eyes as she looked at Puff. "Please, I'm sure you are a perfectly nice dragon, but you can't do this. It's not right. I want to go home."

Someone behind her grumbled that repeating herself wasn't going to make something magically happen.

Nik cringed. He loved his people, but they needed to understand this from the poor girl's perspective. She obviously didn't believe Puff could shift. She probably thought they were asking her to commit bestiality.

"Okay," Nik said, then stopped. Had he spoken aloud? He didn't think so, but then again, his words weren't his own anymore.

He turned to the dragon. "Did you say that? What do you mean, okay?"

A deep sense of loss overcame Nik as Puff headed toward the still stoned-in entrance.

The Maori stepped back, giving him room as Puff grabbed a boulder from the center of the pile and pulled. His tail twitched, but the mound only creaked. Puff opened his mouth and howled at the doorway. The sound echoed through the chamber, bouncing off walls. Many dropped to their knees, grabbing their ears.

Nik tried to calm the swirl of emotions jack-hammering across their bond. He eased toward the screaming dragon. "Boss, you okay?"

Puff snapped at Nik before he threw his good shoulder at the wall, tumbling the upper rocks outward. When the light gleamed through the top of the mound, he pressed his front talons into the pile and the boulders rolled outward. Men on the outside shouted to stop, but Puff hoisted himself onto the mound and squeezed through the opening near the ceiling.

Outside, men continued to shout over the grating sounds of

the boulders scratching beneath Puff's talons. The dragon's immense form closed out the sunlight for a few moments before he pushed his way through. His tail was the last to disappear, leaving a gaping hole at the top of the entrance.

The men continued to shout outside. Two words carried through the commotion.

Another dragon.

Sweat instantly dampened Nik's brow. They'd been found.

His heart pounded in time with his erratic gasps as he clawed to the top of the boulders and slid through the hole. He squinted in the early morning heat, shielding his eyes as the three men they'd left outside circled Puff, yelling and pointing back to the cave.

Puff opened his jaws and bellowed at them. The men fell silent, until Puff's howl was answered from somewhere far above.

"That's what we've been trying to tell you," one man said to Puff. "Another dragon has been circling all morning. That's why we haven't given the all-clear."

Nik slid, tumbling down the boulders. He cried out, and Puff shoved his shimmering tail beneath his *Kotahi*, cushioning Nik's fall.

Heart rattling, Nik paused for three seconds and confirmed there was nothing broken, before the terror in the eyes of the men around them sunk in.

"Are you sure it was a dragon?" Nik slid to the sandy ground.

"Look." One of the men pointed to the sky.

Miles above, a small winged creature glided through the air.

Nik shielded his eyes. "That's a bird."

"It's not. You have no idea how high that is. We saw him circle lower. Believe me, it's a dragon."

The creature above swerved. It looked like it rolled through the air, playing in a way he'd never seen a bird fly before—as if it were enjoying the flight, rather than simply stalking prey.

Even so, that made him no less a hunter.

Nik placed his hand on Puff's neck. "Boss, we need to get you inside. That dragon—"

"Already saw us." Pops stood by the small human entrance to the cave, his right hand shielding his eyes as he looked toward the sky, where the huge winged creature swooped toward them.

Anna pushed past the men removing the remainder of the rocks from the human-sized entrance to the cave. Pops stood outside, partially blocking the door, staring into the sky.

No matter. With everyone distracted by Puff's sudden exit, this might be her only chance to get away. She squeezed through the small space, but cried out when the ground quaked and a loud thump echoed through the clearing.

A colossal blackish-green dragon held its wings high above their heads. The men outside stepped back before crowding around Puff.

Were they insane? Did they actually think they could do something to stop that monster from hurting their dragon?

The green behemoth lowered its neck and bellowed a furious roar at Puff. The smaller dragon elevated his one good wing in a similar pose and growled in return.

"Boss, wait!" Nik held up his hands, but Puff shoved him to the side as the larger dragon howled again.

Puff tapped the dirt, and the two dragons continued their growling and posturing, spinning around each other and somehow managing not to stomp on any of the people doing their best to keep the two creatures apart.

The cacophony stopped as the green dragon raised its head, looked over puff's extended wing, and locked gazes with Anna.

Her breath seized. She pushed herself against the cold stone behind her.

Somewhere deep within, a small voice screamed to run, but the most movement she could muster was scraping her fingernails against the rock wall.

This was it. She was going to die, and she couldn't even find the strength to fight for her life as the green strode toward her.

Puff stepped back, giving way to the other dragon. Had he given up on her, ceded the fight to the first challenger?

Three of the Maori moved between her and the green dragon as the huge beast seemed to shrink, becoming smaller as it stalked Anna. The men gasped, backing away.

The new dragon continued its advance, folding its wings back until they disappeared. Gaze still locked to hers, the behemoth rose on its hind legs as its front talons drew into hands, and its green hide lightened to a creamy gray tone. The creature's dark mane shrank into long, flowing locks covering a rounded, human-shaped head.

Anna hazarded a breath, shaking, as a naked man stopped next to Pops. The older Maori gulped, but didn't seem surprised as the dragon-turned-man's gaze flicked from Pops, back to Anna.

The dragon-man held out his hand. "I've been searching for you. Are you all right?"

The voice—so calm, so demanding, so *familiar*.

Anna tried to clear her thoughts, remembering this face, these eyes, cemented to her sister as they both stood in a bar in what seemed like centuries ago.

She trembled. "C-Connor?"

He held out his arms in a mock curtsey. His guy-stuff dangled unabashedly between his legs. "At your service, my queen."

Her head spun. She steadied herself against the mountain. "W-what?"

His smile did nothing to ward off the bile pushing up into her throat.

Dragons really could shift. They could be monster or man at will. Everything these insane people had been preaching was true, and now there were two of them.

God, was this whole contest-thing really true? Were Connor and Puff going to fight over her, now?

She stumbled, but Puff caught her with one shimmering-scaled arm. Connor glared at him, arms folded and legs held wide, guy-stuff still dangling.

Pops bowed his head slightly. "Mighty Lord, maybe some human clothing would be in good order? We are unaccustomed to meeting shifted dragons."

Connor seemed to ignore him, reaching out and spreading Puff's injured wing. A light whistle left his lips. "That must have hurt."

Puff snapped at him, while Nik placed a hand on Puff's shoulder. "He said hitting the ground hurt worse."

Connor's eyes widened. "*Kotahi?*" He looked back to Puff. "You actually bit a human?"

Puff shrugged.

Connor snickered before his attention drew back to Anna. He spun her away from him. "Gale's claws pierced your flesh. I saw it happen."

Anna trembled as he stroked his palms across her back.

He turned to Puff. "You have been busy. Too bad you can't heal yourself."

Anna rubbed her shoulders. Yesterday's pain ghosted across her skin.

"Can *you* heal him?" Nik asked.

"Me?" Connor cocked his head.

"Yeah. Can't you heal him like he healed Anna?"

"I'm a green. We're not much for healing. Our skills lie more within the pleasure centers."

Nik looked at Puff. His eyes widened as they stared at each other, before he turned back to Connor. "You're a lust dragon? Please tell me that doesn't mean what I think it means."

Anna shrank into a shallow mountain crevice as Connor turned toward her again. Her heart raced in time with her staggered breaths, then settled as their eyes met.

Puff didn't protest as the naked man reached for her. Anna's gaze drew back to the package dangling between his legs. The air around them seemed to suck away, closing the two of them in a hazy void.

Connor lifted her chin, forcing her eyes away from his, umm… stuff. "That's not for you, little one." Puff's growl bit through the haze in Anna's mind as Connor looked back at Pops. "I suppose I will take those pants before my new king bites down on my jugular."

Anna blinked and the fog cleared, bringing her back to the side of the mountain, the people, and the man she'd last seen fully clothed outside the bar.

Connor caught her as she swooned. "You may feel unnaturally drawn to me from time to time, my queen. It's not intentional. I have trouble controlling it."

Anna gulped. Lust dragon. Holy Toledo.

Puff grumbled something.

"He says he wouldn't have hurt you," Nik said.

Connor laughed, slipping on a pair of loose khakis that sat about four inches above his ankles. "I heard him, I'm not deaf."

"My sister," Anna said. "Sybil. The dragon—the *other* dragon…"

"Dropped her." Connor scowled. "Then I dropped you. Forgive me for that, but I knew Joesephutus wouldn't let you fall."

Joesephutus? Her gaze shot to Puff. The silvery-white dragon tilted his head to the right, his eyes large and searching. A light breeze blew through his shiny platinum blond mane. Each hair caught the light, sparkling, just like the ghostly white hair of a boy she'd met in a bar.

Holy shit. Everything they said was true.

Puff grumbled again. But that wasn't just Puff. He wasn't only a dragon. At least, he hadn't been when they'd first met.

Connor turned to him. "Stop complaining. When I dropped her, you'd already broken free from that gray. You had more than enough time to catch her. I, on the other hand, was the only thing between the lovely Sybil and the rocks below."

It was Connor. Connor had snatched Anna from the gray dragon's claws. He and Puff—or Joe, had both saved her.

Anna tried to tame her thumping heart. "So, Sybil is okay? You caught her?" God, she was praying that her sister had been caught by a dragon. She was talking to a guy that was a monster only a few minutes ago. This was the insanest of dreams, and she was ready to wake up.

The power of Connor's gaze pressed against her as if he'd stroked her entire body with practiced hands. "She's more than fine. She's absolutely delicious."

Anna gulped. "D-delicious?"

Nik placed his hand on her shoulder. "Not delicious like that. Greens are, umm…"

Lust dragons. Yeah, she'd heard. "What did you do to her?"

He held his hands out to the side. "I took nothing she didn't offer freely, I assure you. Your sister shows her appreciation in the most agreeable ways."

She screwed a dragon.

Anna's face must have betrayed her thoughts, because Connor said: "She remembers falling, and I miraculously caught her. My wings and talons somehow slipped her mind."

Anna recoiled and glanced at Puff. Could they do that, make you forget?

"Puff wants you to know that he hasn't done that to you," Nik said.

"Joe," Anna whispered. "His name is Joe." Anna shuddered, but only for a second as she accepted myth as fact. She looked back to the dragon. "Those other guys in the bar, were they dragons, too?"

He nodded. Such a human reaction. Why hadn't she believed them earlier?

"Grays. The worst of our kind," Connor said. "The one that took you, Galeptopnor, was our former king."

Nik shifted his weight. "Puff says this Gale guy is *still* king."

Connor's gaze settled on Anna. "Not once we get you to the mountain."

Sweat dampened Anna's brow as she pressed against the rocks, again.

Connor held up his hands. "I'm only here to help, you have no need to fear me."

Despite the fact that he was really a ten-ton reptile in disguise.

She closed her eyes and took a deep breath. She wanted to shut all of this out, to pretend nothing had happened. That was the safe thing to do—to hide until all of this went away. But they weren't going away. These dragons needed a girl, and for some reason they chose her.

When she opened her eyes, Connor was holding Puff's wing to the light. Dark, swirling, identical tattoos scrolled along the edges of Connor's shoulder blades.

"Someone sewed you up," Conner said. "These stitches look practiced."

"I'm a veterinarian." Despite standing nearly six foot tall, Tyler seemed dwarfed next to Connor as the dragon stooped to look at the man's handiwork.

"Do you know how long this will take to heal?" Connor turned to the vet. "More than likely, we'll have to fight our way back to the mountain."

Tyler shook his head. "It's going to be a long time before he can fly. As for fighting, he's as strong as ever. As long as no one touches his wing, he'll be fine."

Connor puffed out a laugh. "Grays have never been known to play fair. Especially Gale." He reached up and stroked the dragon's snout. "If you can shift, I can carry you."

The dragon lowered his head.

"He said he's tried. It hurts too much."

Connor tapped a finger against his chin. His thoughts seemed miles away. "Then you make the journey on foot. I can protect you from the sky."

Nik glanced at Puff, then back to Connor. "He says Gale will gut you."

"Probably. But maybe I can slow him down."

Puff reared up and slammed both front claws on the ground.

"He won't let you sacrifice yourself."

Tyler stood. "How can we increase the speed of his healing?" He pointed at Anna. "What the Great One did to her wounds was amazing. Can you bring back another crystal dragon?"

Connor cocked a brow. "The crystals have been under forced submission since last night." He looked at Puff. "When Gale couldn't find you, he flew back to Dragon Mount and made sure your kin couldn't help you."

Puff ruffled his wings. Not only was he small, but now he was cut off from his people. He was alone, except for Connor.

Anna shivered. She had seen the gray dragons. Connor was huge to her, but he was no match for a gray. What chance did they really have?

Nik ran his fingers through Joe's mane. "Isn't there anyone else who can help?"

Connor straightened. "The golds."

Puff raised his head.

"Golds?" Nik asked. "Puff said the golds would never help the crystal dragons."

The left side of Connor's lip turned up in a grin. "Two days ago, I would have agreed with you. But much has happened since the Seventeen Year began." He backed away and held up his hands.

"Everyone back into the mountain. The grays cannot see in sunlight, but that doesn't mean they will not send others to look for you."

"What are you going to do?" Nik asked.

"I'm going to get help." Connor shimmied down his pants and kicked them off his ankles. He stood in all his naked glory, glancing at the shocked faces around him, before holding up his arms.

The air around him flickered. The Maori backed away as his arms and legs grew and covered with a thick blackish-green hide. The tattoos on his shoulder blades leapt off his skin and solidified as translucent jade wings unfolded from his back and fluttered in the light breeze. He arched his neck as his bones elongated and his mouth stretched into a full-toothed snout.

The dragon grew until it towered over them. Anna had grown to accept this over the last hour, but her heart still throttled and her world spun. She clutched the mountain to keep from falling as the colossus roared once and bounded into the sky.

The Maori held still, most shading their eyes as the enormous beast… no, not a beast… as *Connor* rose into the clouds, quickly escalating to a height where no one would question that he was anything more than a bird.

Incredible. Anna didn't think she would ever tire of seeing such a thing, no matter how terrified she was.

That didn't change anything, though. She had to get out of here.

CHAPTER 15

"I guess we should head back into the cave, then." Nik moved toward the opening, but stopped when Puff didn't follow. "You heard the big guy. We need to get you safe."

I need to hunt. I'm hungry. He glanced at Anna. *I need you to watch her while I'm gone.*

"How are you supposed to hunt with a bad wing?"

Pops and Tyler approached and placed a bundled lump at Puff's feet.

"Our friends on the outside considered that." Pops opened the rags, revealing a very-dead young tahr. A stretch of its shaggy coat lay matted with blood, and one of its stubby, pre-pubescent horns dug into the soil, forcing the animal's gaping muzzle upward. Nik cringed, glad he hadn't eaten yet.

Puff's eyes widened and an itch tingled across their bond. Nik's stomach grumbled at the thought of the fresh kill sliding down his throat. He twitched, shaking the dragon's thoughts away as Puff glanced at Anna. The girl's brow furrowed. Her lips twisted in disgust.

I can't let her see me eat. She's already terrified.

"I kinda agree with you on that one." Nik fell to one knee, rewrapped the bundle, and slipped his arms beneath. He grunted as he stood. "This thing is heavier than it looks."

Glancing over both shoulders, he found a large boulder and some trees that would afford Puff some privacy. He set the burden down and unwrapped it before returning.

He motioned to the rock. "Breakfast is served."

Puff glanced at Anna. He seemed pensive, but no thoughts skittered across their link before he headed toward the boulder. *Thank you.*

Anna held her stomach, her lips still twisted into a frown.

"I think we can probably find something a little more cooked, if you're hungry," Nik said.

She gulped. "I might never eat again."

Anna eyed Puff's twitching tail sticking out from behind the boulder before scanning the rest of the camp. Her eyes kept skirting toward the path they'd followed up the mountain. Not that he could blame her. She hadn't asked for this, but she was a part of it now, just as much as he was.

"No one brought any cars or anything like that up here, if that's what you're looking for."

She closed her eyes and blew out a breath. "Of course there wouldn't be." She glanced back at the boulder. "You seem like the most reasonable person here. Can you try to talk some sense into them? I need to get home."

Home. The whole idea seemed a little transient these past few days. Before the dragon fell from the sky, everything had been crystal clear. Nik's path had been set. Not that he was doing great on that path, but he'd have found a job eventually. Things would have turned around for him. He would have had a *real* life.

Then the creatures from the storybooks became real, and he let himself be bitten by a dragon. Now he had this otherworldly connection to a giant, intelligent reptile that he still barely understood.

However, he did understand Anna's point of view. Two days

ago, he'd have been using this opportunity to smuggle the girl down the mountain while Puff wasn't looking.

But that bite had done more than simply given him the ability to translate for Puff. Nik understood the dragon at a deeper level than any of them could comprehend. The spirit of the Seventeen Year had emblazoned through his bones, becoming part of him. Every time Puff even had a passing thought about the current dragon king, the need to overthrow the beast became all the more concrete. This dragon, Gale, couldn't be allowed to rule. And if bringing this girl up the side of the mountain was the only way to stop his tyranny, then so be it.

The old Nik cringed. Forcing a girl to do something she didn't want grated at his humanity. He couldn't force her. No, he wouldn't. She deserved better. He loved her enough to let her go, if that was what she wanted.

Nik balked, gasping at his own thoughts, when a dragon-shaped shadow fell over him. He breathed a sigh of relief. These weren't his thoughts, but Puff's. Soon, hopefully, he'd be able to distinguish between the two.

He turned to the dragon. "Are you seriously going to let her go?"

Yes.

"But what about all that stuff with Connor? He went to get help."

I will accept any help to heal my injuries. I still want to return to the mountain, even if it will be in defeat.

Nik stepped towards him. "But Gale will kill you."

"What's going on?" Anna asked.

Tell her.

Nik's gaze dropped to the sand at his feet. So many dragons depended on this hunt. Hundreds lay in the back of dark caves under lock and key, hoping for the little dragon they'd sent out as a long shot to come home and save them from their oppressor.

But Puff had failed them. He never had a chance to begin with. He never deserved the hope they had in him.

Grunting, Nik pushed Puff's thoughts out of his head again and advanced on the dragon. "Now wait a goddamn minute. You are not giving up so easily." He pointed at Anna. "You have the girl. You've already won. You just need to reach the finish line."

"I'm not a prize in a game," Anna cried. "I am a human being."

Old Nik looked back at her, understanding. But the part of him that had connected with Puff, the part that allowed Draconic blood to flow through his veins, overpowered him. "This is bigger than you. It is bigger than both of us."

Stop! Puff roared, his growl echoing through the clearing.

The Maori stood silent, staring at them. The dragon scanned the crowd before lowering his neck and caressing Anna cheek to cheek.

"He says that he doesn't care about the Seventeen Year." Nik grimaced. "Something about a bond and wanting you happy."

Puff turned toward Pops.

Nik sighed in defeat. "He says he wants you to send her home."

Tears filled Anna's eyes. She slipped her arms around Puff's silvery neck and hugged him. "Thank you so much."

The Maori broke their statuesque poses. Most of them gaped.

Nik bit his lip, understanding their confusion. He was new to this believing in dragons thing, but most of these people had been waiting their whole lives for a dragon to appear. And then to be a part of assisting the next king, it was the makings of history—a dream come true.

The second Puff fell out of the sky, these people left their everyday lives to help him. And now he was giving up, just like that.

I won't force her.

Puff loved Anna. It wasn't a flighty, childish insta-love, but something deep, mature, and eternal. But how was that even possible when they'd barely even spoken?

I'm a dragon. The second I recognized her as a viable mate, the process began. When I decided to fight for her, the Draconic instincts took over, and by the time I'd plucked her from the sky and won her, it was done. Puff turned, walking toward the mountain. *She will always be mine in my heart, but my dragon soul will not allow me to make her unhappy, no matter the cost.*

Nik started after him. "What about the sadistic guy locking all your people up? What happened to saving all Draconi from tyranny? What happened to bringing dragons back into the open?"

Puff looked over his shoulder at Nik. *I already told you, I refuse to force her.*

Pops gripped Nik's shoulder, pulling him away from the dragon. He spoke loud enough for the congregation to hear. "We'll return the girl, but we cannot head down the mountain so late in the day. We won't make civilization before nightfall." He glanced at Anna, then back to Nik. "We will spend the night once more in the embrace of our sacred caves, and break camp at first light."

Nik shook his head. "I can't believe you, of all people, are giving up, too."

Pops put his arm around Nik's shoulder and walked him away from the crowd. "It is barely two hours past sunrise, is it not?"

"Yeah. So what?"

His grandfather snickered. "We have more than enough time to get down the mountain."

Nik stopped and turned to him. "You bluffed. Why?"

"The Great One has bonded with the young lady, yes?"

"Yeah. He kind of explained the whole thing to me."

Pops watched Puff climb the boulder pile and disappear back into the cave with a sense of childish awe that Nik had lost the second Puff gave up.

"Remember, Nikau, that our new king is quite young, and not yet familiar with just how great his greatness is." He tilted his head back, closing his eyes and allowing the sun to caress his face. "Tonight is the Brigham Solstice."

Nik huffed. He never really paid attention to the ancient Maori elemental calendar. "I guess. So what?"

Pops's eyes opened, seeming somewhat brighter. "Do not underestimate the power of Ruma Marama on the most glorious night of the year."

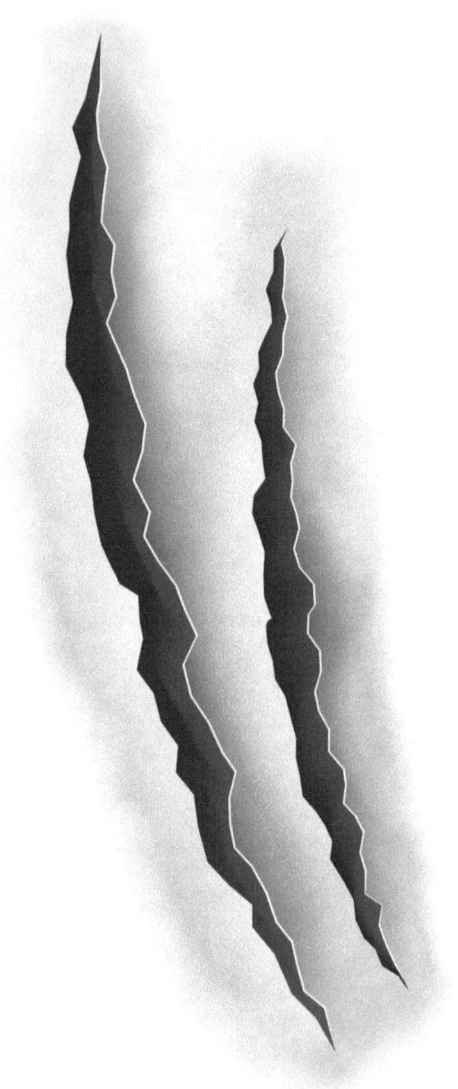

CHAPTER 16

One more night. Anna could do this. She glanced around the cave as the men worked to reseal the opening, blocking them off from the outside. The women milled about, some bringing water and food to the men, and others creating small fires. A slight draft tickled Anna's skin and spiraled the smoke into tiny billows that sucked through a small hole in the ceiling. A naturally occurring ventilation system. Amazing.

The older children helped their parents, while the younger Maori gathered the twigs into neat piles. A few chased flies that had come in before the exit had closed. They led such a simple but backward existence, men doing the labor while the women cooked. They couldn't possibly live like this when they were back in their normal lives.

Anna couldn't help but wonder if this was like playtime to them, like how people dressed up and acted out parts in Renaissance fairs back home. When this was all over, would they all return to the twenty-first century?

"Comfortable?" Nanna asked, easing to the floor beside her.

"I guess." She didn't want to admit that she still hurt from sleeping on the hard ground the evening before. Especially since the older woman never complained, and she hadn't had the luxury of a dragon wing to keep her warm all night.

Nanna's gaze carried across the room, where Puff allowed the younger children to climb on him. "Our dragon seems to have won the hearts of our next generation. It's encouraging."

"What do you mean?"

She shrugged. "I'm not as young as I used to be. I probably won't be here for the next Seventeen Year, but they will be." She pointed at Puff and his throng of young playmates. "More importantly, he will be." Nanna watched for another moment, smiling. "Those little girls will remember this day: his kindness, how warm and comforting he was." She grinned. "In seventeen years, when they are young women, they will probably fight each other to get on the platform, hoping to catch his eye."

Anna's hands fisted and her stomach clenched. A sudden desire to swat all those little girls away from her dragon enveloped her.

Wait.

Her dragon? When had he become her dragon, and why did she care? She folded her arms. Any of those little girls could have him if that meant she could go home.

Anna took in a deep breath and let it out slowly. She *was* going home. Puff had set her free. The Maori would do whatever he asked without question. They just had to wait until it was safe to make the journey. There was nothing to fear anymore.

One of the little girls fell off Puff's side and slammed to the ground. She howled until Puff nudged her. The little girl jumped to her feet and hugged him.

Funny how none of them were afraid of an animal so much larger than them. Didn't any of their history show dragons killing people? If not, weren't they afraid of all those teeth?

Puff sneezed, ruffling his mane. The children giggled and crowded him. Nik stood close, smiling as the dragon seemed to struggle under the kids' weight. The *Kotahi's* expression belayed that the dragon was only pretending to be thwarted, and the children loved every second.

But they were young. Would any of them remember this day, or would meeting the dragon settle into the reaches of their memories, easing back into the realm of myth passed down from generation to generation, until Puff was nothing but a bedtime story told to their grandchildren? Anna looked away, hoping to banish the thought.

Throughout the cave, the Maori churned in constant movement, as if they'd done this a thousand times and everyone knew their task until meals were prepared, eaten, and cleared away.

Anna sat, rapt as Puff stood and allowed the children to defeat him over and over again until her cheeks hurt from smiling. He truly was a gentle giant, despite his small size among the other dragons.

Pops approached and shooed the children away. A collective "Awwwww." rang through the chamber. The old man whispered a few words to his grandson, who glanced in Anna's direction before following Puff toward the back of the chamber and into a dark passage.

Where were they going?

Nanna grabbed the paper plate on the ground beside Anna. "Did you have enough to eat?"

"Yes, thanks. It was great." Well, as great as burnt rabbit and the meat from whatever an *arapawa* was could be. She'd never eaten anything off a stick before, though. The experience was definitely memorable.

Limping slightly, Pops approached. She hadn't remembered a limp earlier, but she had to give the old man credit. The past two days had taken a toll on Anna, and she was less than half his age.

"How has your evening been, Miss Anna?" Pops asked.

"Great, thanks. You've all been so hospitable." Hospitable, even though she refused to be their dragon queen. Every time she turned she expected someone to act out, shout at her, or do something else to force her to their way of thinking. Every single Maori had been overly kind to her, though. She felt at home here, like she truly belonged among them.

"The Great One has moved into the cathedral for Brigham Solstice." Pops looked toward the dark hallway at the back of the chamber. "This is a sacred time for the Draconi. Tonight, when the moon is at its apex, the dragons will be at the height of their fertility." He turned to her. "It would be appropriate if his queen joined him."

Anna's veins iced. "But he let me go. He said I don't have to."

"You may not be returning to Dragon Mount with him, but that makes you no less his queen." He settled on the floor beside her, opposite his wife. "He chose you. That hasn't changed."

Anna's gaze darted to the walled-off exit again, as if her sudden panic might make the giant boulders blocking her escape somehow disappear.

Nanna's hand covered hers. "The Great One asks nothing of you but your company, I'm sure." She glared at her husband, then back to the ground. "He has a good heart, our dragon. A shame really. He would have been a wonderful king."

"Enough of that, Carolyn," Pops said. "That door has been closed."

"But it's still the truth. Anyway..." She turned to Anna and smiled. "No one is asking you to consummate anything with him in dragon form. Goodness knows he wouldn't ask that of you either, but tonight is as holy a night for the Draconi as it is for the Maori. He is alone here, even among so many. He probably would appreciate company other than my Nikau." She cupped her hand over Anna's ear and whispered. "Nikky is a good boy, but he tends to be a bit boring at times."

Anna laughed. These two reminded her so much of her own grandparents. The Maori were all nice, wonderful people despite the dragons and caves and the insanity surrounding the Seventeen

Year. She wished she'd met them all under different circumstances.

She looked toward the dark corridor. "What's back there?"

Nanna stood and held out her hand to Anna. "Like we said, the cathedral room. Large rooms are common in caverns like these, but ours is special. That is why the Maori walled off these caves centuries ago." She took Anna's hand. "It is nearly time. I think the Great One would be overjoyed to experience the solstice with you."

Anna took her hand. As long as no one expected her to spread her legs, she supposed she could spend a little time alone with Puff. She wasn't much into spiritual things, but caves had always fascinated her. She couldn't imagine any cavern room being as spectacular as the cathedral room in Luray, Virginia. She was always willing to bask in nature's artistry though, no matter how ornate.

Nanna and Pops walked her to the beginning of the dark hallway and handed her a flashlight. As she grasped the cool cylinder, she noticed the Maori had fallen silent. Even the children stared at her.

Why? Did they expect her to do something? Was there some kind of ceremony to this Solstice-thing that she didn't know about? She hoped she wasn't breaking some kind of ancient custom by turning her back on them and walking into the dark, but they couldn't really expect the foreign girl to have any idea what was expected of her.

She clicked on her flashlight. The cave hallway cut a hard left, then angled down and to the right. She felt along the cool wall until the passage opened up to a brightly lit chamber. A spectacular display of white, glossy flowstone cascaded down the far wall and disappeared into a crevice in the floor. The massive space echoed with her single step. The sound seemed an unwanted intrusion on the ancient room's silence.

Puff and Nik turned toward her. The dragon jumped to his feet and galloped in place three times.

"He's glad to see you." Nik held out his hand, helping her down prehistoric steps carved into the rock floor.

Puff nuzzled her neck. She giggled. He really was as sweet as the old couple thought he was.

Their lantern flickered, casting a dancing light across the flow-stones. A trickling sound filled the cave, and Anna realized it was a touch more humid down here than it had been in the entrance chamber above.

She lit her flashlight and cast its beam toward the back of the cave, where a slow running stream seemed to cut across the floor and disappear down the same fissure the flowstone emptied into.

"Wow," she whispered.

Puff inched closer, pressing his folded, uninjured wing against her.

"He says he's happy you joined us."

Puff's translucent scales picked up the light reflecting off the water. Seeing him shimmer like that, it wasn't hard to tell why his kind were called crystal dragons.

"So," Anna said. "What's so special about this room? Is it the river?"

"I'm not sure," Nik said. "Pops told me to wait for the exact moment of the solstice, and turn off the lights." He glanced at his phone screen. "Which should be in a few minutes."

They'd done that at Luray when she was a kid. The guide called it "the black light." Since there's no natural light inside a cave, they were left in complete darkness. Anna couldn't even see her fingers wiggling in front of her face. She'd been terrified when the guide didn't flick the lights back on right away. She hoped this solstice-thing wasn't anything that silly.

"Time's up." Nik motioned to her flashlight. "Are you ready?"

She nodded, shutting her light off.

Nik reached for their lamp. "Here we go."

A single click basked them in complete darkness. She tensed, closing her eyes, before Nik gasped beside her.

"Whoa," he whispered.

Puff growled something.

Anna gaped in the darkness, or lack thereof. The cave had come alive around them. It was as if they'd been shot into space and floated amongst the stars. No matter where she turned, small spots of light greeted her, then blinked out. Some twitched, sparkled and glowed, leaving the entire room illuminated by a slight greenish hue.

"Wh-what is this?"

"Glow worms." Nik's face remained turned toward the ceiling. "But I've never seen them on South Island outside of *Te Anau*, and never in these quantities."

As they stared, the lights increased, as if these strange creatures congregated for their pleasure.

Puff flipped his mane away from Anna's face.

"He wants to know if you like it."

"He's kidding, right? This is amazing."

A green shadow cast across Nik's face. "He says the worms have different colors where he comes from, but there are not as many. They only swarm like this for a few days during Brigham Solstice."

Anna couldn't imagine what a million multicolored lights would look like. It must rival Christmas.

Nik cleared his throat. "Puff is a little frustrated. He wishes he could talk to you with his real voice."

Anna blinked away the lights and turned to Puff. Those deep, large, somehow human eyes drew her in, encompassing her with just his gaze. What was behind those eyes? Could a dragon really be capable of love, like he said, or was this something else?

She turned to Nik. "Then let him. Give him your voice like you did earlier today."

His lips thinned. "I didn't give him my voice. He took it."

And from the tone of his words, that was not something he wanted to experience again. The poor dragon did look frustrated with his *Kotahi*, though. If Nik really could feel Puff's emotions, he'd have to understand that.

Anna rustled up her prettiest smile. "Just for a few minutes."

Nik raised a brow before his attention drew back to Puff.

"Please?" Anna entreated. She really needed to know what was going on in the dragon's head, and she didn't want to worry that something might be lost in translation.

Nik pursed his lips before he backed into the shadows, leaving Puff and Anna alone within the growing spectacle of dancing lights.

Anna eased down to the damp, rocky floor. Puff settled beside her and placed his talon on her right hand before he drew it away.

"No," she said. "It's fine. I know you won't hurt me."

"I'm sorry I have to touch you with a claw."

Anna's gaze flicked back to where Nik stood in the shadows, before her gaze drew back to Puff. She had to remember that the voice she heard, while Nik's, was really now her dragon.

The lights above sparkled in Puff's eyes, adding to his brilliance. "It's not a claw," she said. "It's your hand."

"I have a real hand. I wish I could show you."

"I've seen it. You held me in the tavern, remember?"

Puff exhaled a gust of scentless smoke. She wondered if that was the dragon version of a laugh. "I suppose you wish you never walked in there."

"Not at all. I mean, yeah, I spent half the night terrified." She motioned to the glowing ceiling. "But this, you, and everything else has been amazing."

He spun from the lights and looked at her. "I want to touch you. I want..." He turned away and shook his head.

Anna grabbed his muzzle and turned him back to her. "Hey, you're sweet, you know that? You may be the sweetest guy I've ever met, and I'm incredibly honored that you chose me." She ran her palm along his cheek. His scales were surprisingly soft. "It's nothing personal. I just want someone human."

He tensed beneath her touch. "I can be human. You've seen me."

Anna looked away.

Yes, she had. His human form, Joe, wasn't quite what she'd normally look for in a guy. She'd always dreamed of a tall, dark stranger. Maybe not so tall and dark and strange as Connor, but she'd had a vision of a knight in shining armor since she was a kid.

Andrew's easy smile filled her thoughts. She'd thought he fit the bill. She'd even worn that cheap ring he gave her until he could afford a diamond.

Anna grimaced. Fairytales were pretty hard to live up to when you lived in the real world.

She didn't need prince charming, but how about a nice strong guy to take care of her? That sounded primeval, but that's what she'd always wished for. *Gaston*, without the asshole mentality. Connor, without the Connor-ness. But every guy she'd met who looked the part acted the part as well.

Then there was Joe—a short, pale, thin counterpart to Connor's dark alpha-male-ness. He'd never stand out from the crowd, other than maybe to be stared at over his nearly-white hair.

When the fixture had fallen from the ceiling, though, Joe had moved with incredible speed and grace, catching the frame before it fell on Anna. He'd held up the wooden contraption as if it weighed only a few pounds, while the bartender seemed barely able to budge it.

She considered the deeply etched reptilian muscles beneath the shimmering scales on Puff's shoulders. Looks could be deceiving, she supposed.

But none of that changed the truth that Joe was a dragon. A human and a reptile, the whole idea was insane. Even if Puff could shift into Joe once he was healed, that didn't change the fact that in reality, he was another species. It was just *weird*.

Her thoughts drifted back to Connor, a lust dragon.

Had her sister really slept with him? In his human form, she could hardly blame Sybil. He was gorgeous, sure of himself, and sexy in a sleazy kind of way… exactly what her sister liked in a cheap screw.

Did Sybil even know she was sleeping with a dragon? If she did, was she okay with all this, or was Connor really controlling her mind and making her forget about the aerial battle, her falling, and him snatching her out of the sky?

Anna covered her face. All this was a bit much for her to take.

Puff moved closer. "I didn't mean to upset you. I told you I would let you go home, and I meant it." He looked up into the twinkling lights. "I'm glad that we got to share this, though. It will be a fond memory."

Yes. Yes, it would.

Anna tried to remember another time when she'd sat in the dark with a guy who hadn't tried to grope her. In the past few months, several friends had set her up with men they knew; but even on first dates those guys had expected too much.

She supposed there were plenty of girls like her sister out there, ready to lay it all on the table, or the bed, so to speak. Maybe that was normal, now. Maybe Anna was the strange one, looking for a connection rather than just sex.

She leaned her head on Puff's hide, and smiled as his warmth rose and fell with each breath. Why she expected him to be cold, like an iguana, she didn't know. He was the warmest, most sincere creature she'd ever met.

Nanna was right. He would have been a great king.

Puff shifted slightly, and his wing rose and gathered around her. "Is this okay?"

She smiled settling against him as she had last night. "Yeah. Actually, it's pretty nice."

"You're warm, for a human."

Anna laughed. "I was thinking the same about you."

He craned his neck to look at her, before touching his nose to hers. "I know humans think differently from dragons, but I hope you understand how important you are to me. Even when we part, a portion of my soul will remain with you, forever."

Part of her wanted to push away and tell him he was being ridiculous. He was moving too fast. That this kind of connection was impossible between two people, especially two who had just met.

Instead, she stared into his eyes, soaking in the sparkling lights dancing around them. A ball wadded in her throat and twisted. Somehow, she understood what he meant, as if part of her reached out to this dragon, needing to cling to him as if her soul required his presence—like she'd be lost if he didn't wrap his wings around her and protect her from everything that ever tried to harm her.

But again, that was ridiculous, and she allowed the thought to drift up and away, lost to the flickering lights above.

What she wanted was a pipe dream, and pipe dreams, like everything else, exploded.

She leaned closer, and Puff slipped his thick, scaled arm around her. His touch felt strong, sure, and oddly enough, human. She lost herself in his warmth, closing her eyes to the sparkling lights, and shutting out everything other than the intense heat seeping through her skin and warming her soul.

She knew this was more than she should ask for, that sharing this one fleeting moment wasn't fair to either of them, but she cuddled closer, accepted his embrace, and lost herself within the perfection he offered.

Just this once.

$\mathcal{A}$nna woke to the soothing sounds of trickling water, and a commotion from down the stone hallway. Puff stirred beside her, his wing tightening and pulling her snug to his body.

A light clicked on, changing the green, soothing mottled glow to a bright, yellow blast that stung her eyes.

Nik stood beside them, his hair sticking out at the sides. "I heard it, too."

Anna tugged at Puff's wing until he released her.

"He wants you to stay beside him," Nik said.

She glanced between the two of them. After last night, she equated that voice to Puff. It seemed strange, now, hearing the smooth, melodic tenor from Nik's lips.

Torchlight danced along the walls in the hallway before Pops emerged. "Excuse the interruption. Great One, but the mighty green has returned."

Puff glanced at her before he started walking toward the hallway.

Nik followed beside her. "He'd hoped for some more time with you this morning."

Anna smiled, but didn't answer. Something stirred within her, delighted that Puff enjoyed her company.

But why? Once Connor helped his friend, they would leave, and the Maori would bring Anna down the mountain. After today, she'd never have to worry about dragons again.

She shivered as the joy she'd reveled in only moments ago slipped away, leaving her feeling alone and empty even as she stepped into the room crowded with people.

The Maori parted to the sides of the cavern, revealing Connor, shirtless and wearing the same too-short khakis as yesterday.

Nik glanced at Puff, then to Connor. "He says you smell like…" His eyes narrowed. "Exactly where have you been?"

A wry grin lifted the edge of Connor's lip. "As I said, I went to get help, but this morning I flew towards the villages to check on my queen's sister." He kissed Anna's fingers. "She is in excellent form, by the way."

Anna drew her hand back. "You slept with her again?"

"How could I resist? Dragons like beautiful things. She is a gem like no other."

The same questions spun in her head. What did Sybil know about Connor, and why was she sleeping with this strange guy and not calling the cops about her missing sister?

"Did she ask about me?"

Connor's grin spread to his whole mouth. "I assure you, she is unconcerned. I have been keeping her *occupied*."

A tremor of disgust ran down her spine. "Don't hurt her."

Connor glanced at Puff, then back to Anna. He held up his hands. "I swear to you as my queen, all I have done is made her forget about dragons. She thinks you are touring the countryside with the handsome blond stranger you met in the tavern. She, in kind, is enjoying the wealth of pleasure Joesephutus's best friend has to offer her." He held out his arms and bowed low at the waist, his trousers riding higher on his ankles.

Was he really that pompous?

He straightened. "I have a feeling I will be spending a great deal of time in the villages when this is all over. I've grown quite fond of her..." He glanced at Anna's waist, then back to her eyes. "Her finer assets."

Yes, he obviously *was* that pompous.

But he was exactly what Sybil wanted: a mysterious foreign stranger—the sleazier the better. Her poor sister was probably better off not knowing the truth, as long as she was safe.

Connor turned his attention to Puff. "I have procured the help of a few unlikely allies. I'd hoped they would be here already."

A few people outside screamed. A dragon roared.

"It sounds like help has arrived," Connor said.

Puff scampered to the door and pushed through the boulders as he had the previous morning. Connor grabbed Anna's hand and drew her through the human exit with Nik and the others following.

Outside, two identical, young blond men stood in the dark, staring at Puff. Their hair caught the light of the torches, the breeze drifting through the golden layers. Puff's milky mane stood out, ghostly in comparison.

The newcomers' attention darted to Anna.

One approached, narrowing his golden—yes, they were actually golden—eyes. "Is this our new queen?"

He sniffed her hair. Anna squeezed Connor's hand, doing her best not to shudder at the odd greeting.

"This is Shun." Connor pointed to the second boy as he approached. "And this is Takata."

Another dragon appeared. His golden hide shimmered in the torchlight. He hovered before alighting on a rock and staring down at them.

"And that is Pijeth," Connor continued. "They are gold dragons, if you hadn't guessed."

Takata's gaze started at her feet and drew slowly to her face.

Anna couldn't help but feel like a piece of meat in a display case, being summed up by a potential buyer.

"She's perfect." Shun stepped back. "You should take her, Quenor. Bring her back to Dragon Mount and end this."

Anna backed up a step, but was stopped by Connor's iron grip.

"I thought I made myself clear," he said. "The girl belongs to Joesephutus."

And Joe had promised to let her go. She took a deep breath and released it slowly. As long as Connor stayed loyal to his friend, she'd be fine.

Takata pointed over his shoulder at Puff. "Have you seen that tear in his wing? We're golds, we aren't magicians."

Connor held Anna tightly to his chest. "I am well aware of the extent of his injury. The question is, can you heal him?"

"Yes." Takata glanced at his brother. "But not in time. You need to take his place, Quenor. Take her. Take the crown."

"I will not."

"You must."

His grip on Anna tightened. It started to hurt, but she didn't dare to move, as she was stuck quite literally in the middle of an argument between three dragons.

Connor pointed at Puff. "He's bonded to her. Dragon manifesto isn't just a code of decency. It has to do with honor. If I took a female from a bonded male, I'd be no better than the king we're trying to overthrow."

Puff moved beside them, his head held low.

Connor directed Anna to him, and Puff reared up on his hind legs, standing in a nearly human pose.

Anna slipped her arms around her dragon, and felt him sigh as they embraced. His warmth seeped into her, stronger and faster than last night. The right-ness of it left her dizzy.

Takata leaned toward Connor, fire in his eyes. He was dwarfed by the taller man. Anna suddenly realized that these twins were young, barely teenagers.

"Fuck decency." Takata spat on the ground. "It's decency that's kept us enslaved all these years. Decency killed Elor."

Puff released Anna and roared, dropping back to all-fours. The younger dragons stepped back. Even Pijeth, above on the rocks, fluttered his wings as if he might fall.

The torchlight danced across Nik's face as he looked nervously from Puff to the others. "He, umm, wants to know what happened to Elor. Who's Elor?"

Connor took in a deep breath and released it. "Sorry, I didn't want to tell you until all this was over." He glanced at Anna. "Elor flew with us. He was the gold dragon's hope for the crown."

"And our oldest brother." Shun crossed his arms.

Connor grunted. "Elor was Gale's only real competition for the throne. Five minutes into the flight, the grays turned on him."

Puff hissed.

Takata drew up a chord tied about his neck, pulling a long, sharp, black claw from within his shirt. "This talon was lodged in my brother's throat. I yanked it out right before the sentries dropped from the clouds to burn his body." He spun on Puff. "A lot of good you did to save him, fluttering around at the back of the pack, hiding like a coward."

Puff howled in the boy's face, but the young blond barely flinched.

"Don't embellish your anguish. He was my brother. I'm the one who knows the throbbing sting of loss."

Puff grumbled.

"He didn't mean to belittle your pain," Nik said.

Takata turned on him. "Shut up, human. I am not incapable of hearing."

Connor held up his hands. "Gentlemen, this isn't helping."

Shun pointed at Puff. "That prepubescent dragon can't fight Gale."

"Not if you don't help him." Connor moved beside Puff. "I don't know about the rest of Dragon Mount, but I am tired of bowing to the grays. I stand beside my new king, no matter the outcome." His gaze darted between the two boys. "If I die, so be it. At least I will have done my part."

Puff raised his head, straightening his posture as he gazed down at his friend.

Connor ran his palm down his friend's neck. "In two days, we will know our future, and I, for one, hope it's crystalline."

The golden boys stared at him, expressions blank, before they eyed each other in silence. Their gazes then drew to Puff where they lingered, until the brothers separated, sharing a silent, pointed look.

Takata turned to Nanna. "I need a small glass jar, and a cheese cloth. If traditions hold true, you would have had several receptacles prepared for the Seventeen Year."

"Yes, of course, just in case." Nanna's smile beamed. "I'll be right back."

Behind them, Shun held out his arms and a brilliant yellow light encompassed him. Anna shielded her eyes as night turned to day. The dragon's body blurred within the glow before a spectacular golden dragon with dark, coppery horns took his place. Puff didn't flinch despite the dragon being two times his size. Anna couldn't say so much for herself, especially since the dragon still watching them from the rock was even bigger.

Shun bowed to Puff before nosing the smaller dragon's stitches. Tyler held out the injured wing, adjusting the sutures as the young dragon worked what Anna hoped would be a miracle. If they really were going back to the mountain empty handed, Puff needed to defend himself.

She closed her eyes, remembering Gale's monstrous bulk. Would healing him even make a difference? What would these three dragons do when they found out that Connor had lied to them to get their help?

Puff wasn't going back to their mountain to take the crown. At the very best, he'd slink home in shame, and Anna would be on the next plane to the United States, keeping well out of the reach of any dragon still looking for her.

Puff glanced in her direction. Even in dragon form, she could tell he was smiling. Warmth flooded her, as if nothing could ever harm either of them if they were together.

But that wasn't true.

The dragon they feared, Gale, knew she was with Puff. Even with a mended wing, how long would her dragon last if Gale truly was the beast they all claimed?

Shun drew away from Puff's injury and growled a few times.

Takata scanned the crowd. "He needs..."

"The container." Nanna parted the onlookers. "Give an old woman a chance."

She set one glass canister on the ground, and held the other up to Elaina, who adjusted a thin white cloth over the top, attaching it with several rubber bands. The young girl handed the container to Takata before they got to work on the next one.

Takata eyed the jar. "Is this the largest you have? His injury is..."

"Extensive, I know. I helped sew him up." Elaina circled the rubber bands on the next jar. "We followed the customs and brought the jars, we just never expected to have to use them. Glass is heavy to drag up the side of a mountain."

Takata accepted the second container. "They will have to do."

He held both jars out to Shun. The dragon bared long fangs and sunk them into each of the cheese cloths. A thick, syrupy liquid shot from the dragon's teeth until the jars were nearly full.

When Shun released his bite, Takata held the containers out to Tyler. "I trust you know what to do with these?"

The veterinarian nodded. "Boil one into a drinkable form, use the other as a salve." He took the jars, almost reverently. "Thank you. I'm honored."

Shun fluttered his golden wings, and returned to his human

form. "That's all I can do. His wing will mend if you continue to apply the venom, and he'll need the healing draught by tonight."

"I'll get right on it." Tyler turned to his daughter. "Elaina, can you help me?"

Shun watched them fade into the darkness before turning to Connor. "Joesephutus needs to rest. If he exerts himself in the slightest, he'll undo the healing I've done. Then he won't be able to fly, let alone fight."

"It won't be enough," Takata said.

Connor gripped the young dragon's shoulder. "Your generation lacks faith."

"We've never known an age where we had hope, let alone faith that our lives could improve."

Connor spun them both in Puff's direction. "This is what faith and hope looks like. Be warned, though. The fight may not be only his to win. We're going to need to be creative. Especially with this stubborn little buck."

Puff cocked his head and stared at his friend. No one needed Nik to translate to understand the little dragon's what-the-frig stare.

Smiling, Connor turned to Pops. "I hate to ask this, but do you, by any chance, have a dragon spear?"

Pops's smile rivaled that of the dragon. "I am old, but I'm not foolish. This is, after all, the Seventeen Year."

He motioned to the circle of men around them, who each pulled a foot-long, thin metallic rod from their backpacks. Moving as a cohesive unit, the men joined their individual pieces into a long spear that shimmered in the torchlight. Nanna handed Pops the final piece: a sharpened point that clicked onto the end.

A hush fell over the group. The two golden dragons stepped back. Puff gaped, his eyes wide. Above them, the larger gold, Pijeth, howled.

"What is that?" Anna asked.

"The dragon spear." Nik shuddered. "The point has been

mounted on our wall my entire life." His brow furrowed as he stared at the shiny metal. "I never in a million years thought anyone else knew where the remaining parts were, let alone know how to rebuild it." He tore his eyes away from the spear and looked at Anna. "According to myth, the dragon spear evened the odds when the dragons started hunting people. It is one of the few weapons capable of inflicting enough pain to immobilize a dragon."

Anna turned to Connor. "What do you want with that?"

"Simple." Connor pointed to the cave, looking at Pops. "I need you to bring Joesephutus back into the cave, and keep him there. Use the spear if you need to."

Puff roared.

Nik held his ears as if his head might explode. "I don't think I need to tell you guys he's not happy about this."

Connor pointed at the cave. "Go. The gold said you needed rest, and rest you will get."

Puff grumbled at Nik, but the *Kotahi* just shook his head. "The big guy is right, boss. No matter what happens, you need your strength or you're as good as dead."

Nik made way as his grandfather took the weapon and pointed the shimmering tip at the clouds. "I will not dishonor you by using this, Great One. But I humbly ask that you do the right thing and listen to the mighty green."

Anna exhaled as the small dragon looked at her with sorrowful eyes. He growled in an un-menacing tone, before the two boys flexed into dragon form and helped the crystal dragon up the sloped rocks, and back into the safety of the cave.

Connor breathed a huge relief-filled sigh once Puff was out of sight, and the boys had returned to their human form.

Pijeth jumped from his rocky perch. With a flash of yellow light, he shrank into a man as he approached. Anna realized that he was older than the twins by over a decade, or probably more like seventeen years, now that she thought about it.

He addressed his brothers. "The two of you get out of here quickly."

"Why?" Takata asked.

Connor's eyes narrowed. "One thing that will improve with your age, is your hearing."

They both tilted their ears to the slowly brightening sky. One paled, then the other. A dragon roared in the distance.

"Get out of here. Now!" Pijeth pushed them both.

The boys ran, shimmering into dragon form as they jumped into the air, already batting their wings. Pijeth followed close behind his younger brothers.

The roar came closer. Anna's ears rang as the Maori clambered around her, grabbing torches and making their way back into the cave.

Puff roared within.

"Your king calls for you, my queen," Connor shouted, directing the adolescent Maori to the human-sized door as he threw a bolder to the top of the pile, partially enclosing the dragon-sized entrance.

Anna scrambled toward the door, but each step triggered a new sense of panic.

She recognized that roar. The gray dragons were coming.

What if they got here and she was trapped inside that cave? She would have nowhere to go.

Another roar bellowed in the distance, and she stepped back, allowing a woman with three children through the door. She couldn't go in there. They were coming for her. She needed to get away. She hugged the side of the mountain, watching another family of Maori flee within.

Nik seemed to be fighting with Connor in the center of the clearing, when their eyes drew to her.

Connor howled at her to run.

Nik screamed, "What are you doing? Go!"

Her lips parted to answer, but her words caught in her throat.

Nothing made sense anymore—not fantasy nor reality, not standing on a mountain, and certainly not trapping herself inside a cavern. Turning from the opening, Anna ran, leaving the cave, dragons, and the roaring horror in the sky behind her. Her shoes padded on the ground until the trees engulfed her in total darkness.

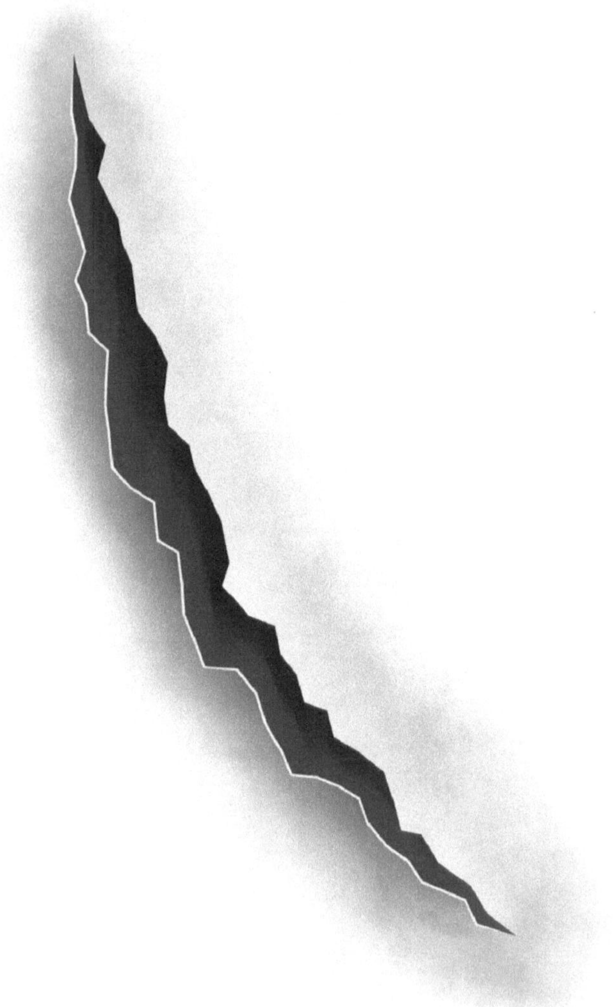

CHAPTER 18

The girl was out of her godforsaken mind.

"Get inside!" Connor yelled at Nik and the remaining Maori.

Nik fled toward the door, but a gargantuan double-column of gray-scaled legs slammed down within the clearing, blocking his escape.

He froze, dimly aware that the remaining humans had stopped running as well. Something whispered within him, keeping him calm, but also still and posed like a doll.

Heart thumping against his ribs, Nik's gaze rose over a rounded, gray belly and up to a mouth of teeth dripping with clear goo. The dragon's wings still fluttered in the air, massive gray sails reaching across the clearing and nearly sweeping the trees on either side. The eyes, yellow and veined, flickered in the torchlight and bore through his soul.

Every instinct in his body shouted to run, to save himself, but no human in the clearing moved.

The beast's gaze drew to Connor, and the weight of a million planets left Nik's frame. Free from whatever had held all of them, Elaina took two steps toward the cave before being stopped by her father. The veterinarian's gaze caught each of them, and he widened his eyes, warning them not to move.

Of course. If they ran to the mountain, they would give away the hidden cavern, and everyone inside.

Many of their faces twisted. A few lips quivered. A man prayed. It was the most any of them could do.

"Hello, Gale." Connor folded his arms and looked up. He feigned boredom well. "Are you lost? I can't believe you'd risk flying so far from the mountain this close to dawn."

The dragon arched his back and shrank. The torches flickered over his ashen hide as it faded to a light, peachy complexion that paled next to Connor's dark, Caribbean tone.

Naked except a hairy chest, back, and legs, looking no less the predator as he had in the shape of a dragon, Gale advanced on Connor. A red, scabbed nub held the place where his right index finger should be.

Takata had shown them the talon they'd pulled from their brother's corpse. If that claw belonged to Gale, the monstrous gray had made the killing blow himself. If Nik remembered his Draconic history well enough, that was a big no-no in the Seventeen Year.

Gale scanned the area. "Where is the runt?"

Connor widened his eyes, somehow managing not to look at the cave. "You mean you haven't found him, yet? By now I thought you'd have ripped the girl out of his corpse's arms and secured your crown." Connor drew a Maori woman to him and whispered into her ear. "I, on the other hand, have been enjoying all the outside world has to offer." He kissed her neck and fondled her breasts. The woman clung to him, but her horror-filled eyes never left the gray.

Gale narrowed his gaze. "You can't mate with that one, idiot. She can't bare your child."

Connor laughed. "It's not all about procreation. It's about the pleasure. You grays need to stop and enjoy the sensations these simple creatures can give you."

Gale sneered. "That is why the greens are always below us. You are misguided by base needs that lead you nowhere."

"That is where we differ. There is nowhere I'd rather be, than between a willing set of thighs." He kissed the girl deeply.

Gale growled. "This hunt has never been about pleasure."

Connor released the kiss. "I am aware of that, but if you thought for a single instant that I was your competition, I'd be dead already. So who is the wiser, the dragons bleeding out on the hillside, or the one listening to the moans of the woman he thrusts himself into?"

Gale angled a brow. "Fair enough. You've never been a problem, but you do have a well-known friendship with a small dragon that has recently caused me a considerable amount of irritation."

Connor shrugged. "What of it? I'm not the one standing in your way." Sniffing the woman's hair, he slipped his hand in her pants.

"So I see," Gale said. "But just in case." He reached his arm back as if to hit Connor, and shifted into dragon form with blurring speed.

Connor pushed the woman to safety, ruining the seconds he had to shift and defend himself. She hit the ground at the same moment the gray dragon's talon met flesh.

Nik cried out as Connor's blood-soaked body fell. He took two steps then froze as Gale turned on him and the rest of the Maori. The dragon howled and spouted a beam of fire into the air, curling the outer leaves of the surrounding trees. Nik turned from the scorching heat, but he knew he was at the beast's mercy.

Elaina and Tyler gathered the people into a huddled mass and waited for the flames to engulf them.

Instead, the dragon roared and took two booming steps toward the helpless Maori. The group scattered as the beast jabbed a claw into their midst. A scream echoed through the pre-dawn light. Nik stood, helpless, as Gale hoisted a thrashing blonde girl into the air.

"Elaina!" Tyler cried, reaching for his daughter.

The dragon garbled something in Draconic before he flapped his wings, extinguishing several torches as he took back to the air.

Nik shuddered in disbelief, even as the roar of the dragon told him the creature had left them far behind.

Tyler fell to his knees, his arms reaching toward the sky as if he could magically will his daughter's return. There was nothing he could do, though. There was nothing any of them could do.

Stunned, Nik surveyed the clearing, realizing the torches were no longer the only source of illumination.

The sky had turned purple as light threatened to peek over the treetops. Dawn had come, and was probably the only reason any of them were still alive.

As Tyler dropped his face into his hands, Nik knew at least one of them might have preferred the dragon's fire over being left in this clearing. He took a step toward the veterinarian, hoping maybe a simple touch or a kind word might ease his suffering, when a woman behind him cried out, "He's bleeding!"

Connor. Shit.

Nik bolted toward the shifted dragon's motionless form.

The woman Connor had kissed knelt beside him. "He pushed me out of the way. He saved me."

Tears ran down her cheeks and dripped onto a blouse covered in red splatter. Nik had no idea if the blood was hers, or Connor's.

Puff's roar blasted through the clearing, but Nik wasn't sure if the sound existed, or if he only heard the scream in his own head. Either way, he closed his eyes, trying to hide the vision of Connor's blood from his dragon.

The damage had been done, though. A resounding boom rattled the side of the mountain. Fire and rock shot from the cave into the clearing. Puff emerged, eyes wide as he galloped to his fallen friend.

Quenor! Puff howled, dirt piling at his feet as he stopped beside him.

The crystal dragon lapped his friend's wounds, but Connor didn't stir.

Nik's chest clenched, his pulse quickened in time with his dragon, but his blood thickened when the gored man didn't stir.

No! Puff batted Connor's side with his snout.

The wedge in Nik's chest folded over until a sob formed in his own throat.

Wake up! Again, Puff slammed against Connor, but this time, the man groaned.

Nik released the breath he'd been holding to ward off the pain and steeled himself, stepping back from the blood-soaked soil.

A deep gash ran from Connor's ankle to his hip. A white area peeked through the blood as Puff continued to lick at the wound. Nik retched, realizing it was a bone.

Another slice ran across Connor's stomach with near surgical precision. Apparently dragon talons were just as sharp as they looked.

The girl kneeling beside him pulled off her blouse. "We need to put pressure on these wounds."

Nik eyed the shirt, wondering how clean it was after two days in the cave, but he supposed it was the best that they had. The Maori milled about, many stumbling from the cave and squinting in the dawn light. Pops brought water to Connor's lips, then spilled the remainder over the gash in the dragon's leg.

If he dies because of me...

"Shut up," Nik said. "He's not going to die."

The girl holding the rag looked at Nik, then glanced at Puff, recognizing that Nik wasn't speaking to her. Which was good, because he didn't have time to explain.

Nik grabbed two water bottles held by the waiting children

and started cleaning the slice in Connor's stomach. Just because it wasn't bleeding as bad, didn't mean it wasn't as severe.

A scream echoed over the trees. Puff lifted his head and looked at Nik before scanning the crowd. *Where is Anna?*

Oh, shit.

She'd run away. She'd never made it into the cave.

Nik opened his lips to speak, but the look in the dragon's eyes told him the dragon had already read his thoughts. Puff looked at his dying friend, his mind in a whirl of conflict.

"I got him," Nik said. "I won't let him die. I promise."

Puff nodded his silver snout before backing between the children bringing supplies. He took one last look at his dying friend before galloping into the woods.

Connor groaned again. Nik shared a glance with the woman helping. Her eyes shared his fear. They'd done the right thing by sending the dragon away, but neither one of them knew if they could uphold their promise to keep this man alive.

$\mathcal{A}$nna pawed at the thin branch that had stopped her fall and kicked her feet, scrambling for purchase. She closed her eyes and took a single, steadying breath. People who panicked, died. All she needed was a small ledge, a rock, anything to support her weight.

She opened her eyes and took in the crevices nature had etched into the sandy slope of the mountain, the three thin saplings jutting out from the mountainside a few hundred feet below, and the rocky bottom a few thousand feet further.

Anna gripped the branch and closed her eyes. When the gray dragon flew away, she thought she was safe, but she was going to die anyway, alone on this cliff, a victim of her own stupid clumsiness.

A panicked roar echoed through the air—a dragon. *Her* dragon.

"I'm here. Help!"

Puff's snout pushed between two massive trees several yards above her head. He sniffed twice before he looked down. His eyes widened as he garbled something in Draconic.

"I'm falling." Anna closed her eyes, sickened that the last words she might say to him were something so obvious that even her little dog, Dixie, would be able to figure it out, let alone a sentient dragon.

A fizzle of smoke trickled from his left nostril as he forced one arm down to her through the two trees. Anna suppressed a whimper. Even if she dared reach for his claws there was still a foot of empty air between them.

Puff snarled. His rear talons slipped and gravel peppered Anna's face as he pushed against the trees. Unable to gain footing on the slope, he tried once more to force his thick torso between the mighty sentries, but they held firm, as they probably had for hundreds of years.

A small pop echoed through the air as one of the roots anchoring the branch Anna clung to pulled out of the mountainside. She looked again for something, *anything* to support her feet, but she only managed to make more gravel and small rocks fall until they were indiscernible in the valley below.

Puff howled and reached through the branches once more. Desperation cascaded through the red fury in his eyes. His gaze faltered before he growled through clenched teeth and drew back, out of sight.

Wind whipped through Anna's hair, mocking her sudden solitude. The morning chill settled deep within, preparing her for the inevitable.

Another root snapped, spraying sand across her face.

"Puff!" She whimpered as the branch cut further into her hands.

She was supposed to be old and gray when she died, surrounded by friends and family. Not young. Not alone.

The valley floor loomed below, pulling at her feet, dragging her down. Her eyes burned and she gritted her teeth.

She didn't have to give in, though. No, she didn't, and she wouldn't.

A rush of adrenaline washed over her. She'd already survived being snatched by a dragon and falling out of the sky. She refused to allow her life to end by falling off a godforsaken cliff.

Taking a deep breath, she hoisted herself up once, then again.

Blood smeared across the bark. Her hands stung, but she clenched her teeth, steeling herself against the pain. Her hands throbbed. She slipped on her own blood. Her feet dangled, swaying in the breeze.

Anna closed her eyes and prayed for something, anything to stop her fall.

A sharp dragon roar reverberated off the rocks followed by a shrill shriek like the sound Dixie had made when she'd been bitten by a raccoon, only a hundred times louder.

Her pulse throbbed in her temples as she envisioned the huge, gray dragon biting down on Puff's pearlescent neck.

Her dragon roared again, not anger, and not the garbled Draconic words like she'd heard in the camp—this was pain, undeniable shrieks of mind numbing pain.

She fought to control her breathing, pulling herself up further as Puff continued to wail. He was dying up there, and there was nothing she could do about it.

Her shoulders ached as she pulled herself higher, but she was still only half way up the branch. The roots shifted, releasing more gravel to fall in her eyes, before the sandy soil gave way, dropping her.

She didn't scream. Time slowed as she hung in the air, shocked, as the roots that had anchored her to the mountain shot into her hand. They were white and fluffy, with small balls of soil still attached to the individual threads. Her heart thumped slowly in her ears as she focused on the treads in the cliff face before her.

Her mind raced, contemplating the depth to the bottom, how long she'd fall, and how quickly it would be over. She hoped Sybil would be okay, and Connor would take care of her.

Sybil hated dogs, though. Who would take care of Dixie?

"Anna!"

She looked up as the silhouette of a man appeared between the trees. A hand shot toward her and wrapped around her wrist. Her body jolted to a stop. Her shoulder exploded in pain.

"I have you," the voice called from above.

She rose, confused, tired, bewildered, and still waiting to hit the ground.

Instead, her body slid up the stone, between the two trees, and over the precipice, until she lay flat against the soil.

The grip holding her released, and someone slumped beside her, panting. Long, flowing platinum blond hair fell across his face before he pulled it back.

"You're okay," he whispered, holding his chest. "We made it."

Anna pushed up from the soil. Hands shaking, she held herself off the ground, blinking against tears and dirt in her eyes as she took in the man's milky-white chest, rising and falling in rapid succession. She reached out to touch him to make sure he was real, and he winced as her fingers met warm, white flesh.

"Joe?"

He blinked, turning his strange, icy blue eyes toward her.

But no, they weren't strange. They were beautiful eyes. Dragon eyes.

He tried to reach for her, but fell back. He winced through clenched teeth.

"Don't." She pulled herself into a sitting position. Her eyes drew down his torso, briefly taking in the rest of his pale, naked beauty. Damn, how could she ever have thought he was scrawny? "You-you shifted."

Tears streamed down his cheeks. "I couldn't reach you. It was the only way."

She wiped the tears from his face. "But I thought you were stuck in dragon form."

He caught his breath. "It hurts." He clutched his stomach. "Anna, it hurts."

"What do I do?"

He closed his eyes. "Keep safe. Stay hidden until the Seventeen Year is over. He'll have no need to look for you after that."

Wait. What was he saying? "I'll be safe, because I'll be with you."

He shook his head. "It hurts *inside*." He took two short, labored breaths. "The change. It was too much."

Just like the gold dragons warned. He knew the risks, but he did it anyway to save her. "You are not going to die. You can't."

He cupped her cheek and tried to keep a grimace from his face. "Promise me you'll hide until the Seventeen Year is over."

She leaned down, and brushed her lips against his. "Only if you promise not to die. Stay with me. Hold on." His eyes fluttered closed again. "No." She shoved him. "Puff, no!" This wasn't happening. He'd shifted to save her, she couldn't let him die for it. "Joe!"

Rocks skidded down the mountain from above as Tyler slid to a stop beside Joe. His eyes widened. "Albinism." He turned to Anna. "The Great One?"

She nodded.

He felt Joe's neck. "He's still breathing."

"Oh, thank God."

"Can you stand?"

"I-I think so."

Tyler looked up the mountainside to the precipice she'd fallen from. "We're down here!"

Several blurry figures slid down the path made from her fall. She allowed herself to cry once they lifted Joe's nearly lifeless form, and started moving back up the mountain.

CHAPTER 20

The glow worms twitched overhead as Nik stared at Puff.

Well, no, that didn't seem quite right anymore. What had the boss said his real name was? Joesen-hopping-on-a-fiat or something like that.

To the Maori, he would always be *Great One*. The name still managed to fit. This pale, sickly-looking guy continued to appear ethereal, like the magical being Nik knew he was.

Anna had been asking over and over for *Joe*, so the guy's name was obviously Joe—it was to her at least.

But how could Nik call him Joe? It seemed wrong, like calling the governor-general by his first name. It seemed demeaning.

It was still Puff's tormented thoughts swirling through Nik's mind, no matter what they called him. A man lay as his feet, but Nik still saw a small, helpless dragon—someone he was bound to so deeply, that he'd known the second Puff made the choice to shift.

The pain had knocked Nik back and sent him whirling into a foggy abyss that continued long after Tyler had found Puff and Anna trapped part way down the mountain.

Nik woke hours later, dragged himself to Puff's side, and took vigil, doing not much more than watching him breathe.

Every few minutes, Puff's—No. *Joe's* face, would contort.

Nik had learned by now that their bond had a two second delay, because right after Joe winced, Nik's mind would explode in a cascade of sharp, slashing pain that seemed to cut into the very center of his being. Now, every time Joe moved, Nik grabbed the side of the nearest stalagmite, waiting for pain and nausea to overcome him. Sometimes it didn't. Most times, it did.

He didn't know what Tyler was doing with all the herbs and salve he spread on the kid's pale skin, but all this ancient Maori healing stuff seemed to work wonders on Connor. For now, Nik could only hope the odd treatment would do the same for his boss.

Boss. That seemed an unnecessary title, things being what they were.

The one and only job Nik had ever done well was acting as a translator. But with Puff human again, the dragon hardly needed Nik anymore.

He pursed his lips. *Say hello to another layoff.* Even though he wasn't getting paid, it still stung.

Joe groaned and Nik placed a cool cloth on his head. A wave of relief coated him, and he knew he'd done the right thing.

At least if he wasn't needed to translate anymore, he could give the doc a decent barometer on the Great One's health, since Nik could still pretty much feel every emotional switch, and he could definitely feel the little dragon's pain.

Tyler sat beside him. "Any change?"

"You can't tell looking at him, but I think he's better."

Tyler felt Joe's cheek. "I think you're right." But a deep sadness grew in his eyes.

"What's wrong?"

"The gold dragons warned him not to exert himself for a

reason. He's hurt even worse now than he was when he fell from the sky."

And with both Joe and Connor out of the picture, there was no one left to challenge Gale. Even worse for the mourning vet, there was no one left to save his daughter.

"But he's going to get better, right?"

Connor limped through the door. The worm-light basked his face in a sickly glow. "He won't heal in time for the close of the Seventeen Year." He slumped to the hard ground. "Neither of us will."

Damning the Draconi to another seventeen years of gray rule.

This was bad. Nik understood that, but somehow he was relieved to know everyone had lived to fight another day.

He glanced at Tyler. Well, almost everyone. It didn't seem right to think that one girl was an acceptable loss with her father sitting right next to him. Nik needed to count something as a victory, though, or all of this would have been for nothing.

Tyler turned to Connor. "Have you tried to shift?"

Connor sneered at him. "Didn't you hear me scream like a dying pig? Everyone else did." He looked away. "No, I can't shift."

"What are you going to do?" Tyler asked.

"There really isn't much to do." Connor glanced at Joe. "I can probably go home once I heal, but he'll have to live in exile."

"Exile?" Nik asked.

Connor leaned back and rested his head on the stone floor. "Gale isn't an idiot. Even if Anna is no longer on the islands, Gale will smell her on Joesephutus. That will be enough to prove he was hiding her." He grimaced. "Gale will kill him for it."

None of this seemed real. Nik felt caught within the plotline of a movie, not living in real life. And this wasn't only about the dragons anymore. How long would the Maori be able to hide Joe before Gale found them and fried them all to cinders?

Joe groaned and blinked his eyes.

Connor winced, pushing back into a sitting position.

Joe's creepy silver eyes widened. "Anna!" He sat up, then doubled over, grabbing his stomach."

Tyler placed his hand on Joe's back. "Sitting up like that is probably not the best idea. You really need to rest, Great One."

"Where is she?" Joe rasped through gritted teeth.

"She's fine. Resting. You saved her. Do you remember?"

Joe nodded, then accepted Tyler's help easing back to the floor. He looked at Connor. "I'm glad to see you're still breathing."

"It takes more than a dragon ten times my size to clip my wings. You should know that by now." He looked at Nik and Tyler. "I would like a moment alone with the boy."

Nik stiffened. Not his reaction, he realized, but Joe's.

Tyler tapped Joe's shoulder lightly, rose, and disappeared into the dark corridor. Nik made to follow.

"No," Joe said. "He stays. He'd hear everything through the *Kotahi* bond anyway. Better to have him here than feign privacy."

Connor's eyes narrowed. "Fair enough."

Joe closed his eyes and breathed deeply. "You called me *boy*. You've never called me boy."

"Because today, for the first time, you acted like a child."

"I am a child."

"You're not!" The roar from Connor's throat reverberated off the walls, as loud as if he'd taken dragon form.

The worm-light flicked out as if someone threw a switch, dropping them in complete darkness, before one by one, they began to glow again. The light betrayed Connor holding his head. They sat in silence until he raised his eyes.

"You doomed the Draconi. You realize that, don't you?"

Joe forced himself into a sitting position. He held his right arm as if it were in a sling. "I couldn't let her die, and I was too big to help her as a dragon. I had no choice."

"You had every choice." He pointed his chin at Nik. "You could have sent your fire-blasted *Kotahi* to help. He's human, unless you'd forgotten. He would have fit through those trees."

"I couldn't send him."

"Why?"

"Because he was busy saving you."

Joe's words hung in the air. Connor's gaze shot to Nik, then back to Joe.

"I was careless," Connor said. "You should have left me to my fate."

"I wasn't going to let you die for me."

"And now you've damned us all. You could have been king."

Joe stared at his friend. "Why do you push so hard? And why me? I'm no better that any dragon who took flight. If anything, I'm worse."

Connor held the younger dragon's gaze. "When you look into the water pool and catch your reflection, what do you see?"

Joe shrugged. "A dragon. A small one."

"True." Connor gathered his thoughts. "But what I see when I look at you, is hope. You are not jaded like the others. You don't want power. You just want everyone to live in peace."

"How does that make me a good king?"

"Because even in your idiocy, your recent actions still tell me that you will choose others over yourself, no matter the cost to you. I highly doubt anyone would say the same of Gale." His eyes softened. "What you probably see as faults, are what the rest of us hold in high regard. If you had made it back to the mountain, others would have stood behind you." He pointed to his chest. "I would have stood behind you."

"I'm sorry I disappointed you."

"I'm angry, not disappointed." He sighed. "I can't fault you for being exactly who I'd expect you to be."

They stared at each other for a few moments. The obvious hung in the air—that none of this mattered, because there was a huge, brutal dragon out there, and neither one of them was in any shape to face him.

Joe pushed off his blankets and stood slowly. He stretched his neck.

Nik stood, steadying him. "Take it easy, boss. You've had a bad day."

"This is encouraging," Connor said. "You looked like you were going to die a few hours ago."

Joe eased back to the ground. "Don't get too excited. That was absolutely exhausting."

"So, now what?" Nik asked.

Connor considered the twinkling worms above. "Now we wait, and pray we still have a home to go back to when the Seventeen Year closes."

CHAPTER 21

$\mathcal{A}$nna fingered her bandages as she watched the sun's decent toward the horizon.

Nanna eased onto the rock beside her. "How are you feeling, my dear?"

"I don't know. Okay, I guess."

"We have a surprise for you." She handed Anna a pair of binoculars and pointed down the mountain.

Looking through the glasses, Anna combed through the trees until the sun reflected off something metal. She adjusted the focus to reveal a silver four-wheel-drive truck parked just north of their original camp where Anna and Puff had fallen from the sky.

"It's a car!"

Nanna took the glasses back. "Yes, my husband called for it the moment the Great One decided to see you on your way."

This was amazing. She could go home! No more worrying about giant, scheming, power-hungry dragons who wanted to use her in the worst way imaginable. She could forget that Gale and the rest of his hoard of giant nasty dragons ever existed.

She stood, ready to make her way down the mountain, but

instead of making a beeline for the trail, she glanced back to the caves. What kind of person would she be if she left the first chance she got, while the guy who'd saved her life was still unconscious?

"Don't get too excited." Nanna stood beside her. "You're not leaving until morning. The trek down the mountain is hard enough in the daylight, let alone trying to drive the jagged trail in the dark."

A few days ago, she may have protested, but now all she could think about was the look on Puff's face as he struggled to get through the trees—the absolute anguish in his eyes as the small branch she held started to give, dropping her closer to death with each passing second. Her little dragon had been afraid of losing *her*, not the contest; and he'd proven that by doing the one thing that ensured the crown would never be his. He'd shifted, trapping himself in human form.

Even if they could leave now, she didn't think she'd be able to go without at least saying goodbye.

Pops approached from the trees. He smiled at them. "The Great One is awake."

Anna nearly dropped the binoculars. "Can I talk to him?"

"In time. At the moment, he is in conference with the mighty green."

More likely, Connor was giving Joe a piece of his mind. Tyler had explained that Joe's sudden shift had done incredible damage to his musculoskeletal system, and that he would probably take weeks to heal.

Neither Connor nor Puff would make it back to the Seventeen Year on time, and it was her fault. But now, at least, she was completely off the hook. If neither one of them could make it up the mountain, they also couldn't change their minds about forcing her to be part of this insane contest. Which left her that much safer than she'd been yesterday.

Anna shuddered. When had she become so callous? Connor had nearly died, and Puff took a huge risk to save her. She should be mortified that all this had happened because of her.

The end result gave her exactly the outcome she'd wanted, though. She was free to go. She glanced in the direction of the cavern entrance. For some reason, knowing she'd soon be free didn't give her the comfort she'd expect.

"I need to see him." She handed the glasses back to Nanna and took one last look at the darkening purple sky before heading back to the caves.

Making her way through the Maori, Anna kept her head down so she could avoid their accusing stares. There gazes still seeped into her, though, chilling her as effectively as if they'd reached out and slapped her.

Within the main chamber, people were preparing for another night in the caves. Yet many stopped as she entered.

"How could she." A woman scowled.

"Such a shame," another whispered.

Most of them simply looked away as she passed.

What a huge reversal from only the night before. They probably thought Anna would stay since she'd spent the night with their Great One. If she was honest with herself, she *had* changed her mind. Her heart had, at least. Not that it really mattered anymore. They had to stop blaming all this on her. They needed to understand that sometimes things didn't go the way you wanted them to.

"Are you hungry?" A little girl held up a wrapped bundle. "I just made these. They're still warm."

Anna accepted the gift. The aroma of spice and meat wafted from the folded towels. Her stomach grumbled, and she realized she hadn't eaten today.

Her breath hitched. In all the commotion, had anyone thought to feed Puff?

She eyed the small stack of similar bundles at the girl's feet. "Do you think the Great One would like something to eat?"

A smile burst across her face. "You can bring him these." She grabbed five packages and held them to her.

"Wouldn't you like to bring them to him yourself?"

She shook her head. "I think he'd rather you brought them, Ma'am."

A woman placed her arm around the girl. "We'd be honored if you'd bring the Great One the fruits of our labors, Ms. Anna. It isn't our way to seek appreciation."

Anna's eyes narrowed, but there seemed to be no malice in the woman's tone. She and the little girl were excited to be a part of this, no matter what the outcome.

Warmed inside far more than the food could provide, she accepted the bundles before feeling her way through the dark corridor. After the fourth turn, a faint green illumination lit her way to the cathedral room.

Connor and Nik stood at the end of the hallway.

"How's he doing?" Anna asked.

"He's a stubborn little buck. He'll be fine." Connor glanced into the cave. "I wish I could say the same for the Draconi."

Not him, too.

Anna squeezed the packages in her hands. "You are about the tenth person to say something like that to me, today, and it's really starting to piss me off." She ignored his widened eyes. "I get that the big dragon in charge is an ass, but if that's the truth, stop complaining and do something about it."

Connor cocked his head. "We *were* doing something about it. This is the Seventeen Year. We flew in hopes of..."

"That's a bullshit excuse and you know it. If the dragons are willing to sit back and wait another seventeen years to get rid of this guy, then this is their own fault. Nothing is stopping them from overthrowing this asshole anytime they want."

"You saw the size of Gale, and he is just one of many gray dragons. It would be a slaughter."

"If your people actually believe they don't have a chance even if they work together, then they don't really want to be free."

Connor opened his mouth, but stopped himself, glancing a Nik.

Anna pushed past them. "Get out of my way."

She tromped into the cathedral room and found Joe gripping a stalagmite, trying to stand.

"What are you doing?" She placed her bundles down and helped him back to a bed of pillows and rags spread out on the floor.

"I heard shouting."

"Yeah, sorry about that. I'm getting a little tired of…"

Her words trailed off when she caught his gaze. His eyes, Puff's eyes, glistened with the blinking worm light. His silvery-white hair drifted around his face in easy waves, softening his sculpted features.

He was *beautiful*. How had she not seen that when they'd first met?

"Tired of what?" he asked.

She looked away. "Nothing. I'm sorry." Shit, what kind of egomaniac was she? This wasn't a game to these people. What she'd been talking about was revolution. Gale was the worst kind of dictator; and like Connor said, he was enormous. Would she be able to stand up to him if she were in their place?

She looked into the twinkling lights above, knowing the answer. It was easy to shout about doing the right thing when you weren't the one with your life on the line.

Joe made room for her on the soft padding. "You look upset. Are you sure you're all right?" He winced as he shifted to the side.

The rest of her anger faded, slipping away as if someone splashed her with a bucket of cold water. Joe was in pain, and he still worried about her more than himself. She was an ass. Worst of all, she didn't deserve his kindness or concern.

Embarrassed, she looked away and grabbed one of the bundles. "They gave me food. Are you hungry?"

He smiled, lifting a weight from Anna's mind. "Yes, actually I am." He opened the cloth wrapping and looked inside. He seemed to hesitate.

Anna tensed, remembering how Nik had moved the carcass behind the boulder so she didn't have to watch Puff eat a fresh kill. "Can you eat cooked food? Maybe I can get something else for you."

He held up a hand. "It's fine. I was actually enjoying the smell. We don't have spices where I'm from."

He motioned to the space beside him again. She eased onto the jumbled mess of cloth and pillows, sinking into their warmth. The worms twinkled above, constant company in the cave's cool comfort.

It was odd, how at ease she felt beside Joe, when so much had gone wrong in her life since meeting him.

She'd been kidnapped and thrown in the middle of a dragon war against her will. She should hate him simply for being a dragon. At the bare minimum, she should be terrified of this ancient beast masquerading as a man. Yet she wasn't. In fact, she couldn't remember the last time she felt so at ease. Was this sense of comfort all him, or was it the magical essence of the sparkling creatures covering the ceiling?

Maybe it was a bit of both.

Anna slipped a piece of the meat between her lips. The flavor exploded across her tongue in a tangy mix of lemon and cayenne. The taste was unexpected, like the hospitality of the little girl and her mother, Anna's coziness with Joe, and the magnificence of this cave. "It's really beautiful here."

Joe nodded. "It makes me miss home."

But could he go home empty handed? "What happens if no one

finds a girl, to, you know…" *Mate with.* Jesus, it was like an entire race living in the Stone Age.

"Gale will remain king. That's why I'm hoping he'll allow me to return after the close of the Seventeen Year, since all he really wants is to rule."

But even if he did allow Joe to return, Gale staying in power was bad for the dragons. This all sucked.

"Don't look like that," Joe said. "If I brought you back to Dragon Mount, Gale would have challenged me for you anyway." He glanced at the sparkling ceiling. "Even if I was in my dragon form, he still would have slaughtered me. I'm just too small."

"You don't know that."

He looked at her, his expression stern and sure. "I *do* know that, and then he would have taken you from me, and killed you as well as soon as he had what he wanted." He closed his eyes and looked away. "It's better for both of us this way."

This kind of thinking is what had kept the dragons under Gale's sharp claws for all these years. None of it seemed fair.

But she'd seen what Gale had done to Connor with just one swipe of his talon. She didn't blame the rest of them for being terrified.

"I'm not upset I found you, though." Joe smiled. "I've enjoyed the time we've spent together."

"You mean the last five minutes sitting here?"

"No, the time we spent together when I was a dragon." He smiled. "I liked the wonder in your eyes when you looked at me, and the sound of your heartbeat when you nuzzled under my wing, and that adorable noise you make when you sleep."

"The noise I make?"

He mimicked a snorting and gurgling sound.

"I do not sound like that."

"You do." He ran his hand along her cheek. His fingers were soft, as if he'd never labored with his hands. "It's a wonderful sound. You shouldn't be ashamed of anything that makes you, you."

She never considered snoring anything that made her, her. It warmed Anna, though, knowing that he thought something so embarrassing was cute.

They ate for some time in silence; the twinkling worms the only distraction in the dimly lit cavern. Anna tried to soak it all in, because tomorrow morning she'd be driving down the mountain and back to civilization. Odd, how something that had started with the terror of being snatched off the street by a dragon, was ending with such peace, quiet, and contentment.

Joe turned away from the blinking ceiling. "Do you think it would have worked between us if we'd met under different circumstances?"

Wow, that was a loaded question. Back at the bar that night, she'd barely given Joe a second look. Now she was keenly aware of his closeness, his strength, his sincerity. Had she been so blinded by her sister's agenda that she'd sheltered herself from something that could have been great?

If Gale hadn't walked in after the glasses fell from the ceiling, would Anna have sat with Joe and had a drink? And what if she had?

"I don't know," she admitted. "If we'd had more time to get to know each other before all this…" She might have noticed the dimple in his cheek when he smiled, or how the same adorable mark disappeared when he was sad, like now.

But who was she kidding? She might have shared a drink to be nice after he'd saved her from the falling fixture, but then she'd have gotten out of that bar as soon as possible. She hadn't been looking for a man. She still wasn't.

Anna's stomach clenched. It was the truth that she hadn't been looking for someone. However, she'd found a guy who'd saved her life more than once in the few days they'd known each other. He'd trapped himself in human form while there was a giant dragon out there, gunning for him, and his only reward was knowing that Anna would live another day.

She forced her gaze away from him, from the ceiling, and from the package on her lap. She closed her eyes and centered her thoughts on the car, on getting down the mountain and back to her life. But the notion no longer held the strength to keep her turned away. She looked back at Joe, and the knot in her stomach unraveled.

Home meant sitting in a college classroom, taking required courses neither she, not her professors cared about. Home was traffic and lines and alarm clocks. Why in God's name did she want to go back to that when she could be here, with him?

Joe wove his fingers through hers. "I guess kidnapping isn't the greatest way to start a relationship."

Unless the guy you start the relationship with is the one who saved you from that kidnapping. She looked from their clasped hands to his face. Yes, this sweet, unassuming guy had saved her life, and she knew he wouldn't hesitate to do it again, even though she was about to walk out of his life forever.

Anna pulled her hand from his. "I wish we'd met on a regular day. I wish we'd had time to talk and get to know each other." No dragons, no evil dictators, no Seventeen Year.

Joe closed his eyes and lowered his head. "I wish that, too."

Because he was already emotionally invested. Connor had explained to her that once Joe had chosen her, she became part of him. She was his in a way far deeper than exchanging rings and making a few vows neither expected to keep.

"This bond-thing, will it go away?"

He shrugged, chewing a bite of meat before taking a deep breath. "I will always know where you are. If you stay in America, my heart will always look northeast." He turned to her. "But know that when you are lonely, I will know, and wish I could be there for you. If you are sad, I'll wish my arms were longer so I could hold you." He looked down again. "You'll be in my thoughts forever."

Anna swallowed the ball building in her throat and wiped the dampness from her eyes.

"I didn't say that to make you cry. I'm sorry."

"No. That's not why I'm crying." But why *was* she crying? Was she happy to be going home, or dreading the loss of what she'd be leaving behind?

He tossed the remainder of his meal to the side and held out his arm. "Would it be too much to ask you to spend one more night with me? I'm sorry, but I won't have wings to keep you warm this time."

She laughed. "I guess we'll have to manage."

He leaned back on the pillows, and she placed her head on his shoulder and settled beside him. Above, the glow worms danced for them, a final bit of magic before returning to the safety of reality.

Anna slipped her arm around Joe's chest and clung to him, hoping he didn't notice that her tears had begun to dampen his shirt.

***

Blinking in the greenish glow, Anna shifted off Joe slowly so as not to wake him, and felt her way along the dark hallway until the she saw the soft yellow glow of the main chamber. She eyed the drop cloths hanging on the far side of the room and shivered, considering the buckets they concealed. She hadn't thought anyone could come up with something worse than a porta potty until now. But she still had to relieve nature's call.

She tiptoed past sleeping children on the rocky floor, cringing as the scent of bleach and smells that couldn't be covered strengthened. There had to be a better way. She held her breath, lifting the lid off one of the buckets.

Someone clicked on a flashlight, and she jumped, dropping the lid.

Tyler smiled at her and whispered, "I've never been able to do my business on a bucket."

Anna smiled, backing away from the stench. "I was hoping to avoid it, myself."

"Me, too." He motioned to the entrance. "It's dawn already. I was heading outside if you'd like to find a nice, solitary bush."

Anna never thought she'd hear herself say this, but, "A bush sounds lovely."

They carefully shifted a few of the stones covering the human entrance and Anna followed him into the narrow crevice.

Half way through the makeshift hall, Tyler stopped and looked back at her. "You spent the night with the Great One, again?"

Sandwiched between two stone walls, his eyes blazed in the low light. He tilted his head, as if demanding a response to the question he obviously knew the answer to. "Umm, yeah."

"Have you changed your mind about returning with him to Dragon Mount, then?"

The word *yes* hung on the edge of her lips. The enormity of those three letters sent a flash of perspiration across her skin.

What was she thinking? She had a life at home. College. A dog who loved her to pieces. No. She couldn't even consider this. It was crazy.

She closed her eyes and released a breath. It didn't matter, anyway. Joe was hurt. It would be long after their deadline before he returned to that mountain, and by then, Anna would be half way home. They'd both made their peace with that. Like Joe said, it was safer for both of them this way.

She met Tyler's gaze and tried to stand taller. "I'm going home as soon as it's safe to get down the mountain. Nothing has changed. I'm sorry."

He pressed his lips together, staring for a moment before he turned back toward the exit. "I'm sorry, too."

Tyler's flashlight cast a narrow beam into the darkness when they left the cave. A chill blew on the breeze, startling her. If it was dawn, why was it so dark?

Tyler stopped walking and turned back to her, lowering his flashlight beam.

"What's wrong?" Anna asked.

Something moved behind her, and Anna turned as a torch blazed to life. A man with long hair and a dark jacket stood between her and the opening of the cave. A wicked smile crossed his lips.

Oh, shit.

Anna turned to run, smacking right into a second man who wrenched her arms behind her back.

"Don't struggle and I won't have to hurt you," he growled into her ear.

She remembered that voice from the bar, right before Gale had dragged her outside. Cain. These men were dragons.

Anna continued to twist, and Cain's grip tightened. Her arms throbbed under the pressure.

Tyler's pained gaze met hers. None of the dragons tried to restrain him, or even gave him any notice.

A deep dread centered in her chest when she realized there was no sign of sunrise. He'd lied.

"Why?" she whispered.

The flashlight dangled loosely from his fingers. He turned from her and looked into the darkness. "I've done what you asked. Where's my daughter?"

"Relax, human," Cain said. "Your king keeps his promises."

Another dragon stepped out of the darkness and shoved a blonde girl at Tyler.

Elaina. Holy God!

The girl stumbled into the veterinarian's arms. She clung to him, crying.

Tyler mouthed the words "I'm sorry" to Anna. Her legs weakened. She wanted to tell him it was okay, but it wasn't.

Bile rose in Anna's throat as Cain sniffed her hair. "You do smell delicious. I understand our king's interest."

The Earth trembled as an immense weight dropped behind them. Cain spun them, and she winced as she faced the glowing yellow eyes of a huge, gray dragon.

CHAPTER 22

Anna!

Nik bolted upright. The blanket covering his shoulders slipped to the stone floor. Around the chamber, many Maori stirred, some rubbing their eyes.

Anna!

A thunderbolt of pain ricocheted through Nik's shoulder and side. He cried out.

Anna!

Was he still dreaming? Why was that girl's name repeating in his head?

"Great One, what's wrong?" Nanna stumbled from her blankets toward the back of the room.

Nik brought himself to full height as Joe stumbled into the chamber, holding his side. "They took her."

"Who took who?" Nanna asked.

Nik didn't need to listen for the answer. The deep ache sinking in his chest was not his own pain, but phantom terror filtering through the *Kotahi* bond. Even in human form, Nik and his dragon were still connected, and there was only one person whose loss could have affected Joe this much.

"Where's Anna?"

A blast of heat seared Nik's face. He stepped back as people screamed and ran from the entrance, where bright orange and yellow flames spewed into the room from the human doorway like someone pointed a flamethrower through the opening.

Blankets blazed to life. Smoke fogged the chamber. A child wailed.

Nik squinted in the chaos, backing away from the heat, but Anna's long, dark hair was absent from the scrambling Maori. Finding the girl, though, was the least of their worries as a foggy, gray haze filled the room.

"Get down!" Nik yelled over the commotion. "Lay on the floor. The smoke will rise."

His grandmother ran past him. "The cathedral, it will be ruined."

What she thought she could do about it, he didn't know. He grabbed her and tugged her back. The wind wafted from his lungs as she landed atop him.

"The sacred lights," she cried.

"They're just worms, Nanna." They weren't just worms to her, but right now they had the lives of human beings to worry about. A couple thousand blinking larvae would have to wait.

Nikau, help me! Puff's voice exploded in his mind. Nik scanned the scrambling people, and found a Joe-shaped silhouette within the thickening smoke. He worked with a few other men, pulling at the rocks that had collapsed, blocking the human entrance. He still had trouble connecting the dragon's inner voice to the platinum-haired man before him, but he needed to contain his awe. If they didn't unblock the exit, everyone hiding in this cavern would die.

"Stay down. You'll be able to breathe better closer to the floor," Nik told Nanna, before stumbling toward the piled stone.

He winced from the heat coming off the rocks, but the flames had stopped, thank goodness. With dozens of uncontained fires still burning throughout the room, though, the smoke had thickened like a murky blanket, hiding everyone's movement until Nik was nearly atop them. One of the men at the door was wrapping a torn, red cloth around his hands, while Joe and Connor grabbed boulders no human could lift alone and threw them to the side.

"Cover your hands," Connor told Nik, before grabbing another stone.

The first man tied off the red cloth and handed Nik the rest of the fabric. The thick gray cloud burned Nik's eyes and stung his lungs. He coughed, but it only seemed to deepen the pain.

Hands covered, Nik grabbed a side of a steaming boulder and helped shift the weight so it could be rolled. A few people tried to get through the narrow opening, but they pushed and shoved, allowing no one to exit.

A child fell, lost in the smoke.

A woman called out for someone named Stephen. No one answered her.

From every direction, the sound of panic and coughing bounced off the columns of smoke.

They had to work faster.

A vision of Anna laughing filled his mind before winking out. Shame struggled against a wrathful despair that cut deeper than the searing smoke. Joe fought alongside them, helping to widen the opening, but the only human he wanted, no—*needed* to save was no longer among them.

The certainty of Anna's absence overwhelmed Nik. Somehow, even through the commotion, he could feel the lack of her presence. The knowledge tore holes through Joe deeper than the smoke and fire ever could. Anna was his to protect, and he'd lost her.

A whoosh of cool air filtered into the chamber as Joe and Connor rolled the largest free boulder from the entrance.

Coughing people and crying children ambled past Nik and through the opening they'd created.

Joe stumbled, but Nik and Connor grabbed him, easing him to the ground outside the cave.

The smoke still rolled over their heads. Rags and boxes that had once been beds lay charred and smoldering inside. Several bodies littered the cavern floor. Such a senseless loss.

Joe held his head, staring at the ground. "I told her I'd keep her safe. Why did she go outside?"

Nik didn't question how Joe knew she'd left. He barely understood the *Kotahi* link, but it was the most powerful connection he'd ever felt. He couldn't even imagine what the bond would be like between a dragon and his intended mate.

Nik wished he could think of something to say that would actually help. 'I'm sorry' sounded so trite, so obvious. Joe hadn't just lost a girl, but handed her into the talons of a creature that would most likely rip her to shreds once he was done with her.

"I can't let that happen," Joe said.

Nik eyed the red stain dripping down the pale man's side. With a wound like that, now worse from the exertion of widening the entrance, there wasn't much Joe would be able to do about Gale taking Anna, and they both knew it. "We need Tyler."

"He won't be joining us." Connor eased down beside them. "There are two badly-burned bodies out here. I'm fairly certain one is him. The other is a young female."

No, it couldn't be. "Has anyone found Anna?" Nik asked, as Pops approached.

"It's not her," Joe whispered. "I can feel her terror. She's hurt. She's alone." He grunted, standing slowly. "I need to help her."

Pops pushed Joe back down with a two-fingered shove. "You are still the Great One, but not so great in health at the moment. You won't be saving anyone."

Joe winced, holding his side as he stood again. "I can't leave her there."

"But going to help her is suicide, and you know it," Connor said.

Joe grunted through clenched teeth, shoving Connor with what looked like all this strength, but the older dragon barely moved.

Joe fell back to the rock behind him. "You've never chosen a female for more than an hour of pleasure. You have no idea what I'm going through."

Connor pursed his lips. "I don't know, I just might." He lowered his eyes. "It seems I may have paid a few too many visits to my queen's sister's bed."

"Sybil?" Joe asked.

Connor nodded. "I noticed a strange sensation the second time I went to her. After the third, I started to sense her." He rubbed his eyes. "Last night she went to bed upset because I hadn't come to her like I'd promised. Her emotions hit me worse than if I'd been staring into her beautiful eyes."

Joe glanced at Nik, then back to Connor. "Then you understand, this isn't a choice for me. I *have* to go after Anna."

A stiff silence hung between them as the Maori threw partially-charred blankets over the dead. Dragons in movies were thrilling and fantastical. Dragons in real-life were the makings of a modern-day horror. Except for the two seated here, in their human form, talking about their human girlfriends.

Nik fingered the charred edge of his shirt. No one would believe any of this if he ever found the courage to tell someone.

Connor sighed. "I'll help retrieve the queen."

Wait. What?

Nik stood. "Are you two out of your minds? Neither of you can shift." He pointed at Joe. "He's bleeding again, and we've lost the closest thing we had to a doctor."

Pops moved between them and jabbed a silver pole into the ground. The gleaming metal hummed with the effort.

"Even your odds," Pops said, folding his arms.

Connor inched back from the dragon spear. "Neither of us can touch that."

Nik stared at his reflection in the shiny metal. How many times had he stared at the head of this spear when mounted on their family room wall, and dreamed of being a dragon slayer like in the movies? In his childhood fantasies, though, the spear was never this long, and he was a muscular, accomplished hero, not an unemployed factory worker.

Joe stirred, pulling himself to his feet. He seemed to steel himself, before reaching for the spear.

"Wait." Nik held up his arm, keeping Joe from the spear.

What was the legend?

The spear had been forged with normal metal, but mixed with ground-up talons and the venom from an amethyst dragon, which was acidic, especially to other dragons. Exactly how they'd been forged so long ago, without technology, was lost to time—part of the reason Nik always considered the relic a fraud. From the looks on Joe and Connor's faces, however, it seems he was surely mistaken.

Nik drew his fingertips along the cool metal, before seizing the etched grip and yanking the spear from the ground.

Joe gaped, his eyes lowering to Nik's hand.

No, boss, there's no pain. Nik considered the silence hanging in the air. Connor and Joe exchanged a glance.

Yes, the *Kotahi* stood among them, human and weak, holding the only manmade weapon that the two of them knew could harm a dragon.

What he wouldn't have given for a gun, or a goddamn rocket launcher. Not that he knew how to use either.

Anyway, here he was, weapon in-hand with a damsel in distress hidden somewhere in the mountains. In his fantasies, the beautiful girl was always his, and he'd never failed to save her.

Anna belonged to Joe, but the trickle of need sparking across the *Kotahi* bond itched into Nik's soul. As insane as this all was, he needed to save her as much as Joe did.

The pressure in his chest lightened as his shoulders relaxed, but his heart still managed to pummel his ribcage. He took a steadying breath. "I'll carry the spear. I'm going with you."

CHAPTER 23

The Maori helped stuff backpacks for each of the three men while Pops trained, or *tried* to train, Nik on how to throw an ancient javelin. They made it look so easy in the movies, but it took a good hour before the shaft of the spear didn't tilt and bang Nik in the back of the head.

What was he thinking, volunteering for this insanity?

Across the clearing, two women rubbed Shun's dragon venom over Joe's wounds. One of them gave him the second potion by mouth before placing both jars in Joe's backpack.

Connor stood beside his younger friend, arms folded, but the large dragon's gaze was centered on Nik, undoubtedly gauging the puny human's progress with the art of the spear throwing, or lack thereof.

The only positive from the past few hours seemed to be Joe's rapid healing. While still wounded, he was no longer limping, and the sense of pain ambling across the *Kotahi* bond had lessened. If neither Joe nor Connor could shift by the time they reached the mountaintop, though, their chances were still slim.

Nanna approached, smiling. "Everyone has gathered. It is time for the ceremony."

Of course it was.

Nanna and Pops had ceremonies for everything. The thought of waving goodbye and wishing people luck wasn't enough for them.

Joe's voice bubbled into his mind. *Be courteous. Maori traditions have carried your ancestors through the centuries.*

Nik cringed, glancing across the clearing to where Joe slipped his white t-shirt back on. Nik's thoughts might never be private again. He'd have to learn to control his inner snark as well as he controlled what he said aloud.

Connor left Joe's side and approached Nik and Pops. "We need to go or we won't make it by nightfall."

Pops waved him off. "A short blessing won't make or break you, Mighty One. Your king has agreed, and so should you."

Connor grunted his disapproval, but still strode alongside them to the front of the cavern.

The dead lay piled beside the opening, covered with blankets and towels. Nik couldn't imagine what they were going to tell the authorities, or how they would get all the bodies back down the mountain.

Nanna and Pops bowed to the dead, before turning to the semicircle of Maori gathered to see them off. A row of children sat at their parents' feet as if ready to hear a story.

This wasn't a fairytale, though. Nik glanced back to the bodies. The horrors of this tale were all too true.

Pops elevated his staff. "Our histories tell us that when the gray dragons took power, they broke the treaties humans and dragons placed in effect to protect these islands. All life was hunted nearly to extinction, until we fought back with this." He lifted the dragon spear in the air. "The fight was hard. Dragons were few, but mighty. We nearly destroyed both our races in the struggle." Pops glanced around the gaping onlookers.

Nanna placed her hand on Joe's shoulder. "The previous rulers, the wise crystal dragons, made a pact between the ruling grays and the Maori to end the bloodshed." Her eyes lingered over them. "The dragons would recede into the mountain, and the Maori would raise livestock along the ridges. The dragons would take no more than 25 percent to feed their kind."

Nik balked. He'd been taught in school that 25 percent of the livestock along the mountain pastures disappeared yearly. Investors pushed the Maori to move their herds elsewhere to decrease the risk and increase profits, but his people always refused. Now he knew why.

Pops stepped forward. "But the grays found new ways to abuse their power, subjugating the Draconi to their merciless rule." Pops turned to Joe. "But the rebirth of the crystal dragons is at hand, and the Maori support our new king, by offering one of our own."

Nanna coaxed Nik forward.

As all eyes fell on him, he couldn't help but feel like a piece of meat—a sacrifice, just like the girls up on the podium a few days ago. However, seeing the sparkle in the eyes of the children, the look of absolute awe, he couldn't help but feel pride in representing his people in what had become almost a holy venture.

The adults in the circle, though, wore a countenance of skepticism. He was, after all, Nanna and Pops' freeloading grandson, the one who couldn't hold down a job. The one who counted on old people to keep him off the streets. None of them expected him to come back, let alone succeed, but their expressions were clear: *better him than me.*

Pops sprinkled water on Nik, Connor, and then Joe. "Take with you the blessing of the Maori. May our futures see the day when dragons and man walk the Earth together once more."

Nanna kissed each of them on the cheeks. She hovered over Nik, holding his face in both hands as their gazes locked. Pride beamed from her eyes, filling him. He gulped down the ball building in his throat. If it was in his power to help Connor and Joe see this through to the crystal dragon's coronation, he would do it. If not for them, then for her.

Two men helped disassemble the dragon spear and placed the pieces into Nik's backpack. "Reassembly is easy," one said. "They fit together in any order. Just keep the pointy end at the front."

Pointy end.

Front.

Got it.

Nik seriously needed to see a psychiatrist when this was all over.

Pops held up his staff again. "And now, my final gift to you, Great One, until we meet again."

The crowd parted to reveal golden-haired Pijeth in human form, and his younger brothers, Takata and Shun. They each bowed to Joe.

"How did you get here?" Connor asked.

Pijeth's lips thinned. "Apparently the ancient Maori ties to the Draconi are still strong among the gold. We were—" He glanced at Pops. "*Summoned.*" His emphasis on the last word betrayed he wasn't quite happy with the idea.

Pops smiled. "And your king appreciates your swift arrival."

"Leaving was not easy." Pijeth turned to Connor. "Gale plans to solidify his rule tonight after the lights of Brigham Solstice go dim. We can't take you closer than a mile to the entrance. I won't risk being seen with the dissenters." He bowed to Joe again. "No offense, my king."

Joe crossed his arms. "None taken." But a touch of anger trickled across the bond. They referred to him as king, but he wasn't a king. Not really. Not yet. No one could make that claim until Gale was removed from power, and grays weren't much on giving up anything they held dear.

Pijeth held out a hand to Joe. "Are you ready?"

"I suppose." He adjusted the strap of his backpack. "I guess you didn't bring a saddle."

A what?

Behind the oldest gold, Shun shifted into dragon form and arched his shimmering wings to the sun.

They had to be kidding.

He looked at Pops. "You can't actually expect me to ride one of those things."

Takata approached. "No gold would lower themselves to let a human ride them."

Shun took flight and hovered over Connor. The little gold was half the size of Connor in his natural form.

"This should be interesting." Connor raised his arms. "Ready."

Fluttering, Shun wrapped his talons around Connor's shoulders. Connor grabbed the dragon's legs before they rose into the sky.

Nik gulped. "You have to be shitting me."

Joe shrugged. "The flying part is actually fun. I can't say I've ever been carried before, but it shouldn't be much different." He nodded to Pijeth. "Let's go."

The oldest gold backed into an empty space and shifted. He was probably double the size of his brothers.

Mimicking Connor's actions, Joe raised his hands. Pijeth snatched him without ceremony and then rose into the sky.

"I suppose that leaves us," Takata said.

"I am *not* letting you carry me."

"Did you expect to *walk* to Dragon Mount, human?"

"Not exactly." He glanced down the hill to the SUV that they'd called to take Anna down the mountain. Nik had assumed they'd be driving.

Takata arched an annoyingly golden-blond brow.

Why did he have to end up with the cocky S.O.B. dragon?

No matter. "Let's just get this over with." He shoved his arms into the air.

"Do try not to scream, and for Brigham's sake, don't thrash or squirm." Takata backed into the clearing, smiling. "I wouldn't want to accidentally drop you."

The air around him shimmered as the dragon began to shift. Nik closed his eyes and took a deep breath as the creature's talons wrapped around him. A breeze kicked the musty smell of dry soil into the air as Takata took flight.

Choking down the bile that leapt into his throat, Nik followed Connor's lead by grabbing the dragon's legs as the ground dropped out from beneath his feet. Nik clamped his jaw shut against the scream begging to release, and did his best to remain still while every reflex in his body begged to twist, thrash, and escape the mythical creature carrying him toward certain death.

The cold lashed Nik's cheeks and bit into his lungs. His heartbeat drummed in time to the dragon's beating wings until he hazarded opening one eye.

A few meters in front of him, Connor dangled from Shun's talons. Nik couldn't see Joe, but could sense him somewhere behind them, at ease and trusting of the creatures who held all their lives in their lizardy-grip.

Nik glanced down and immediately regretted it. His stomach turned, but the dark within his closed eyelids only seemed to make it worse. He opened his eyes, narrowing his lashes against the wind.

In the distance, the huge peaks of a purplish mountain came into view. He didn't know the modern name for the rolling summits, but all Maori knew its ancestral significance—the mythical, colossal, Dragon Mount.

CHAPTER 24

Anna pulled against the shackles over her head. Dammit! Honest-to-goodness medieval shackles! Torches burned along the walls, scorching the stone behind them and casting flickering shadows through the cave.

This had to be a sick joke. She ran her fingers beneath the thick metal collar chaining her neck to the wall. Dragons were bad enough, but this *Game of Thrones* crap was a little much.

She giggled a tiny, nervous, crazed sound as Gale crept toward her. His jeans rubbed against his long, dark coat, making a scraping sound that cut though her with each advancing step. Behind him, the walls reached into a cathedral ceiling that seemed to have no apex, except for a scattering of multicolored glow worms that blinked high above, feigning the night sky.

A smile spread across Gale's face as he neared. "Comfortable, my love?"

Back in the alley, that first night, he'd done something to her, hypnotized her into wanting him, into being completely at ease with his touch. Now, he wasn't so merciful. Now, she knew him for the monster he truly was.

"I am *not* your love." This animal probably wasn't even capable of love. She elevated her chin, doing her best not to quiver.

"True enough. We're not even bonded."

"And we never will be." At least, she hoped not. Deep within her, she could feel a longing, a pull to something in the distance. Puff's big, icy-blue eyes filled her thoughts, warming her from within. He'd bound himself to her. She didn't know how, or why, or even if he'd had a choice in the matter. But his essence ran through her, comforting her even in his absence.

They were intertwined, melded in a way that she never dreamed possible. She wouldn't give up this beautiful sense of belonging, and she certainly didn't want any of this magical Draconic blessing tainted by the sicko leering at her. "Keep away from me."

His smile turned wry. "Fear not, lovely. I have no intention of bonding myself to you. It's far too inconvenient." His gaze flicked to the floor, where a circle had been etched in the stone around her. He remained on the outside. They all did, come to think of it. But Puff hadn't kept away. They'd spent each night together with her snuggled under his wing. Then, when he was a man, she'd cuddled against him, drinking in his warmth.

"Proximity," she whispered. "You can't come close to me, or you'll bond."

His eyes flashed. "Smart girl."

But it must have something to do with the *amount* of time, as well. She hadn't bonded to Gale while he'd carried her, and she hadn't bonded to the dragons who'd tied her up here. The ring must have just been a precaution.

The chains jangled as she reset her footing. She'd spent an entire night trapped inside Puff's wing after he'd saved her from Gale, and then she'd slept covered by that same wing each subsequent night. Every morning she'd felt closer to him, more at ease.

She was as bonded to her little white dragon as he was to her.

Gale prowled back and forth in front of her, stepping over the chain that anchored her right ankle to a chain that disappeared into the floor several yards away from the wall. "Luckily enough for me, I don't need the bond to plant my seed within you. I need only to touch you when we mate, and when you give birth to my fledgling."

She gulped. "And then what?"

His eyes darkened. "You'll do what every good mother does. You'll feed him."

She had a bad feeling he wasn't talking about nursing the baby.

Anna yanked against the shackles, choking down the terror building in her chest. "You can't do this. I belong to someone else."

But he didn't care. She could see it in his eyes. She was a means to an end for him, nothing more. Puff be damned.

She looked up toward the ceiling, where several flying dragons circled in their own private sky. "Help me, please!"

"They're my people," Gale said. "They've come to see me confirmed ruler once more." His gaze lingered on their lazy flight pattern. "The only help they'll provide, is holding your legs apart, if I ask it of them."

A whimper escaped her throat, and she hated herself for it. Yes, he held all the cards, but he would not conquer her soul. She needed to keep her wits about her. Eventually, one of these godforsaken reptiles would be careless. It might only happen for a split second, but it *would* happen. She needed to find her chance to get away, and take it.

A dragon roared somewhere, followed by another. Streams of flame blasted through the sky, lighting torches mounted to the rockface for what looked like a mile overhead.

The walls began to move.

No, not the walls. Dragons. Hundreds of dragons sat perched on shelves lining the bulwark high into the darkness above. The worms no longer comforted her with their light.

Gale turned from her. "Brigham Solstice has ended!"

The dragons bellowed in answer, the sound echoing off the stone walls.

"Once again I stand before you, as your king." He pointed to a line of gray dragons on the floor, some small, some large. "My sons will soon have another of my brood to teach the ways of governance and law."

Those were all his sons? How long had he been king, and where were the previous mothers?

Gale's words hissed through her mind. *You'll do what every good mother does. You'll feed him.*

Jesus, he wasn't just trying to scare her. He was serious.

Anna propped her foot against the wall and pulled. Dammit! Shackles always came loose in the movies. Why not now?

The dragons drummed their talons on the rocks. The sound reverberated off the stone like the march of an army. When she turned, she no longer faced Gale the man, but the largest dragon in the room.

Anna's back slammed against the wall, and she realized she'd retreated. The dragon lowered its head until its eyes were level with hers. She wasn't going to back down, though. If Gale wanted her, she was going down fighting.

Joe's icy-blue eyes filled her mind. She reached to them for comfort, for the warmth she'd relished in the caves, but the vision broke away, splintering until nothing was left but the sight of the yellow-eyed monster before her.

Gale's gaze bored into Anna, making promises and threats that she knew he had every intention of keeping. But she found life in those threats, new meaning. A haze coated the room as his warm breath encompassed her, she reveled in the essence of smoke and endless power.

She was his queen, the only woman in New Zealand who could bear him a child. And she would.

She sighed, breathing him in, knowing he'd soon make her his.

Lolling her head, she bared her neck in submission, accepting him. Wanting him.

Gale raised a talon, snagging the edge of her pants.

"Yes," she whispered, leaning back and exposing herself to his might.

"Gale, stop!" The voice rang through the chamber. The drumming of talons stopped, leaving the air empty and wanting.

Three men stepped into the light. Two dark, and one fair with ghostly white skin.

Gale lowered his talon.

Anna weakened from the loss of his touch. "No," she begged. "Please."

The dragon ignored her, turning to the newcomers, growling.

The pale man lifted a torch into the air. "This female is mine, bonded to me by right. She was taken unlawfully and forced here against her will."

Gale roared at them. The heat of his breath tingled through the room, Anna twisted, coating herself in his glory.

"I will not back down, Gale. She is mine, and I will not allow this."

Throughout the room, the dragons galloped in place. Gale puffed three times, snickering.

Who was this boy to challenge a full-grown dragon? Blood would be spilled today, and Anna thrilled at the thought.

She laughed, swinging from her bindings. "He's going to kill you," she sing-songed. The massive gray dragon glanced back to her, and she leaned toward him. "Do it. Slit his throat and be done with it."

The dragon growled and spun on the intruders. The pale boy took a step back, but his gaze remained pinned to Anna's. His forehead wrinkled, his eyes weary and pleading.

Did he think that she'd want him? Ridiculous, when she already had someone so magnificent.

Anna blinked, and the haze about the room cleared. Gale had

his back to her. His tail twitched at the floor between her feet. She shook her head, clearing the rest of the fog before the remainder of the room came into focus.

Joe's presence screamed into her psyche, calling, caressing, and promising to end this madness.

No, not Joe—Puff. Joesephutus. Her dragon. He'd come for her.

CHAPTER 25

*N*ik shuddered as the dragon's gaze hovered over each of them. Beside him, Joe reset his footing, easing his right side away to hide the severity of his injury as Gale loomed overhead.

The dragon bellowed. Hot, rank, smoky breath rolled over them as the creature grunted and clicked.

Joe tilted his torch, illuminating Nik's face. "This man is my *Kotahi*, blood and mind bound to me." He pointed the torch at Connor. "And this dragon chooses to stand beside me as second."

According to Connor, another dragon could legally stand as Joe's second to aid him due to Joe's current handicap—being trapped in human form. But with both of them stuck as humans, and Gale very much a six-ton dragon, Nik didn't see how having a second set of hands would help much.

Gale shook his patchy gray mane. The air around him wavered, like looking through the heat of a campfire, before the dragon shrank into human form. He was taller than Connor, with sallow skin and dark brown hair that threatened gray at the temples. His smile sent a shiver down Nik's spine.

"I am not unreasonable." Gale spun, addressing the dragons in the circular theater above. "This crystal pup was too young to fly in the competition, yet in the interests of sept harmony, we didn't object. Now this insignificant toddling has delusions of being king."

The grays roared in protest, while the rest of the dragons sat on their perches, quietly watching.

Gale turned back to Joe, his gaze hovering over the wound he'd ripped into Puff's hide with his own claw. "I give you the chance to step back and rejoin your people without retribution, runt." He glanced at Connor. "All of you. Our numbers are small. We should not be fighting among ourselves."

He'd said that almost like he gave a damn. Hate seethed across the bond between Nik and Joe, but the boss managed to keep his cool. Well, on the outside, at least. Inside, his mind whirled, cataloging each possible weapon a human could use against a dragon, noting the ledges above, the torches within reach, the chain running along the floor, anchoring Anna's ankle to the platform behind Gale, and counting the distance and how long it would take to get to her.

Nik had to give the kid kudos for bravery. The only thing Nik was looking for were the exits.

Joe waved his torch, casting mottled shadows on the lower walls. "Gale is a dragon murderer and not fit to be king."

Okay, that was a bit blunt and to the point, and not at all what they'd discussed him saying. Connor glanced at Nik and reset his footing. Nik agreed, the kid needed to keep to script or he was going to get his head bitten off before he made his point.

The cavern erupted in growls and hisses from all angles.

Gale's eyes narrowed. "You better have proof to back that up, boy."

Joe quaked inside, but stood his ground. "When the dragons took flight for the Seventeen Year, Gale and his sentries knocked Elor from the sky."

A collective growl rumbled the room. The section of yellow-ish-gold dragons clawed at their perches.

Gale sneered. "Ridiculous. Stand back. Your adolescent fool-ishness will only stay my patience for so long."

Joe pointed to the gilded dragons. "The golds had a strong contender this Seventeen Year, and the grays knew they couldn't outfly him." He turned to Gale. "Elor barely made it past the leveling range before no less than seven adult grays set upon him." He reached into his backpack and withdrew a long, dark claw. "This was found lodged in Elor's corpse before Gale's sentries burned the evidence." He pointed the claw at Gale. "Missing something?"

Gale fisted his right hand and drew it behind his back, hiding his missing digit from the dragons overhead. His eyes flashed. "Enough. If you are going to challenge, do it so I can finally disembowel you."

Like the asshole wouldn't have done so earlier, had he seen the chance, but here, at what Joe had just turned into a dragon version of court, there were rules that even their dictator-king needed to follow.

Joe handed the torch to Connor, his eyes not leaving his oppo-nent. "I challenge in the name of the crystal dragons, and Draconic law." He pointed at Anna, careful to keep Gale fixed in his sights.

Nik looked at her for him and sent Joe calming thoughts that she was okay, that they'd gotten to her in time. The last thing his boss needed was to be worried about the girl, when there was a larger, seething problem a few feet away, gunning for blood.

"The female is mine," Joe continued, "and your life is forfeit to the golds in exchange for the future you stole from them."

Yup, all those years of being forced to study Draconic law, what Nik thought were just boring fictional tomes, had paid off. He'd been able to help Joe and Connor craft the perfect speech to rally the rest of the dragons to their cause. He wasn't sure about those above, but the golds shifted and scratched their perches, their eyes reddened in what could only be fury.

Joe took a gutsy step forward. "Your reign is over."

Gale roared, the sound echoing through the compartment as if he'd taken dragon form, but it was a human fist that swung at Joe. Boss tried to duck, but Gale's fist skidded across his jaw. Joe hit the ground, and bounced to his feet before Gale landed on him. They rolled, Joe squirming away, using his slight stature to his advantage as he evaded Gale's flailing fists.

Connor swayed slowly beside Nik, his hands clasping and unclasping. His movement mirrored the swaying anticipation of the dragons above. It must be killing Connor, not being able to shift and bite Gale's head off to be done with this.

Joe skirted a blow, but Gale countered with a hook that landed on Joe's injured side. Boss huffed out a breath and fell to his knees, wheezing as he held his side.

Nik's breath hitched as Joe's pain rolled over him, stinging and burning as if he'd taken the blow himself. Gale hissed, kicking Joe's injury repeatedly until the kid stopped fighting.

Nik dropped to one knee. His lungs seized. His chest stung.

A smug grin covered Gale's face as he dragged Joe up by the hair.

"Enough." Connor yanked Joe out of Gale's grip.

The boy sprawled across the floor, lifeless beneath the ledge holding the growling and hissing gold dragons. Nik cringed as the ribbon of energy floating between him and Joe blinked out, then eased back like a tired ooze. Boss was alive, but just barely.

Connor hazarded a glance at Nik, his nose flaring.

Jarred by the sudden attention, Nik slid toward Joe and grabbed his boss's backpack. The drumming of the gold's talons pounded louder beneath their perch, echoing off the stone walls.

"Boss!" He pulled Joe up and leaned him against the wall. "Don't give up on us now. We've got that bastard right where we want him."

Yeah, right. Even playing nice in human form, Gale still had the power of a dragon, while Connor and Joe were injured, and Nik was just, well, *Nik.*

He rummaged through the pack until he found the jar of salve Tyler had made out of the dragon venom. Shaking, he poured the thick black liquid over Joe's bare, bleeding side. Nik was no doctor, but the gaping red wound didn't look good.

The venom sizzled over the blood.

Nope, not good at all.

Connor shuffled his feet, keeping himself between Gale and Joe. His muscles stretched against his plaid shirt, as if his dragon form lay just below the surface, waiting to spring free.

"Ah, Quenor." Gale's smile was the stuff of nightmares. "You know, several dragons called you out as a contender this year. What you lack in girth, you even out with strength, yet you didn't use this to your advantage. I find this puzzling."

Gale tried to circle him, but Connor kept pace, keeping himself the only thing defending Joe's unconscious form. He'd have to get through Nik too, of course. Nik tried his best to not think about the possibility of Gale tearing out his meager human innards and throwing his lifeless body to the side before slamming a killing blow against the defenseless kid in his arms.

He stiffened. No. Not on his watch. He unscrewed the lid from the second potion.

"Why would I stand out as a contender, when that would only put a target on my tail?" Connor said.

That's it, bro, keep that psychotic reptile talking. Nik tilted Joe's head back and opened the kid's slack mouth, pouring the potion between his lips. He hoped Joe was cognizant enough to swallow.

Gale's snicker radiated through the room, which had grown strangely quiet. "So you took up with the runt."

Joe's body convulsed, knocking the container from Nik's hand.

He scrambled for the jar, but the black liquid had already spilled to the ground. Dammit!

Connor snarled behind him. "I took up with someone worthy, someone I would be proud to call king."

"That scrawny, weak…"

Nik brushed Joe's long, silvery hair back from his closed eyes. He was breathing, but barely. Did he even swallow what Nik had given him?

"Strength alone does not make a good king." Connor's voice boomed through the hall. "You've proven that well enough to everyone."

Gale howled.

The air wafted and blurred before a bright light flashed, blinding Nik. He blinked the spots from his eyes, refocusing as Connor dodged the thrashing, clawed tail of a huge, gray dragon where human Gale had once stood.

Cheating bastard!

The drumming of the dragons above began anew. They hissed and their gravelly voices echoed through the chamber. The cacophony shrieked like a freight train's brakes slicing through the room.

None of the other dragons moved to stop the fight, though. Nik tried to recall the ancient tomes he'd studied. Somewhere it had to say that fighting a man in dragon form wasn't allowed.

Connor slammed his shoulder into Gale's leg, and the dragon slid across the floor. Gale roared and stepped back, favoring the limb Connor had hit. Maybe the fight wasn't as one-sided as it seemed.

Joe groaned, startling Nik. "Boss!" He shook the unconscious boy. "Come on, snap out of it."

Gale opened his wings and whipped his tail. Connor dropped to his knees before reaching up and grabbing the edge of Gale's wing as it passed over his head. He held on as Gale arched his back, lifting Connor into the air.

"Nik." Joe's eyes fluttered open, his voice barely audible in the booming theater-like cave. He rolled his arms one at a time, as if making sure they were still attached to his body.

"You're all right," Nik told him. "Just take a few deep breaths." *And please do it quickly.* He tensed as Gale roared again behind him.

Every ounce of Nik's flesh crawled and twitched, prodding him to run for his life. But he had to trust Connor, and he had to trust that the dragon venom would prove the miracle they all expected. The little voice in his head told him their plan had too many holes, though, and the boss getting taken out so early made their predicament even worse.

Joe's pain seeped through the bond. Nik did his best to block out the phantom burn searing his side as Joe's chest rose in a deep breath and fell. The kid's eyes widened before he grabbed Nik by his collar.

"Duck!" Joe pulled Nik to the floor.

A whoosh of air rolled over them before rock and dirt cut into Nik's cheek as Gale's tail slammed into the wall where they'd both rested. Gravel and a massive hunk of stone fell to the ground.

Joe coughed, his eyes on Connor's back as the older man readied for another lunge. "I see Gale didn't keep his temper long."

"All of about three minutes." Nik helped Joe to his knees. "Are you going to be all right?"

Joe nodded, but the apprehension spiking through their bond told Nik otherwise. He stood slowly, his gaze carrying to the far side of the room, where Anna yanked against her bonds. The air between them vibrated with the need to free her.

Nik grabbed Joe's shoulder. "Hey, stay with me. We can't help her until we get past the big ugly dragon."

"She's hurt," Joe whispered. "We need to get to her."

With a screaming roar, Gale flung his arms outward, sending Connor careening through the air to slam against the rock wall behind them. He slid down the damp surface until his lifeless body rested on the floor. Blood oozed from a deep, open wound in his stomach.

"Help him." Joe wove the dragon talon between his fingers and moved toward Gale.

Nik eyed the spilled potion on the floor. "I can't." They'd had more than enough elixir for several hits, Connor had even marked the jars into four rations, but all that remained lay soaking into the floor.

The ground trembled and Nik spun to find a golden dragon standing behind him.

Gale roared at the gold. Draconic gibberish rose through the air, grating Nik's ears until the soft translation filtered from Joe. *"Take one more step, youngling, and I'll consider it treason."*

The gold tensed. Its spiraling eyes centered on Nik for a moment. It was Shun, the one who'd healed Joe and given them his venom. He looked back at Gale, puffed smoke from his nose, and continued to make his way toward Connor.

"Your fight is with me." Joe held up the talon. "Leave the gold to his healing."

Hissing, Gale batted Joe to the side. He made to lunge at Shun, when a larger gold fell from the sky, landing on Gale's neck and slamming the larger dragon into the floor.

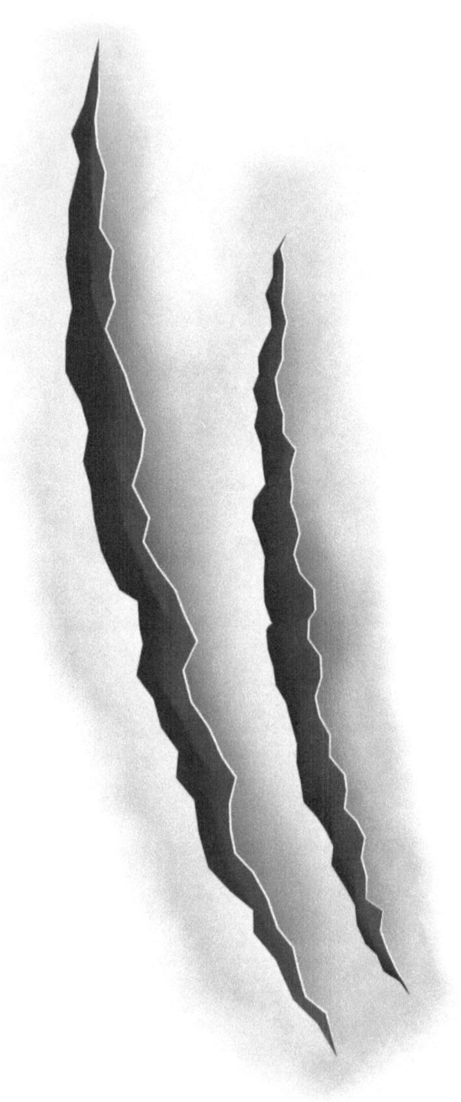

CHAPTER 26

$\mathcal{A}$nna's wrists bled as she pulled at her chains. Across the room, Joe ducked as the gold dragon snapped and clawed Gale. Above, hundreds of other dragons clambered and growled. If Gale was such a terror, why weren't more willing to help?

Beyond the theater, blood stained the far wall where Connor had hit the unforgiving stone. Shun's golden wings loomed over him, blocking his patient from her view. As long as the young dragon stayed there, risking his own life to help, Anna knew Connor was still alive; but now Joe was out there again, with only luck keeping him from getting squashed by two fully-grown dragons rolling across the floor.

Turning back to her shackles, Anna propped her free foot against the wall and yanked. Her hands ached, the metal cold and unforgiving in her grip.

Her muscles quivered as she pulled again, but the bolts holding the chains didn't budge. She needed a new plan.

A waft of air hit her on the right and a small red dragon, only a little shorter than she was hit the ground only inches away. She gasped and stepped back as the creature wrapped its talons around the chain attaching her left wrist to the wall, and tugged.

Anna took three seconds to process that the little dragon was trying to help free her, before adding her own grip to the metal coils.

They pulled together, but the restraints still held firm. Anna growled in frustration as the gold dragon, who she took for granted was Shun's brother Pijeth, took a hit from Gale's tail and sprawled across the floor. She was running out of time.

She turned to her little red comrade-in-arms, but a thud sounded behind her, accompanied with the tell-tale waft of air she'd forevermore assign to dragon wings. She spun and faced a formidable, adult-sized red dragon, only slightly smaller than Connor. The creature looked past her and howled at the fledgling, who spat and hissed back. The younger dragon took a defensive stance, while the adult angled its wings.

Trapped between them, she flattened against the cold stone.

Her breath hitched as the larger dragon snapped twice at the smaller, while the little dragon pawed at the air and hissed. Growling, the larger dragon wrapped its talons around her waist and pinned her against the wall.

She gasped as the wind expelled from her lungs.

They weren't here to help. They were going to fight over her!

Anna struggled against a strength she wasn't built to master as the claws tightened. Maybe they weren't going to fight. Maybe they just wanted her dead.

The little dragon lunged for her throat.

"Joe!"

Her voice barely sounded above the clatter of the fighting dragons, but Joe still spun. His eyes widened when he saw her, and he dodged Pijeth's tail as he sprinted toward the platform. Two seconds of relief were shattered as Gale's giant fist slammed down on the floor, blocking Joe's path. He skidded to a stop.

Anna tried to fight the ravenous baby dragon, but it overpowered her with ease, gnawing and thrashing. Her metal collar afforded her the only protection as the sticky sensation of blood dampened her neck.

The giant talon of the larger red turned her face to him. The beast hissed and smoky steam clouded her vision.

Rat bastard!

She took one hand off the savaging baby to push the adult away. It hissed again, but made no move other than directing her face toward it with the razor-sharp spike.

Another hiss.

But wait, was that a hiss? The smoke cleared and she stared into the creature's eyes. The cold, soulless stare she expected wasn't there. The wedge of scales where the dragon's brow would be creased as it hissed again. It wasn't a hiss, though, but more like a Shhhhhhh.

Anna glanced over to the theater, where Pijeth yanked Gale's wing back, steering the beast away from Joe as he scurried across the floor.

Gale's cold, yellow eyes met hers—eyes that glared death and menace. That demonic trait was missing in the eyes that held her pinned to the wall, while its baby rooted for her jugular.

Unless that wasn't what they were doing.

Shhhhhhh, the dragon cooed again.

The baby could easily have sunk its teeth into her flesh above the collar. Either one of them could have attacked her face for a death blow with far more efficiency. Unless this was a parent training a baby how to rip out a throat. Those eyes, though, there was humanity there. If not humanity, then at least humanitarianism.

If she was wrong, she was dead, but tied to a wall, her only choice was to act on instinct. Steeling herself, Anna dropped her hands.

The baby growled, intensifying its attack, yet still thwarted by the metal collar. Anna kept her eyes trained on the adult, biting her lip against the sting in her throat, trusting that...

Pop!

The baby retreated, and the talon holding her face drew down her neck, and flicked the collar. The weight slipped from her neck and Anna released the breath she'd been holding as the blood-stained metal clanked against the wall, hanging from the chain above.

She gulped and looked from the adult, to the baby. "Thank you."

The baby wagged its tail like a puppy before snapping at her wrist. She held her arm to the wall for leverage as the creature gnawed at the thinner metal until the restraint snapped and fell away.

The baby reached for her other arm, when a deafening roar echoed through the chamber. Gale held Pijeth down with one foot, but his eyes were trained on Anna and her treasonous new friends. The red snatched the baby with one clawed hand and slashed the chain holding Anna's other wrist, leaving her hand free, but still incased in iron. It then pushed off the floor and flew up into the rafters and away from Gale's poisonous gaze.

Pijeth took advantage of the gray's distraction and stabbed his forked claws into Gale's chest. The huge gray's cry reanimated the dragons above, who stomped their talons on their perches.

Joe jumped onto the platform and gathered Anna in his arms. "Are you all right?"

She nodded. "The red dragons."

"I saw. Be thankful reds are egg bearers."

"Why?"

"Otherwise that baby would be a seventeen-year-old adult and too big to gnaw that collar off."

Cupping her cheeks, his gaze roamed her face. Joe seemed to reach through her eyes as his essence ran over every part of her body. Her wounds tingled, while some of the ache in her bruises disappeared completely.

This joining, this sense of connection was almost too much to bear, though. She needed to touch, to feel and connect in a human way to center the rampant energy pulsing through her. The chain hung loose from her wrist as she ran her hand down Joe's uninjured side, drinking in the warmth radiating from his skin and relishing its embrace.

He glanced at her mouth and leaned toward her. All the unease about dragons and humans and her current altered reality slipped away, drowned by his overwhelming Joe-ness. Anna licked her lips. She closed her eyes and relaxed despite the dragon battle still raging a few steps away, and surrendered as he lowered his mouth and… rubbed his temple against the side of her neck.

Anna's eyes shot open as he drew away.

He checked the battle behind him. "You're fine. I've healed what I could."

"Oh." Anna blinked. Her cheeks burned.

Why had she even dreamed he would kiss her when Gale could still bite their heads off at any minute?

Across the room, Nik fumbled with something beside his backpack. He wiped his brow, and his face twisted in concern before he rose slowly, gaze fixed on the dueling dragons.

The flickering torches caught the furrow in his brow and the grim, straight line of his mouth. He opened and closed his left fist. His right remained in shadow until he stepped further into the arena, allowing the torchlight to dance across the shimmering length of the dragon spear.

No one is born a hero. They become heroes, either by courage or necessity. At least that's what Nik had been taught as a kid. Facing a dragon the size of a house, though, sent his courage running down the mountain, leaving him alone with necessity, and a pulse throbbing like the incessant beat of an alarm clock buzzer in his ears.

Throughout the theater, the onlookers jabbered and roared, slamming their claws against their massive box seats. On the platform, the boss had managed to scare off the two red dragons and free Anna's hands and throat. The chain on her left ankle still seemed securely shackled as she and Joe stared at him from across the dragon-dueling mayhem.

He adjusted his grip on the spear. The weapon's energy surged as if it had a life of its own, cooling and heating beneath his grip.

Even a touch from the spear will burn a dragon, the history books said, and from the way Joe and Connor had reacted in the spear's presence, at least some of that had to be fact.

He needed to do more than just burn Gale, though. It was obvious that Pijeth was faster than the gray, but not stronger. The gold dragon was still fighting because Gale hadn't managed to land more than a few hits, but Pijeth's blows weren't doing enough damage.

Nik's grip tightened on the tingling metal as the gold dragon spun around the hulking gray. The plan had been for Nik to throw the spear as Connor distracted Gale. Stuck in human form, Connor was a much smaller obstacle than the huge gold.

If Nik threw, and hit Pijeth, this competition would be over, and he would be to blame. Gale lumbered, but the gold's constant movement fluttering between Nik and the gray dragon's hide was a variable Pops hadn't accounted for when teaching him how to throw.

Faith was all he needed, but not something easily achieved in the face of mythological monsters.

I have faith in you.

Startled, Nik's gaze carried to Joe, who'd stopped yanking on the chain holding Anna to the floor to stare into his eyes.

I've always had faith in you. If I hadn't, I never would have chosen you.

Nik choked down the lump in his throat. "If I hit the wrong dragon—"

You won't. End this for me. Joe's gaze moved beyond Nik, to where Connor still lay motionless against the wall. *End this for all of us.*

The throbbing in Nik's temples heightened before seeping into the background. Even the sound of the dragons snapping and growling sucked away, as if he heard everything through water.

Just one hit. That was all he needed. Gale was a huge target. He could do this.

Taking a deep breath, he tilted the spear up, letting a portion of the heavy metal fall behind him for balance, and then he flung the quivering javelin toward Gale's spine.

The lines etched in the weapon's shaft glowed with the firelight, promising the swift death for which the lance had been forged over a thousand years ago. The point arched, then fell with an ethereal grace of a silent stalker, never seen until it struck.

Nik's heart swelled as the weapon dropped toward its target. He drank in the heady sensation, thrilled that he'd done the impossible, until Gale roared and flapped his wings. The metal shaft clanged against bone, knocking the spear back into the air where it landed, impaled along the edge of a balcony above, surrounded by wide-eyed blue dragons.

There it remained: the greatest weapon ever forged against dragons, lost when they needed it most.

Pijeth managed to get his jaws around Gale's throat, but the larger gray tossed him off as easily as he'd thwarted the spear. Joe and Anna stood, motionless and gaping. Anna stared at the spear in the rafters above, while Joe centered on his *Kotahi*. Nik waited for his boss's voice to boom within his head, shouting encouragement, but silence prevailed. Joe's shoulders slumped as he lowered his gaze to the floor.

Nik clenched his teeth. "No," he whispered. "This is not over."

Spinning away, Nik felt along the wall for something to grab onto. People scaled rocks all the time for fun. He was in decent shape. He should be able to climb up to at least the first platform, where several golds now stared down at him with cold eyes.

It was their challenger that Gale had killed during the competition. The golds had more reason than any to want the gray dead.

He only needed to convince one dragon to fly up and get the spear. They would listen to him. He knew they would.

Nik considered the shiny, sleek stone. Getting up there so he *could* convince them was another matter.

One gold sprang from its perch and landed beside Nik, hissing. He recognized those condescending eyes. "Dammit, Takata, I don't have time for your shit." Unless he could persuade this annoying little dragon to go up there and...

Growling, Takata snatched Nik's wrist in one claw and flung him into the air. The world spun. His heart throttled and Nik howled, before a massive black dragon leaned off his perch and snatched Nik's waist in its jaws.

Nik thrashed against teeth and slobbering goo before the beast tossed him back into the air. He flew across the theater and slammed chest-first onto a hard platform.

His hands trembled on the stone. The sound of the two dragons fighting echoed in the vast space, and the air seemed cold and thin. He wasn't on the gold's perch. He was much, much higher.

Nikky's seatbelt constricted as his mother's scream filled the car. His dad hollered one of those words Nikky wasn't supposed to say. The wheels screeched. The car jiggled, jumped, and slammed through the guardrail.

Mommy reached back, holding Nikky in his booster seat even though he was already belted. "It's okay, baby. Hold on."

Her eyes didn't look okay, though. Nikky wailed as the windshield shattered, and everything went black.

Don't look down, he told himself, shaking as he stood. The spear jutted out from the edge of a perch two spans over, and one tier up.

He'd have to climb higher. Shit.

It's just altitude. Mind over matter.

Taking a deep breath, he lunged for the next perch. His heart rattled, knowing no seatbelt protected him this time. His mind screamed until his right hand caught the ledge, but his left slid on loose gravel. Nik dangled God-knows-how-high off the ground.

He steeled himself. This was no different than climbing the ladders at his last job. Focus on your destination, eyes up, not down. His stomach still twitched though, perfectly aware of what was and wasn't below him.

The gravel sprinkled from the edge as Nik grappled for purchase. His right hand slipped, and sweat drenched his back and dripped down his temples. He could do this. No. He *would* do this.

He reached for the ledge again, but a gray dragon with a jagged scar across one foggy white eye peered over the precipice. Hot breath puffed against Nik's face, coating him with the smell of decayed flesh. He struggled to hold his breath as veiny, yellow eyes promised him a swift death.

Dammit! Why wasn't this one with the other grays? The revolting beast growled as it reached down and grabbed Nik's flailing left hand. Nik gripped the ledge tighter with his right, waiting for the dragon to fling him from the perch.

Below, the audience roiled in excitement, half the eyes drawn to him, the remainder on the battle still raging below. Nik slipped and the dragon growled. This murderous, shit-for-brains lizard was playing with him, waiting for the perfect moment before it dropped him into Gale's waiting gullet below.

A flash of cobalt and wind fluttered past as a blue dragon alighted to the right of the gray and shifted into a woman with long, dark hair covering her... *Jesus*, covering her naked *everything*.

"The ancient gray is injured," she called to Nik. "He can't pull you up. Give me your other hand." She reached down to him.

Nik looked from her, to the crazed yellow eyes of the gray dragon. If he released his grip, this gray bastard, who could be Gale's brother for all he knew, would drop him. There was no way he was letting go.

The woman waved her open palm at him. "Come, human. There is no time!"

Naked Lady's fierce gaze filled him with hope, but the stinking gray dragon... was trembling. Its bloodshot eyes implored, as if it was in pain. Shit. It wasn't trying to kill him; it was helping.

Nik let go and shot his hand into Naked Lady's grip. She yanked him up with strength no woman should have. She stumbled back and Nik fell on top of her, one hand beside her shoulder and the other full-on grabbing her boob.

"Shit!" He scrambled off her. "Sorry. That was completely unintentional."

She smiled at him, rising to her full, naked glory. "Dragons do not have modesty, or alarm concerning one part of our bodies over another."

That made sense, he guessed.

She inclined her head as she walked toward the edge and dropped to her hands and knees. "Mount me. Quickly."

Nik's gaze carried over her perfectly sculpted ass. "Excuse me?"

The air about her rippled, and her beautiful derriere morphed into an even more beautiful sparkling blue array of scales.

Oh! *Mount* her. Idiot. He climbed up and wedged his nutsack between two menacing black barbs on her back. She growled at him, and he took that as a warning to hang on as she jumped off the perch.

He winced, sliding forward, the crotch of his jeans jamming against the razor-like protrusions on her spine, before she settled a few feet from where the spear had landed.

He rolled off her, holding his crotch as she shifted back into human form. Her breasts hung in his face as she nudged him.

"Get up, human."

Nik blinked, forcing his gaze away from that incredible rack, and stared at her. She pointed to the edge of the perch, where the spear glistened, imbedded in the stone.

Shit, yeah, the spear. Dizzy, he shook his head to clear out the remnants of pain and inched toward the edge.

"I GOT YOU, LITTLE BRO." A MAN OUTSIDE THE CAR WINDOW CALLED TO

Nikky as he tried the door. He said one of those bad words when it wouldn't open.

Nikky cried for Mommy again. Why weren't she and Daddy scaring away the stranger? The car shifted, sliding down the side of the mountain before jolting to a stop.

Nikky struggled to breathe through his sobs, closing his eyes to hide from the voices and muffled shouting outside. Mommy and Daddy said they were all going to see Nanna and Pops. Why were they here?

The man appeared at the other window. "Look away." He called, hauling a big rock in the air.

The car jiggled again, and the man cried out, dropping the rock. He stumbled, waving his arms before he disappeared. Nikky froze as he saw him again through the windshield below, falling until he was only a spec in the distance.

NIK'S HEARTBEAT THUDDED IN HIS EARS AS HE INCHED TOWARD THE edge. Behind him, the blue dragons scraped their claws on the rocky shelf.

His voluptuous friend stepped beside him. "What's wrong with you? Take the spear."

Sweat dripped from his hairline as the edge blurred. His mind spun and he stepped back. The edge—shit, the edge!

TEARS BLURRED NIKKY'S VISION AS ANOTHER MAN APPEARED BY HIS window. The guy tested a rope tied to his waist and clunked a giant metal alligator mouth against the door. Nikky howled, hiding from the monster as it ate the side of the car.

The metal crunched and Nikky hid beneath his palms until warm, human hands cupped his face, released his seatbelt and lifted him from the car.

The window jarred as he slipped through. The man said a bad word, crushing Nikky to his chest as the car creaked and rolled until it flew through the air and dropped, leaving Nikky alone with the man tied to a rope.

Nikky screamed for Mommy and Daddy as he twisted against the stranger's grip and reached for the valley far beneath them.

But the car was gone, taking Mommy and Daddy with it.

Nɪᴋ ꜰᴇʟʟ ᴛᴏ ʜɪꜱ ᴋɴᴇᴇꜱ, ɪᴍᴍᴏʙɪʟᴇ ᴀꜱ ᴛʜᴇ ᴅʀᴀɢᴏɴꜱ ᴅᴜᴇʟᴇᴅ ʙᴇʟᴏᴡ. The shaft of the spear stuck out of the edge, mocking him, less than a step away.

The woman shoved him. "Take it, human. Use the height to your advantage."

The height. Yes, height would normally be an advantage, at least to other people. With a clean drop from overhead, the spear would pick up speed as it fell. A throw from here would be ten times as deadly, and Gale would never see it coming.

Nik drew in a deep breath and crawled half a pace to the edge. Heavy with sweat, his shirt clung to his chest and arms. He stopped, panting.

Naked Lady knelt beside him. "I cannot touch the spear. If you are ill, remove your shirt and I will use the cloth to try to pull the weapon free, but you must hurry."

A dragon shrieked below. The high pitch had to be Pijeth. Nik didn't have time to take off his shirt and hope the spear didn't hurt the pretty naked dragon. He needed to do this now. He had one job to do in this godforsaken crazy plan, and he sure as hell was going to do it.

He slid to the edge on his stomach, his hands shaking on the cold stone floor.

"Lᴇᴛ ᴍᴇ ɢᴏ! Lᴇᴛ ᴍᴇ ɢᴏ!" Nɪᴋᴋʏ ꜱᴄʀᴇᴀᴍᴇᴅ.

The man only tightened his grip as the people above pulled the rope, hoisting them up the side of the mountain.

Dragging himself across the floor, the shaft now loomed inches from Nik's face. He could do this. He could save everyone with one throw of the ancient weapon. But the hilt blurred and doubled, jumping from left to right. Nik closed his eyes. It was an illusion. The spear was right there. He needed to finish this. He was the only one who could.

Nanna hugged little Nikky to her. "It's going to be all right, Nikau."

He struggled in her grip. "It's not okay. I want my Momma!"

She brushed the damp hair from his eyes. "The sun has risen on a new day, my strong Maori warrior. It may not seem like it now, but you are destined for great things. You will do your parents proud."

Nikky fell onto her shoulder, sobbing. How could anything ever be great again?

Nik squeezed his eyes tighter against the memory. He *was* destined for great things. He was a *Kotahi*. The first in generations. He'd been chosen, and his dragon, and every dragon in this theater was counting on him. He wouldn't let them down. He'd never let anyone down again.

He reached out and grasped cold steel. The shaft pulsed in his grip, beckoning, begging for blood.

"Pull it out, human."

Nik gulped, opening his eyes.

Below, Joe and Anna tugged on the chain connected to her ankle. Joe would struggle with a chain that thick even in dragon form. He wasn't freeing her anytime soon. To their right, Gale pinned Pijeth to the arena floor. His spine was a huge target. Nik wouldn't even have to throw. At this height, he could just drop the heavy weapon and let gravity win the day.

He yanked on the spear, but at the odd angle, he had no leverage.

The room spun.

The ground beckoned to him.

His head and arms drew down as if weighted, or the ground below was sucking him in.

Nik closed his eyes again. Nothing was moving, and the ground wasn't alive and plotting his death. He knew it. He just needed to convince his eyes, his mind, his *everything* that there was nothing to fear.

"Hold tight, human." Naked Lady wrapped her arms around his waist, towing him from the edge.

His hands slipped along the cool shaft. His shoulders burned. Clenching his teeth, he tightened his grip. They could do this. *He could do this.*

"Come on!" Nik shouted at the ancient weapon, adding his strength. The shaft creaked, jimmied, and then slid free.

He stared at the spear, a long dark cylinder over the torchlight from behind, until the metal began to hum again, as if powering up for its impending flight.

Joe looked up at him from Anna's platform and nodded to his *Kotahi*. He shouted something to Anna and they attacked the chain anew. Pijeth snapped at Gale's face, and his tail slapped the larger dragon's back. The huge gray growled, slamming the gold's head to the floor, baring Pijeth's neck.

Joe leaned back, yanking Anna's restraints until the baseplate dislodged from the floor, leaving a hole in the platform where the chains had been anchored. Both he and Anna stumbled and fell, but she was free.

If Nik was going to do this, now was the time.

He stepped to the edge. The gray dragons staring at him from the opposite platform froze. He raised the spear, held his breath, and readied to drop the weapon on Gale should any of them bathe him in fire, but the entire section of the king's kin sat and watched. The only fire came from their yellow eyes. Nik smiled, more aware than ever of what a monster the beast below must be, before he drew the spear back and threw.

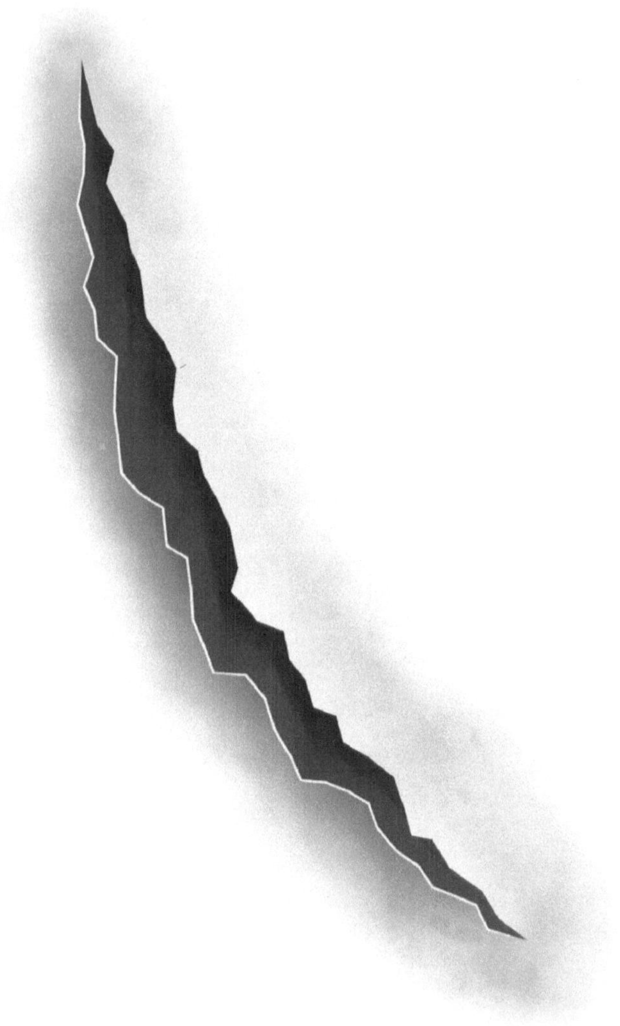

CHAPTER 28

The weapon glinted in the torchlight as it fell toward them. Anna clutched Joe, holding her breath until the spear pierced scale. Gale reared up like a colossal, shrieking demon as the wound smoked and sizzled at the point of impact.

Pijeth slipped out from under the huge gray, favoring his right front leg. The gold flared out his wings, but Gale only ducked.

Joe and Anna stooped below Pijeth's swishing tail before Gale reached back and yanked the spear from his shoulder.

Her stomach dropped.

No. It wasn't possible.

Nik had hit Gale. This insanity should all be over.

The stadium grew silent. Smoke rose from Gale's fist and a sickly, ashen smell hung in the air as he aimed the spear at Pijeth. Anna's grip on Joe's shirt tightened. The spear was burning the mammoth gray, but not enough. That had been their one and only chance at victory.

A howl echoed through the chamber as Nik jumped from the ledge above. He seemed to fall forever before he slammed onto Gale's back. Anna gasped as the *Kotahi* wheezed out a breath and shook his head as if he couldn't see.

Eyes blazing with fury, Gale turned toward the intruder as Nik scrabbled up the dragon's hide and wrapped his arms and legs around the monster's neck. Gale growled and spun, snapping at him.

The spear slipped from Gale's grip and clanked to the floor. Could they be so lucky?

Joe stepped back as the shimmering weapon rolled toward him.

Anna stopped it with her foot. She grasped the shaft, hefting the cool, dense metal with both hands. Her biceps stung from the exertion as Gale continued to spin, clawing at Nik.

"I can't throw it," Anna shouted over Gale's roar. "It's too heavy."

Joe reached for the shaft. As his fingers met the metal, he gasped and drew away, shaking his hand.

Gale stood on his hind legs, still trying to knock Nik off, when Pijeth reared up, shoving the larger dragon.

Anna's eyes widened as the drum of her heartbeat slowed in her ears. Her vision tunneled, focusing on the deep hole in the platform where her chains had disappeared into the floor.

"Help me!"

She hefted the weapon, dragging it across the ground as Gale faltered. Joe grabbed the shaft, grimacing as smoke and the nauseating stench of burned flesh rose from his grip. They reached the hole, shoved the aft of the spear into the floor, and held the humming rod steady as Gale stumbled towards them, drawn down by Nik's extra weight. The huge beast toppled back, and Joe tackled Anna to the floor as the colossus fell.

Gale's roar filled the stadium as Nik dropped off the gray's neck and rolled to safety before the spear pierced Gale's hide. The beast's momentum drove the weapon clear through his back and out his reptilian chest.

The gray convulsed, clawing at the metal and howling. Flames spewed from his mouth, igniting the air with the beast's fury. The dragons above roared and slammed on their perches, sounding like an army of horses charging into battle.

Smoke rose from the wound. Dark, boiling ooze bubbled down the dragon's gray hide until his arms and head dropped to the floor.

An eerie silence fell over the chamber.

Nik stood, favoring one leg.

On the far side of the room, Connor balanced against Shun's wing and clutched his stomach with his other arm.

Pijeth nudged Gale's body twice, then bellowed, shooting flame toward the ceiling. The room erupted in howls and Draconic prattle as three brilliant purple dragons hovered over the carcass, shooting what looked like water from their mouths, coating the former king with a sticky goo. Within seconds, Gale's skin bubbled and smoke rose into the heights of the theater. Anna covered her nose from the stench as the carcass shifted and oozed. The bones caved in on themselves, puddling into a thick black liquid that seeped into the floor and disappeared, leaving no trace of the former king.

It was over. He was actually gone.

The smell dissipated. Anna choked out a breath and grabbed Joe. He clung to her, shaking.

She tightened their embrace. When Gale flew her away from their mountain, she'd thought that was the end, that her own idiocy and stupid trusting nature had doomed herself and the Draconi. Then Joe had appeared like an avenging angel. Now they stood together on the same platform where she'd been bound, victorious.

The roar in the theater was deafening as a duo of gold dragons left their perches and slammed to the dais, shaking the ground.

Joe pushed Anna behind him.

"What's wrong?" she asked. "It's over. We won."

"No we didn't. I didn't kill Gale. Pijeth did."

Anna gaped. "But we held the dragon spear. He died because of us."

Joe shook his head. "It was Pijeth's battle. He toppled Gale, not us. They won't care who set the spear."

The largest of the golden brothers limped toward them, a menacing figure despite his injury. Two speckled gold guards held sentry at his flanks.

Joe's grip tightened as Pijeth's gaze hovered over them. The larger dragon took a step toward her, and Anna's blood iced.

She was still the dragon queen, and now she belonged to the wrong dragon.

There had to be a way out of this. They just needed a second to think it through.

The guard on Pijeth's right raked the floor with his talons.

Pijeth garbled something in Draconic and Joe released his grip on Anna.

She grabbed his shoulder. "What are you doing?"

"He's the king, Anna. It's over."

That's it? He wasn't even going to fight for her?

"Gale is dead and golds don't kill their mates." Joe looked back at her. "You're safe. That's all I ever wanted."

Her chest twisted. "But what about what I want?" She grabbed his hand. "Whatever this is between us, I don't get it, but think I lo —" She stopped herself, and a small part of her heart shattered. She'd been fighting her growing feelings for days, but now she wanted to cling to her little pale dragon forever. She never expected this thing between them to last, but if it had to end, she wanted it to be under their own terms, amicably, as they'd agreed. And if she had to stay, she wanted Joe, not this gold dragon she barely knew.

Pijeth erupted in a flash of light, shifting into his human form. He dropped to his knees, wincing and holding his thigh. He brushed off the two guards who tried to help him and stood on his own, managing to look regal even through the pain.

He held out his hand to Anna. "Do not fear me, my queen."

She recoiled. "No. I don't belong to you." She grabbed Joe's biceps, taking comfort in his warmth.

That comfort seemed so ethereal now, so frivolous. But it was something she wanted desperately. What she wouldn't give for one more night in his arms.

Pijeth eyed them both for a moment and smiled. Anna gritted her teeth, wishing she could scratch that smug grin off his face. Bastard.

The gold dragon turned and shouted into the cave's heights. "A new day dawns for all Draconia."

The room erupted in roars and sprays of fire. The crystal dragons sat quiet and still. If Anna's heart wasn't throttling so hard, she might feel sorry for them, coming so close against all odds, only to lose the throne on a technicality.

Pijeth lifted one arm, silencing the room. "Today, I take the honor bestowed upon me through right of combat." More cheers as he spun back to Joe and Anna.

Joe straightened. "I can't do this." He pulled Anna back behind him. "You're mine. I'm not giving you to another."

Her dragon quivered beneath her hands. What would happen to Joe if he didn't give her up? Would their stupid ancient rules require Pijeth to gut him publicly?

A shiver ran over her skin as she moved back to his side. She wouldn't let Joe sacrifice himself.

Pijeth's smile broadened.

"Quenor trusted you," Joe said.

Anna glanced at Connor, whose gaze darted between Joe and Pijeth. What would he do, if Joe and Pijeth came to blows?

A single, ear-shattering roar filled the theater. The ground quaked as a massive, tattered gray slammed to the ground. The beast considered those around him with one blazing yellow eye. A scar cut across the other, coating it with a milky film. It was obvious none took that as a handicap.

An elegant blue alighted by the gray's side and fluttered its wings in Nik's direction. The *Kotahi* straightened. A blush stained his cheek before the gray lumbered forward, blocking Anna's view.

The two golden guards beside Pijeth parted, bowing to the gray as he approached.

Joe's eyes reflected the megalith. His lip trembled slightly.

Anna tightened her grip. "What? Who is that?"

Joe gulped. "Ugaron, the Ancient One. The only living former king."

Jesus, was this guy going to stake a claim, too?

Pijeth, struggling against his limp, held his chin high and approached the beast. Pretty ballsy, when Ugaron could swallow someone in human form whole.

Joe tapped Anna's hand on his arm. "Ugaron is here to transfer power to the golds. The fighting is over."

Anna shivered and leaned her cheek on Joe's shoulder. He said he wouldn't give her up. What did that mean for him? *What did it mean for us?*

Connor stepped behind them, putting a hand on each of their shoulders. He tightened his grip when the gray's yellow eyes fixed on them.

Pijeth turned to them as well, that god-awful smile still leeched to his face. Anna's jaw clenched. That rat bastard had been planning this all along. He was just waiting for someone else to get her to the mountain so he could muscle his way in.

The scheming gold led the gray back to them. He gestured to Anna. "The blood right queen stands among us, Ancient One."

Anna took a step toward him. "And she is going to scratch your eyes out if you come any closer."

Pijeth's eyes widened before he laughed.

The bastard actually laughed!

Joe pulled her back. "Don't make this worse."

Ugaron leaned in and smelled her. She gagged on the stench of decay as the beast garbled something in Draconic.

Pijeth nodded.

Joe straightened as the section of gold dragons started howling. Two of them spit fire in the air.

Anna covered her ears. "What's going on?"

Conner pulled her tight to him. "He just said you smell like Joesephutus."

Joe's hands fisted. He took a step forward. "She is mine, Ancient One."

Several crystal dragons jumped into the arena. The two gold guards raised their wings and howled at them. Connor backed her away.

She thrashed in his grip. "Let me go."

He grunted before grabbing her face. "You are hurting me, but that will not stop me from keeping my promise to protect you."

Protect her? Anna's gaze shot back to the center of the arena. Ugaron bellowed into the sky, silencing the room.

Pijeth called his guards back as he faced Joe.

Anna refused to let this happen. She elbowed Connor in his injured stomach. He doubled over, dropping her. She sprinted back out and forced herself between Joe and the gold.

Pijeth's self-righteous grin returned as he grabbed her. "Take note, all those within the sound of my voice!" He faced up into the theater. "The Ancient One has confirmed the girl can carry the seed of the Draconi."

Screw this. She didn't give a damn that she had a special blood type. The gold was not her dragon. If Pijeth thought she was going to be an easy lay, he had another thing coming. She twisted and pulled, but he barely budged.

Pijeth's smile widened, and he whispered, "Feisty, an admirable quality in a queen." He shoved her into Joe's arms and raised his palms into the air. "The golden sept recognizes and accepts the crystal dragon's claim to the throne." He turned to Joe and bowed low at the hip, splaying his hands at his sides.

Joe tensed beneath Anna's touch.

The hush in the room hovered like a hatchet waiting to fall before Pijeth looked up.

Joe huffed out a breath. "Wh-what?"

"Place your hand on my head, boy. Quickly."

"But you won. The mountain is yours."

"And it is also mine to give away. I wasn't battling for the crown. I was keeping that murderous gray from killing another one of my brothers." His nose flared. "Now accept my offer before I change my mind."

Still trembling, Joe reached out and placed his hand on Pijeth's head. Anna breathed a sigh of relief.

The room erupted in a thunderous cacophony again as Ugaron touched his head to the floor at Joe's feet. Then the shimmering blue dragon beside him bowed, followed by the crystals that had jumped to the stage, followed more reluctantly by the golds.

Anna pressed her hand to her chest, holding back the joyous ache as dragon after dragon bowed to the gaping, wide-eyed, pale man beside her.

Cradling his now even more injured stomach, Connor limped to Joe and kneeled.

Joe made to stop him. "You don't bow."

Connor held up a palm. "Today, I bow. Tomorrow I will return to being a talon in your side, my king."

Anna's heart swelled. More shouts echoed through the room as Connor's head touched the floor.

Pijeth stood and reached out to shake his new king's hand. Joe showed the gold his blistered, bloodied fingers left from grasping the dragon spear. Pijeth smiled, spit into his palms, and rubbed Joe's wounds until they disappeared.

"Thank you." Joe accepted the older dragon's hand. "The crystal dragons recognize your sacrifice."

"You found the girl. The throne was always yours." The gold shrugged. "And I'm more the brute strength type than the ruling type. I think I could much better serve our people as the head of your guard."

Joe smiled. "I accept, with great honor."

Pijeth grabbed Joe's hand and thrust his fist into the air. "Our new king!"

The dragons around them roared in a deafening thunder that reverberated through the chamber. Joe pulled Anna tight to his side as dragons continued to make their way to the stage and bow.

The red baby dragon scuttled to the front of the assembly, followed by the adult who'd tried to help free Anna. The larger dragon shifted into a man with coppery hair and a beard.

The red bowed to Joe. "Please allow us the honor of removing the remainder of the queen's bonds. I'm sure a crystal dragon has no desire to have her shackled while you mate."

Joe's neck twitched. He glanced at Anna, then back to the red. "You're correct, but I'm sure we can find the key."

"True." The red placed his hand on the baby's head as the youngster sat and wagged his tail like an expectant puppy. "You will understand this more when your queen gives birth, but my fledgling wants to help. He'll be shattered if he can't finish what he was brave enough to start."

How adorable was that? Anna's heart warmed, despite the *giving birth* comment.

She held her wrist out to the baby. The chain dangled, the links massing on the floor. "I'd be honored for the help, little one."

The red smiled as the child started gnawing on the shackle. "You are going to be the greatest of queens. I'm overjoyed that we will get to know you."

Because if Gale won, the psychotic tyrant would have screwed her, tied her up somewhere until she gave birth, and then fed her to the baby. God, that was screwed up. Why had all of them allowed this to go on for so long?

The metal bracelet fell from her wrist with a clunk, and the baby jumped to the ring around her ankle. The child grunted and tugged, his tail wagging with excitement. He was kinda cute for something that would grow into a two-ton predator.

She wouldn't get to see him grow, though. Not if she left as planned. She looked up at the expectant faces around her, some human-looking, but mostly dragons. They hadn't dispersed after recognizing Joe. Probably because there was still one little matter to attend to that involved Anna and her womb.

Joe's brow furrowed as he watched the baby toil with the last shackle. He hadn't expected to take the crown. Now that it was his, would he backpedal on his promise? Would he keep her here and force her to have his child to placate their archaic customs?

The anklet popped and the baby savaged the metal as if giving a killing blow. The dragons roared and scraped their talons on the stone. The shifted dragons applauded.

Joe took a deep breath. His hands clenched and unclenched. Their gazes met. His crystalline eyes were wide and shaky. This was it, the moment she'd been dreading since she found out about the Seventeen Year.

A sharp pain started in Anna's throat and deepened. Joe wanted to let her go, she could tell, but now that they were here, he had no idea how to get her out of this.

The sound abated around them, until the onlookers stood in silence.

The red shooed the baby behind him and inclined his head to Joe. "There is the matter of impregnating the queen, Sire."

Joe drew in another breath. "I am aware of that." He took in the crowd before returning his gaze to Anna. "I will not take her publicly. This is an intimate moment, one I look forward to enjoying in private."

The dragons hummed and garbled over what must have been a huge change in tradition. Was Joe simply biding her time to escape, or had he decided to go through with this? She retreated a step.

Joe grabbed her wrist, pulling her back. He whispered in her ear. "I made you a promise, and I intend to keep it. Do you trust me?"

Did she trust the guy she only met a few days ago? The answer should be obvious, but it wasn't. Simply looking into Joe's eyes left her with an overwhelming calm and a sense of freedom. She moved closer and smiled.

The red lowered his chin. "May I suggest, Sire, that you take your queen back to your sept residence." His nose twisted. "I doubt you will find the condition of the royal chambers to your liking."

Anna cringed, imagining what horrors Gale left behind for them.

"Very well, then." Joe offered Anna his hand. "Shall we, my queen?"

AT THE TOP OF THE STONE STAIRS, ANNA AND JOE HESITATED AS A large, shimmering, white dragon landed on the platform and shifted. The man left within the sparkling flash had hair as white as Joe's and eyes only a touch darker.

Ignoring the fact that he was naked, the man embraced Joe. "You have done your sept proud, my son." He released Joe and bowed to Anna. "You will have to forgive us, my queen. We were not anticipating such esteemed company, and my mate and I have just completed a breeding cycle." He looked from Joe, back to Anna. "She needs to remain in dragon form for at least another hour. She will have to greet you as a dragon. I hope you understand."

Joe wrapped his arm around Anna. "I trust that means I can be expecting a brother soon."

A bluish hue touched his father's cheek. "That is our hope, yes." He looked down the hallway. "I will need to prepare your mother. When you didn't return the first night, we thought the worst. She doesn't even know you're alive." He hunched his shoulders, possibly embarrassed by that admission, before passing through the doorway and into the darkness.

Joe took Anna's hand. "These corridors are not made for human eyes. Let me guide you."

Within three steps the light disappeared as if someone had thrown a switch. Choking down her panic, and need to reach out and feel for the walls, she strode beside Joe until an open doorway bathed the dragon-sized hallway in light once more.

The moment they entered, a large silver snout touched noses with Anna. She froze, her breath hitched as Joe wrapped his arms around the dragon's neck and whispered to her.

The creature cooed in Draconic. Anna's heart warmed and she smiled. Who'd ever have thought such a massive, horrifying beast could be so affectionate?

When the dragon turned back to her guest, Anna waved her hand. "Umm, hi. It's nice to meet you."

The dragon ruffled her glossy, white mane and licked Anna's cheek. Anna cringed, but did her best to hide her disgust before the dragon bumped her toward the rear of the room.

Joe's father motioned them through a doorway. "We will do our best to give you both the privacy you ordered, my son. Please call out if you need anything."

"I will. Thank you." Joe dropped a thick, leathery door over the opening, blocking them inside. The room was a small cave not much larger than Joe would be in his dragon form. A small pile of trinkets glistened in one corner. The remainder of the room was filled with a huge pile of dried leaves and grasses with a well-worn dent in the center.

Anna found herself stepping away from what looked very much like a nest. "You said to trust you. I'm still trusting you."

Joe pulled her into his arms and rested her head on his shoulder. "As you should. I have no intention of going back on my word."

Her chest tightened. She'd made her wishes perfectly clear, but here they were, alone in his room and hugging beside his bed. She pulled him closer, taking comfort in his earthy smell as her muscles finally gave in and relaxed.

The rightness of it all should have sent her clambering for the exit. Instead, she stole another deep, content breath before leaning back. "All these feelings I have, are they mine, or are you doing something to me?"

Joe held out his hands in submission. "I haven't done anything intentionally, but you are my mate, whether or not we act on that." He glanced at the nest, big enough for ten people, let alone two. "It is possible that you're feeling the bond. I'm not really sure." He looked back at her. "I'm sorry having these feelings displeases you."

Her eyes shot open. "No, no, no. It's not like that. It's just..."

She felt her own gaze draw to the nest, wondering if it were comfortable, wondering how it would feel to lay in his arms within its simple embrace.

He drew a line with his fingertips across her collarbone, up her neck, and settled on her chin, tilting her face toward him. Those crystalline eyes seeped into her again, holding secrets she'd never discover.

She trembled as he placed slow, tender kisses along her cheek, her temple, and her ear. His lips were soft and tentative, but sure and strong. She drank him in, knowing this might be the only tender moment they'd spend together.

Joe released her, and smiled as he wiped a tear from her cheek that she didn't realize she'd shed. "My people need to believe we've mated. One more night is all I ask. Then I will bring you back to the village."

"Oh." She swallowed and dropped her gaze to the floor.

Her hands quaked as he drew her toward his nest. Her cheeks burned, realizing how comfortable she was with him in these strange surroundings, in everything about this guy and his foreign, mythical world.

Anna's chest ached as she snuggled into his shoulder and tried to commit to memory his smell, the strength of the arms wrapped around her, and how for the first time in her life, she felt safe.

CHAPTER 29

Brightly colored rooftops marked the town amongst the trees as a final gust of air wrapped around Anna. Shun fluttered his golden wings before setting her gently on the grass.

Anna grabbed her chest and took a deep breath of the warmer air on the ground. A few minutes into the flight, her terror subsided, but the lashing cold continued to berate her. She'd shouted a few questions to Shun, but he couldn't do much more than grunt in response.

Pijeth beat his massive wings as he set Joe beside her. He then alighted on a nearby boulder. Takata dropped Connor from a few feet up. The large man scowled, grabbing his already wounded abdomen while the dragon released a set of grunts that sounded quite a lot like laughter. If this were true, Connor was far from amused.

The two younger dragons settled on either side of their larger brother. Their muzzles angled across the small clearing and, from their vantage point, probably beyond.

Connor glared at them, rubbing his bandages before turning to Joe and Anna. "I'll wait over here and give you two a moment to..." He waved his hand between them, as if that summed up all the possible ways to end that sentence, before he backed away.

"Connor is going to take you the rest of the way to the town." Joe studied the dirt at his feet.

Anna's eyes widened. "Oh. I-I thought that..." Joe would take her to town. She'd hoped they could have a drink and talk for a few minutes, somewhere far from the dragonly chaos. This guy had, after all, saved her life, and then let her go when it was completely in his power to keep her prisoner.

What would happen, she wondered, when the other dragons realized she was gone, and Joe hadn't produced a child for them?

She took his hands in hers. "Can't you walk with us for a bit?"

Joe tilted his head towards the three dragons behind him. "My new security detail was quite adamant about me getting back right away. Something about me being too vulnerable to hostiles stuck in this form."

Hostiles, meaning humans. But she could understand. If they lost Joe, the grays would probably pounce and take back power. It was going to be a struggle as it was, let alone with Joe not being there to keep the peace.

"You've got a lot of work ahead of you, huh?"

"Yeah." His gaze rose to meet hers. He parted his lips to say more, but closed his eyes, the words lost.

Maybe because she'd stated the obvious. Maybe because right now, these few moments were theirs and theirs alone before they parted forever, and she couldn't find something nice to say to the guy who'd risked his life to save her. *You've got a lot of work to do.* How thoughtless.

But what *could* she say to make things right? "This is going to sound completely trite, but I'm going to miss you."

Joe took a deep breath and let it out slowly.

"I'm serious."

He smiled. "I know." He looked away again. "*Miss* isn't a strong enough word for what I'm feeling." His eyes were red when he turned back to her. "Do you really think things may have been different between us if we had more time to get to know each other?"

She was afraid he'd ask that again. And she was even more afraid of her answer, knowing the bond they now shared seemed to tie in to her emotions. She'd never be able to keep a secret from him, and for some reason that comforted her.

His gaze remained latched to hers, and she wondered if he was doing it now—reading her reactions, waiting for a lie.

Damn, his eyes were beautiful, the kind of beauty that dove deeper than simply their strange, icy color. The eyes were a window to the soul, as they always said. She'd never really understood what that meant until now. This boy, no—this man, now a king, would do anything for her. Her heart twisted, struggling within her chest as if fighting to stay behind.

But she wasn't a dragon. She couldn't fall in love that quickly. She couldn't make decisions that would affect her entire life just because she had the right blood type.

Joe's eyes narrowed for a moment before centering again. He could feel her struggle. She knew it. She also knew that his feelings stemmed far stronger than the need to reproduce. He wanted her mind and soul first. Everything else was secondary. And he was proving this by letting her go, giving up probably his one and only chance to have a child, and maybe even giving up the throne.

"Yes." The word left her lips before she was aware she'd uttered it. "Yes, I think things would have been different. And I wish they were." Her stomach knotted, joining her treasonous heart. She needed to leave before she changed her mind and did something stupid.

Joe took in another long, deep breath. "May I ask a favor?"

"Of course."

"I'd like to kiss you, just once. I know it's out of—"

"Yes."

She was beginning to sound like a trained puppy, but screw it. *Woof.*

Kissing him, of course, was probably the most foolish thing she could do. If the kiss was bad, it would ruin her memory of him. Even worse, if it was good, she'd stew over those lost sensations for the rest of her life. But she wanted to kiss him. If for any other reason, just to say thank you.

That's what she told herself, at least.

She hardened herself against her annoying conscience. Thank you and goodbye. That's all this was. "Yes," she reiterated. "I would love to give you a kiss."

Her breath hitched as Joe closed the distance between them with startling speed. He stroked her chin, smiling, and Anna was vaguely aware of Connor approaching behind her.

Joe's breath tickled her lips as he stared into her eyes. His gaze betrayed desires they'd never be able to share. Anna trembled, already mourning their loss as his lips touched hers. So soft. So hesitant.

Connor's hands grasped her shoulders, and she stiffened before Joe deepened the kiss. Berries and a hint of smoke overcame her senses as she gave in, opening to him, tingling as his tongue glided over hers. A sparkle shot through her, as if he'd breathed his dragon fire through her lips and into her soul. Heat reached down through her body, stinging and biting and digging, as if Joe seated part of himself into her core.

He drew away suddenly, holding her cheeks. "I love you," he whispered. "Always remember that, even when you've forgotten me."

Anna's world spun. Connor tightened his grip on her shoulders as her ankles buckled beneath her. The three dragons bellowed, their roars echoing through the sky. She blinked, struggling against Connor's hold as darkness crept in on all sides.

"Joe?" She reached for him, the only thing she could still see.

"Shhhh," he whispered. "I hope, one day, you'll forgive me for this."

All terror eased away, lost as if she fell into a tranquil void.

"You're sure you want to do this?" Connor's voice asked.

"Absolutely."

"You do realize this could end badly."

Anna waited for an answer that didn't come. Her body lifted into strong arms before the last of her consciousness faded away.

CHAPTER 30

The dragons in the boss's escort bellowed above the ledges that led to the king's chambers. Nik waited as Pijeth lowered Joe to the hidden balcony outside the royal meeting space. The large gold dragon grasped the enforced ledge as Joe spoke to him in hushed tones. The dragon nodded in a decidedly human way.

Nik shielded his eyes as the dust kicked up from Pijeth's massive golden wings as the dragon took back to the sky.

Joe spared Nik a glance before he strode deeper into the caves, eyes down and hands in his pockets. Saying goodbye to Anna had been agony for the new king. Nik had felt the pain firsthand, even though the village they'd flown Anna to was miles away.

Nik followed him inside. "You love her."

"What of it?" Joe picked up some sort of speckled rock and tossed it to the side. "I need to have someone come in here and get rid of all this." He waved his hand around the piles of trash and odd trinkets cluttering the floor.

"Don't change the subject."

"What subject?"

"Anna."

Joe finally graced Nik with his attention. "I let her go. Nothing else matters."

"It's me, remember? You can't hide what's really going on in your head."

Which was a whole lot of gut-wrenching regret. Nik got it, though. If you love someone, set them free and all that horseshit. Chivalry wasn't always good for the one being chivalrous.

He picked up a slab of what appeared to be rawhide. Not wanting to think what the hide may have been made of, he dropped it back to the table. "Trying to ignore how you feel isn't going to work."

Joe sighed. "It certainly would have been easier if I didn't have to think about her for the rest of her life."

The rest of *her* life? Just how long did dragons live?

"Are you seriously just accepting this? Do you think the dragons will accept this? They're not stupid."

"No, they're not, and you're right, there are certain expectations of a king."

And those expectations were pretty damn big. He was king because he brought back a girl. Now he was expected to do something with that girl.

"No offense, but if you lose the throne because you're a nice guy, then all of this was for nothing."

Joe threw another trinket over his shoulder. It landed on top of a pile before sliding to the floor. "I have no intention of losing the throne."

"Then how do you plan to keep it?"

Joe's gaze carried back to the ledge Pijeth had alighted on. "I'm a king, now, Nikau. Just because I stand here, with you, does not mean my plans aren't unfolding elsewhere."

CHAPTER 31

Smooth, cushy warmth enveloped her. Anna stretched and rubbed her eyes as soft light filtered through her bedside window.

Someone stirred next to her. "She's waking up!" a male voice called.

A guy?

She bolted upright, squinting in the light that now seemed a hell of a lot sharper. She lay in a queen-sized bed, the sheets gathered at her waist. Another queen-sized bed sat a few paces to her left, and a television sat on a table on the far wall.

She was in their hotel room. But...

A huge, dark shape loomed next to her, shrouded in the sunlight beaming through the window.

She blinked. "Who, where?"

The man grabbed her shoulder. "Take a deep breath. You've been through a lot." His thick New Zealand accent seeped into her, putting her instantly at ease.

"Oh my God, Anna!" Sybil flew toward her from the hallway and gathered Anna in her arms. "You scared the shit out of me. Are you okay?"

"Umm." *Was she* okay? Anna closed her eyes and breathed slowly. She was trembling, but she had no idea why. Anna leaned back. "What's wrong? Was I sick?"

The man sat on the edge of her bed. "The doctor said you had an acute case of dragon fever."

"Dragon fever?" She blinked a few more times, and his form finally took focus. Long, dark hair waved along the sides of an angular, solid face and eyes that felt like lances. "Who are you?" Anna asked.

Sybil rubbed her shoulder. "This is Connor, don't you remember? We met in that bar." Her hand stopped rubbing as her eyes met the stranger's. "He's been helping me through all this. It's been scary, you being gone. He's kept me *occupied*."

Anna cringed at her emphasis on the word occupied. Sybil and Connor shared a soft smile before Anna glanced at the rustled blankets on the bed beside her.

Gross! Had they *done it* while she was asleep in the other bed?

Connor placed his hand over Sybil's as he spoke to Anna. "The doctor said you'd be fine, and to let you rest."

"What doctor?"

Sybil's eyes widened. "It was the weirdest thing. Connor called for a doctor, and a second later the doorbell rang. You don't get service like that in America."

Connor massaged the back of his neck. "Doctor Pijeth said the condition needs to run its course, and it's normal to have some short-term memory loss." He leaned toward her. "What is the last thing you can remember?"

Anna twisted the white woven blanket in her fingers. Everything seemed so jumbled—like boxes of color scrambling through her head and trying to re-glue themselves.

"Last night, I guess. I remember going into the bar with Sybil." She looked at her sister, and then Connor. "Is that where she met you?"

Connor released a breath before a small smile formed that melted away in a blink. "Yes, it was."

Sybil's brow rose. "But that was almost a week ago. You disappeared right after."

A flash of heat swept over Anna's skin. "What?"

"Yeah, we were talking to Connor and that cute platinum blond, and all of the sudden you were gone." She closed her eyes and pinched the bridge of her nose. "Wait, that's not right. Something else happened."

Connor eased beside her and placed his arm around her shoulder. "Your sister had a bout with the fever as well, but it seems she only lost about an hour or two."

Sybil shook her head. "Something else happened. I remember being scared."

Connor rubbed her shoulder and spoke softly in Sybil's ear. "Of course you were scared, darling. The drinking glasses fell from the ceiling. My friend Joe stopped them from falling on your sister."

"Glasses?" Anna shivered. How could something like that happen without her remembering?

Sybil's thoughts seemed miles away. "Yeah, the glasses. That must be it." She raised her gaze to Anna. "Do you remember that? Do you remember Joe?"

"Joe?" The name felt familiar on her lips. A warmth spread over her, as if this person, Joe, was someone important to her. She reached into her mind, struggling to match the wonderful, sparkling feeling spreading through her to a face, but nothing appeared. "I don't know. I can't seem to remember."

"You left with him." Sybil glanced at Connor. "At least, that's what Connor told me. I can't really remember much more than being scared."

"Joe was going to show you the mountains," Connor said.

Anna narrowed her gaze. "I left with a guy I'd just met?" Bloody unlikely. But somehow, even with the huge void in her head, she knew that she'd go anywhere with Joe, that as long as she was with him, she'd be safe.

She pushed the thought from her head. This stinking fever must have affected her more than they all thought.

"Connor found you collapsed just outside of town and brought you back here."

"After being gone a whole week?" Anna's vision tunneled. She held her head. "That's crazy. What day is it?"

"It's Saturday."

Anna stared at her, waiting for a punchline that didn't come. "Are you telling me we're leaving tomorrow? I feel like I just got here."

Sybil looked at Connor. "About that." She returned her gaze to her sister. "Doctor Pijeth said that you are clear for air travel as long as you wake up within twelve hours of your flight, and you did. So, you should be fine. And, umm..."

Why was she hesitating? Could there be anything Sybil could tell her that would be worse than losing a week of her life?

Sybil cleared her throat. "I'm not flying back to The States. I'm staying here, with Connor."

Okay, maybe there was *one* thing. "Are you crazy?"

"A little, I guess." Sybil wove her fingers through Connor's. "But I think I've found something special here, and I want to give it a go."

Sybil lifted her chin in that *I've made up my mind and screw what everyone else thinks* way.

"What am I supposed to tell Mom?"

"Tell her the party girl is finally considering settling down."

In New Zealand.

A hundred gazillion miles away.

This wasn't going to go over well.

But Anna had to admit, there was a little something different about her sister. She seemed more—what was it—relaxed, poised, calm, sure of herself?

Whatever it was, she had to admit, it looked good on Sybil. Anna wasn't ready to trust this Connor guy, but she couldn't discount his effect on flighty Sybil.

Maybe New Zealand was just what her sister needed to finally grow up.

Unfortunately, Sybil's newfound adultism meant a fourteen-hour plane ride back to the USA, alone.

Maybe that would be a good thing. Maybe if Anna closed her eyes and thought long enough, she'd be able to remember all the time she'd lost.

Where in God's name had she been for a week?

And who was this mysterious Joe?

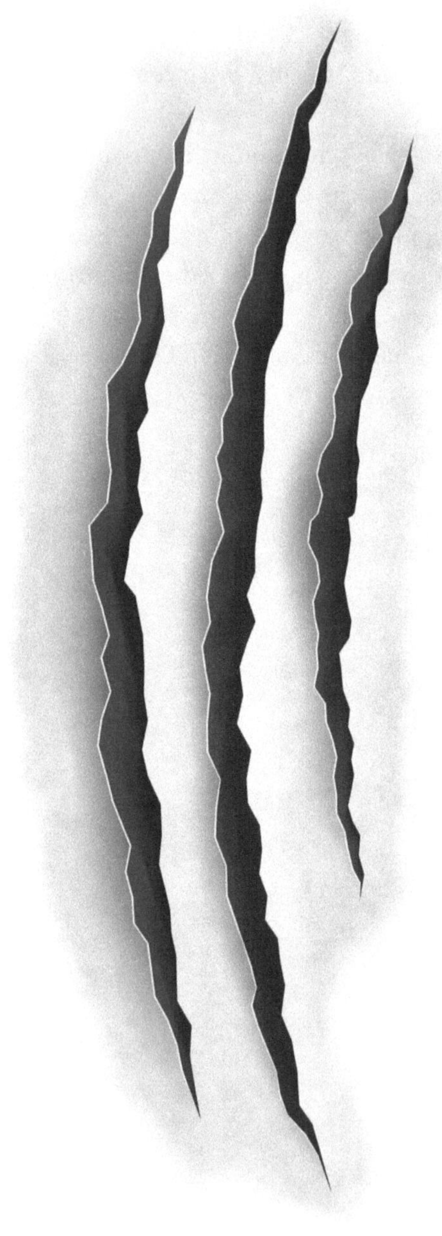

CHAPTER 32

*N*ik had been trying to wrangle a dragon to fly him home, but no matter which color he approached, they either ignored, laughed (if you could call that odd sound a laugh) or growled at him. One even had the gall to spit fire at his feet. He supposed the translator was only a valuable tool when there were humans around to translate for.

He stomped down the dragon-sized hallway toward the king's chamber. Well, at least he *tried* to stomp. The stone barely made a noise as he slammed his feet against the floor.

The small yellow dragon standing sentry opened the door as he approached. Good thing, because he was pretty much poised to hand out a bucketful of whoopass at this point, even if his opponent could burn him alive with its breath.

On the far side of the chamber, Joe threw something into a pile. He grabbed a box from the shelf and dusted it off, not even looking up at Nik. "You've been trying to secure passage down the mountain."

That stopped Nik in his tracks. He'd thought Joe had completely forgotten about him. He relaxed his stance. "Yeah. I figured I'd outstayed my welcome."

Joe looked up. "How so?"

"I'm human, remember?" He pointed a thumb over his shoulder. "And not all those dragons out there seem friendly."

"Are you alive?"

Nik narrowed his eyes. "Yeah."

"Then trust me, they're being friendly." He tossed the small box on the pile. "Since you are so eager to leave, tell me, what are your plans once you get down the mountain?"

Nik shifted his weight. He hadn't had any plans at first, but the more trouble he had securing passage off this rock, the more he realized that he needed to get back to civilization. It was time to grow up. He was done being the perpetual child.

Joe arched a brow, waiting for an answer.

Nik shrugged. "I don't know. Get a job, for starters. I can't keep freeloading off my grandparents. I need to be my own man, take accountability—hell, maybe even become someone Nanna and Pops can be proud of."

"They're already proud of you, and you know it." Joe snatched a clear, blue stone from the floor and held it up to the flickering torchlight.

"Yeah, but I guess I need to be proud of myself, too. I need to find my place in the world." Funny, he'd never really thought about having a place in the world. Living was just what you did day by day, doing the same things. He'd never really wanted more than a job to pay the bills, and a house he could call his own. But now he wondered if there was a way to get more out of life.

Joe tossed the stone in the air and caught it. "I'd like to show you something." He headed for the exit without checking to see if Nik followed. How *kingly* of him.

Nik trailed after him through the dragon-sized door and through another dragon-sized, stone hallway. Everything about Dragon Mount made him feel dwarfed, despite walking beside Joe, who didn't seem dwarfed at all, even though he was nearly six inches shorter than Nik.

They turned into a narrower hallway, and stopped short, blocked by a blue dragon. Startled, Nik retreated a step, but the boss barely budged as the creature shrank into human form and pushed back her long, dark hair.

Nik's lips parted, taking in Naked Lady in all her God-effing-damn glory.

She dropped to her knees, arms splayed. "Forgive me, my king. It was not my intention to be in your presence in dragon form."

Joe huffed out a breath. *They've been doing this all over the mountain. Apparently Pijeth decreed it rude to be a dragon in my presence until I can shift again.* He looked back at the girl. *I think they all expect me to lash out like Gale.*

Do you blame them? You gotta admit, Gale was a dick.

The girl didn't move. Her dark hair shrouded her face and hid her beautiful chest. What. A. Shame.

Joe pulled her to her feet. "Please, bowing isn't necessary."

"I apologize for the intrusion, my king, but I have been looking for your *Kotahi.*"

Nik's eyes widened. "Me?"

She smiled and took a step toward him. Yeah, she was definitely still naked.

"When you jumped off the ledge and onto Gale's back, that was courage like I've never seen from a human."

Courage? Maybe, if he ignored the part where he almost puked.

She turned back to Joe. "I want him."

Joe's brow shot up.

Nik coughed. "Come again?"

"You interest me, human. Male dragons are not the only ones who like to play."

Sweet God. Please, please, please make her be talking about what I think she's talking about.

Joe laughed, blushing. "Forgive me, but I do believe you need to be looking for a Draconic mate. We have no shortage of males."

She straightened, pushing out that spectacular rack.

Thank you, boss, for ticking off the beautiful girl.

"I would never fly circles around my duty." She grabbed Joe's hand and pressed it to her bare stomach.

His gaze shot to hers. "You're already clutching. Congratulations. Who's the father?"

"Blues do not concern ourselves with trivialities. There were five males in my nest, all strong and healthy."

Five? Damn.

"I hunger for something else now." She turned from Joe and ran her fingers through Nik's hair. "You will come to me. Tomorrow, when our king no longer needs your service."

Did the air just suck out of the room? "I-I…"

Joe folded his arms. "My *Kotahi* is planning on leaving. He may be gone tomorrow."

Her eyes narrowed. "Then I will have him tonight."

Joe laughed outwardly.

Her nose flared. Damn, that was sexy. *But can we stop pissing her off, now?*

Boss grabbed her shoulder. "I have some business with my *Kotahi*. Once we are done, if your offer interests him, I will have him brought to the blue sept. Is this agreeable?"

She nodded. "Of course, my king."

Joe shoved Nik past her. *Sorry about that. Blues are very…*

Straightforward?

Joe smiled. "That's a way of putting it."

"I'm certainly not complaining."

A soft blush still flashed over boss's cheek. Hopefully he wasn't poking around in Nik's head, because when Naked Lady dropped to her knees back there…

Dammit, he should have asked her name.

A slick sheen of dread drifted across their bond, blotting out thoughts of the beautiful, candid blue dragon licking his neck, chest, and lower. Joe's mind thickened, even darker now than when they planned their strategy against Gale.

That shouldn't be a surprise, though. He was a king without a queen. No matter how much he trusted the golds, the fact that Anna was gone wouldn't stay secret forever.

The hall opened into a larger room devoid of furnishings with a colossal wooden door on the far side guarded by two black dragons. The huge beasts quickly bowed and made way for Nik and Joe, one pushing the massive door open for them.

Joe grabbed a torch from the wall and one of the dragons ignited the tip for him. Once inside, Joe lowered the flame into a small circular font, and the fire took on a life of its own, running along a channel, up the walls, and through the ceiling until the entire chamber exploded in light.

Squinting against the sudden glare, Nik gaped. The brightness wasn't all caused by the flames. The room glinted with shimmering piles of gold towering over Nik's head. Ancient trinkets mixed with what appeared to be doubloons littered the floor. There had to be millions, hell, billions of dollars in artifacts let alone gold.

"Ho-lee-shit."

"Yeah, what can I say? Dragons like shiny things." Joe set the torch into a holder on the wall and turned to Nik. "I have a proposition for you."

Nik drew his gaze away from the mountains of treasure. "A proposition?"

Joe tossed the blue stone he'd taken from the royal chambers into a pile of glistening gems. "I'm not crazy about this human form. I'm little enough as it is." He held out his arms. "But this is pushing it."

Nik inched up his brow. What was boss getting at?

"I want to open up lines of communication with the humans. I don't want to hide anymore. We're going to make ourselves known, and I want to do it as a dragon."

Holy hell!

"Boss, that is *not* a good idea. People are going to panic. I don't know if you realize this, but dragons are pretty goddamn scary." He pointed out the door. "And humanity has changed a lot out there. It's not spears you need to worry about, now. It's guns, and missiles, and nuclear bombs."

"That's why I want to officially hire you as an interpreter. I need the humans to see that you are comfortable with us. You can explain there has been a transfer of power, and that we're not a threat."

But the dragons *were* a threat. At least humanity would see it that way. There was no way the world leaders would stand for not being at the top of the food chain anymore.

"Consuming humans is illegal. It has been for generations."

Nik balked, still not used to this short, blond guy reading his thoughts. Joe needed to understand that even the fact that there *was a law* against eating people would make parents hide their children under their beds at night. "I seriously think you should reconsider."

"Your objection is noted. When I take my proposition to the Draconi, you should feel free to voice your opinion. I hope you will stay long enough for the proceedings."

Nik breathed a sigh of relief. Proceedings meant he was going to take time and talk this out with someone. He wasn't thinking of flying into downtown Auckland tomorrow and saying '*Hi, we're here!*'

Jesus, the hysteria it would have caused.

"I understand your concerns. I have them, too. But the Draconi have been trapped in this mountain long enough." He picked up a golden pitcher and placed it in Nik's hands. "I hope you can understand my position, and I hope I can convince you to stay on."

The firelight flickered off the ancient artifact. Was it Incan? Egyptian?

"It's yours," Joe said.

Nik startled.

"Not enough?" Joe reached into the pile and grabbed a fistful of gold coins. A red-stoned necklace hung from his fingers as well. "How about now?"

Nik snapped his jaw shut. "You're serious. You're talking about a job, a *paying* job?"

Joe nodded. "Do we have an agreement?"

Nik gaped at the gold in Joe's hand. That might be enough for a down payment on a house. A big house. But there was also an enormous catch to all that glitter, as there always was.

Joe had every intention of outing the dragons and Nik knew there was no talking him out of it. This young king was ready to take caution to the wind to set his people free. As frightening as the prospect was, Nik was kinda proud of him for stepping up. Maybe the kid was more of a leader than either of them had realized.

No matter what happened, this was going to be the event of the century, and New Zealand would be at the heart of it all. Every country in the world would flock here to gauge the threat and make alliances. To pass this offer up would be turning his back on the opportunity of a lifetime.

"So, you accept, then?"

Let's see, a real, honest-to-goodness job, one that would make a difference to the world, let alone himself; or go back to scrolling through job postings and maybe get hired as a cashier or a stock clerk.

The easy road would be to stay the person he'd always been, to lead a normal life and live paycheck to paycheck like everyone else.

The hard option would be to accept. Yes, it seemed the money would be good, but was Nik ready for this kind of responsibility? He'd be thrown into the spotlight. For the first time in his life, he'd actually be accountable for something. Was he really the right man to place so much trust in?

Joe stood, unwavering. The fistful of gold still shimmered in his hand.

The new king obviously believed in him. There was no apprehension slithering through their *Kotahi* bond. The young dragon had made his choice, and that decision was already final.

Joe's conviction seemed odd since they barely knew each other. Then again, they'd been living in each other's heads for the past week. They probably knew each other better than anyone else at this point.

And that was an interesting fact, come to think of it. Despite seeing inside Nik's royally effed-up brain, Joe still trusted him. The kid hadn't considered anyone else for the position, and he never would. For some odd reason, they were both completely comfortable with that.

Not to mention that there was a beautiful blue dragon waiting for him somewhere in this mountain. Yeah, that part of the equation was a little hard to overlook.

Nik smiled. "When do I start?"

A wave of relief ricocheted off Joe and into Nik. "We'll meet with all septs of the Draconi in a few weeks." Joe dropped the gold into Nik's ancient pitcher. The coins clinked as they settled at the bottom. "In the meantime, I have a very important matter to take care of."

nna clutched her carry-on as she stared at the screen displaying flight departures. One by one, the times faded out and were replaced by the word *delayed*.

And then *bloop*! There it was, flight 128 to Houston: *delayed*.

A collective groan resounded through the terminal, and she agreed. Changing all the departure times without any explanation was downright rude. Would an estimate of what *delayed* meant be too much to ask for?

The flight at the top of the list changed to *canceled* and the passengers held a collective breath until a moment passed and the rest remained simply *delayed*.

What would she do if her flight got cancelled? A fourteen-hour flight was bad enough. Now she'd have to spend even more time finding another flight with everyone else who was stranded here. Not to mention finding another connecting flight to get to Philadelphia. What a nightmare.

And how in God's name was she supposed to get her luggage back?

Adjusting the bag on her shoulder, she made her way past the complaining passengers until she found a restaurant that hadn't yet been trounced with angry, anxious travelers.

She took a seat at the bar.

"What can I get you?" the barkeep asked.

"Ginger ale would be great, thanks."

Above, the television screen flicked to a reporter standing in front of a fire. The caption below read: *Christchurch International Airport.*

Her jaw fell open. She was sitting in Christchurch International Airport. What the hell?

The guy at the other side of the bar yelled, "Hey, turn that up."

The barkeep complied.

The reporter held a finger in one ear as wind hit her from the side. "And, as you can see, the flames are spreading. Airport personnel have confirmed every single runway is on fire and all arrivals and departures have been either delayed or cancelled."

Well, that certainly explained things.

The man bussing the tables threw a towel over his shoulder. "My son was working the runways when the fires started. He said it was dragons."

The people within earshot laughed.

"Well, hello." A guy with shoulder-length platinum blond hair slipped onto the barstool beside Anna before turning to the man. "Dragons, you say? Did he get any pictures?"

The busser grimaced. "No. My boy said they suddenly disappeared as soon as they'd come." He straightened. "I believe him, though. My son is not a liar."

The guy at the other end of the bar piped in, "I saw some pictures of a few nudists running from the flames. I bet they'll have some interesting stories to tell the police, if the cops ever catch 'em."

The platinum-blond leaned around Anna. His nearness seeped through her, as if his heat reached out and staked a claim. Disconcerted, she inched away.

"So, the nudists weren't caught, then?" he asked.

"Nah. Slippery little naked bodies. Lucky suckers."

The blond suppressed a grin. "Good to know."

The reporter on the screen continued. "Amazingly, there seems to be no damage to the buildings, or people. Somehow this fire has been completely contained, harming nothing more than surrounding grass, and flight plans."

She said that as if grounding every flight in an international airport was no big deal. Anna had already been through security, and her bags were out there waiting to be loaded into a plane that probably wouldn't take off anytime soon. She was trapped, and things in this airport were probably about to get ugly.

When would Air Traffic Control decide which planes would remain delayed, and which would be completely canceled?

"What can I get you, bro?" the bartender asked the blond.

He glanced at Anna's glass. "Whatever she's having looks good."

"I'm guessing these fizzies will start being spiked before the night is out." He drew the soda and handed it to the guy. "Where you headed?"

The blond gestured to Anna. "The lady and I are on our way to Philadelphia, by way of Houston, Texas. Flight 128."

Wait. What? "How do you know I'm going to Philadelphia?"

His eyes narrowed as he considered her for a moment. "So, it's true, then. You really don't remember?"

Anna leaned away. "How do you know I—"

"Connor told me."

She felt her jaw drop. "Connor?"

The guy took a few seconds, staring into her eyes. "You really don't remember anything at all—not even the bar?"

Anna shook her head.

"Well, then, this is a little uncomfortable, isn't it?"

He took a sip of his drink, but Anna was sure he was hiding a smile. "Who are you?"

He set his glass down. "Well, I suppose that would help a bit." He offered his hand. "My name is Joesephutus, but you call me Joe."

She stared at his outstretched hand. This was the guy Connor and Sybil said she'd been with all week. "You're Joe?"

He nodded.

And he was here. Now.

On his way to Philadelphia.

Apparently with her.

The light from the artificial candle on the bar flickered across his face. The firelight seemed somewhat familiar on his very pale skin. How could she not remember any of this? "What happened all week? Where were we?"

He pushed back his drink and turned to her. "Well..." A smile crossed his lips. "You were kidnapped by a huge, ugly gray dragon who wanted to make you his mate. I saved you, and then we spent a few nights in a magical, Maori cavern before I returned you to your village."

She stared at him for a moment. "No, seriously."

He only smiled wider.

"That's a nice story." Anna took a sip of her drink. The bubbles tickled her nose. "Are you going to tell me what really happened?"

He held up his hands. "That's the gist of it. I'm sorry you don't remember." He tapped his finger on the edge of the glass. "No, that's not the truth." He turned to her. "I'm not sorry that you don't remember, because now I get to fall in love with you all over again."

Hol-ee. "Love?"

He continued to look at his glass. "I'm going to be honest with you, Anna."

Thank God, because the whole getting saved from a dragon thing was a bit far-fetched.

"You told me it was too soon to be in love."

Well, at least she'd been in her right mind while she'd been with him. Love wasn't as simple as everyone made it out to be. Her feelings for Andrew had grown over time. Years. She'd never been the type to fall in love on a whirlwind vacation, and she didn't expect to turn into that type in the future.

However, here this guy was, sitting beside her. "If we weren't in love, then why are you coming back to Philly with me?"

He shrugged. "I didn't say we weren't in love. I said *you* weren't in love. Not yet, at least." He glanced at the fires on the television screen before returning his gaze to her. "You said you wished we had more time. So I'm giving it to you."

That sounded a lot like her. If she didn't like him at all, though, she would have told him to take a flying leap off the nearest cliff. Apparently that didn't happen.

Would she be that careless, though, especially after the Andrew disaster?

Andrew.

For months that name had brought her nothing but agony. But now, it was meaningless… just another word.

When she'd arrived in New Zealand she'd still been broken. She couldn't imagine her life without him.

But now… nothing.

How could she have gone from utter desolation to indifference in a week?

Her gaze carried along Joe's sculpted shoulders before meeting his striking eyes.

With Andrew, it was all about what *she* could do for *him*. How *she* could make his life easier. That was all Anna knew.

But this guy, a man she just met, was more than ready to get on a plane for her. Whatever had happened between them must have been huge. At least to him. Too bad he was hiding behind a ridiculous story about a dragon.

Anna looked away. "This is stupid. I feel like I don't even know you."

Joe placed a finger on her chin and eased her gaze back to him.

"Like I said, this just gives us the opportunity to fall in love all over again."

She sat back, struck by the sincerity in his eyes. That wasn't a cheap come-on. He meant it. Her heart took flight in her chest, as if part of her were ready to soar with him in the sky. But that was irrational, wasn't it?

The bartender stared at a computer screen. "Looks like you'll have plenty of time." He looked up at them. "Flight 128 to Houston just hit the cancelled list, with about a dozen others."

The traffic outside the restaurant shifted, the people switching stream and now heading out of the terminal. They probably had the right idea. All this lunacy aside, Anna still needed to find a way home and get on with her life.

"Can I get my check, please?" Anna asked.

"Your check?" Joe asked.

"Yeah, I need to find another flight."

Panic lit Joe's eyes. She turned away, again. Whatever had happened between them, he needed to understand that she couldn't even remember meeting him, let alone spending the week together.

The bartender handed her a bill. "Right now you'll be rushing to wait in line with everyone else. Trust me, they won't have this sorted out for hours. No one is going anywhere."

Joe tapped his knuckles on the bar. "He's right." He turned to Anna. "How about we have some dinner?" He gestured to an empty table. "This probably won't be as romantic as roasting rabbit over a campfire, but it will have to do."

Anna rolled her eyes. This story just got deeper and deeper. As if she'd actually eat something they'd just caught out in the mountains. Something about the thought, though, made her sigh, as if she could feel the fire warming her face.

That was crazy, though. She didn't even like camping.

But what had they been doing out there, and how did she catch this crazy dragon fever?

He slipped his fingers around hers and drew her from her barstool. Even his touch felt familiar, strong, and unbelievably right.

He led her to a table in the back as a few other travelers filtered into the restaurant. She told her feet to stop moving, that she should be more worried about flight plans than eating, but something drew her along. There was such a sense of ease about Joe, like she'd known him forever.

He pulled out her chair and she sat as he took his place opposite her. His long tresses framed his face in soft waves that were closer to white than blond, and his large, knowing eyes were light blue, nearly crystalline. He almost didn't look real. A smug smile crossed his lips.

Anna blushed, hiding her eyes. "I'm sorry for staring. You must get that a lot."

His smile widened. "I do, actually, when I visit the city. Where I come from, everyone looks like this. Well, at least everyone in my clan does."

Did that mean the hair, the eyes, or those etched features? He almost looked Elven: all grace and perfection. She'd have to convince him to pose for a selfie before they parted ways.

Her breath hitched as a pain twisted in her chest. Why did the thought of leaving—of leaving him, suddenly put her in a panic? She had to go home, didn't she?

The word *no* exploded in her head. She gasped.

Joe reached across the table and caressed her hand. "Are you all right?"

As soon as their fingers met, she relaxed, as if his touch made everything wrong in the world okay. That was ludicrous, though.

She massaged her temples. "I feel so strange."

"Dragon fever can do that to you."

She drew her hand back. "Do you know anything about dragon fever? Will I get my memory back?"

"It's different for everyone, but even if you don't remember…"

He reached for her hand again. His touch was so gentle, so warm. "We can create new memories."

She smiled. "I don't think we'll be able to create anything as exciting as you saving me from a dragon."

"Maybe not." He wove his fingers through hers. "But I'm really looking forward to trying."

The sincerity in his gaze drew her in, lulling her into the deepest sense of ease she'd ever experienced. Andrew's eyes had always been somewhat distant, as if his mind was elsewhere.

Joe was here emotionally as well as physically, and his every thought, his every concern, was her. She trembled as the hugeness of that swept over her, but then she eased back into the ethereal rightness.

The familiarity in his touch, the warmth she felt simply from being in his presence—was it possible that her body remembered what her mind had forgotten?

Her chest thickened, and a deep ache settled at the base of her throat. There were emotions there, sitting on the edge of her psyche, waiting to be tapped. Strong emotions for a guy she couldn't even remember.

A stream of guilt flooded her, and her eyes blurred with tears.

Joe tightened his grip on her. "What's wrong?"

She tried to pull away, but he only gripped harder.

"What's wrong?" She puffed out an ironic breath. "Everything is wrong. You, me, everything."

She dropped her forehead onto her other palm. Dammit! Why couldn't she remember?

Anna raised her gaze. "I felt something for you. I know I did. I just can't remember what." She closed her eyes and swallowed. "I feel horrible that I can't recall…" *How safe I felt in your arms, how you listened when I prattled on, how your heartbeat lulled me to sleep at night.*

Anna shivered at the memory. No, not really a memory, but the sensation of a memory. She'd slept beside him, and she'd never slept so soundly. She suddenly yearned to pull his arms around her, to bask in his warmth, to drink him in and never let go.

Everything he'd said was true. Well, maybe not the part about saving her from a dragon, but she'd get the truth about that later. Anna looked into his eyes, and her heart leapt when she saw the raw emotion there, the heat, the undeniable adoration. She didn't know how it had happened, but they were in love.

She couldn't go back to Philadelphia. Not now, at least. If she went home, if she took *him home*, they'd be sightseeing and running around and meeting people. That wasn't the way to get to know Joe again. She needed to know everything, and to find out why these intense feelings existed.

More people filed into the restaurant, looking for a place to stay until they figured out their flight plans. It wasn't right for her and Joe to use this table when they weren't going anywhere.

She stood. "Let's go. I don't want to have dinner here."

Joe rose slowly. The pained, frightened expression returned to his eyes. "Wh-why not?"

"I want you to show me the mountains. I want to eat at a campfire. I want to see this magic cave." She wanted it all. Everything. Like he'd said, she wanted to fall in love with him all over again.

A smile burst across his lips. "What about getting home to your dog?"

Her mom could watch Dixie for a few more days. Anna had another week of vacation coming to her, and she couldn't think of a better way to use it.

Joe was right, though. She needed to think about her little pooch. "Do you like dogs?"

Joe grimaced. "I don't have a problem with dogs, but they don't tend to like me."

"Seriously?"

"Yes. They tend to run away." His lips turned up slightly. There had to be a story behind that adorable grin.

"That won't happen with Dixie. She loves everyone."

Anna thought about the hissing-barking incident last year when her neighbor's iguana got loose. That hadn't gone over well.

As long as Joe didn't have a big pet lizard they would do just fine.

She took a deep breath. "I'll have to call my mom and let her know." She grabbed Joe's hands and gazed deep into his spectacular eyes. "I'm staying." At least for now, but the rustling inside her left her wondering if *for-now* would end up *for-ever*.

Joe's smile reached deep into her heart, swirling up all the emotions hidden inside and basking her in a warmth that trumped all worries of her life back home. Something new skittered on the edge of the horizon.

Something exciting.

She hugged Joe's arm, her heart thumping in anticipation of starting fresh, experiencing new things, and falling in love with this amazing person all over again.

Maybe finding a guy in New Zealand wasn't so crazy after all.

Did you enjoy flying through the clouds? Well, how about a race through space? If you love Joe, you'll flip for David, a teenaged extraterrestrial pilot stranded on Earth.

Pick up FIRE IN THE WOODS and help Jessica outsmart the Army in a race to get David home.

A sneak peek at the first five chapters is included at the end of this book.

By the way,
Thanks for reading!
I hope you enjoyed the book.
Dragon Kisses!

ACKNOWLEDGMENTS

Writing Dragon Mount to a strict 6 month deadline was like a roller coaster ride. Thanks to the Sisterhood of the Traveling Pens and the MNBKA Authors for listening to me whine and for cheering me on to the finish line. Big, sloppy dragon kisses, ladies.

My family never ceases to amaze me with their support. Yes, you can be jealous—My husband cooks and cleans to make sure I stay on schedule. Thanks for giving me the support to keep typing. And typing. And typing.

Thanks to Anna and Jenny for beta reading in high speed chunks. Sorry for the rush, ladies. This was a tight one, and you guys totally stepped up to the plate.

Sharon, thanks for swooping in on the edge of a dragon's tail after the soft release, and confirming what I knew was true. Everyone who likes the new cut-to-the-chase beginning… that's thanks to Sharon. Dragon snuggles!

Victoria Cooper rocked the cover art. You totally brought Anna to life. And thank you for not taking offense that the first dragon looked like he was about to bite Anna's face off. [Giggle-giggle, snort]

And finally, the last eyes on this Draconic tome: Tandy Boese of Tandy Proofreads... because the Good Lord gave me a gift to tell a tale, but did not grant me with the ability to spell, nor the skill to place a comma in the right spot. Ever.

You know what... while I'm doing all this mushy stuff... THANK YOU for reading. Without you, none of this would be worthwhile. Dragon hugs!

ABOUT THE AUTHOR

Jennifer M. Eaton hails from the eastern shore of the North American Continent on planet Earth. Yes, regrettably, she is human, but please don't hold that against her.

While not traipsing through the galaxy looking for specimens for her space moth collection, she lives with her wonderfully supportive husband, three energetic offspring, and a duo of poodles who run the spaceport when she's not around.

During infrequent excursions to her home planet of Earth, Jennifer enjoys long hikes in the woods, bicycling, swimming, snorkeling, and snuggling up by the fire with a great book; but great adventures are always a short shuttle ride away.

Read more from Jennifer M. Eaton

www.jennifereaton.com

By
Jennifer M. Eaton

CHAPTER 1

The walls shook. My favorite sunset photograph crashed to the floor. Again.

Why the Air Force felt the need to fly so low over the houses was beyond me. Whole sky up there, guys.

I picked up the frame and checked the glass. No cracks, thank goodness. I hung the photo back on the wall with the rest of my collection: landscapes, animals, daily living, the greatest of the great. Someday my photos would be featured in galleries across the country. But first I had to graduate high school and get my butt off Maguire Air Force Base.

One more year—that's all that separated me from the real world. The clock wasn't ticking fast enough. Not for me, at least.

Settling back down at my desk, I flipped through the pages of August's National Geographic. Dang, those pictures were good. NG photographers had it down. Emotion, lighting, energy …

I contemplated the best of my own shots hanging around my room. Would they ever compare?

Another jet screamed overhead.

Stinking pilots! I lunged off the chair to save another photo from falling. The entire house vibrated. This was getting ridiculous.

Dad came in and leaned his bulky frame against my door. "Redecorating?"

"Not by choice." I blew a stray hair out of my eyes. "Are they ever going to respect the no-fly zone?"

"Unlikely."

"Then next time you have my permission to shoot them down."

"You want me to shoot down a multi-million-dollar jet because a picture fell off the wall?"

"Why not? Isn't that what the Army does? Protect the peace and all?" I tried to hold back my grin. Didn't work.

He grimaced while rubbing the peach fuzz he called a haircut.

So much for sarcasm. "It was a joke, Dad."

A smile almost crossed his lips.

Come on, Dad. You can do it. Inch those lips up just a smidge.

His nose flared.

Nope. No smile today. Must be Monday—or any other day of the week ending in y.

The walls shuddered as the engines of another aircraft throttled overhead, followed by an echoing rattle.

Dad's gaze shot to the ceiling. His jaw tightened. So did mine. Those planes were flying way too low.

My stomach turned. "What—"

"Shhh." His hand shot out, silencing me. "That sounds like ..." His eyes widened. "Jessica, get down!"

A deafening boom rolled through the neighborhood. The rest of my pictures tumbled off the walls.

Dad pulled me to the floor. His body became a human shield as a wave of heat blasted through the open window. A soda can shimmied off my desk and crashed to the floor. Cola fizzled across the carpet.

My heart pummeled my ribcage as Dad's eyes turned to ice. The man protecting me was no longer my father, but someone darker: trained and dangerous.

I placed my hand on his chest. "Dad, what..."

He rolled off me and stood. "Stay down."

Like I was going anywhere.

As he moved toward the window, he picked up a picture of Mom from the floor and set it back on my dresser. His gaze never left the curtains. How did he stay so calm? Was this what it was like when he was overseas? Was this just another day at the office for him?

The light on my desk dimmed, pulsed, and flickered out. The

numbers on the digital alarm clock faded to black. That couldn't be good.

Were we being attacked? Why had we lost power?

The National Geographic slid off my desk, landing opened to a beautiful photograph of a lake. The caption read: *Repairing the Ozone Layer*. I would have held the photo to the light, inspected the angle to see how the photographer achieved the shine across the lake—if the world hadn't been coming to an end outside my window.

I shoved the magazine away from the soda spill. My heartbeat thumped in cadence with my father's heavy breathing. "Dad?"

Without turning toward me, he shot out his hand again. My lips bolted shut as he drew aside the drapes. From my vantage point, all I could see were fluffy white clouds over a blue sky. Nothing scary. Just regular old daytime. Nothing to worry about, right?

"Sweet Mother of Jesus," Dad muttered, backing from the window. His gaze shot toward me. "Stay here, and stay on the floor. Keep the bed between you and the window." His hands formed tight fists before he dashed from the room.

Another plane soared over the roof, way too close to the ground. My ceiling fan swayed from the tremor, squeaking in its hanger.

I trembled. Just sitting there—waiting—it was too much. I clutched the gold pendant Mom gave me for my birthday. If she was still with us, she'd be beside me, holding my hand while Dad did his thing—whatever that was.

But she was gone, and if all I could do was cower in my room while Dad ran off to save the world again, I might as well forget about photojournalism right now.

Wasn't. Gonna. Happen.

Taking a deep breath, I crawled across the floor and inched up toward the windowsill. Sweat spotted my brow as my mind came to terms with what I saw.

Flames spouted over the trees deep within the adjacent forest, lighting up the afternoon sky. The fire raged, engulfing the larger trees in the center of the woods. I reached for my dresser to grab my camera and realized I'd left it downstairs. *Figures.*

I gasped as the flames erupted into another explosion.

The photojournalist hiding inside me sucker-punched the frightened teenager who wanted to dash under the bed. This was news. Not snapping pictures was out of the question. I flew down the stairs. The ring of the emergency land-line filled the living room as I landed on the hardwood floor.

Dad grabbed the phone off the wall. "Major Tomás Martinez speaking."

The phone cord trailed behind him as he paced. His fingers tapped the receiver rhythmically—a typical scenario on the days he received bad news from the Army. I stood rapt watching him, hoping he'd slip up and mention a military secret. Hey, there's a first time for everything. I'd have to get lucky sooner or later.

"Yes, we lost power here, too … Yes, sir … I understand, sir … Right away, sir." He hung the receiver back on its stand and glanced in my direction. "I told you to stay upstairs."

"What'd they say? What's going on?"

"I'll tell you after I find out." He snatched his wallet from the counter and slipped the worn leather into the back pocket of his jeans.

"You're leaving? Now? Did you hear that last explosion?"

"I know. That's why I'm being called in." He picked up his keys.

"For what? You're not a fireman."

His gaze centered on me. I shivered. Dad in military mode was just. Plain. Scary.

"It's a plane. A plane went down."

The memory of the low-flying jets and the rattling of what must have been gunfire seared my nerves.

"Went down or was shot down?" The journalist in me started salivating.

"That's what I'm going to find out."

The door creaked as he pushed down the handle. The blare of passing sirens reverberated through the room.

"Why would they shoot down a plane?" I glanced at my camera bag perched on the end table. My shutter finger itched, anticipating juicy photos to add to my portfolio.

"Everything will be fine. For now, just stay in the house."

"Stay in the house? But this is like, huge. I want to take some pictures."

His jaw set. That gross vein in his neck twitched. "You can play games later. Right now, I need to know you're safe."

"No photojournalist ever made it big by staying safe."

"Maybe not, but many seventeen-year-olds made it to eighteen that way. Stay here. That's an order."

The whooting of a helicopter's blades cut through the late afternoon sunshine. Butterflies fluttered in my gut as Dad disappeared through the screen door without so much as a backward glance.

Seriously? He expected me to just sit there—with the biggest photo opportunity of my life going on outside?

I ran to the window and brushed the curtain aside. The Air Force pilot who lived across the street ran to his jeep, a duffle bag swinging from his arm. Lieutenant Miller from next door left his house and exchanged nods with Dad as they both slipped into their cars.

The sound of another explosion smacked my ears. The ceiling rattled, and I steadied myself against the wall. How many times could one plane explode? I took a deep breath and forced myself to relax. I lived on a military base for goodness sake. The Army and the freaking Air Force were stationed next door. You couldn't get much safer than that.

Flopping onto the couch, I clicked the power button on the remote control three times. The blank television screen mocked me. *No electricity, idiot.*

Another siren howled past the house. My gaze flittered back to my camera case. When in my lifetime would I get another chance to shoot pictures of something like this?

"This is crazy." I slid my cell phone off the coffee table and dialed my best friend. No service. Ugh!

I grabbed the corded phone. Her voicemail answered: "Hey, this is Maggs. You know what to do."

"Maggie, it's Jess. Where are you? The whole world is coming to an end outside. Call me."

Another helicopter zoomed over the roof. How many was that now? Three? Four?

My gaze trailed to the name above Maggie's on the contact list. *Bobby.*

The part of me that feared the chaos outside yearned to call him. Bobby would come. Leave his post if he had to. Protect me. But did I really want Bobby back in my life?

Not after he and his MP buddies beat up poor Matt Samuels. All the kid did was take me to a movie. It wasn't even a date, but Bobby didn't care. If he couldn't have me, then no one could.

I gritted my teeth as I slipped my phone back into my pocket. Suddenly, I wasn't as scared as I thought.

Tucking back the living room curtains, I snooped on the neighbors gathering outside their houses. Mrs. Sanderson and the lady across the street both herded their kids inside, their faces turned toward the sky. The fear in their eyes struck me. What an amazing photograph that would have been.

A few guys began walking toward the thruway. One of them held a cheap, pocket camera in his hand. He had to be kidding. What kind of shot did he expect to get with that?

I let the curtain fall. Staying in the house was just too much to ask. This was the story of a lifetime. I couldn't let it slip by without getting something on film.

Grabbing a black elastic band off the end-table, I twisted my hair into a pony tail. One brown lock fell beside my cheek, as it always did. I clipped that sucker back with a barrette and slung my camera case over my shoulder.

I hesitated at the front door. A picture of my parents hung askew beside the window. I straightened the frame. Mom's smile warmed me, but Dad's eyes bored through me, daring me to face his wrath if I touched the doorknob. I stood taller, strengthening my resolve. He'd understand after I got into National Geographic.

The odor of smoke and something pungent barraged my nose as I opened the door. A fire truck wailed in the distance, warning me to keep away. But I couldn't. I pulled my collar up over my nose to blot out the smell and headed toward the main road.

A parade of emergency vehicles whipped by at the end of the street. Lights flashed and sirens blasted through the neighborhood.

The cacophony froze me for a moment. Nothing like this had ever happened before. We lived in New Jersey for goodness sake, not Saudi Arabia. I glanced back at the house. Keeping it in view made me feel safe, but I knew I needed to get closer to get a good shot.

This was it. The big league. I could do this.

Turning left toward the airstrip, I watched the last fire truck become smaller before its whirling lights passed through the gates onto the tarmac. The fire blazed well within the tree line, maybe even farther than I originally thought. The smoke reached into the sky, blotting out the sun. I raised my lens and waited for the clouds to shift and give me the perfect lighting—until a smack on my arm ruined my setup.

Maggie.

A smirk spread across her face. "Hey, Lois Lane. I figured you'd be out here."

I sighed, watching a flock of fleeing birds that would have maximized the emotion of the shot—if I'd taken it.

"Lois Lane was a reporter. Jimmy Olsen was the photographer."

"Whatever." Her golden curls bounced about her face. "This is like, crazy. My dad took off like World War Three or something."

"Yeah, mine, too."

I shielded my eyes. The smoke rose in gray billows. Almost pretty. I raised my lens.

"You want to know the scoop?" Maggie's perky form fidgeted like a toddler who couldn't hold in a secret. She loved eavesdropping on her father, the general. Unfortunately, that kind of gossip could get you carted off by the MPs. Never stopped her though, and I adored her for it.

"You know I do. Spill it." I brought the clouds into focus and snapped the shutter three times.

Her grin widened as she feigned a whisper. "It's not one of ours."

"What do you mean?" The stench in the air thickened. I covered my nose.

"The plane. They don't know whose it is. Isn't that exciting?"

"Heck yeah." I raised my camera and clicked off ten successive shots. If a terrorist got shot down over American soil, Jess Martinez was going to have pictures to sell. This was the kind of break every photographer dreamed of.

I adjusted my camera-case beside my waist. "I'm going in closer."

The air around us grew hazy. Maggie coughed. "Are you nuts? This is close enough for me."

"Stop being such a wuss." I tugged her wrist. It never took much more to convince her.

Maggie prattled on while I shot off round after round of gripping photographs. My heart fluttered as each preview image appeared on my screen. For once I was actually doing it. I was being the journalist I was meant to be, not the caged-up little girl Dad wanted. And boy, did it feel good.

The closer we came to the chained-link fence surrounding the runways, the more people gathered around us. A man, ignoring the whimpering Labrador on the end of his leash, gawked at the clouds. *Click.* Two women caught excited children and dragged them away. *Click.* The MP from down the street shouted, "Yes sir, right away sir," into his cell phone and jogged from the scene. *Click*—all amazing images to add to my portfolio.

Pushing to the front, I slipped my fingers through the metal fencing. The paved tarmac sprawled before me, backing up to the trees. Soldiers on the far side of the airstrip formed barricades against the tree line. I centered my lens between the silver links and chronicled their maneuvers.

A breeze whipped up. The heat slapped my face like sitting too close to a campfire. I covered my lens to protect the glass as the people around us flinched and backed away. One woman ran, crying into a hankie.

"Should we be able to feel the heat from this far away?" Maggie asked, shielding her face with her arm.

I shrugged, unease settling on me as the smoky cloud arched toward us. The breeze stretched the formation, driving it north over our heads and toward the houses.

My stomach did a little fliperoo. The spunky, fearless photo-journalist slipped away, leaving a scrawny, slightly-unsure-of-herself teenager behind. "I gotta go."

"Why?"

"My Dad told me to stay inside. He'll be calling on the house phone any minute to check on me."

"The major's getting more neurotic every day. You're almost eighteen for goodness sake."

"I know, but I still get the *While You Live Under My Roof* lecture every day."

The ground rattled. Another billow of fire wafted into the sky. I steadied myself, transfixed by the sheer magnitude of the ever-growing bank of smoke.

Wow, did I want to just stand there and use up my memory

card—but I wanted to not get grounded more. I began walking backward, snapping off shots with every step.

Maggie strode beside me. "Do you ever stop taking pictures?"

Click.

"Not if I can help it."

I SHIMMIED OPEN THE FRONT DOOR. ON THE FAR SIDE OF THE LIVING room, the corded phone rattled on the receiver, mid-ring. My keys clanged to the wood floor as I sprang toward the table to grab the handset. "Hello?"

"Where've you been?"

"Nowhere. I was—in the bathroom." I clenched my teeth, holding my breath. Would he buy it?

"Are you okay?"

"I'm fine. Why?"

I could imagine his Major Martinez no-nonsense expression on the other side of the phone. "Listen, it's really important that you stay inside tonight. I'm sorry I can't be there, but I need you to lock the doors, and stay away from the windows."

I crinkled my forehead. Sweat settled across my brow. "Why? What's wrong? There's nothing, like, nuclear or anything, right?"

There was a pause on the line. "No—nothing nuclear."

I drew the curtain back from the rear kitchen window. The smoke cloud over the woods had darkened. The smell of burning pine tickled my nose as a humming tone on the other end of the call agitated my ear.

Dad spoke muffled words to someone else. "Jesus H. Christ," he whispered, returning to the phone.

"Dad, is everything okay?"

"Please just promise me you'll stay inside tonight."

Yikes. His Major Tomás Martinez voice had drifted away. That was his 'daddy's scared' voice. I hadn't heard that tone since the night Mom died. I shuddered. "Dad, if things are that bad, shouldn't I be with you?" Silence lingered, and a scratching noise reverberated in the background. "Dad, is someone else on the line with us?"

"Jess. I am asking you to stay inside and lock the doors. Can you do that for me … Buttercup?"

Buttercup?

My breath hitched. Crud. That meant something. Buttercup was a word he and Mom used when something was wrong. Something was definitely up. "I got you, Dad. I'll stay inside. I promise."

"Thank you." He paused. "I'll be home as soon as I can."

"Yeah, okay." My hand trembled as the phone clicked back into the cradle.

I checked the front and back door and ran to the stairs. The fire cast a magnificent glow behind the trees outside my bedroom window. I slid down the screen and clicked off a few rounds of shots, hoping to catch the eerie blues and pinks behind the shaded leaves. Whoa. *New favorite sunset shot for sure.*

Settling down on my bed, I started scrolling through today's pictures. Something was weird about the fire, but I couldn't quite place my finger on it. Flipping through June's National Geographic, I glanced through the photographs of the explosion in Nanjing China. The colors in my shots were so much more vivid, more dynamic, more, well, *colorful.* Not that I knew anything about explosions, but something itched that little button inside that told me I had something special.

The lights suddenly flicked on. I gasped and laughed at myself. Perfect timing. I settled at my computer, hooked up my camera, and started the upload. I couldn't wait to enlarge those babies.

CHAPTER 2

rumpets! My eyes popped open as round after round of incessant choruses of Reveille echoed over the base PA system, shocking the world and demanding everyone get up and take notice that the ungodly time of O-six-hundred-hours had arrived.

A groan escaped my lips as I pushed up off my desk. Every muscle in my neck and back screamed at the same time. I must have fallen asleep waiting for my pictures to upload. Rubbing the back of my neck, I stood as the last trumpet bellowed its obnoxious call.

God, I hated that stinking song.

The screen-saver flicked off when I jiggled my mouse. The website from last night was still waiting for me to confirm my order. I smiled and clicked the button. I'd be a few hours before the store opened and I could pick up the pictures that would change my life. Once I added the best of yesterday's shots to my portfolio, no one would dream of refusing my college application.

The sun sparkled through my windowpanes. In the distance, three dark birds circled over the forest in a beautiful, blue sky. A thin tendril of smoke trailed from the trees, a small reminder of yesterday's chaos. The coolness of the glass enlivened my skin as I pressed my forehead against the window. Despite the unbelievable shots I'd taken, I was glad it was finally over.

I stumbled through the hallway and peeked in dad's room. His bed hadn't been slept in. So much for his day off. Ignoring the grumbling of my impatient stomach, I treated my sore muscles to a shower and got dressed.

The digital clock on my dresser blinked four-seventeen. So much for the fool-proof back-up battery. I made a mental note to fix the time later.

While liberating a few knots from my hair, I made a beeline to the refrigerator. Fruit, eggs, milk … Boring. I shoved aside a few food savers and smiled.

"Bingo."

I slid out a plate of German chocolate layer cake. Smacking my lips in anticipation, I plopped back in front of my computer and scanned the photos I'd sent to the drugstore print shop. I could hear Dad now, "Why don't you just send the pictures to the PX. It's cheaper."

Yeah, they're cheaper all right—and pixely.

Not to mention the fact that they might confiscate a few of the shots I'd taken of the soldiers. My brow furrowed as I scanned the photos of the platoon gathered near the edge of the forest. In every shot, the soldiers were facing the woods. If they were there to keep the people safe, wouldn't they be facing out?

Swallowing down the last bite of cake, I walked downstairs and peeked out the front window. No sign of Dad yet, but I wasn't about to sit there and wait for him. I dialed up his cell, but his voicemail answered.

"Hey Dad, it's Jess. Everything's fine. No problems last night. I'm going to walk down to the drugstore to pick up some pictures, okay? Don't worry, I'm going in completely the opposite direction from where the fire was, so I won't be anywhere near the cleanup. See you later."

I hung up and grabbed a notepad and pen. Standard Major Martinez protocol dictated a note as well as a message. I flipped to an empty page and let him know where I was going, sealing it with a smiley-face.

Outside, a summer breeze caressed my face. I inhaled the crisp morning air and crinkled my nose at the slight hint of smoke lingering from the fire. Yuck.

Quiet greeted me throughout the compound, as if yesterday's calamity never happened. Funny, how quickly everything adjusts back to normal. I guess the fire really wasn't as big a deal as I thought.

The heaviness still hung in the air, though. Not that I thought a plane crash would take it away. Everything about Maguire, and the other three military bases I'd lived on, stifled me like a prison without walls, and the pressure seemed to tighten every day.

Day trips with Mom used to help, but now that she was gone, and with Dad sinking further and further into his shell ... Well, things just weren't the same without Mom.

Relief swept over me as I passed the guard shack and walked into the real world. I laughed at myself. I was only a few feet away from military ground, and most of those houses were probably still Army or Air Force families all squashed together since they merged Fort Dix with Maguire. It was civilian land, though, and it smelled like freedom. Well, smoky freedom at the moment, but still freedom.

I headed toward the woods and allowed my thoughts to drift up and away, clearing my mind and letting it wander. Senior year began in a few weeks, and I'd have to start looking for colleges.

Looking ... funny. There was only one choice. Columbia. Their arts department was the tops. My application was already filled out, and these photographs were going to cinch it for me.

Dad dreamed of me going to West Point. We'd already sent in the paperwork, but I didn't care that every Martinez since my great-grandfather went there. I had to live my life, not his.

A larger than life advertisement on the side of a passing NJ Transit bus made me smile. *Fire in the Woods, starring Jared Linden and Chris Stevens. In theaters September tenth.* Jared leaned forward in the photo, ready to pounce off the side of the bus. Chris Stevens stood beside him, shirtless with hands in pockets and beautiful blond tresses falling seductively toward one eye. I loved Chris's new haircut, and Jared—Yum. Five foot ten inches of pure tall-dark-and-handsome. They were both just to die for.

A sudden movement drew my attention from the bus. I skidded to a stop. To my right, maybe a hundred feet from the forest, stood the most beautiful buck I'd ever seen. I held my breath trying not to move as he stared me down. A majestic twelve-point rack of antlers scrolled from his head, and his white and brown tail flickered incessantly. After a long, breathless wait, his mouth swirled in a chewing motion. Nature in its most beautiful form.

An eerie shadow cast across the grass as the sun shone through his rack. The silhouette formed little fingers that seemed to reach for me. Wow. If I took that picture at just the right angle ...

Shoot. My camera sat safely at home, not attached to my hip where it should have been. Diversity in the portfolio was a must. I needed a picture of that guy. I inched forward and the buck raised his head, shifting the shadow from sight.

"It's okay," I whispered. "I won't hurt you."

I reached into my pocket and fumbled for my phone. The aperture on the camera feature opened, and I lifted the screen toward him. Without warning, the deer sprang into the air. It flipped its tail toward me and bolted into the woods.

"Awe, man."

Clutching my camera-phone, I ran to the trees and squinted into the brambles. The buck's dark, shiny eyes blinked within the brush. He chewed twice before he trotted deeper into the foliage.

"Come on, dude, I just want a picture."

I ramrodded my way into the forest, the branches whipping back as I set them free. The morning warmth gave way to cool, damp air beneath the trees as I hopped over a group of fallen logs and ducked under a giant poison ivy vine climbing up a tree. I paused, listening to the woods. Silence greeted me, followed by the chirps of two birds chasing each other from tree to tree in the upper canopy. I slowed and fought to catch my breath. He was gone.

My chest throbbed as I leaned my hands on my knees. Sheesh, he was fast. I chuckled to myself. What was I thinking?

A puff of smoke rose over some brush on my right. I pulled the bushes aside and found the remains of a small smoldering campfire. Some people were so irresponsible. I tossed dirt on the embers until they winked out. Good deed for the day: done.

Turning to head back out of the woods, I froze. A noise blasted through the forest, screeching like a smoke alarm gone haywire. A stabbing pain tore into my brain. I slammed my hands over my ears, but I couldn't fight the drills boring inside me. Head pounding, I howled, but my own voice fell victim to the vibrations within my mind.

I dropped to my knees. "Please stop! Make it stop!"

The squalling encompassed everything. Tears pooled in my eyes, blurring my vision before trailing down my cheeks. I wailed in misery.

Until it stopped.

I shook, reeling from the unexpected silence. A faint hum lingered, a frightening reminder of the sound's intensity. Hands still covering my ears, I sucked in a short breath and dared another. Holding as still as possible, I scanned the trees.

What the heck was going on?

Sobbing, I blinked back fresh tears and wiped my cheek clean. A leaf fell to the ground at my feet, but the rest of the forest remained motionless. The chirping birds had vanished. Nothing stirred to disrupt the eerie quiet—not even a gentle rustle of the wind.

I cringed, frightened by a thrash behind a large fallen tree. Ignoring the instinct to flee like the buck, I inched forward and peeked over the log.

A guy, maybe seventeen or eighteen, lay curled in a ball on the ground. His hands pressed against his ears as he whimpered through twisted lips. A tight-fitting white tee-shirt clung to his back, slightly untucked from his faded blue jeans. His soulful whimper clawed my heart as he rocked steadily on the woodland floor.

Biting my lip, I mustered up the courage to speak. "Are you okay?"

He grunted. "Please stop! Make it stop!"

"The noise? But it's gone now."

He twitched and moaned. The brush beneath him crunched with every movement.

"It's okay," I said. "Just breathe. It's over. Everything will be all right."

Panic centered in my chest, as if something reached inside me and tugged. A haze seeped into my thoughts, and I shook my head to clear it. What was wrong with me?

The boy hadn't reacted to my questions, almost as if he couldn't hear me. A helpless, panicked swirl within my ribs gave me pause. I had to do something, but what?

My hands balled into fists. "What's wrong?"

I shoved aside a stray branch and jumped over the log. The boy stopped rocking as I approached, but his body quaked with long, labored breaths.

"It's okay. It's over."

He didn't respond. I looked through the tree trunks and over the bramble and ferns … only leaves and vines and trees blending into more trees for as far as I could see. There was no one else to help him. I ran my fingers through the hair at my temples, massaging the sensitive skin where my brain still pulsed with a dull ache.

Pull yourself together, Jess.

The guy pushed up on one arm. His long, dark bangs fell over his face. Cautiously, I placed my hand on his back.

"Hey, are you all right?"

His entire body flinched. He popped out of his crouch, shifting away with a cry of alarm. He kicked his feet against the leaves and dirt, backing himself away. A murmur escaped his lips as he smashed against a tree trunk. His turquoise-blue eyes widened. His gaze darted in every direction.

Were his eyes actually turquoise? I tilted my head to the side. Yeah, they really were. Must be contacts or something.

I raised my palms, keeping my distance. "It's okay. I won't hurt you."

He focused on me, mouth open, taking in huge gulps of air. His right hand reached up and held his left shoulder as he bit his bottom lip. Beautiful white teeth grazed his slightly tanned skin before he closed his eyes and swallowed hard.

I stepped closer. "Are you hurt?"

The guy scrambled away, sliding beside the tree.

I raised my hands. "Okay, okay. I was only trying to help." I eased down on a patch of moss. "What do you think that was anyway?"

His eyes centered on me—freaking me out with their odd color. I wanted to look away, but I couldn't. My eyes burned and grew heavy—until he blinked.

A waft of air entered my lungs, and I let it out slowly. Why was I holding my breath? I rubbed my eyes. What was wrong with me? I felt, I don't know, different—like a cloud covered me. No, like a blanket. A nice, safe blanket.

A wince contorted the boy's face as he stretched his neck. He crinkled his nose, his breathing settling to a more normal pace.

His gaze seemed to search through me, and the foggy feeling deepened. I relaxed, taking in his strong round cheeks and delicate jawline. I must have won the lottery or something ... stuck in the middle of the woods with a guy who—come to think of it—looked a lot like Jared Linden.

"So," I began, trying not to focus on those muscular arms nearly busting out of his tight tee-shirt. "What's your name?"

"Your name?" His hair fell in loose waves along the bangs, flipped back over short-cropped sides ... exactly like Chris Stevens's hair, but much darker—almost black.

"Yeah, you know—your name." I pointed to my chest. "I'm Jess."

I waited for an introduction that didn't come. He just looked at me, blinking hard like something was stuck in his eyes.

"And you are?"

He squinted. "David?" His eyebrows arched, almost as if he were making sure his name was okay.

"Are you asking me, or telling me?"

A maddening grin shot across his face. Jared Linden eat your heart out. Damn, this guy looked like he should be on a magazine cover, not out traipsing around in the woods—or whatever he was doing out here.

"David," he said. "My name is David."

"Okay, now that we got that out of the way, are you all right? Is your shoulder hurt?"

He shifted to the left. A grimace twisted his lips. "My shoulder? Umm, yeah. It hurts in the back."

"I took first-aid last year. Do you want me to take a look at it?"

"Take a look at it?" He blinked twice.

"Yeah. You'll need to take your shirt off, okay?"

"Shirt off?" He placed his hand down, crushing the jagged leaves of a fern.

"Okay, did you hit your head or something, because you're, like, repeating everything I say."

He blinked his eyes hard again. His breathing came in shallow wheezes, as if every lungful hurt. I half expected to find a gunshot wound, but I'd probably have seen the blood by now. At least I hoped so. It'd be embarrassing if I passed out and he ended up taking care of me instead.

"Here. Let me help you." I reached for the bottom of his tee-shirt and helped him lift it over his head.

"Ouch." David grabbed his shoulder before I could get the shirt over the other arm. The white fabric hung in the crook of his elbow, dragging the ground and picking up a few pine needles.

"Sorry, I didn't mean to hurt you." I shifted to kneel behind him. His gaze tracked me like I had a knife or something. "Okay, let's take a look."

I chewed the inside of my cheek and took the longest look of my life. He was flawless. Absolutely flawless. Slightly bronzed, unblemished skin covered strong shoulders. He almost seemed air-brushed. I reached out to touch him, and his muscles rippled and tensed.

A gasp escaped my lips. Dang. I mean seriously: Da-ha-hang. If I didn't distract myself, I was gonna drool all over him. "So, what do you think that loud noise was?"

"Loud noise?"

"There you go again, repeating me." My jaw fell open. "Holy cow. You weren't in the plane crash were you?"

"Plane crash?"

"Still repeating."

He shook his head. "No. No plane."

A light wind blew overhead, bringing life back to the forest. The birds resumed chirping as I slipped beside him. "Did you see it, the crash?"

He nodded. "Yes."

"You didn't get hit by shrapnel or anything, did you?"

His lips formed a word, but stopped. "I, I don't know."

"Crap, talk about picking the wrong time to be in the woods." I moved behind him again, and ran my hand along his back. I couldn't find any trace of injury, but his skin seemed hotter than Hel…well, really hot.

"What's the last thing you remember?"

His shoulders twitched. "You asking if I was okay."

"Don't you remember holding your head and screaming in agony?"

He rubbed his forehead. "Oh, umm, yeah. It was … strange."

"Strange is kind of an understatement, don't you think?" I removed my hand. "I can't see any swelling. Where does it hurt?"

"In the shoulder middle."

I ran my hand across his back lightly once, and applied gentle pressure in the center of the blade.

He cried out.

"Oh, Sorry." It hit me that I'd barely passed first-aid class. I had no idea what I was doing.

He grumbled, flinching. "Can you first aid it?"

I laughed. "First aid it?"

"Can you help me?"

I sat back, just missing a daddy long-legs scurrying across the ground. "David, I think you need to go to a hospital."

He raised his hand. "No. No hospital."

"But you're hurt. You probably need an x-ray."

"No. I definitely don't need one of those." He stood and cried out, clutching his arm.

"Listen, are you in trouble or something? Are you running from the police?"

"No ... not the police."

I propped myself against a small tree. "So you *are* running. From who? You're not, like, a criminal or anything, right?"

"No. I just don't want to be found." His gaze drifted downward.

Way in the back of my mind, a little trickle of doubt and fear struggled against an overwhelming need to help him. I should have done the smart thing and run, but I couldn't just leave the poor guy there.

"Listen. You don't have to tell me what's up, but you're hurt. You at least need some ice."

He looked up. "Ice?"

"You know—to keep it from swelling."

A deep furrow crossed his brow. "Can *you* get me ice?"

"I guess. Do you want to walk back to my place with me?" I shuddered. Did I just invite a guy I didn't even know back to my house?

"No. Bring it here."

Relief washed over me, but not because I was afraid of David. I was more afraid of Dad finding me alone with a boy. Bring ice? No problem. I glanced around the trees, no longer sure which way I'd come from.

"The only problem is I'm not sure I'll be able to find you again. I'm not even sure if I can find my way out."

He motioned behind me. "You are six-hundred and twenty-seven point five meters north east of where you entered the woods."

I stared at him as my geek-meter went haywire. "You're kidding, right?"

He paled slightly and shrugged, glancing away. "Yes, of course. You did come from that direction, though."

He was probably some kind of a math nerd or something. Damn cute math nerd, though. "Okay. I'll be right back." I started walking.

"Jess?"

My hair grazed my check as I turned back toward him. "Yeah?"

David eased himself against the log. "Thank you."

"No problem." *As long as my dad isn't home, that is.*

I imagined all the possible Major Martinez interrogation questions. None of them ended up good. I turned to the woods and quickened my pace. I had to get in and out of the house before Dad got home.

CHAPTER 3

I sprinted down my street and stopped at the edge of the sidewalk. Busted. Dad's car sat in his favorite parking space, still creaking as the engine cooled. How in God's name was I supposed to sneak a bag of ice out of the house with Dad home? The back door!

The handle of the rear screen door clicked as I tiptoed into the kitchen.

Dad's voice came from the living room. "I did tell her to stay home. Mom, I just don't know what to do with her anymore. She doesn't follow orders at all."

Why was he talking to Grandma about me? Didn't matter. I had to get that ice. I inched toward the freezer.

"I know she's not one of my soldiers. Believe me. If she was, she'd think about the big picture and not focus on herself all the time. And she wouldn't do such stupid things. I swear she does this to piss me off."

I gritted my teeth and slid the ice tray out of the freezer. What dad considered *stupid things* were all the things that were important to me that he didn't understand. If he'd look up and beyond that stupid uniform he wore all the time, he'd realize there was more to life than—

"And this dumb photography thing—dammit Mom, I wish you never bought her that camera."

I froze. My heart wiggled its way into my throat.

"Give her space? Let her make her mistakes? What kind of advice is that?"

Photography wasn't a mistake. It was my life, my passion, my—

"Mom, I need help with her. I thought I could manage it alone, but I can't. All I'm asking is for you to come for a week or so, just until school starts. There's too much going on and I just can't trust her anymore."

Can't trust me?

Grandma?

My stomach did a somersault and missed the landing. The ice container slipped out of my hands and crashed on the floor.

"Mom, she's back. I gotta go."

I dropped to my knees, taking deep breaths as I scooped the slippery cubes off the linoleum. My hands shook. Why couldn't he understand how much that camera meant to me? Why couldn't he understand that his dreams weren't the same as mine? I shoved the container back into the freezer and sat down at the kitchen table. I doodled the deer's antlers on the edge of a pad, trying to calm myself down as I prepared for the impending fight.

Dad barreled around the corner. "Jess, where have you been?"

"I told you, I went to the store."

"You were supposed to stay home."

"You said last night. I went out this morning."

His face reddened. "When I tell you to stay home, I need you to stay home."

"I left a note and everything, didn't I? And I called, like a good little soldier, but as usual, you didn't pick up the phone. You never pick up the phone."

"Don't you try to turn this around on me."

"Don't worry. I didn't do any more stupid things." I pushed past him and stormed up the stairs.

"Jessica!"

I slammed my bedroom door. The covers poofed up around me as I flopped onto my bed. Only think about myself? Dumb photography? What did he know? I rolled over and hugged my pillow. It was the same argument, different day. Nothing would change. Ever.

By now, Dad was probably half way to counting to a hundred

to calm down. He'd need to get to two-hundred before he'd come up here and give his stylized lame apology. God, I hated that part.

I rubbed my face, remembering why I'd come home in the first place. I needed to find a way to smuggle some ice past Dad. But how? There was no chance of getting out of the house again until he stopped focusing on me.

A prisoner until the game played out, I decided to kill time with Maggie. I slipped my phone out of my pocket, and dialed her up. "Hey girl."

"Hey, you. What's up?"

"My dad as usual, but guess what just happened in the woods? I was chasing after a deer—"

"Again?"

"Yeah. Anyway, there was this noise, and it felt like my head would explode, and then there was this guy, and he heard it too."

"A guy?" She giggled. "Okay, now I'm interested. I thought you were going to tell me another stupid *Jess chases an animal* story. So, fess up. Was he cute?"

A sigh slipped from my lips. "Didn't you hear about the noise? I mean, it was really loud. Did you hear anything?"

"Nope, no noise. Now spill it about the guy."

I rolled over onto my stomach. "His name is David."

"Isn't David the name you made up for your dream prince?"

I giggled. "Omigosh, how'd you remember that? We were, like, thirteen."

"I remember those juicy stories you made up about him—all tall, dark and Greek-God delicious."

The more I thought about it, David actually did look a lot like—

"So was he running through the woods taking pictures of animals, too?"

"No. Can you keep a secret?" I rolled onto my back. "He's hiding out there from someone."

"Hiding? Girl, you're not hooking up with a serial killer or anything, right?"

"He's not a serial killer. He's like, seventeen, eighteen tops."

"Didn't you see that movie *Scream*? Those two were—"

"Can we come back to reality please?"

"Okay. Okay. Okay. So, what's he running from?"

"Dunno." I rubbed my fingertips, remembering the heat radiating from his skin. "He said it wasn't the cops. I'm hoping he talks to me when I go back."

Maggie snickered. "You're going to meet him again in the woods? Miss Goody-Two-Shoes, are you finally going to do something naughty? And without me?"

I sat up, knocking the pillow off my bed. "No. I just want to help him. He's hurt."

"I bet you want to help him." She giggled.

"Stop. You are so bad."

"But seriously, Jess. You don't know anything about this guy."

I chewed the top of my lip, thinking about Dad's conversation with Grandma. Was I being stupid? I needed to make a good decision here. "You know what? You're right. Can you come out there with me?"

"You know I'd love to meet your prince charming but I need to go school shopping while my mom's credit card is still squeaking, and tonight is family movie night. No getting out of that in the Baker household."

"Oh yeah, I forgot." Oh well. So much for reinforcements.

"You know what? Just don't go. Tip off the MP's that someone's out there, and they'll find him."

"You want me to turn him in?"

"No, not turn him in, but if he's in trouble … You know … They have shelters for kids like that. Confidential and all. They won't call his parents."

I fingered the chain on my neck. "No. It doesn't feel right. He needs my help."

Someone knocked on my door three times.

"Maggs, I gotta go. My Dad's revving up for another pep talk."

"Okay, but be careful if you go out there, okay?"

"Yeah, whatever." I clicked off the phone and opened my door.

Dad's hand was poised at eye level, about to knock again. His chest expanded for the obligatory breath before an apology speech. "Jess, I don't want to fight with you. I just wish you'd listen once in a while."

I folded my arms. "I only went to the store." With a little side-trip into the woods.

"It's not just that and you know it." He ran his palm across the top of his cropped hair. "You know it's been hard without your mom here, but I'm trying."

"I know." Dang he was good with the guilt trips. An uncomfortable silence lingered, stifling me like an invisible curtain.

"Listen. I've never been able to keep you cooped up, and I realize you're into all that photography stuff, but until things die down and I can confirm everything is secure, I need you to stay in the house."

Crap.

You see dad, I can't stay in the house. There's this drop-dead gorgeous guy in the woods, and I promised to bring him ice. Nah. That wouldn't go over well. Certain things a girl should just keep to herself.

"Dad, what's going on? And what was all that *buttercup* stuff about last night?"

He rubbed his face with his palms. "You weren't really old enough when your mom and I came up with the word buttercup. I was hoping you'd understand what I was trying to say."

"Mom told me once to listen if you ever said buttercup during an emergency. That's all I remember."

"Well, we were in an emergency. You did good."

"There was someone on the phone, wasn't there? They were making sure you didn't tell me anything."

Dad leaned against my doorframe. "You know I'm not allowed to talk about work."

"Work smirk. I don't care about security clearance."

"There was a possibility of danger. I just needed to know you were safe" He kissed my forehead. "I gotta get back."

"You're leaving again?"

"Yes. I'm sorry, but the whole base is on alert status."

"For how long?"

"It depends on how long it takes us to find …"

I waited for a word that didn't come. "Find what?"

His head tilted to the side. "Nice try."

"Can't blame a girl for trying."

So, the army was looking for something. Interesting.

"I'll be back in the morning for a bit. We'll have breakfast, okay?"

"Uh-huh."

Dad headed down the stairs, and I counted to a hundred before following.

So, the army was all jacked up in another one of Dad's top-secret operations. I still had no idea what Dad did in the army, but what I could gather from Maggie's eavesdropping habit, Dad's division dealt with dangers of the "who" kind, not the "what" kind. They called my dad to track people down. If Dad was involved, whoever they were looking for had to be pretty big potatoes.

David was hiding from someone, and he was hurt. Could he be running from the military? A vision of David's bright eyes and the perfect cut to his jaw flashed through my mind. I shook my head. Why would Dad be hunting a kid? He certainly had better things to do. Terrorists and the like were out there. Real criminals. There was no way Dad could be looking for David. My gaze settled on my camera case. I grabbed it … just in case.

Shooting over to the kitchen, I opened up the cupboard, pulled out a gallon-sized Ziploc and filled it with ice. The bag fit neatly into the bottom of my backpack. I threw together a few peanut butter and jelly sandwiches and tossed them in with a couple bottles of water and my camera. The ice chilled my back as I threw the pack over my shoulder.

I hesitated, my hand on the front door. Dad wanted me to stay home. *Until everything was secure.* That meant that there was a safety risk, and if Dad was involved, it had to be a pretty big one. He expected me to be a good little soldier and stay inside. But how could I?

David was out there, alone. Hurt. I couldn't just leave him there, especially if there was some kind of dangerous fugitive on the loose. I'd made him a promise, and I had to keep it.

I yanked my jeans free of a thorny bush. I swear I had to be crazy. Just that morning something screeched in the woods so loud it almost burst my eardrums. But here I was, wandering around in those same woods, probably lost, bent on finding and helping a boy I didn't even know. My chest ached with pressure from my short, choppy breaths. Why did the forest seem so much more sinister than it normally did?

"*Auoi calinart, est.*"

The gruff, masculine voice echoed through the trees. The language was odd, musical. Kind of like singing, or maybe Norwegian—or maybe a Norwegian guy singing. I couldn't decide.

An elderly man wearing a long, dirty winter jacket slapped a tree branch as he sped-walked around a bush. He nearly plowed into me.

"Sorry," I said, backing off the path.

The man gazed up at me. His nose crinkled as if a foul odor suddenly hit him. He blinked and continued on his way, but his icy cold countenance hung with me for a minute. And his eyes … No one had eyes so blue. Except maybe David.

I shivered. Not sure why, but the old dude creeped me out. His head bobbed as he moved through the bushes. He had to be delirious, wearing that warm coat in the middle of August.

"Pardon me." A woman with gorgeous long blond curls ran up the same path. Her jacket brushed against me as she passed. When she caught up to the old guy, she grabbed him by the arm. They muttered, heads close, before he shoved her away and continued down the trail. The woman turned her face toward the sky, fisted her hands, and continued on after him.

The dude had to be her father or something. Why else would

she take that kind of crap from him? I sniffed out a laugh. I hoped that wouldn't be me and my Dad in twenty years.

I pushed through the brush and plodded on. The trees were probably laughing at me, because I was pretty sure I'd seen the one with the big black knot in the bark at least three times, now. Stinking, stupid, big, black, knotty tree.

A rustling of leaves deep within the trees startled me. I froze, and stared down another gorgeous, enormous buck. Or was it the same one as that morning?

"Hey, beautiful," I whispered.

Swirling antlers blended with the landscape. He barely seemed to notice me.

"Good boy." I clawed for my camera, slipping it out of my pack. "Just stay right there." I pressed the picture button and zoomed in. *Click.* Gotcha. But a closer shot would be even better.

I inched forward. Majestic black eyes emitted a sense of serenity, calming me from within their gaze. *Crack.* The twigs broke beneath my feet. Dernit. The deer's ears twitched.

"It's okay buddy. It's me, remember?"

Two little baby steps brought me closer. I held my breath, trying to keep quiet, but my phone vibrated, the ringtone reverberating through the trees. The buck bolted.

"You're not going to chase him again," I told myself. A grin broke across my lips. "Oh, yes you are."

Jumping over fallen trees and stomping in muddy patches, I followed him deeper into the woods. My phone finally stopped ringing, but the buck was long gone … again. I laughed and leaned over, resting my hands on my knees. I was starting to make a habit out of this.

"Jess?"

I screamed and whirled toward the voice.

David raised his hands. "Sorry. I thought you saw me."

"Saw you? I was looking at the stinking deer." I held my hand to my heart, willing it to stay within my chest. "You scared the crap out of me."

His lips contorted into the cutest pout as he settled onto the ground. "Sorry."

"Well, wear a bell or something next time. Geeze!"

Okay, heart. You can slow down now.

I caught my breath. "Are you feeling any better?"

"Maybe." He rotated his shoulder. "Either that or I'm numb."

Dirt and pine needles scattered in a puff as I dropped my backpack beside him. "Okay, let's get to it, then." I grabbed the Ziploc bag.

"What's that?"

"Ice. What did you think?" The cubes scraped together inside the plastic.

"Umm …" His eyes widened.

"If your shoulder is swollen, and you won't go to the hospital. You need a cold compress."

He swallowed hard. "Okay."

David bent forward. I brushed traces of bark and dirt clinging to his back as I knelt beside him. The muscles in his neck and arms tensed.

"Loosen up. It's just ice." I carefully placed the bag on his injury.

David trembled. He steadied himself against a sapling, gripping the slim trunk in a shaky fist. "It burns! Owe, it burns!"

I pulled the bag away from his skin. "How can it burn? It's cold." I set the Ziploc on my leg and let the ice chill my skin. "Look. No burn. You can't be such a big baby. This is supposed to help. Can we try again?"

David nodded, but flinched as I lifted the bag.

"Okay, tell you what …" I picked up his tee-shirt from the ground. "Let's get this back on you."

His head popped through the opening, and a gentle tug brought his right hand through the armhole. I elevated his left arm as slowly as I could, but he still stifled a groan as the rest of the shirt slid on.

"This is like torture," he whispered.

"Sorry." I gently replaced the bag. "Your shirt should protect a little against the ice but still leave it cold enough to stop the swelling." I smiled, proud of myself for remembering something from first aid.

David grimaced. "It's still pretty cold."

"It's supposed to be. That's the point."

David's eyes closed. He took in a deep breath through his nose, and his lips parted slightly to release it. I watched the tight, white cotton expand and retract across his back with each breath. Holy shmoley. *Okay, Florence Nightingale, get a grip.*

David's body quaked, and he grunted through clenched teeth. He grabbed the sapling, snapping it in two.

"Hey, what'd that tree ever do to you?"

His hands formed into trembling fists. He shook like a rocket trying to take off until he bolted upright. The ice fell to the ground.

"I c-can't," he stammered. "It's just too cold."

"All right." I picked up the bag. "But I don't think it was on there long enough to help you."

"Then I'll have to deal with the pain. I'll get over it." He grimaced, settling back down on the ground. "Eventually."

He rubbed his shoulders. His gaze seemed distant.

"Are you okay?" I asked.

"I can't seem to get warm."

"Warm? It's like eighty degrees. It's gorgeous out here."

"I know, but I keep getting a chill." He scuffed the dirt, making an imprint with the front of his sneaker. A spider shimmied from the divot and crawled up a tree to his right.

The sun funneled through the canopy, flickering splotches of light into his hair. What was it about this boy? I just wanted to sit there and stare at him. Well okay, he was gorgeous, but it was something more than that. I felt compelled, like a gentle tug inside, drawing me to him. I bit back a grin. It's called hormones, Jess. Let's just keep it together and don't make a fool out of yourself.

The wind blew lightly through the treetops, rustling the branches over our heads as I slid down beside my bag. "Are you hungry?"

"Yes, famished." His eyes lit up, the color actually brightening. It must have been the sun.

"Great. I made a few PB&J's. I hope that's okay."

"I guess."

I handed him a sandwich. He flipped it over, squinting at the jelly running down the crust. Okay, so, I wasn't Betty Crocker. Get over it. I removed mine out of the plastic wrap, and David followed suit. He watched me take a bite before tearing into his own.

What did he think, it was poisoned or something?

"This is good." He swallowed and nodded. "Really good."

A snicker escaped my lips. "I guess anything would taste good if you hadn't eaten since yesterday."

"Mm-huh. Thank you." He finished the last bite and ran his tongue slowly along his pointer finger, licking off a glob of jelly.

I shifted my weight, watching his tongue glide across his skin.
Wow.

I bit my lip and cleared my throat.

Get. A. Grip. Jess.

Looking away—definitely a good option. "Listen, you can't stay out here. There is some kind of dangerous fugitive or something on the loose."

"Or something?"

The spider beside him dangled from a branch before swinging back up, a stream of silk glistening behind it.

"That's about all I know. I just thought you should know. You know?"

Ugh. How much dumber could I sound? Why did I act so goofy around this guy? Pfft. It had nothing to do with the perfect tan, the washboard abs, those unbelievable arms …

"So, what does this fugitive look like? It's not a young girl with long brown hair and blue eyes, is it? Because that would kind of suck."

I laughed. "If I were a fugitive I wouldn't be making PB&J for some sappy guy in the woods."

"Well, I guess today's my lucky day, then."

He licked another finger. I forced my eyes back up to the spider web. The sunlight caught the square outline of the miniature piece of art before it disappeared, fading in and out like a mirage.

My stomach churned anxiously. "So, do you want to tell me why you're out here?" *Please, please, please don't tell me you're a dangerous fugitive.*

He looked down. "I told you …"

"I know. You don't want to be found. I get that, but the Army is out there looking for someone suspicious. If they find you …"

David's eyes sprang open. He leapt to one knee, just missing the spider web. "Where are they looking?"

"I don't know. Around, I guess."

A refreshing breeze blew through the woods, invigorating me, but a shiver rattled David's shoulders. "It's getting colder."

Dark clouds wafted over the treetops, shrouding the forest in a dim gray before the sun broke through once more.

"It might rain, but it's still, like, eighty degrees."

He wrapped his arms around himself and sat hunched over. A pang deep within my gut warned something wasn't right, that I should run, but the sensation quickly ebbed away. As if erased.

I knelt beside him. "Are you sure you're okay?"

"I'm just cold."

"Maybe you have a fever? You should really see a doctor."

"No. No way." He raised his hands in a defensive position.

"All right—if you tell me what's going on, maybe I can get help, but we're not really getting anywhere here with me doing all the talking."

"Okay, let's talk." He looked to the right and moved closer to the web. He seemed to focus on each strand the spider spun.

The sunlight sparkled in his dark hair and gleamed within the web. I couldn't help myself. I grabbed my camera and adjusted the focus so both David and the web popped crisply from the outlining scenery.

Whoa. The preview looked like a magazine ad. The lines in his face, his nearly pore-less skin—just perfect.

David smiled as I raised the lens again. I set off the shutter on high speed repetition, hoping to get some of the sparkle from the spider's web.

"You like to take pictures, huh?"

"Yeah. It's an obsession of mine. You don't mind, do you?"

He shook his head, and I snapped some more. The last one had a beam of sunlight in the background. Damn if I couldn't sell those as pictures of Jared Linden and gotten away with it.

I closed the lens. "I'm still waiting for your story. I love photography, but I'm not that easily distracted." Well, not right now, at least.

"I'm not sure where to begin. Do you get along with your dad?"

I leaned back, surprised. "I guess. I mean, most of the time. He's a little judgmental, though."

"Mine too. In a big way."

"Is he the reason why you're out here?" A fly buzzed my ear. I swatted it away.

David shrugged. "Indirectly. If he'd just listen, just try to understand ..."

"I know what you mean. My dad's got this crazy idea I can't make good decisions."

"Yeah, mine too. He said I was worthless, and I've never done a selfless thing in my life. What does that mean, anyway?"

"My dad thinks I don't listen."

David propped his elbow on his knee and rested his chin on his fist. "Well, you're listening now."

I smiled. A little girly tingle jittered through my chest. He was cute, and said the right things. Score another notch in that lottery ticket.

My cheeks burned up in a flush under his sparkling gaze. Those eyes—so darn blue. I broke our stare, clearing my throat. "So, you had a fight with your dad, huh?"

"Something like that. I tried to prove I was worth something."

"Did it work?"

He took a deep breath and let it out in a puff. "If it did I wouldn't be here."

The fly buzzed around David's head and darted toward his right, snagging itself in the spider web. The more it thrashed, the more the webbing ripped and covered its wings ... until the struggle abruptly ended. The web seemed to wink in and out of existence as the spider inched toward its prey.

Despair settled into my gut. The thought of being totally over-powered—and to die like that—it just didn't seem fair. The clouds drifted, and the web faded once more. So beautiful, but nothing more than an elaborate trap.

David's gaze moved from the spider back to me. He seemed to search through me, and his brow furrowed. Did I surprise him somehow, or was that confusion in his eyes?

His expression faded into a smile. "Jess, you ..."

Another cooling breeze encircled us. David clamped his arms around his shoulders. His hands shook as they rubbed his skin.

The hair on my arms stood on end as the sky darkened ominously overhead. "David, are you all right?"

He wheezed, his body trembling as he bent over into a ball.

"Okay, that's it," I said. "I'm getting you out of here." I lifted him to his feet. He barely struggled, but drew away once we were standing.

"I can't leave the woods," he said.

"Oh, yes you can."

I nestled my camera into my backpack and flung the bag over my shoulder. David's body seemed rigid as I pulled him to his feet.

"Jess, please don't ..." His words were lost between chattering teeth.

"Don't nothing. You need help."

I yanked on his arm. Luckily for me, he was too busy trembling to fight me. We slunk through the trees, stopping each time David's chill shook him too hard to walk.

This is insane, Jess. You don't know anything about this guy. Lord knows what's wrong with him, and ... A moist tap hit my head, then another. I glanced up. The clouds thickened. Another raindrop grazed my nose as a few birds flew for cover.

Great. A rainstorm was all I needed at the moment.

David studied a drip run down his arm, and turned his eyes up to the trees. "What ..."

"Come on," I said, giving him a tug. "The trail is this way." At least I hoped it was.

Ferns scraped against my jeans as I pushed branches away from my face. I stopped once to untangle David's shirt from a sticker bush before the woods opened up to the dirt path beside the road. It wasn't where I'd come in, but it was close enough to get home.

David tensed as we stepped away from the trees. Small circles appeared on the ground, darkening the sand from tan to brown as scattered droplets fell from the sky.

David retreated toward the woods. "I can't ... I can't."

"You don't have much of a choice now, do you?" I led him forward.

His muscles relaxed, but his eyes told me it was in defeat rather than agreement. David hunched his shoulders, ducked his head, and stumbled as I nudged him forward. I slowed my pace, hoping it would help him keep up.

This is crazy, Jess. Just bring him to the ... I stopped, alarmed by the movement at the gates to the base housing. Two men in uniform tossed their packs beside the door to the guard house. One fumbled with keys.

In the entire four years we'd lived on that base, I'd never seen guards stationed at the entrance. A wave of adrenaline swept through my body. Sweat formed at my temples.

David gripped my arm. Turquoise eyes, wide with fear, met mine.

A twinge in my gut forced my whole body to tremble. I was right all along. It was him. He was the guy they were looking for. We were in deep shi ... well, we were in a lot of trouble. Or was it just me? Was I in trouble? Was David dangerous?

I forced a smile. Every part of me screamed to run, to flee to the guards and tell them, but when I looked into David's eyes, the mistrust melted away, disappeared.

Wait. Why did it disappear? I was scared to death a minute ago, wasn't I?

His eyes softened me. I was safe with him. I always had been.

"I'm not going to turn you in. I promise."

His shoulders relaxed. "Can we please go back to the woods?"

"There's no way to warm you up out there. Now come on, and act natural."

I kept watch on the guard house as we walked toward the gate. One of the guys talked on a cell phone while the other unpacked his bag. *Just keep walking.* A large raindrop pelted my shirt, then another.

David brushed away a rain droplet dribbling down his cheek and looked toward the sky. He gaped, his eyes questioning. Why did rain freak him out? Everybody's seen rain, right?

His nose and lips distorted before he ducked his head down again. Not really as inconspicuous as I'd hoped for, but at least he was keeping up.

Relief washed over me as we passed through the gate. I couldn't believe it. We'd actually …

"Excuse me."

Oh. Crap.

Every muscle in my body tensed. I could feel David's bicep contract as I turned toward the MP. "Yes?"

"Can I see some ID please?"

"Oh, umm, yeah."

I reached into my pocket and grabbed my wallet. He made note of my driver's license on a clipboard.

The MP motioned to David. "And yours?"

"He doesn't have his license yet," I stammered. "He's only sixteen."

My tense muscles got even tenser. There was no way David would pass for sixteen. He looked eighteen, nineteen. My brow furrowed. Just how old was he?

A crack of thunder boomed overhead. David nearly jumped into my arms. The wind whipped up. I glanced to the MP. *Please let us go, dude.*

David turned from my shoulder and stared at the MP. The officer moaned and blinked his eyes. He looked up at the sky and handed my license back.

"Okay. You're cleared. Thank you." He walked back to the booth, massaging his forehead.

No way.

I shoved my license back in my pocket. "I don't believe it."

David didn't comment beyond a tremor as I maneuvered him across the street.

We'd been incredibly lucky. The guy hadn't even made a note of David. Maybe MP training wasn't as hard-core as I'd heard.

We moved past a bush near the edge of the sidewalk, and a sparrow hopped out. The bird fluttered its spotty brown wings as it snatched a squiggling worm on the concrete.

David reared back, nearly knocking me over. "What the …"

I tightened my grip on his arms. "Dude, it's only a bird. Chill out!"

"I'm sorry. It frightened me."

His eyes remained on the little brown-spotted minion-of-doom as it hopped onto the road. What kind of idiot got spooked by a bird? I didn't push it. David obviously had serious issues. Hopefully they weren't the homicidal kind.

I cringed.

No. He was just a guy who needed help. No homicidal anything.

David's gaze shifted from left to right. "Where are we going, anyway?"

"Don't be so scared. It's not like the whole world is looking for you. What are the chances of your father just happening to be on Maguire, and driving down this road at this very minute?" I tried to gauge his reaction, but his expression didn't change. He was worried about more than his father, I could tell. Was it really the MPs? The regular police? Worse? Maybe eventually he'd open up to me.

As we turned onto my street, an open-top jeep sped toward us. David cried out and jumped away from the road. One of the soldiers inside waved as they drove by.

"I really think I need to go back to the woods," David said.

The jeep turned the corner, not even hesitating at the stop sign. "It's nothing. They're only going to work. You need to lighten up."

You should bring him back to the gate. Turn him in. This is bigger than you, and you know it. If the Army is looking for him something is seriously up.

I scoffed at my own idiocy. Paranoia was so un-cool. He'd be fine. He was just out of sorts with a fever or something. Besides, if he was a fugitive, and I helped him, I may just be setting myself up for the story of a lifetime.

Or a lifetime behind bars.

I decided to go with the first scenario. Much better karma.

Head tucked down low, David allowed me to guide him while I kept a careful watch on the neighbors' windows and front porches. The last thing I needed was a nosy housewife calling my dad.

David dug in his heels as we turned up my walkway. He wrenched against my grip. "What's that?"

"My house."

"Your house?"

"Yeah, this is where I live. David, are you delirious or something? Where did you think I was taking you?"

I placed my hand on his arm. Perspiration beaded on his brow and his tee-shirt seemed far damper than it should have been in the light rain.

Sweat?

David scrunched his eyes closed and stumbled foot over foot. A torrent of unintelligible words streamed from his lips as his body went limp.

My knee slammed on the pavement as I reached down to catch him—but he was nowhere near as heavy as I expected. Weird.

His eyes opened and rolled back into this head. He coughed once before his gaze re-focused on me.

"You're done. I'm calling an ambulance."

He grabbed my arm. "No! I just need to get warmed up."

I shook my head and helped him back to a standing position. "I think it's more than that, and something really strange is—"

"I promise you, I'm just cold. Please just ..." His words lost themselves inside a moan, and another shaking chill brought us both to our knees. David's shoulders stiffened between my hands, becoming board-rigid before shaking fitfully.

"Shoot," I whispered, rubbing his arms in a fruitless effort to warm him.

The sky opened up. Rain pummeled us. The sound roared through the compound.

David's pupils fixed on a point behind me. His jaw vibrated in time with the tremor. Dark wet tresses matted to his forehead. Water trailed from his bangs and down his cheeks.

I gripped his face and pointed it toward mine. "David. David, listen to me. I need to get you into the house."

His eyes didn't focus. His teeth chattered.

"Okay. Let's hope you heard me." He grimaced as I hauled him to his feet. His shiver tightened his joints. The stiffness in his body fought against me as we made our way to the door.

CHAPTER 5

Beneath the overhang, I fussed with my keys and pushed the door open. With some finagling I dragged his trembling form inside and into the family room, where he collapsed on the couch.

"Stay here." Like he was getting up anytime soon. "I'll get some blankets."

I sprinted up the stairs, leaving muddy footprints on the carpet. Yeah, that wasn't going to get me in trouble or anything. I threw open the linen closet.

"Okay Dad, it's like this," I whispered to myself. "I know I wasn't supposed to talk to strangers, but he was really cute so I figured it was okay ... then he got sick. I couldn't just leave him out there."

Yeah, that'll work. You are in deep dog-poop, Jess.

I threw two towels over my shoulders and grabbed a stack of spare blankets before padding down the stairs. Drying David's clothing proved fruitless, but at least his hair wasn't dripping anymore. Dad had left his gray sweatshirt hanging on the back of a chair. I peeled David's wet tee-shirt from his back, trying to be careful of his injured shoulder, and pulled the warm fleece over his head.

Still stricken with the chill, David rolled himself into a ball. I unfolded the blankets with a flourish and swaddled him in pink and yellow fuzz.

"Okay. If that doesn't warm you up, nothing will."

I admired my domestic-ness until the covers began to quake again. He had to have a fever. I cranked the thermostat up from seventy degrees to seventy-five.

"David, I'm going to get a thermometer."

Chattering teeth answered me.

Just call an ambulance, Jess.

No. No ambulance. He'd been clear on that. No hospitals. Until I found out what was going on, I needed to keep that promise.

I walked right by the telephone to the bathroom and grabbed the thermometer from underneath the toothpaste in the medicine cabinet.

Closing the door, I cringed at my reflection. Yesterday's eyeliner oozed down to my cheek. My bangs hung wet, lifeless, and clinging to my forehead. Lovely. I ran a fingertip under each eye, alleviating most of the raccoon syndrome. Who was I kidding? I'd never win a beauty pageant anyway.

I uncapped the thermometer as I returned to David. He groaned. His chill rattled the coils in the couch.

"David, I'm going to stick a thermometer under your tongue." I had no idea if he could hear me over his shivering.

After pressing the button to clear the digital readout, I pried his mouth open to slide the prong between his lips. His hand clutched the edge of the blanket. His fist shook against his chest.

"Come on David. Snap out of it."

His eyes squeezed shut. His mouth formed a pained, straight line.

"It'll be okay." A puff of air blew out of my lips. Saying the words didn't help me to believe them. What if I was wrong? What if he really needed a doctor? What if he died?

I touched the chain on my neck, twirling the links around my fingers. The phone sat on the end table. One call to 911 would bring an ambulance, which was what he really needed. I reached for the phone and sighed. He seemed petrified of the hospital. But was it right to let him die just because he was afraid?

The clock on the wall ticked, filling the room with its cadence. David's teeth rattled against the plastic tube in his mouth. What was taking that thermometer so darn long to beep?

I grasped my pendant, willing myself to do the right thing—if I could just figure out what the right thing was.

My mother's words seeped into my mind. "I had this necklace blessed. You'll never have to worry about anything while you wear it." Her image soothed me like a hug. I closed my eyes and fed on her strength.

"All right, Mom," I whispered, "here goes nothing."

Another tremor rocked David's body as I unhooked the chain and refastened the clasp behind his neck. I touched my fingers to the golden oval.

"Please God," I whispered. "Please help him." The shiver subsided, but his breathing seemed labored.

Darnit. What was I supposed to do?

I frantically searched the room for something to help. Pillows, magazines, remote controls, everything a good Jersey home should have other than something to stop a person from freezing to death.

Three logs lay unburned beside the fireplace, leftover from the spring thaw. Perfect. I placed one of the logs on the steel grate and shoved some newspaper beneath it. Luckily, the dry wood caught quickly. I checked David's blankets and glanced at the thermometer's digital readout. *112. 113. 114.* "What the ..."

David convulsed and bit down, snapping the thermometer in two.

"Holy crap!" I picked up the half that fell on the blanket and tossed it on the table. My finger shot between his lips, and I pried his mouth open, praying he didn't bite me by accident. I dug the rest of the thermometer from under his tongue and threw it over my shoulder.

His head fell to the side, his body as limp as a rag doll. I did my best to hoist him to a sitting position as his eyes rolled back, exposing ghostly white orbs.

"Omigosh, this is not happening. David! David!" No answer. I slapped his face.

His eyes sprang open, centered on me, and froze. His lips clamped together. His body shook as if it were preparing to explode. His muscles hardened like bricks beneath my fingertips. The skin around his eyes crinkled. The set of his eyes screamed for help.

"Come on, David. Snap out of it. Come on!"

His eyes remained fixed on me until the convulsion subsided. A blink told me he was still in there. I eased him back until he rested on the couch without my support. His gaze locked with mine. Color returned to his face.

I reached out and touched his arm. My fingers trembled. "Please tell me it's over."

David closed his eyes and rubbed his chest, taking in several long, full breaths. He blinked and squinted as if the light hurt his eyes, before scanning the room.

His movement seemed hesitant and sleepy, as if he'd just woken up. The licking flames in the fireplace caught his attention. His lips turned up in a grin.

"Warm. Thanks," he whispered.

I ran the back of my hand across my forehead, dabbing away the sweat. "Thanks, nothing. You have, like, a hundred and fifteen-degree fever. We need to get you to a hospital."

His eyes darkened. "No. I told you—"

"David, this is serious."

He reached out and touched his fingers to my chest, just below the collarbone. "I am serious." His irises seemed to brighten beneath his dark lashes.

A soothing sensation rolled over me, relaxing my muscles one at a time. My apprehension slipped away, while something deep in the recesses of my mind begged me to run. I blinked and allowed the calm to overcome. "All right, but I'm not a doctor, you know. I have no idea what I'm doing."

"I don't need a doctor."

Yeah, so he'd told me. I kneaded my hands together, doing my best to remember what they taught in my first aid class. "So, okay, fever. A tub of ice, right? Ice water will break a fever?"

He raised his palms and leaned away. "No! No more ice. Please …"

"But David you're really sick."

"No, I'm not." He rubbed his temples. "I, I … have a disorder."

"A what?" The fire crackled behind me as the room continued to heat.

"It's … thermo-nucleic disorder. Have you heard of it?"

"No." I crossed my arms.

He straightened. The pink blanket fell to his waist. "I have an extremely high body temperature. I don't do too well in the cold."

"You're trying to tell me you're always that hot?"

He placed his hands on his lap. "Pretty much. I'm feeling better, though. Thanks for the fire."

I kept my arms folded. Seriously? He must have thought I was a …

His smile warmed me more than the fire, and I relaxed.

A disorder, of course. It made total sense—unless he was pulling my leg.

His smile faded as he tugged the chain of my mother's pendant out of the sweatshirt. He fingered the golden oval. "What's this?"

I scooted aside the blankets and sat beside him. "It was my Mom's. She gave it to me when I was twelve. She told me that whenever I wear it, I could hold it tightly and know that she was with me … that everything would be all right."

David ran his thumb over the etching and turned the charm over. The starburst cross on the front glistened in the firelight. "That's beautiful. Why did you give it to me?"

I shrugged. "At the moment you kind of needed it more than I did."

"The fire warmed me, not the necklace." He reached for the clasp behind his neck.

"No. Keep it for now … until I'm sure you're okay."

The fire cast a light glow on the right side of his face. "If you can help me stay warm, I'll be giving this back to you pretty quickly."

I narrowed my eyes. "Wow, I can't believe this. You really can't take the cold? At all? What do you do in the winter?"

He laughed. "I try to dress more warmly."

I fiddled with my thumbs, recapping and sorting through everything that'd happened. Despite being completely relaxed, I knew something was very wrong. I fought back the feeling of ease as it tried to overtake me again. Why was I being so complacent when something was obviously up? What was wrong with me? Focus. I needed to focus.

"David, why are they looking for you?"

"You mean my father?"

I stood. "No. I mean the Army. Is it because you have some kind of funky disease? Am I in any danger? Did you break the law? What—"

"I'm going to have to take notes if you keep asking questions without letting me answer."

I folded my arms. "Then start answering."

He pursed his lips. "I'm not contagious, and I would never hurt you."

"So you *do* have some sort of freaky disease. Is that why they're looking for you?"

He chewed his upper lip, his face pensive. "I promise I'll tell you everything, but right now I don't think it would do either of us any good. Can you please just trust me for now?"

"I don't know you. I'm not even sure why I brought you here."

David stood and curled his fingers around my hands. "Trust me. We're alone. If I wanted to hurt you, I'd have done it already."

"But David …"

He stepped away from me and grabbed his temple.

"Please don't tell me you're getting another chill."

"No." He sat on the couch, jostling the pink blanket. "Just dizzy."

He closed his eyes and stretched his neck as I sat beside him. "David, I don't know what to do."

"I think I'm just tired." He cuddled into the corner of the couch.

Shifting the blankets out from under me, I stood and threw one over him. David blinked and smiled, sending a rush of tickling energy through me, heating my cheeks. What was it about that smile? Why did I turn into a heaping sack of melted jelly when he barely even looked at me?

My hands shook. Distraction. I needed a distraction.

"Tell you what. You get some rest. I'll see if I can scurry up something to eat for dinner." Yep. Food. That would work. Nothing helps a girl keep her calm and focus like a good old-fashioned dose of carbs and calories. I walked toward the kitchen. "I can always make peanut butter and jelly again if I need to."

David drew the blanket up under his chin. "I'd rather have more PB&J if you have it. That was great."

I turned, leaning on the doorframe. "That's what I said."

His lashes flickered closed, and his face softened. A placid rhythm developed in his breathing.

Maybe he was more tired than I thought. I walked back and sat beside him on the couch. Trailing my fingers across his forehead, I brushed back his long, dark bangs.

Who was he? Why was he here, and what the heck was going on? I rubbed my chin. He asked me to be patient, but all these questions were killing me. Was I sitting on the story of my life, or was I setting myself up for disappointment, and perpetual, eternal grounding?

The firelight cast a stunning shadow behind him. Eerie, ethereal. I pulled out my camera and rattled off shots from several angles, but the photos in the preview screen did little to convey what my eyes saw in real life. Maybe they'd look better when I downloaded them later.

Making my way into the kitchen, I opened the cabinet and reached for the peanut butter and a loaf of bread. I slathered as much jelly as I could without it sloshing out the sides of the sandwich. Admiring my finished masterpieces, I licked the jelly that still clung to the knife. Waste not, want not, Mom always said.

I smashed a quarter wedge into my mouth and placed the rest on a napkin, leaving it on the coffee table beside David. His lips rose in a half-smile as he slept.

Boiling hot skin met my fingertips as I touched my hand to his forehead. I winced, fright overtaking me for a moment, before I settled myself.

Duh. Of course he was going to feel warm. Temperature disorder, remember?

The sun broke through the clouds outside. Cheerful sparkles glimmered on the water droplets still clinging to the window screens. At least the rain was over.

I eased into the armchair and watched David sleep. So many questions muddled inside my mind. What was he running from? What's really wrong with him?

Although the storm outside had abated, the storm inside still slumbered on my couch. I should have been terrified of him, but I wasn't … and it drove me crazy.

And what about Dad? He could burst through the door at any moment. What would I say? How would I deal with the unavoidable life-long punishment? I covered my face. *Crap.* I was in way over my head.

The rhythm of David's breathing transfixed me, lulling me to sleepiness. I blinked twice, and grabbed my phone. I Googled 'rare temperature diseases' and scrolled through listings of pointless topics. Raynaud's syndrome. Nope didn't make your temperature high. Lyme's disease … nah, didn't seem likely. Cold urticaria … allergic to cold temperatures, causes hives in the cold. I glanced in his direction. No, there was never a mark on him, and they didn't say anything about constant high temperatures.

I clicked off my phone and rubbed my eyes. The sun had gone down, and the last embers in the fire had died out. I spied a carton of synthetic logs under the kindling newspapers. I added one to the grate to keep the fire burning.

David rolled over in his sleep, his bangs falling toward his right eye. I brushed them aside and sat on the floor staring at him. Was he telling the truth? Could he really have some sort of freaky temperature problem?

The clock on the wall clicked to nine-thirty. I tousled my hair and found it damp from the heat. Sweat beaded on my chest and dripped down into my bra. Gross.

David's cheek was warm, but not sweaty. His breathing remained deep and regular.

He may have felt fine, but I felt like I was going to yack. I headed up the stairs to my bedroom and hoisted the window open, letting in the cooler outside air. A light breeze blew the curtains beside my shoulders, refreshing me from the heat in the house. I rested against the sill and turned my face to the sky. A thousand lights in the heavens glinted and sparkled, settling my uneasiness. I breathed deeply, enjoying the sweet scents of Mrs. Miller's garden until a star overhead winked out. Then another.

I grasped the windowsill and pushed against the screen—holding my breath as the stars wiped away before my eyes. A deep, dark blanket stretched out over the house, consuming the sky quickly and more completely than any cloud cover.

I reached for my necklace. Startled by its absence, I froze until I remembered it lay safely around David's neck. My gaze drew back to the sky. A black mass hovered over the houses, continuing to blank out the stars. One by one the little pinpricks of light returned as the form passed overhead and moved toward the airstrips.

No lights. No landing gear. Just black—And really, really slow. A blimp? In the middle of the night? And no noise at all?

I shivered and backed away from the window. Keeping an eye on the mass, I fumbled for my phone and dialed Maggie. I recounted my entire day, right up to the apparition that'd just flown over my house.

"Did you see it?" I asked.

"So they flew a plane over your house. It's not the first time."

"Have you been listening to a thing I've said?"

"Come on, girl. I don't care about the plane," Maggie said. "I want to hear about the hottie. He's actually there in your house? Right now? And your Dad's not home?" Her giggle always sounded maniacal. "Are you going to *do it?*"

"No! Maggie, come on."

"But seriously. What are you going to tell your Dad?"

I shook my head. "I was thinking of the truth. I can't send David back into the cold, and I can't really hide him either. Right now he's passed out on the sofa."

"Holy cow. The major's going to have a brain aneurysm."

"Believe me, I know." I tucked back the curtain and peeked up at the stars. Everything seemed perfectly normal—now. "Maggs, that plane, or whatever—it was weird. I mean, really weird. I couldn't even hear it, but it must have been huge."

"Hon, maybe you were dreaming."

"I wasn't."

She held a long pause on the line. "Are you going to deal with the real problem, here? What do you think is wrong with Prince Charming?"

I checked the window again and slumped onto the bed. "I have no stinking clue. He says he has this funny disorder."

"Okay, so what is it?"

I rolled onto my back. "He said it was something like thermo-dynamic disorder. Or maybe it was thermo-nuclear disorder. I don't know ... something that makes him really hot and he freezes when it gets cold out. I tried to Google it but I couldn't find anything."

"You already knew he was really hot."

I ignored her. "It was so bizarre. I couldn't get him warmed up, no matter what I tried."

"You know, if it happens again, you can always smother his body with yours."

"What?"

"Seriously. I see it in the movies all the time, and they told us that in first aid class too, remember? Sharing body heat and all." She snickered. "And I hear friction ..."

"Maggie!" I sat up and tossed my pillow back to the head of my bed. Not that the idea of snuggling up with David was all that gross, but I didn't need her to know that.

"Okay, okay, but I'm going to research it to make sure he doesn't have the plague or something."

"Whatever. I'll talk to you tomorrow."

I smushed my forehead against the window screen again and counted stars. Not that I knew how many were supposed to be up there, but tallying them made me feel better. Scattered light clouds left from the earlier storm dotted the sky, but otherwise the stars shone as brightly as any other night. I closed the window, pulled the blind down, and leaned against the edge of my dresser. I knew there was no way I was going to be able to sleep.

I grabbed my comforter and pillow and padded down the stairs. Throwing the bedding on the chair beside David, I placed my fingers on his forehead. Still hot. *Duh – Temperature disorder, Jess.*

First things first: I needed to make sure Dad didn't have a conniption when he walked through the front door so he didn't shoot David or something. I grabbed the note pad from the counter and scribbled: *Don't be mad. I'll explain in the morning* on the yellow-lined sheet. I taped the note on the couch behind David.

Lame, but it was all I could come up with. Tomorrow was not going to be fun.

I eased back into the chair beside David and yanked the lever to raise my feet. Using the blanket to prop up my side, I cuddled into my soft down pillow and watched David sleep. So many questions … but tomorrow I'd get some answers.

Hopefully David would comply. If not, Dad might beat the answers out of him.

<hr>

I really hope you enjoyed the preview of
FIRE IN THE WOODS.
You can pick up your copy of this and other great adventures by
Jennifer M. Eaton at your favorite booksellers

By the way,
Thanks for reading!

Joe says, "Goodnight."

www.ingramcontent.com/pod-product-compliance
Lightning Source LLC
Chambersburg PA
CBHW050613170726
48283CB00001B/229